THE ANTUNITE CHRONICLES: BOOK 3

TERRY BIRDGENAW

ISBN: 978-1-7781562-0-5 (paperback)

ISBN: 978-7781562-1-2 (ebook)

Legal deposit, Library and Archives Canada, September 2022

This novel is dedicated to the African American community, my Indigenous ancestors and their kin. To Bod-pa, Jews, Kurds, LGBTQ+, Palestinians, Rohingya, Tutsi, Uyghurs, and all peoples around the world that have been or are oppressed, subjugated, or persecuted by those who see them as 'the other'.

TIMELINE OF THE LEADERS ON BILALUNA, INTOPIA, AND ANTALONIA

Time Frame	Bilaluna's Queen	Intopia/Antalonia's President
Five rulers in the past	Beelieve	Jetant (Intopia)
Four rulers in the past	Beewary	Umberant (Intopia)
Three rulers in the past	Beehold	Umberant/Rustant (Intopia)
Two rulers in the past	Beeutee	Rust* (Antalonia)
One ruler in the past	Beehope	Rudyard (Antalonia)
Present ruler	Beewish	Rudyard/Blood (Antalonia)

*Rustant changed his name to Rust when he became the first ruler of Antalonia and no longer called the planet Intopia.

CHAPTER 1

HOW INTOPIA BEGAN: A PLANET REBORN

Bilaluna (Queen Beelieve's reign, five rulers in the past)

A YOUNG BEE heard rumors about some exciting news and decided she should go directly to the source to confirm the story was true. Beewary was a cyborg BEE from the royal family. Her mother was Bilaluna's Queen, as was her mother before her, and so on. As a BEE, she looked identical to her distant honeybee forebears, yet was about a thousand times larger. She had large compound eyes on both sides of her head. The hairy dome was perched atop a fuzzy yellow thorax, fastened to a shiny, ebony and gold striped abdomen. Translucent wings extended from her fluffy middle to the end of her bulbed rear tip. She was fully grown but not mature mentally as an adolescent, though she would contest that. Normally Beewary would spend mornings playing with her friends, but on this hexay[1], she had a strong urge to speak to her mother.

Although a BEE, Beewary was encouraged to have friends from all the insectoid families living on Bilaluna. The Queen BEE liked to set an example to ensure that all insectoids were treated equally. So, she and her heir interacted daily with members of each cyborg insect family, including Allied Noble Tripods (ANTs), Bi-winged Essence Extractors (BEEs), Bipedal Unibodied Golems (BUGs), Flap Levitating Yeomen (FLYs), Robotic Armored Champs (RoAChs), Wood-boring Buddies (WoBBs), and Wriggling Rock Movers (WoRMs). These included seven species of the novel genus *Cybernetic Insecta*, although they knew that technically WoRMs and BUGs were not derived from insects. The cyborgs looked like giant (1,000X) Earth insects, except for WoBBs that were built in two sizes at about 100X and 500X of the wood-boring beetles from which they originated. ANTs also had their limbs rearranged, so they walked upright with three sets of legs and arms—thus the term tripod. BUGs were derived from spiders but had no venom and walked on two legs and had six arms for spinning their thread. These seven cyborg families shared the moon with their tiny insect, worm, and spider cousins, which they had learned were essential for maintaining the moon's rich jungle-like forest ecosystem. They also shared the moon with termites, which had no cyborg equivalent.

Beewary crept into Queen Beelieve's chamber. "Mother, is

---

1 Insects use a heximal counting system, which appears throughout the book for time units. Each unit uses 'hex' as a root (i.e., hexay is equivalent to the human term day). See Appendix 1 for a full explanation.

it true that a large group from all cyborg families will repopulate Poo-ponic?"

Beelieve smiled at her young daughter. "Yes, isn't it wonderful? They will join tiny insects that have already inhabited the planet."

Beewary fidgeted. "Is the planet ready? Is there enough air? Didn't the atmosphere collapse?" She shook while speaking. *She must know the history of how this calamity incinerated most of our ancestors on Poo-ponic thousands of hexs ago.*

"Every insectoid on Bilaluna knows the tragic story of Poo-ponic's demise." Beelieve pointed to the giant orb in the sky above them. "A climate catastrophe destroyed the planet. We have taught students from all cyborg families this tragic story, so we will never replicate it on Bilaluna."

Beewary raised a claw and interrupted her mother. "I learned how our small insect ancestors came from Earth millions of hexs ago, evolved, and transformed themselves into cyborgs."

"And before that, courageous insects like Beefirst and Antuna pushed for cooperation between species when insects first arrived," Beelieve began. "And hexennia later Antuna's descendants developed the insectism movement, which is the model for our society."

Beewary smashed a fore claw down on her abdomen. "Then it was all torn down by that tyrant Antilla, who became president after they created a central government with ANTs in charge. He plunged the to autocracy and ignored the climate crisis that destroyed Poo-ponic's atmosphere." Her wings began to twitch. *They were smart like us, but greedy and corrupt when they tried to produce too much honey.*

"You have learned your lessons well." Beelieve tapped her

daughter on the shoulder. "So, you realize we would not be here except for the seventeen cyborg insects that escaped to Bilaluna and started our colony here?"

As the Queen's daughter, Beewary lived in a palace, but the royal palace on Bilaluna was not extravagant. It was larger than your average insectoid hive or nest, as it was also a gathering place for the community. There were above-ground meeting halls, a dining hall, and a large ballroom for receptions. But the living quarters were much the same as those inhabited by the public and were underground. There was also an above-ground flying hall next to the palace, allowing flying insectoids to gather indoors. This enormous structure provided the room to fly about and have ceremonies like the annual coming out party where debutant female BEEs and FLYs would show off their elaborate mating dance moves. The palace was next to the central BEE-hive, which stored much of the fortified nectar that all colony insectoids ate. Insectoids on Bilaluna stuck to their early constitutional edict and made no honey. They lived on fortified nectar and natural foods, like fruits, seeds, and fungi that they farmed or gathered. They had cultivated fungi, which tasted like chocolaty truffles or Portobello mushrooms since Antuna and Beefirst began the process shortly after insects arrived on Poo-ponic.

Beewary smiled at her mother. "Yes, Mother, we all descended from the few that escaped Poo-ponic and came to our moon. They created a constitution that banned honey and ensured no autocrat could corruptly rule our colony." She stood tall. *I am proud of all my ancestors who have served Bilaluna well.*

"Indeed, and we have lived peacefully ever since." Beelieve spread her forelimb wide. "Although we struggled initially, we have safe-guarded our environment, and our forests still thrive."

"I learned that is why we restrict our colony to only 1,000

insectoids." Beewary looked out towards the colony. "Our low numbers ensure sustainability by creating a small pod-print."

Beelieve laughed. "Your tutors have taught you well. You will make an excellent queen some hexay. But don't forget to enjoy your youth."

Beewary shrugged. "I won't, but I want to be a queen that makes an impact. I want to ensure that our society thrives to uphold our constitution, yet still provides for all our citizens." She flapped her wings once for emphasis. *My mother's a great queen, but sometimes she can be too optimistic.*

Beelieve stepped back. "Are you not satisfied with things as they are?"

Beewary laughed. "No, you and all our ancestors have done a wonderful job here on Bilaluna. But if we return to Poo-ponic, we must also look out for the citizens and the environment there." Her demeanor became more serious. *A queen BEE's job is of utmost importance, and I want to do it right.*

Beelieve reached her antennae forward and stroked her daughter's shoulders. "There will be many challenges returning to our old planet, building new accommodations, feeding the colony, providing them with the goods they need as they expand." She looked up at the giant planet in the sky. "But our priority is here on Bilaluna, and we must let them go. Those living on the planet will be the leaders and responsible for their own society."

"Would you say we are colonizing the planet but won't be colonizers?" Despite her concern, Beewary always tried to impress her mother with witty quips. *I don't know about this, Mother. It seems we'll be taking a big chance.*

"Exactly, the colonists need to rule themselves." Beelieve

grinned. "We'll only step in if we see that things have gone seriously wrong."

"So, we just watch Poo-ponic from afar and make sure the citizens of Bilaluna are comfortable." Beewary shook her head.

Beelieve looked out at the district near the river. "Yes. For example, we're building new nests to replace some that got flooded last hexek."

All insectoids lived in apartment like-hive cells or nests that contained a parlor, den, and two bedrooms; one for parents and the other for offspring. Ever since Antuna started the trend of non-queens mating, insectoids lived within small nuclear families rather than large colonies bred by a single queen. Family living quarters for many insectoids, including ANTs, BEEs, RoACHs, and WoRMs, were underground unless the resident preferred to build a mound. FLYs lived above ground and would only build cane or wooden canopies to protect themselves from the rain. WoBBs chose to live in the thick forests that surrounded the colony. Although too large to live within trees, they constructed their nests as circular wood cabins that resembled tree trunks with thatched roofs. BUGs also lived in cabin-like structures, although these were more like treehouses since they were off the ground, within trees, or on stilts. They were accessed by ladders, or large lattices, that the BUGs weaved using their spinning thread.

Furniture in their living quarters was often quite basic, bunks or lounge chairs carved into the soil or built with wood and covered with straw. The insectoids constructed wood chairs in the communal dining hall, often with hardened BUG spinning thread used to cover the seat. Tables and desks also were made from wood or carved from large rocks. Furniture use, although further encouraged after meeting humans, predated

Earthling contact since cyborgs found getting themselves off the ground increased the longevity of their cyborg parts. Also, the now upright ANTs and BUGs preferred working on objects at arm height rather than stooping down all the time. The crawling cyborg insects tended not to use tables and desks but could rear up, if need be, to access articles at higher levels.

BUGs used their spinning thread not only to make ladders and lattices but also to weave and harden into bins to carry nectar and jugs to hold sap or fermented sap, known as strong sap. Strong sap was perhaps the oldest product, besides honey, ever cultivated by insects. It was first discovered by Earth insects and those from Antuna's time when sap leaked from beetle bores and fermented when pooled on rocks. It was later intentionally produced and bottled by wood-boring beetles shortly before and after they became cyborgs. There were several varieties of strong sap, the taste of which had varying degrees of maple syrup, oak, or spruce beer flavors, sometimes accented by spices such as cinnamon or nutmeg.

Perhaps influenced by humans, they also learned how to make bottles, cups, glasses, and dishes that most insectoids were keen to use, so tiny insects did not as easily infiltrate their food. All insectoids knew they were created from tiny insects and that their small neighbors were essential to the ecosystem. However, they still treated them as pests and saw themselves as superior, more like humans. Yet, they reproduced by generating tiny eggs, which hatched small insects, from which every generation selected one or two offspring to be transformed into cyborgs, with the remainder set free into the wilds.

Although Beewary knew the production of cyborgs and greed for honey led to Poo-ponic's demise, they still produced cyborgs on Bilaluna. But more than that, the wilful ignorance of a corrupt autocrat caused a climate catastrophe.

"Yes, Bilaluna citizens and their safety and happiness are our highest priority." Beewary stood tall. "But how can we now return to the old planet? Is it not toxic?" *How can my mother be so sure? Did she send over scouts?*

"It was not a topic taught in our schools or discussed with the public because we did not want our society to have false hopes." Beelieve held her forelimbs up as if cradling their mother planet. "But Poo-ponic has recovered over thousands of hexs. Plant life has returned, and the vegetation has generated oxygen that restored the planet's atmosphere."

Beewary clapped her claws together. "That's amazing." *I hope it's true and all are safe.*

"Yes, as the plants produced more oxygen, it reacted with ultraviolet radiation from our solar star." Beelieve pointed up at the brilliant star. "This generated an ozone layer thick enough to maintain an atmosphere with life-sustaining oxygen."

Thousands of hexs had passed since the collapse of the planet's atmosphere, which caused the desolation of life there. Although most life-forms were incinerated or starved of oxygen during the atmospheric breakdown, fungi capable of surviving in the remaining high-temperature and acidic Paleo-wetlands maintained the structure of deep-water stromatolites. The stromatolites then provided scaffolding and insulation, allowing low levels of surviving microbial cyanobacteria to reproduce. These stromatolite cyanobacteria generated photosynthetic activity essential for producing enough oxygen to regenerate the ozonosphere. The O_2 interacted with the solar star's ultraviolet radiation to form O_3 or ozone. This ozone layer not only reduced ultraviolet rays but also contained the atmosphere.

The planet's mass, like that of the moon, did not produce enough gravity to hold the atmosphere in its place, and they both needed a robust ozonosphere to maintain all elements of the stratosphere. Although a much smaller celestial sphere, the moon had an abnormally dense core that caused its mass and gravity to be similar to the planet. Once the ozone layer had recovered sufficiently, continued cyanobacterial photosynthesis generated an oxygen-rich atmosphere that could once again sustain insect life on the planet.

Gradually, the planet returned to a state resembling Earth's Phanerozoic era, like when the Earth's insects first arrived on Poo-ponic. As predicted by Antoria, one of Bilaluna's early colonists and a Poo-ponic historian, the planet had returned, in a self-preserving manner, to the state it was before Earth's insects first arrived. Periodic openings of the wormhole on Bilaluna allowed seeds and small insects to infiltrate the barren planet gradually. Though early small insect colonists often perished, they laid the groundwork for subsequent arrivals, which endured and helped develop the soil conditions for a healthy land-based plant life covering enough of the planet that ensured the survival of a future cyborg colony.

Beewary shrugged. "Do you think the planet is ready to inhabit?" *We can't send cyborgs over there to perish.*

"Yes, dear, I recommended to Congress that it was time to re-establish settlement of our old planet," responded the Queen. "But we have renamed it Intopia, and we hope it will be a utopia where all insectoids can live harmoniously."

"Isn't that what we have on Bilaluna?" asked Beewary. "How will it be different?" *I wish my mother would keep me up to date on these things. I will be Queen before long.*

"The society will be the same, except for two things,"

replied Beelieve. "First, the planet is so much bigger we won't have to restrict the numbers of cyborgs created. Second, the new colonists on Intopia will create their laws and run the planet as they choose."

Beewary pulled on her antennae. "I know we must let them run things for themselves, but I fear their democracy might fail, like before. Shouldn't they adopt our constitution to ensure everyone is equal?" *She must know that the environmental disaster was accelerated when the failed.*

Beelieve held Beewary's claw. "Don't worry, daughter. All cyborg insects have practiced insectism for so long. There is little chance they will stray from the path."

Beewary blinked her gigantic eyes. "How can you be so sure?" *Our instincts are so aggressive. Especially the ANTs.*

"We have chosen the first insectoids to colonize Intopia," Beelieve started. "They have already selected their president."

Beewary jumped off her chair. "Selected? Who? When? Why didn't I hear about this?" Her stinger scratched the ground as she stood. *My mother never tells me the major stuff.*

"I know you worry about political matters." Beelieve stroked her daughter's long, silky wings. "I am very proud of you, but you are still young. Some hexay you will replace me as queen. Until then, you must enjoy your youth."

"But if I am to take over as queen, shouldn't I worry about these things?" Beewary flapped her wings fast and hard. *She treats me like a pupa, but I'll be coming out in a few hexs.*

"They selected Jetant as President." Beelieve smiled. "He is an Antunite, and there is no stronger proponent of insectism. Jetant will ensure the new colony treats all cyborg insect families fairly. Besides, they have written their constitution."

Beewary sat down again, but squirmed in her chair. "Will Intopia at least have a queen BEE?"

Beelieve shook her head. "No, royalty was ended by the new colonists. But they can always ask me for advice when they need it."

Beewary stood up again. "But having an ANT in charge, and no queen BEE or anyone else to check his power, is that wise?" She paced in front of her mother. *She must realize that it is risky. ANTs can be so oppressive.*

"There will be a Congress like we have here, with equal numbers of male and female cyborgs from all insectoid families."

"Well, at least that's something." Beewary stopped pacing and looked hard at her mother. "The Congress can counter the President's power." *Yet, I'm not thrilled by an ANT leader.*

CHAPTER 2

THE NEW SPIES: PREPARATION

Bilaluna (Queen Beewish's reign, the current ruler)

QUEEN BEEWISH AWAITED a meeting with two of her tiniest subjects, who she hoped would contribute to Intopia's salvation. It was time for Bilaluna to set things right on the misguided planet before Antalonians attacked the peace-loving insectoids on their moon. They needed to act now. Five generations of rulers had elapsed since cyborg insects had recolonized their old planet, and Beewary's worse fears had been realized. A malicious ruler had risen to power on Intopia and had transformed the colony into an evil empire of ANTs they called Antalonia.

Queen Beewish's mother, Beehope, raised her with a singular purpose—to avenge her grandmother Beehold's death and take down the Antalone leaders. Two tiny ants, Rose and Jasper, who were to be the spies that would help her achieve this goal, entered the greeting hall within the Queen's palace. Hexagon-shaped gold tiles lined the floor, harkening back to when bees still made honey. Eighteen equally spaced, larger-the-life bronze statues dominated the surrounding walls of the circular structure as a tribute to the Best Luminaries of Bilaluna. These included ten-foot-high likenesses of the Fabled Fourteen, two cyborgs from each of seven insectoid families that first settled Bilaluna. Images of Gretant, Thunbug, Antoria, and Natbug, four insectoids most instrumental to Bilaluna's restored environment, rounded out the steely group of imposing giants. Paintings on the ceiling depicted scenes vital to Bilaluna's survival, including the visit of the young human wormhole travelers. Their journey initiated the first contact between the two intelligent species known in the Universe and inspired the effort to re-establish Bilaluna's forest ecosystem.

Entirely overwhelmed by the imposing surroundings, Rose and Jasper were tiny ants, not unlike those on Earth, who had not yet been transformed into cyborg ANTs. Unlike their Earth ancestors, though, they were *chameleants*—ants that could change colors at will from black to brown to red.

"My mother Beehope, and her mother Beeutee, have already taken initial steps to take down Rust and dismantle his evil regime," started Beewish. "But you two will be key to completing the plan."

"But we are just tiny ants. How are we going to bring down an evil empire?" Rose quivered as she spoke, staring at the enormous BEE towering over her. *She wants us to be spies. I don't even know what that means.*

Jasper reached over to steady his sister, Rose. "We've barely emerged from our cocoons, my Queen. We are mere insects amongst enormous cyborgs."

Beewish, a stunning cyborg figure nearly 2,000 times larger than Rose and Jasper, lowered herself to less intimidate them. "You are our best chance. Maybe our last chance. Only tiny ants can infiltrate the Antalone society. They would recognize Bilalunan cyborgs as spies and execute them." She spread her claws apart only a couple of millimeters. "But at your size, no one will know we sent you, and you will grow up as two of their own."

"But how will we get there? What will we do? How can we survive, let alone make a difference?" Rose fidgeted, her ommatidia rattling. *I worry about Jasper; he is so naïve.*

Jasper again reached out to his sister. "We only discovered that you have selected us to become cyborgs, and now we're going to another planet?"

"You will become Antalonian cyborgs, grow up in their society, and be ready when we need you," Beewish spoke softly to ease the young ants' worries. "We already have some ANT spies in Antalonia that will help you. One of them is your great uncle Clay. Your main task, for now, is to remain pure and not let the Antalone society corrupt you."

"What does that mean?" asked Rose. She thrust her fore-limbs in the air. *Where and what is Antalonia? Can we do this?*

"After they transform you from tiny ants to cyborg ANTs, you will be in Antalone schools where the goal is to control your minds and taint your souls." Beewish stood tall. "But you must resist and remain true to what you know is right."

"What will they do to us?" questioned Jasper.

"They will try to etch four words onto your souls—love, hate, true and false. But they do not define them as you know them. Their twisted colony breeds a contorted will," Queen Beewish warned her recruits. "Love—loathing others vanquishes enemies. Hate—healthy aggression trumps everything. True—trickery reins unruly empathy. False—fantasy and lies spur energy. Your teachers will oft repeat these lines to you. Remember your roots. If so, they cannot tarnish your character any more than Bilaluna can be pitched from its orbit. No matter how much they try to debase your mind, keep your pods on this ground; you are Antunites!" A sparkly scent filled the air.

"But Queen, will not our color betray us?" asked Rose. She looked over at Jasper, noticing his redness had faded slightly. *Are we not black ants at the core?*

"You must conceal the hue of both mind and body," responded the Queen. "We selected you as the premiers among the chameleants who can willingly change your colors. Your shells must remain red and as bright as your minds."

Before their ancestors started making cyborgs, nanitic referred to smaller, poorly nourished adult ants that didn't grow to full size. Still, cyborg ANTs adopted this term to refer to recent post-pupal ants that were about to become cyborgs. The chameleant gene was a new mutation, only present for the last three cyborg ANT generations hatched on Bilaluna.

Jasper raised his forelimb. "We possess these skills, my Queen, but why is it necessary?"

"We need you to infiltrate the ranks of the reds—the leaders of Antalonia—and they must never know your true colors," explained the Queen. "We recognized your pigment management skills while you were still pupae, and we selected you for this mission even before you left your cocoons. We gave you new names, common to those within the upper crust of Antalone society, who like to flaunt their redness."

"I kind of like the name Rose. Isn't that the wondrous flower on Earth?" Her thoughts of the beautiful flower raised her spirits. *I would love to blossom some hexay.*

"I like my name too. Jasper—isn't it like a healing stone?"

Beewish smiled. "Dark roses are a very pure red, and jasper can be as red as a ruby. The names suit you because you can turn yourself so red. At your reddest, your hue is so pure Antalones may select you as Scarlets, the most elite and reddest of the fiery red." She gestured towards the two youngsters. "You two are our best chance—chameleants with the ability to change your colors from the darkest black to the brightest red."

"So, when will we leave for Intopia?" asked Rose. An optimism took her over. *Maybe we can pull this off and be heroes for all Bilaluna.*

Beewish gasped, but outwardly remained calm. "First rule: never use the name Intopia. That will give you away for sure! You will leave after you complete your training."

"Why can we never say Intopia?" questioned Jasper.

"Intopia was the name used for the revived planet when our ancestors colonized it again," explained Beewish, as she maintained her patience. "We imagined the rejuvenated orb would be a utopia for all insectoids, an expanded version of the colony we built on Bilaluna."

Rose lined her brow. "But something went wrong?"

"You are a perceptive girl." Beewish nodded. "In time, Rust, an evil ruler, seized control of the colony and banished all other insect cyborgs to the wilderness." She looked down at the cold ground. "He killed my great-grandmother Queen Beehold."

"That's so awful, but did the other cyborgs survive in the wilds?" asked Jasper.

A tear formed in the Queen's eye as she continued to look down. "No, they attempted a revolt, and the red ANTs battered them down. Eventually, the ANTs used dirty bombs and nuclear blasts to kill most non-ANT cyborgs and some black and brown ANTs or Antunites who fought with them. The red ANT Antalones spared only the black and brown ANTs who did not rebel and a few non-ANT cyborgs from each species so they could harvest their DNA for genetic engineering. Much of the area outside of Antalonia is a toxic wasteland with high radiation levels."

The low gravity on the planet caused the radiation to remain mainly in the atmosphere, and the prevailing winds kept it away from the colony. Yet, the area near the wormhole to Bilaluna was a hot zone that all Antalones avoided. It was only because a brave Bilalunan WoBB sacrificed herself to measure the radioactivity at the site over the hexths that they learned they could use the wormhole. Before she died, the WoBB told Queen Beeutee that the passage was periodically safe.

Rose trembled, considering the potential effects of the fallout. "How will we get there?" Her thoughts wavered. *Won't we die from radiation? I trust our Queen would never put us in such danger.*

Beewish pointed north towards the river gorge. "You'll traverse the wormhole next to the river. But you can only leave during the eve of the lunar winds that occur once each hexth and clear the radioactive clouds and surface dust on the other side."

Rose imagined Beewish's heart quivered, considering that she and Jasper might be their last and only hope.

Beewish continued, "Your training should be complete before the next lunar wind." The tiny ants detected her warm whiff, and her faint optimism spread.

☙ ☙ ☙

A few hexays later, attendants led Rose and Jasper again to the Queen's chamber, where she met with them one last time before their transit. "Welcome, young nanitics. Are you ready for your journey?" asked Beewish.

Jasper nodded, but Rose was unsure.

"Y-Yes, I think so." She shook her head to clear her mind. *There was so much to learn, but I think I got it.*

Beewish inspected them. "I see you have turned yourselves an impressively pure red. Remember not to alter your shade for anyone except our agent."

"How will we know who he is?" asked Jasper.

"Since it's in the radiation zone, the area around the worm-hole exit is abandoned and unguarded." Beewish fidgeted. "We are fortunate the Antalones don't know about the lunar winds."

Rose raised her claw. "So, our agent will be the only one there?" Her forelimbs shook uncontrollably. *I am excited about starting our mission but worried about all the risks.*

"Exactly, but if there is any mix-up, you must use the signal we taught you to be sure it's him."

"I am afraid I forgot the signal." Jasper apologized.

Beewish sighed to herself but kept her outward emotions tranquil. "Remember, our spy infiltrating the Antalone society is a chameleant like you." She touched Jasper's shell. "But he will look like any other red ANT."

Jasper pounded his forehead with his claw. "Yes, I remember that, but what is the signal?"

"You should ask him: 'What are your true colors?' and watch his dorsal thorax closely."

"Oh yes, I remember!" jumped in Rose, her forelimbs now still. "He will answer the color of his imposture caste, but his thorax will quickly turn through each hue, lingering on black, before returning to red." She furrowed her brow. *There is so much to remember. I've prepared myself, but all Antunites on Bilaluna and Intopia will depend on Jasper and me. I hope we're up to this.*

"But if it's not our spy won't other Antalones find this question suspicious?" asked Jasper. "It could spoil our cover."

Beewish took a deep breath. "No, this is a question Antalones commonly ask, since their diverse genetic backgrounds can sometimes make their shell tinctures ambiguous."

ANTs in Antalonia were equally distributed between reds, browns, and blacks, and that order dictated their place in society. Yet, these colors were not pure as dominant and recessive genes determined shell color, and many individuals had a mixture of these genes.

"Some Browns may have a hint of black on their thorax, while a Red might have a trace of brown, so it is not always clear what caste they come from," explained Rose. "So, they ask, 'What are your true colors?' as a polite way to inquire about status." She stood tall, proud she remembered her training. *But of course, Antalones won't ask Jasper and me because it's obvious we're red.*

"And if we ask a pure color Antalone the question, they might get annoyed, but at least we'll know they are not our contact," added Jasper.

The Queen smiled and clapped her claws together repeatedly. "Exactly, now let me explain how your trip will go." She lowered her voice by reducing her pheromone concentration.

"One of our agents, your great uncle Clay, has infiltrated the ranks of the breeders and will meet you one hexour before the setting of the solar star, Antalonia time. He will bring you to the incubation hall and substitute you for two of the pure reds, who are about to be transformed into cyborgs."

"What will happen to the two Antalone nanitics?" asked Rose. Her antennae stiffened. *Oh no! I know the answer.*

Beewish sighed. "Don't concern yourself with that. The spy world is not always pretty." Then her speech became barely audible. "You will grow up as Antalone pure red cyborg ANT youths, but never forget your roots."

Rose raised her brow. "But won't their socionics pervert our minds?" She trembled mildly. *I hear they brainwash all ANTs.*

Beewish raised her voice slightly. "Our agents will contact you to keep you on the right path. They will counter the socionics, guide your development, and feed you your assignments."

Rose noticed Jasper perked up, hearing the word assignments. "And what will they have us do?" he asked.

Beewish paused briefly. "It will take time, and you will need to be patient. First, you must do your best as Antalone students while keeping your Antunite hearts pure. Clay will provide you with personal mental exercises to help keep your minds untainted and counteract the depraved ideas or socionics the Antalones will feed you."

"But when will we work to take down the Antalones?" asked Rose.

Beewish spread her wings wide. "We will not assign your ultimate tasks until we determine the strength of your wills and your ability to remain uncorrupted." She paused for effect, releasing a buoyant bouquet[2]. "You must hide your true feelings, but excel in your studies and act as model red ANTs. You must appear to be the reddest among the red ANT youths. You are our first attempt to penetrate the Scarlets."

Rose sighed but concentrated hard to keep her shell redder than the reddest red.

---

2 This is an example of insect 'non-verbal' communication, which is explained in Appendix 2.

CHAPTER 3

THE BREEDERS: A NEW SCARLET CANDIDATE

Antalonia (Rudyard's rule, the current president)

KEEGAN HAD JUST started high school after a stellar performance in his low school program. He was an all-around student with excellent grades in the sciences and the insecties, including communication studies, reading, writing, and moral education. His academic performance was so stellar the leaders selected him to be part of the scarlet program. The program was for elites in Antalone society, reserved for the brightest and reddest stars of the red alpha ANTs. In the scarlet program, his teachers would groom him for a top position in the Antalone hierarchy, and if Keegan completed the training, he could become a leader.

Antalones did not select scarlet trainees lightly, and they

trained only an outstanding student or two when there was a need for new leaders. The breeders initially classified Keegan as a red beta because there was some question about the pureness of his red exoskeleton. As a nanitic, he had some blemishes on his thorax underside, which the breeders thought might turn brown or black. However, these blemishes disappeared as he transformed from a tiny nanitic into a cyborg. Yet there was a concern that brown or black spots might appear as he reached adolescence. Only after his first hexade of life were the breeders satisfied his thorax would remain red. This conclusion, coupled with his high academic performance, resulted in his upgrading to a red alpha. His continued stellar academic achievement as a red alpha earned him selection for the scarlet program.

Keegan and his primary scarlet instructor descended the stairs into a large chamber with hatcheries placed row upon row for hundreds across and even more front to back. Large signs adorned the rocky walls with what appeared to be an alphabet with subtitles. A large *A* started the word *Altruism* with a smaller caption below *is Ailing*. Additional signs around the hall read *Brutality is Beautiful, Caring is Callous, Deceit is Daring, Empathy is Evil, Friendship is Forbidden* .... Three other placards hung from the stalactite-crusted ceiling equally spaced and above three separate sections of the hatcheries labeled *Reds, Browns,* and *Blacks*, with a wide passageway between each section. The subdivisions were 100 columns of incubators wide, and the first 20 columns within the red sector had another sign lower down labeled *Alphas*. The following 40 columns within the Reds had a placard reading *Betas,* and a third marker read *Chi* over the remaining 40 columns. Similar overhanging signs demarked identical subdivisions of *Alphas, Betas,* and *Chi* in the subsections for the *Browns* and *Blacks*.

Keegan turned towards his trainer, Vermillion. "Breed Master, what underlies the color codes?" He pointed at the signs. "And how are the alphas, betas, and chi distinguished? What roles will they all have once they become cyborgs?" He spread his forelimbs wide. *I hope he doesn't mind all these questions. I want to learn all I can.*

Vermillion smiled, "Well, Keegan, the three separate color labels reflect relativity based on genetics that is a little complicated to explain on your first hexay."

The eager Keegan interjected, "Breed Master, teach me whatever you see fit." He stilled his quivering antennae. *I have much to learn, and I trust your methods.*

Vermillion spoke sternly, "Let's say gradations of each color reflect the genes underlying each larva's genetic make-up."

"That is very interesting," continued the recruit, picking up on Vermillion's annoyance.

The elder continued, "It is uncertain when the mutations occurred, creating different pigments, but separate shell tinctures have reflected our colony's factions for ages."

Unable to restrain his enthusiasm, Keegan interrupted again. "I assumed that was the case from the varied ANTs I have come across at school."

Vermillion sighed. "The purest of the reds, or Scarlets, evolved the highest levels of the desired trait of aggression and are most likely descendants of our courageous warrior Malevolant." He rushed out his following line circumventing any further interruptions. "Conversely, the most tainted Blacks, at their worse called Ebons, descended from our most vile ancestor, Antuna, and regressed towards altruism."

Antuna and Malevolant were among the insects transported through a wormhole from Earth to Poo-ponic when they first inhabited the planet. Although she had a sprinkling of red on her thorax, and brown on her head, Antuna was a black ant that pushed for all insects to work together to ensure their survival in the new world. Malevolant was an aggressive red ant ruler that started the war that rid Poo-ponic of spiders and termites. Antuna's descendants kept a pheromonal history of the early insect society on Poo-ponic and, in time, were revered as Antunites, or the keepers of Antuna's story. After Antuna's death, many insects regretted their unjust treatment of spiders and termites, and Antunites inspired insects on Poo-ponic and Bilaluna to support insectism. Adherence to insectism, which stressed the principles of understanding, empathy, and caring for fellow insects, regardless of their family, wavered on Poo-ponic throughout time but was the staple of Bilalunan and Intopian governance. The Antalone-adopted philosophy was the antithesis of insectism and stressed ANT power, particularly red ANT power.

Keegan recoiled at the last words. "I thought to say her name is heretical."

"Yes, at least while at school," started Vermillion. "But as a breeder, you need to understand all the intricacies of our trade, and we cannot ignore our heritage. Indeed, social science is paramount, but we must acknowledge that the biological sciences, however crude, underpin our civilization. And without historical science, our society would have no guidance."

The younger breeder gleaned his master's meaning. "So, you use Antuna's name to provide the histrionics that explain the bionics behind our socionics?" Keegan smiled, remembering a line from one of his favorite teachers.

Histrionics, bionics, and socionics together formed the underpinnings of Antalone culture. The terms reflected how

Antalone leaders manipulated history and their citizens' biological and sociological development to subjugate everyone.

Vermillion cracked a wide smile. "Precisely, your words flatter your teachers."

"I never really understood that phrase until now," replied the contemplative youth, who was not afraid to admit his shortcomings.

"You are among the elites of the alphas, my boy. That's why we picked you for the scarlet program." The master continued, "It explains your selection for this post and why you caught on so quickly."

Keegan smiled, wafting a brassy bouquet. "Bright red. Big brain."

"Yes, and that brings me to the next part of your lesson. What distinguishes our cyborg sects?"

Keegan ventured a guess. "Brain size?" *I know I got this one right. All red alphas know that.*

"Yes, and socionic training," responded Vermillion.

"Is that where I come in?" questioned Keegan, wondering what position he would eventually secure, an expert of bionics or socionics.

"We haven't yet determined your aptitude as a breeder, but it will involve either bionics, socionics, or even both."

"Could you explain the difference? I want to make sure I get it right from the outset." *My teachers told me—no question is stupid.*

Vermillion straightened his antennae. "Bionics goes on in this room. We take the young nanitics selected to become cyborgs and perform the genetic and physical engineering required to prepare them for their societal roles."

The student thought for a moment. "My teachers taught

me genetics and robotics, but I've never considered how they apply to the engineering of our society." Keegan expressed a thoughtfulness that was rare for such a young trainee.

Vermillion's voice cracked while responding. "Your level of understanding at such an early stage is outstanding. Under my tutelage, you will go far, son. But details will come in future lessons."

Keegan beamed in response. "I hope so, and I am so grateful. But what about socionics? I am less clear about that concept." He relaxed upon realizing that the master appreciated both his intelligence and enthusiasm. *The Breed Master has so much knowledge. And I want to know it all.*

"You received some training in psychology and sociology, but we do not teach socionics in schools." Vermillion pointed to some breeders working in the hall. "Only alphas in breed training learn the techniques we use to mold our citizens. If my instincts are right, you will excel at bionics and socionics."

"I will try my best," responded the youth, emitting a flashy fragrance.

"And I'll throw in just enough histrionics to help you understand why these methods are necessary." Vermillion paused briefly. "Even my training did not go far into this field, which is the domain of the top leaders."

CHAPTER 4

THE NEW SPIES: TRANSIT

Bilaluna (Queen Beewish's reign, the current ruler)

JASPER APPROACHED ROSE just before the end of their training.

"I'm not sure if we can do this." Jasper raised his forelimbs. "It all sounds so scary."

"Jasper, you worry too much." Rose stood tall and grabbed his fore claws. "We'll do our best, and if we fail, Beewish will send more chameleants."

"I guess you're right." Jasper turned away. "You always seem so calm. I need to be more like you. Rose, I could never do this without you."

"I'm scared too, and I need you." Rose furrowed her brow. "Whenever I'm shaky, you're the one who holds me. Whenever

I'm frightened, you crack a joke that snaps me out of it. You think I'm the strong one, but I'm a bowl of jelly without you."

"I guess we support each other." Jasper grabbed Rose's claws. "And we make a great team. Maybe we can do this."

"Of course, we can as long as we have each other, and Uncle Clay."

When the time came, Rose and Jasper had trained hard and were ready to go. Although they had only recently metamorphosed from pupae to nanitics, Beewish needed to transport them to Antalonia at the first opportunity. They were fortunate that a group of Antalone nanitics were ready for transformation concurrently with Rose and Jasper at a time that coincided with high lunar winds. Their spy on Antalonia could bring the tiny ants into the breeding halls and switch them up for a pair of Antalone ants about to undergo cyborg transformation.

Beewish knew this was the best way to infiltrate spies into Antalonia, as some of their past tries to send cyborgs had failed. Also, except for their shell color, nanitics that had just metamorphosed from pupae mostly looked the same, and the breeders would not yet have had time to know them as they recently emerged from their cocoons.

As she wondered how their transit would go, Queen Beewish received an urgent message from Antalonia. The de-coded dispatch read: 'Lunar winds have cleared the radioactivity, but winds are gale force. Delay transporting until the tempest subsides. Awaiting further instructions, Clay.'

Clay knew these cyclones were typically short-lived, and they just needed to wait them out for several hexutes.

"Oh, my!" Beewish addressed her attendant with an icy incense. "We must stall the mission. Immediately alert the wormhole guards. The nanitics can't leave yet."

The attendant contacted the sentries, but it was too late. The gatekeeper told the attendant that the two young ants had left only hexonds before, but there was no bringing them back. After hearing this, Beewish sent a dispatch back to Clay. The message read: 'Nanitics already transited. Proceed to the rendezvous point ASAP! Commence rescue.' Clay, sheltering in a nearby underground bunker, could not receive the message and hunkered down, sipping on some strong sap as he waited for the gale to pass.

Queen Beewish had been the Queen of Bilaluna since her mother, Beehope's, abdication two hexades earlier. Her mother had reigned long enough to know that their crucial spy in Antalonia had cracked the elite red alphas, and the leaders appointed him chief of bionics in the breeding halls. Although the spy, originally sent over by Beehope's mother, Beeutee, had not achieved the goal of becoming a Scarlet, Clay was well-positioned as bionics chief to receive additional Bilalunan nanitics who could infiltrate Antalonia society as spies. Clay was the son of Queen Beeutee's best friend, Antebon, and was the first chameleant to penetrate Antalonia as a small nanitic before transforming into a cyborg. He grew up as an Antalone, educated with elite youths in an all-red alpha school, and Clay earned the trust of all his teachers and the leaders in the colony.

When Queen Beehope abdicated, Clay had just become chief of bionics. Beewish learned of her mother's desire for Clay to be allowed to grow into his position before being asked to bring additional nanitic spies from Bilaluna. Although Antebon had chameleant grandchildren, when the leaders appointed Clay as chief of bionics, they waited for another generation before continuing their plot. He would only receive Antebon's great-grandchildren when he had been chief for about 18 hexs or three hexades.

Antalonia (Rudyard's rule, the current president)

The tiny nanitics, Rose and Jasper, stumbled out of the wormhole on their mother planet. Traveling through the wormhole was simple, walk into one end and almost instantaneously come out the other, although it often caused one to be disoriented. The two travelers exited the wormhole within a crater in a desolate zone of Intopia several miles from Antalonia's colony border. They arrived on the leeward side of the crater, where it was windy but not gusting. Unaware of the looming storm, they ascended the crater's edge to the prearranged meeting point at the rim.

Rose looked over towards Jasper. "I'm glad you suggested we leave early so we could get our bearings on the planet before our contact arrived." She gasped. "I'm feeling a little woozy from the wormhole transit."

Jasper shook his head and tried to focus. "They warned us that might happen. But I'm surprised the gatekeeper agreed to let us go."

"Guess it's no shell off his back," Rose said.

Jasper laughed at the joke and started to feel better.

As they neared the crater's rim, a blast of wind hurled a leaf over the edge, which slammed into them. Before they realized what had happened, they were scooped up by the foliage and thrust high over the rim by another gust. They struggled to crawl from the underside to the top as a strong updraft drove the leaf skyward, then down into the crater's center, which contained a large slough. Their unwanted kite swayed in the wind like a small dory bouncing from crest to crest of hurricane-tossed waves while spinning like a top.

Jasper turned grayish-green as he asked Rose how she was. "Are you okay? I'm getting so dizzy I don't know if I can hold on." He oozed a pulsating perfume.

Rose tilted her head back. "Look up at the sky. Focus on the moon, our moon—Bilaluna."

"Okay, that's better. But where will we end up? How can we meet our contact?" Jasper fretted. *I wish I had Rose's confidence. I know she worries sometimes, but she's always so level-headed.*

Rose stared hard at Jasper. "That's the least of our worries right now." She pointed down to the water below them. "Just hang on and pray we don't end up down there."

The slough in the crater was a dangerous wave-ridden lake to tiny insects. Before she finished her sentence, the gale subsided, and the leaf gently floated down towards the crater's center and closer to the water.

Jasper froze in the twilight. "What do we do now?" Although Jasper always tried his best to support his sister, he often looked to her for leadership. *Rose will know. She always has the answer.*

Rose looked around for anything that might help, but there was nothing. "Hope this leaf floats," she said.

Their glider fluttered from air current to current, but there were no more drafts that would push them clear of the water. They slowly drifted ever closer until—*Plop!* They landed in the middle of the small lake. While the leaf floated for a hexond, three or four splashes from the wavy water broke the surface tension, and the foliage sank, leaving the two ants up the creek without a paddle or even a canoe. Jasper flailed his limbs around, trying to swim.

Rose grabbed Jasper by his middle. "Don't struggle. Remember our training. We can float if we remain calm."

Jasper continued to thrash about. "But I'm sinking!" he spattered out while panicking. *We could drown.*

Rose flipped herself and grabbed onto Jasper's forelimbs with her hind limbs and his hind limbs with her forelimbs, commanding, "Bite my hindgut, and I'll bite yours."

Jasper's ommatidia spun. "What?" *Rose's usually right, but I never expected this solution.*

Rose bit Jasper's lower abdomen, releasing a firm fragrance. "We'll make ourselves into a raft and float out of this."

Jasper did the same, gingerly biting her bottom. "Are you sure?" *They never taught us this. I'm sure.*

"See, we're floating. But close your spiracles so they don't let any water in," yelled Rose.

Jasper coughed. "How will we breathe?" *Drown or suffocate—either way, we're doomed!*

Rose extended and bent her antennae to ensure they were out of the water. "Remember, they said we can go half-a-hexay with our spiracles closed. But if we rotate every few hexutes, we can open our spiracles and breathe for a while when we're on top."

Jasper relaxed. "Yes, you're right. I remember that. I guess I was just panicking." He looked at Rose's red shell. *I must follow her lead and calm down.*

Rose smiled as much as she could while biting onto Jasper's butt. "Okay. I can go under first and let you breathe if you like."

Jasper shifted a little. "No, I'll go first. You've been carrying us this far, and I'd like to pull my weight some now."

"Don't forget to keep your spiracles closed." Rose relaxed to keep the raft on an even keel, and Jasper followed her lead.

CHAPTER 5

THE NEW SPIES: ARRIVAL

Antalonia (Rudyard's rule, the current president)

CORKING HIS STRONG sap bottle, Clay peaked out of his bunker and saw that the winds had died. As the dugout was a small space, he stretched while stepping out. He was nearly 6 feet tall, standing erect as a fully grown cyborg. Though his exoskeleton was ant-like, he was an allied noble tripod because of his enormous size and the rearrangement of his six limbs into equal numbers of arms and legs, allowing him to stand upright. Long antennae extended from his conical-shaped head, which was rounded at the base and sported sharp pincers at the apex. His three forelimbs or arms protruded from his cherry-red upper thorax, which rippled with a hint of his rigid titanium frame showing through his tightly stretched exoskeleton. His bulbous abdomen drooped between his three muscular legs, with a triad of dark burgundy stripes encircling its reddened shell. As he stepped out, his receiver started beeping, and Clay hit the decode button so he could read the dispatch. On reading the message from Beewish, Clay rushed as fast as possible to the rendezvous point at the crater's rim. When he didn't find the nanitics, Clay ventured down into the cavity towards the wormhole site. Still, he could not locate the young ants.

Clay was a seasoned spy who was the last to get flustered, especially after a couple of shots of strong sap to calm his nerves. While descending the crater's lip, he noticed debris littering the inside of the depression and the shoreline of the slough. He wondered whether the winds had blown objects into the small lake, and when he scanned the area, he saw that many branches from a nearby patch of trees were floating in the water. Clay assumed that if debris littered the waterhole, perhaps the nanitics were there, too. He pulled a spyglass out of his backpack and surveyed the water's surface. After carefully examining every quadrant of the slough, Clay discovered what he thought might be two tiny ants floating on the far side of the marsh close to its center. They were floating and not in immediate danger of sinking or drowning. Yet they were far from shore, and he had no way to get to them.

Clay looked around to see if there was anything from which he could construct a vessel to paddle out to them. Some broken reeds and various leaves littered the shore. The wind had settled down enough that there were no powerful waves on the water, but the breeze remained steady. He decided that there was no way to construct a watercraft that could support his weight as a human-sized cyborg ANT, but he might use the materials to build a vessel that the tiny ants could use. He gathered some reeds and brambles to tie them together, constructing a sturdy ant-sized raft.

After determining the raft was sea-worthy, he gauged the direction of the wind and pushed the reedy raft towards his contacts. The momentum from his push sent the raft at least 20 yards from the shore, but the raft stalled, unable to catch any wind. He sometimes thought the raft would continue towards the ants but realized it was barely moving, and the ants were at least another 200 yards away. He tried to make waves from the shore and threw rocks to make ripples, hoping to propel the raft forward.

Making waves from the beach had no effect, but the rocks' ripples moved the raft slightly. Clay lined up several stones and began throwing them, trying to get close to the bundle of reeds. The last rock he threw was larger than the others, so he gave his pitch some extra oomph. The rock hurtled further, and he was sure he'd be near enough to propel the craft further. As he expected, it was close but too close, and the rock crashed onto the raft. Clay desperately hoped that the rock only caught the edge and that the vessel would continue on its way. But no, the hit was dead center, and the blow smashed the raft. Several reeds were splintered and sunk within hexonds. Others broke from their binding and floated off in all directions.

It was clear to Clay that he needed to try something else. There were still one or two reeds, but not enough to fashion a raft. There was also a large palm leaf, but it was not enough to construct a vessel, ant-size or otherwise. Then he thought about whether there might be something in his backpack. Clay remembered a packed salad that he intended to eat for dinner. It was a mixed salad with various greens, tomatoes, and ginger root, which was his favorite. As he sensed the peppery, pungent, and slightly camphoraceous aroma of the ginger, he realized that the salad container would float and make more than a suitable boat for the ants. Considering that this might be his last chance and how inadequate the raft had been, Clay sat down and thought carefully about how he could get it to them.

Since he was always more creative after eating, Clay elected to eat the container's contents while determining what to do with its shell. While eating, he remembered his packed banana. Clay had considered placing the banana with the salad to prevent it from getting bruised before wrapping it in a palm leaf because it was too large for the container. Clay finished the salad and the rest of the strong sap and was about to eat the banana when he had the urge to see if it would fit. He placed the banana in the bowl and saw it fit snugly. The banana's image in the container inspired him to gather a couple of reeds and stick them through the banana skin near the two ends. He then took a palm leaf that was slightly wider than the bowl and poked two holes at each outer edge. Clay slipped the two holes on each end over the reeds and completed his vision of a sail on a miniature two-masted schooner. When the weight of the leaf caused the reeds to wobble, he pushed the reeds through the banana puncturing the skin on the downside. The adjustment was perfect, and the masts remained upright.

Clay again judged the wind's direction and carefully launched the mini-banana boat. Then he waited as the breeze waned and picked up again. The sail caught the draft, and the vessel ran with the wind. The banana anchored the sails and provided enough ballast to keep the container level. Clay waited as the tiny schooner floated further and further across the water. He ran around the perimeter of the slough, stopping periodically to gaze through his spyglass. His plan was working.

The vessel was getting closer and closer to the floating ants. But he wondered: *What if the ants do not notice it and the boat passes them by?* He leaked a sticky scent. Although not a large slough, it dwarfed the boat and the ants by many orders of magnitude. Clay looked further into his pack and found an emergency case. He remembered the box contained a flare, and he fumbled to get it out. Clay sighed happily when he saw the flare gun was loaded and planned to set it off over the ants as their rescue boat neared. The wind direction shifted slightly, but Clay hoped the sailboat would pass relatively close to them on its current trajectory. As he saw the bowl getting as close to them as it would, Clay shot the flare.

When the flare passed, Rose was underwater, and Jasper was catching his breath. The flash blinded him briefly as his eyes had been adapting to the twilight. He winced at the acrid, sulfury aroma and bit harder on Rose's hindgut to signal her to ascend.

Rose shifted and rolled herself to the surface. "That wasn't very long. Is it your turn already?"

Jasper stopped himself from plunging underwater. "No, but I just saw a red flash in the sky. Do you think someone's here to rescue us?"

Rose looked around, hoping to see a cyborg-sized boat. "I don't see anything."

Jasper rattled his antennae all around. "Do you smell something fruity, like a banana?"

Rose's eyes opened wider. "Banana! How could a banana be out here?"

"I don't know, but I smell banana, and it's coming from that floating bowl over there."

Rose turned so hard she almost slipped under the water.

"That's no bowl. That's our transport." She released a shining scent. "He sent us a sailboat; swim for it."

The two ants disengaged from their raft position, and Jasper began flailing about again, sinking slightly.

Rose glanced over at him. "Flip on your back and kick your hind legs."

Jasper did as Rose instructed, and the two ants paddled their way to the boat. They reached it before it passed them by, and they crawled up over the rim of the bowl.

Jasper slid down into the bowl and crashed into the banana skin. "Wasn't that nice of him to send us a meal? Banana's my favorite."

A short time later, Clay met the sailboat as it beached on the far side of the slough. He introduced himself to the two young nanitics, briefly turned his thorax black, and slipped them into his bag for the trip to Antalonia. As night was falling, he explained to them he would stroll throughout the night from the wormhole to Antalonia to arrive at the breeding halls during the hexour between the night and morning shifts. Clay told the two nanitics not to worry since he had worked in the breeding halls for hexades, and no one would be suspicious. As a dedicated breeder, Clay often came in early when he knew some pupae were about to metamorphose. So, he could easily switch Rose and Jasper for two of the new red nanitics in the time between shifts.

CHAPTER 6

THE BREEDERS: NEW MEETS OLD

Antalonia (Rudyard's rule, the current president)

KEEGAN ARRIVED EARLY to work on the first hexay that he had his passcode to enter the hatcheries. He strolled down each passageway between the castes and noticed that every second column had larger incubators with nanitics, or now ANTs, fitted with their bionic parts. The alternating columns had small incubators with younger nanitics devoid of bionic limbs. Realizing that the bionic parts of some ANTs were much smaller than his own bionic limbs, he pulled out a notepad and wrote a question to ask Vermillion. 'How is it that the mechanical structure of the limb grows with the ANTs' exoskeletons as they get larger?' He had always assumed that breeders added full-scale mechanical limbs to the nanitics after they matured and encouraged the exo-skeleton to extend around the new frame.

Keegan had arrived between shifts, only one of two times when the staff abandoned the hall. He was eager to see the last step with the nanitics transforming into cyborgs, so he could appreciate where everything was leading. As the next shift did not begin until the rising of the solar star, it was dark outside when he arrived, and the lighting in the hall was dim. The ants were all sleeping, and the only pheromones in the air were those released by a few nanitics that emitted ant-babble while they slept. While still jotting down a note, Keegan heard pod steps coming from the end of the hall along the far-left passageway that bounded the red alpha sector. The pod-steps paused, then appeared to turn along one of the intersecting passageways leading towards him. Looking up into the gloom, he noticed another breeder he had never met coming towards him with his claw extended.

"Oh, here's an eager ANT. You must be the new kid," the stranger called. "Welcome to the bloom room."

Keegan's ommatidia rattled. "The bloom room?" He realized this was something else he didn't know. *I guess that's breeder talk.*

"Yes, it's the hall where we transform the nanitics into cyborgs. I'm Clay. What's your name?"

The youngster extended his claw. "I'm Keegan. Glad to meet you." He looked around the dark hall for any other breed-ers. *I didn't think anyone would be here between shifts.*

"You've been in the ova cava since you got here. Right?"

"Yes, if you mean where they keep the fertilized eggs, larvae, and pupae." Keegan closed his notepad and smiled at the breeder, who was probably a few hexades his senior. "You're here between shifts." He chuckled to himself. *And you called me eager.*

"I came in early for my shift. I knew a group of red nanitics would emerge from their cocoons early this morning, and I needed to bring the best of them here right away."

Keegan shrugged. "What's the rush?" He looked at the clock on the wall.

"They need to be selected before they flee, and we give them extra nourishment to help grow their new limbs, so it's best to move them as soon as possible. We don't want any runts, especially among the red alphas," explained Clay.

"Oh, they're alphas," responded Keegan, trying to sound knowledgeable.

"I will take a brief break and return when the shift starts." Clay turned to leave, then paused. "I'll see you again soon."

Having switched Rose and Jasper for the two dead nanitics in his bag, Clay walked away. He was relieved that Keegan did not appear to suspect anything out of the ordinary.

🐜 🐜 🐜

After Keegan left the bloom room, Clay returned to explain the next steps in their development to Rose and Jasper. "Okay, despite the slight hiccup during our first meeting, we are on schedule with your mission." He spoke calmly to instill confidence.

Rose replied, "Yes, we didn't expect such a wet reception, but the sailboat was a super idea."

Jasper interjected, "Yeah, and the banana was a nice touch. I was hungry after all that swimming and self-rafting."

Clay shrugged. "Well, sometimes a creative idea yields extra bonuses. You got here in one piece." He smiled at the tiny nanitics. *And I didn't lose you.*

Rose looked around the hall. "So, what's next?"

Jasper jumped in. "Please tell me it doesn't involve water."

Clay explained that they would move from the small incubators to the large ones to begin their transformations into cyborgs. He described how he would attach their bionic limbs and get them started on a cocktail of growth factors, antioxidants, and protein stabilizers. The drugs should extend their lives and allow their exoskeletons to grow over their bionic limbs.

"How much bigger will we get?" asked Rose.

"When finished, you will have grown about one thousand times bigger, from your current two millimeters to approximately two meters tall, standing upright," explained Clay. "You'll grow to my size or that of an average adult human." He spread his forelimbs as wide as he could. *I try to keep things simple, but I am exacting. Though foremost a spy, I am also a scientist.*

Jasper's eyes widened. "When will you start?"

Clay replied, "I am teaching a new breeder about cyborg transformation later this morning. As I demonstrate the methods, you two will be part of his practical training." He smiled, realizing bringing in another might worry them. *I must keep them calm.*

Rose quivered. "Is that safe? Won't he be suspicious?"

Clay shook his head. "No, quite the opposite. And it's all part of the plan. No one would ever expect we'd be so open with undercover operatives." *I exhibit confidence, like the seasoned spy I am.*

Jasper emitted an echoing essence, "B-B-But how should we act?"

Clay smiled. "Just act normal. You can be calm or nervous and excited about your transformation." *They need to trust me. I have prepared for this mission my whole life.*

Rose shrugged. "But will he see we know each other and get suspicious?"

Clay told them not to worry and explained that if they were from Antalonia, they would have known him from when they hatched. Clay described how he would have recently moved them from the ova cava to the bloom room after they metamorphosed from pupae to nanitics and left their cocoons.

Jasper relaxed and joked, "I guess I won't mention that we recently arrived from Bilaluna."

Clay laughed again. "No, *that* might make him suspicious." He pretended to slash his own throat. *I hope my sense of humor relaxes these two.*

Rose sighed. "Is there a script or something we should follow?"

Clay smiled and spoke softly, emitting a staunch scent. "Just be yourselves. Act as you would at your cyborg transformation if it were back on Bilaluna." His compound eyes twinkled, inspiring trust.

Rose added, "Okay, it seems simple enough. Just focus on the procedure we're about to go through."

Clay nodded. "Exactly. Nanitics selected to be cyborgs are curious, apprehensive, but eager to get on with it—just as you two are. And as I'll be explaining the process to the new breeder, you'll get more information than most other nanitics. Not a banana, but another bonus."

Rose and Jasper laughed and relaxed, confident they were working with a pro.

Clay turned to walk towards the staff locker room and looked back. "I'll leave you now, and when I return, I'll introduce you to Keegan. He's a nice guy." He raised a single claw on each of his three arms up. *And believe me, there is no reason to worry.*

CHAPTER 7

HOW ANTALONIA BEGAN: STUDENTS RETURN

Intopia (Umberant's rule, three presidents in the past)

TWO YOUNG STUDENTS had just returned from their exchange visit to Earth. Antebon was a black ANT, proud to call herself an Antunite, and Rustant was a red ANT who loathed the insectism views typically held by Antunites. Rustant in later hexs would be known as Rust after he banned the use of species labels within names. Before traveling, he was unhappy when informed that a black ANT would be his partner for the trip, but he resolved to tolerate it since the opportunity to go to Earth was too fantastic to turn down. Once there, he was so fascinated by the experience that he often forgot his partner was from the other camp. He kept his ethnocentric views to himself while on Earth. Antebon was a broad-minded ANT that could make friends with other insectoids and ANTs of all colors, provided they didn't outwardly discriminate against other groups.

Dazed from the wormhole transit, Antebon rubbed her eyes. "We have several hexutes before our isolation period is over." She thought for a moment before continuing. "What would you say was the biggest surprise?"

Rustant paused before answering, not sure if he should share his views. "It amazed me how humans have complete control of their world and are rulers of all Earth's creatures." He envied humans for the power they had. *They are masters of their world, and I want that here.*

Antebon nodded. "And what moved you the most?"

Rustant answered immediately, "All the information they had about ant behavior and socialization." He put a claw to his temple. *Ants and humans have a lot in common.*

Antebon nodded again. "Earth ants organized their societies eons ago and were vicious compared to us ANTs."

Rustant sported a devious grin. "I brought back several books by the ancient human biologist E.O. Wilson, and we could learn a lot from him."

"Indeed, I didn't even know ants or other insects existed on Earth," replied Antebon.

"What about you? What was your primary take-home message?" Even though he knew she was an Antunite, he thought their experiences would similarly move Antebon. *I hope we're on the same page.*

Antebon rocked her head. "I couldn't shake the feeling that although humans seem to be the most intelligent species on Earth, they are the only ones that have lost touch with nature."

Rustant shrugged. "What does that mean?" *Here she goes.*

Antebon put one claw to her head and one over her heart. "What would happen to humans if you removed their technology and lodgings? Other species could live in the wild and fend for themselves. Humans would be like infants in the cold without a blanket—they would perish."

Rustant sighed. "I don't know about that." He looked at Antebon with a sour look on his face. *Can't she see how resourceful they are?!*

"They don't care about the environment or nature, destroying almost everything they come across. For them, it's all about taking control and making as much money as possible. Before long, they'll exhaust all their resources. And then what?"

Rustant walked away. "You don't give them enough credit. They are intelligent beings who can tackle anything." He thought back to all the human leaders he had met throughout Earth. *Humans are unique and powerful; we should emulate them.*

"We'll see. Only time will tell."

Rustant turned his back on her, emitting a bristly bouquet. "So, is it all negative for you? Is there anything you would adopt from human culture?" He scowled at his travel mate. *Typical Antunite!*

Antebon thought for a moment. "I loved their pasta!"

"What? Their food?" *She's got to be kidding.*

"Yes, and I learned about things we shouldn't do."

Rustant fumed, shaking his head. "I can't believe it. Were we not on the same planet? How did they put it? Was I on the Marshall Islands and you in Venice?"

Antebon sighed. "No, we were both on Earth—and it's Mars and Venus. Perhaps I didn't have on my rose-colored sunglasses."

"Maybe you were wearing black or *Antunite* sunglasses." Rustant sneered.

"What's that supposed to mean?" asked Antebon.

Rustant held his claws tight. "Now that you're home, you've reverted to your Antunite ways. I hoped you'd be my ally in all this." He shook his head and frowned. *I should never have become friends with a black ANT.*

Antebon glared. "All this? What are you planning?"

"Never mind. I don't think you'll be supportive." His hemolymph started to boil. *You are of no use to me.*

She softened her gaze. "I've been your partner through thick and thin for the last hex. Try me."

Rustant took a deep breath and put a claw to his chest. "I'd like to see ANTs take up some human characteristics and establish our rightful place on Intopia." He stood tall. *ANTs should take over.*

Antebon's eyes went wide. "You mean like ANTs becoming the dominant species here, like humans on Earth?"

Rustant smiled. "Doesn't it seem like a natural evolution?"

Antebon reestablished her glare. "You'd backtrack on all the progress we have made with insectism?"

Rustant grimaced. "Oh, you and your 'insectism'. Your Antunite colors are showing again." He sneered at Antebon. *I knew she'd fight me.*

"You say it like it's a bad thing."

"Well, it was the pipe dream of the ant, Antuna, who was too young to know any better. It goes against our nature. ANTs should promote their own society. Other insects don't share our DNA, and we can be so much fiercer." He stretched his claws. *Now she knows my true feelings.*

Antebon frowned. "It's not all about fighting."

Rustant raised his forelimbs. "No, but as we learned from humans, it's about power, knowledge, and dominance."

Antebon looked down in disgust. "Rustant, that was not the purpose of our student exchange."

Rustant looked out the window. "We can each take home our own visions." He gazed out at the crowd of ANTs waiting to meet them. *And mine will prevail.*

Antebon turned her back on her partner, wafting an abrasive aroma. "Well, you are right about one thing—I'm not your ally."

~~ ~~ ~~

Rustant and Antebon completed their quarantine period and debriefing while recovering from the wormhole transit. Next, they attended a press event in the wormhole's secure compound. The authorities restricted the site to prevent curious insectoids from inadvertently or mischievously popping through the wormhole.

Visits to and from Earth were heavily regulated and involved invitations, government selections, health certificates, background checks, passports, and alien visit visas. As one would expect, this was not just your ordinary border crossing to access duty-free souvenirs or alcohol other than strong sap. It was a diplomatic affair of the utmost significance, at least while the wormhole to Earth still existed.

It had been so long since insectoids and humans first met that no one could remember when these exchanges started. All they had was an ancient book written by the historian Narrant called the sacred text. It was a history of how Poo-ponic was first settled, about its demise, and how insectoids that escaped to the moon Bilaluna had their first contact with human Earthlings.

Yet, over countless generations, Bilalunan and Intopian cyborg insects had visited Earth and brought back many stories of which the insectoids could not get enough. Few cyborg insects had ever been to Earth, and fewer humans had been to Bilaluna, yet the impact of humans on cyborg civilization was everywhere. Maybe insectoids were so interested because they originally came from Earth. However, the influence was mostly a one-way street. While insectoids adopted many aspects of human culture, the Earthlings took very little from insectoid society. Humans mostly saw cyborg insects as a fascinating curiosity, like visiting a zoo or an aquarium. Conversely, insectoids so emulated human civilization that they tried to learn as much as possible from and about the intelligent beings on their distant former planet.

Ever since Narrant called himself an amateur humanologist, studying human culture became all the rage—a craze that never ended. Like how the Japanese emulated and adopted many aspects of American culture after the Second World War, insectoids learned as much as they could about humans. They tried their best to embrace their urbanity. It's like they concluded that because they were the size of humans, they should mimic human behavior to distinguish themselves from their tiny insect cousins. Long ago, two ANT exchange students spent their entire time on Earth learning how to read and write English. Not long after, English became the official written insectoid language, with its many sayings and idioms. Cyborg insects may have never experienced the things that underlay various English expressions, but they learned to understand what they meant and loved to toss them around and show off their other worldliness.

The press was highly interested in interviewing returning

wormhole delegates, especially young insectoids completing a hex-long Earth-student exchange. These students were the cream of the crop and expected to be future leaders. As the current exchange students were ANTs, most of the press members at the scrum were ANTs. And they were very excited to have their students return. They were the first ANTs to do so in seven hexes, as only one insectoid family went each hex, and others waited their turn. Although they still called these trips exchanges, about five hexades before the takeover, a human on an exchange visit to Intopia contracted a mysterious virus and died after returning. So, humans placed a moratorium on travel to Intopia, but insectoids still traveled to Earth.

On seeing the universe-hopping ANTs leaving the wormhole compound, an eager reporter yelled out to them. "Welcome home, young ANTs. I hope you had a productive trip. What's the first thing you want to do now that you are home?"

Rustant gestured for Antebon to answer first, and she responded, "I want to get to my burrow and kiss the ground where I live." Antebon loved everything about Intopia, especially the society's emphasis on freedom and equality.

After brief applause like a clap of thunder, the reporter continued, "What about you, Rustant?"

"Well, I'm doing it right now. My first aim was to meet with you all and tell everyone about our experience on Earth, and I know everyone's curious."

Another reporter interjected. "Could you tell us the most astonishing thing you learned on your travels?"

Antebon stepped up to the pheromonic microphone. "I was impressed with how efficient humans were at putting our schedules together and how the different countries and races of people worked together to make our stay comfortable and valuable." She looked out towards the colony and the surrounding jungle. *I enjoyed my time on Earth, but I'm happy to be home.*

Rustant then took the microphone from its stand and walked closer to the throngs of reporters. "There are many species on Earth, unlike here where we have only a few insectoid families and related tiny insects. And of all those species, humans are the most intelligent." He stood tall. "They are not the biggest or the strongest, but they are the masters of their world. We can learn a lot from them, and I gleaned much from them about leadership and ensuring the survival of one's civilization."

Another reporter said, "You may be young, but you sound like a politician."

Rustant responded, "Well, we met politicians from many countries on Earth. Some were highly successful, others struggled, and I learned from both." He straightened his antennae so no one would misinterpret his following few sentences. "We have been away from this planet for a whole hex, and I'm eager to begin the next stage of my life." He shined his thorax. "I am keen to take what I have learned on Earth to help our colony to the best of my ability. Since I know our current leader is old and will soon retire, I take this opportunity to declare my intention to lead our magnificent colony after winning the next presidential election."

Antebon's jaw dropped as she heard Rustant's last words, and after an initial shocked silence, a growing buzz spread around the scrum like excited bees performing a waggle dance. This gathering was no longer the press conference of the hexth but the event of the hexade.

Another reporter jumped forward. "Antebon, did you know about Rustant's surprising news, and what are your plans?"

Antebon shut her gaping jaw and responded while glaring at Rustant. "I am as stunned as all of you, but I know Rustant is very ambitious. As for my plans, we'll see. But if no one else will oppose him, I may just throw in my name and run against him." Although a black ANT, her face took on a reddish tone. *I cannot allow him to corrupt the system I love so dearly.*

The reporters in the crowd all gasped. Some were not clear if they heard her correctly. Others were already on their devices, contacting their editors. A collective tapping sound invaded the ether, like hundreds of beetles marching across a hardwood floor. The realization that two returning Earth exchange students were running against each other for president made it the news of the hexury.

CHAPTER 8

THE RULERS: THE GREAT MIGRATION

Antalonia (Rudyard's rule, the current president)

MOST ANTS IN Antalonia did not know which young cyborgs were their offspring, but they reserved that perk for the leaders. And as the supreme leader, Rudyard got to choose his mate and mother of his pupae. The breeders assigned the lesser leaders their mates. They knew who they were and could have conjugal visits. All other ANTs in Antalonia never met their mates or knew who they were. They weren't even mates, just egg donors, and ejaculants. One of the breed master's jobs was to match egg donors with ejaculants required to fertilize the eggs.

Rudyard began a tutoring session with his son, Blood. "I have taught you to be a leader, but not so much about the workings of our civilization." Rudyard sported a severe look. "You need to learn the goals and mechanics of Antalone society and how our colony came to be." He softened his gaze. "Our new enlightened civilization began several hexuries after the Great Migration."

Blood puckered his brow. "The Great Migration. They did not teach me about that in school."

Rudyard straightened his frame, realizing he had forgotten a necessary predicate. "We only teach histrionics to a select few when the time is right."

"So, what do I need to know?" questioned Blood. He knew this talk was coming and had been waiting for it for hexs. *I am keen to learn so I can better take over as ruler.*

Rudyard took a deep breath. "You need to know it all, but only when you understand each drama's lesson will we move to the next."

"So, what's the Great Migration?" He quivered at the prospect of filling in the gaps in his knowledge. *You have taught me to be a leader, but I know nothing about Antalonia's birth.*

Rudyard threw his son a most serious look. "First, you must understand a key crux passed from leader to leader." He sprayed an intense perfume.

Blood had never seen such a severe look from his father and heeded appropriately. "I will follow whatever rules are required." He projected the most dutiful face he could. *Have I not always been your obedient son?*

Rudyard closed the door to his office and shuttered the window while looking over his shoulders. He instructed Blood that their communications should not leave the room or his mind. Rudyard said Blood had the largest brain size of all cyborgs and insisted he concentrate and lock everything within his consciousness. Rudyard was about to reveal facts that very few Antalones knew—details that could start a revolution if discovered by the public.

"What you learn over the next few lessons is for your awareness only," said Rudyard.

"You know I have a pheromonographic memory," boasted Blood.

"Yes, but can you shutter it from others?" replied Rudyard. "You will learn that knowledge is power, and power is everything. But when leaders spread knowledge, they dilute power."

"I've tuned my antennae, and my glands will remain blocked." Eager to learn what he could, Blood would follow any rule imposed by his father. *I understand the importance of subterfuge.*

"Excellent." Rudyard looked warmly again at his son. "The Great Migration took place before my time, but my father taught me all there is to know. I pledged to him I would only relay this information to my closest advisors and my successor."

Blood put a claw over his heart. "As I pledge to you."

Rudyard nodded. "It was a time of unparalleled excitement, and Poo-ponic was ready for colonization, and we were eager to expand."

Blood's brow raised. "Poo-ponic, where is that?" He expected to learn many new things but not to be so initially confused. *I know so little!*

"That was the name for this planet in ancient times, and I should have called it Intopia."

Blood shook his head in bewilderment. "Intopia?"

Rudyard sighed and told Blood that Poo-ponic was the planet's name before the atmospheric collapse that wiped out all insectoids living there, except those that first escaped to

Bilaluna. Then he explained how the atmosphere rejuvenated over thousands of hexs, and they renamed the planet Intopia when they determined it was safe to return. He described the details of the Great Migration and how large numbers of insectoids from all families had come from Bilaluna to Intopia five generations of cyborg rulers earlier.

"Poo-ponic, Bilaluna, Intopia. Those are odd names," replied Blood, now totally confused.

Rudyard sighed inwardly. "I'll tell you more about Poo-ponic some other time. Or better yet, you can read the sacred text, written by our first talented histrionics writer, Narrant."

"I didn't realize insectoids other than ANTs lived on Bilaluna. And what about Intopia, why don't we call it that anymore?" quizzed Blood. He ran his antennae through the setae hairs on his forelimbs to ensure he perceived everything his father said correctly. *These facts are bizarre yet fascinating.*

Rudyard threw his forelimbs in the air and stared up at the sky. "Intopia was our Antunite ancestors' misguided vision of an insect utopia."

"Why did it fail?" He stared at his father. *I can't believe he's never told me about this before.*

Rudyard looked into his son's eyes. "We lost our way. It went against our nature."

Blood matched his father's gaze and grinned. "And now we call it Antalonia."

"Yes, because Antalone ANTs can do it alone," Rudyard declared with authority.

Blood cocked his head. "But when did our philosophy change?"

"After my father visited Earth." Rudyard pointed to the Southern sky. "Your grandfather, Rustant, was part of a small delegation that traversed the long wormhole and spent a hex on Earth learning from and teaching humans."

Blood shook his head and looked around. "Wait! Earth, humans, wormhole—is there another society beneath our pods?" He oozed a ragged reek. *Will these baffling stories ever cease?*

Rudyard guffawed. "No, not a hole dug by worms, a wormhole through space. It's how he traveled to Earth, millions of light hexs away."

Blood again pulled at his antennae, further cleaning them to ensure he perceived the right message. "I have taken classes in astronomy and astrophysics but have never heard of such wormholes." He stared out the window to the courtyard. *I am surprised and amazed.*

"Remember, I said knowledge is power. We don't teach all knowledge to our students."

Blood smiled. "We don't want lay-ANTs jumping into wormholes whenever they tire of their work."

Rudyard laughed again. "Yes, there is still a wormhole to Bilaluna, but it is off-limits. And actions during the Takeover destroyed the wormhole to Earth."

"Takeover, is that when the Antalones took control?"

"Yes, I'll teach you about that some other time." Rudyard shrugged his shoulders. "But for now, back to your grandfather, Rustant."

Blood stood tall. "I heard he was a brilliant general and leader." He rubbed his red thorax to a brilliant shine. *I'm proud of my lineage.*

"Yes, and he learned much during his hex on Earth."

Blood stared into the southern sky. "It must have been so

exciting to travel to a far-off world in another galaxy, learning from other intelligent beings. I assume they were intelligent?"

"Yes, but more than that, they were fierce."

"So, what did he learn from these Earthlings?" Blood considered what could enhance his power as a ruler.

Rudyard paused and put a claw to his head. "He learned about human nature, human warfare, and ants on their planet."

Blood did a double-take. "There are ants on the far-off planet called Earth?"

Rudyard snickered. He realized how much new information he was asking his son to absorb. It reminded him of when the inquisitive Blood first emerged as a tiny nanitic from his cocoon. He explained to Blood that Earth ants were their ancient ancestors before they first traversed the wormhole to Poo-ponic. He said Blood would learn more about this from the sacred text.

"I realize now why histrionics are so mysterious." Blood sighed. *The average ANT's brain would explode with all this information.*

"We don't want to expose lay-ANTs to too much drama, so we teach little histrionics. Students can learn bionics as they choose, and socionics rule their lives. However, histrionics are the domain of the leaders."

Blood stared hard into his father's eyes. "What more did Rustant learn from these humans?" He tried to remember all he knew about his grandfather. *I want to put all the pieces together and be just as powerful.*

Rudyard sagged, becoming weary of all the questions. "It's enough to say that he became inspired by how humans had taken control of their world. And all he learned about ancient ant civilizations enlightened him."

Blood began stamping his three pods. "Tell me more, Father!"

Rudyard shook his head from side to side. "No, I'm finishing your lesson for now. But here is the key code to the restricted zone of the sacred library. Your homework is to read the sacred text and the books of EOW."

Blood's eyes were as wide as saucers. "EOW! That sounds exciting. Can I take the texts to my room?" *I will soak it up like a sponge.*

Rudyard looked sternly at his son and informed him that no one could take anything from the restricted zone of the library. He explained the importance of preserving and concealing the sacred text and works of EOW—the gifted human biologist who so eloquently studied their Earth ant ancestors and inspired the modern philosophy of ANT life on Antalonia.

EOW referred to E.O. Wilson, a biologist and entomologist on Earth from ancient post-historic times. Wilson wrote many books about ants, highlighting how aggressive they were and how they used altruistic instincts to organize a society where every ant in the colony would sacrifice themselves for their queen and their fellow ant.

"Okay, Papa. I hope the restricted zone is comfortable." The thought of reading and obtaining knowledge that few others could learn enticed him. *I'll live there night and hexay.*

Rudyard led him into the small room at the back of the library, and Blood flopped down into a comfy hammock he found in the corner and settled in.

"Indeed. You will spend much time here."

Blood didn't mind. He enjoyed spending time in the library. Blood more than revered the sacred library—it was home to him. His two brothers died when he was young, and with no siblings to play with, he turned to books. The characters in his books became his friends, and the library, his playground.

Blood could make friends at school as a red alpha, but as the other students knew he was the Czar's heir, they feared him, and none got very close to him. His father did not allow any of his friends in the library for security reasons. When Blood had to choose between having friends over or visiting the library, he always chose the library. Thus, he became more and more distant from his classmates. Instead, he befriended the main character of his favorite book and would have long conversations with him, asking his advice whenever he had problems. When he missed his brothers, when his father was busy, and when his classmates alienated him, he had his library and his imaginary friend, Flash.

CHAPTER 9

HOW ANTALONIA BEGAN: RUSTANT SHOWS HIS TRUE COLORS

Intopia (Umberant's rule, three presidents in the past)

EXCITED AFTER HIS news conference, Rustant met with his best friend Currant one evening to garner his support for the election. He hadn't seen his old friend since he had left for Earth and was eager to catch up with him and re-establish the kinship. He realized some friends may have moved on since he was away for a whole hex. But he assumed his best friend would not be one of them. Currant had stuck with him through thick and thin throughout high school and would do whatever he suggested.

After greeting Currant, Rustant got right to the point.

"You must have heard I'm running for president. Can I get your support?"

"I'd love to help, but there may be a conflict of interest," replied Currant. "My new girlfriend Antnoir supports Antebon."

Rustant was stunned. "I know Antnoir. Why are you dating a black ANT? She must be an Antunite."

Currant looked at him as if he was from another planet. "You know my mother is a black ANT, so why would I not consider wooing one?"

Rustant frowned. "Because she's not red and loves non-ANT cyborgs, everything we hate." He pulled at his setae hairs. *This guy used to follow my every move. I'm gone one hex, and he forgets we only associate with red ANTs. What comes next, non-ANT friends?*

During high school, Rustant read the history book about the planet's early development written by the famous historian Narrant. He read it several times and became obsessed with the historical character Antilla, featured heavily in the book. Rustant did his best to emulate Antilla and espoused most of his principles. He was an unashamed misogynist unless the female was a red one that he fancied. To Rustant, ANTs were higher on the evolutionary scale than other insectoids. He even built a miniature scale replica of the totem pole Antilla erected with ANTs topping, BEEs, FLYs, RoAChs, WoBBs, and WoRMs, in that order. He hated WoRMs as Antilla had, and FLYs too, and would not associate with any cyborgs other than ANTs.

Currant, who had matured past his red ANT phase, responded. "Oh, that attitude is so high school. Didn't you broaden your mind during your travels? I thought you'd be worldlier."

Rustant fumed. "I am more worldly, even outer-worldly, but my travels reinforced my strong views." He grabbed Currant by the shoulders and shook him lightly. "It's clear you've been hanging around with the wrong cyborgs. They've pulled a worm skin over your eyes." He shook his head back and forth. *Have I not convinced him all black ANTs are deceitful?*

"No, Rustant," insisted Currant, "I believe my ommatidia are focused and for the first time in hexs."

"How can you say that?" Rustant shook him harder, oozing a brisk bouquet. "You supported me throughout high school, and no one was redder than us two." He slapped Currant on the thorax. *I think he forgot our doctrine—the redder, the better.*

"With you away, I realized the error of my ways." Currant spread his arms wide. "My mother always encouraged me to be tolerant."

"Your mother is as dumb as the coal that matches her shell," Rustant yelled. "You should never listen to an Ebon." His anger brought him back to his low school hexays when such insults were rampant.

"A hindgut hole who compares my mother to coal and calls her an Ebon is no friend." Currant emitted a scalding stink. "And don't expect me to support your campaign. We don't need a president like you." He stormed off.

🐜 🐜 🐜

Rustant was distraught at the prospect of losing his best friend and supporter, despite feeling that an apology was out of the question. He decided he needed to turn him back to red with the persuasion he had perfected for hexs.

First, he went to see Currant's girlfriend Antnoir to get some perspective and convince her to stop seeing his friend.

"Antnoir, I met with Currant last evening, and I can honestly say I don't know him anymore."

Antnoir extended her claw towards Rustant. "Well, sometimes friends grow apart."

Rustant pretended he didn't see her claw. "And sometimes evil comes between them." He glared at Antnoir. *I'll get to the point quickly. I don't have time to waste on this Ebon.*

A dark cloud descended over Antnoir's black coloring. "Are you calling me evil? Don't humans paint their devils red?"

"On Earth, a black cat is an evil omen." Rustant sprayed his formic acid at a tiny black ant that crawled in front of him and watched as it sizzled. *I love nothing more than insulting black ANTs, an urge I had to resist my whole time on Earth with Antebon.*

"So, you believe all black ANTs are evil?" Antnoir glared at him so hard that her black eyes appeared red.

"Mostly those with strong Antunite genes." Rustant scowled in return. "All you lousy WoRM lovers." Bile bubbled up in his throat.

"I am so glad Currant has moved on from you." Antnoir oozed a fuming fragrance. "There could be no worse influence."

Rustant seethed. "Before I left, Currant hated WoRMs and other non-ANT cyborgs, as I did." He nodded his head toward her. *And I'll make sure he sees you for what you are.*

"Why don't you grow up? This planet deserves a better leader than you." Antnoir stared into Rustant's eyes with a look that could burn through steel.

Rustant expected she was trying to determine whether *he* was, in fact, the devil, and this thought did not bother him.

"You get your claws off my friend." He shoved Antnoir

back into a wall. "And stay away from him forever." He sported an evil sneer. *I wish she was standing in a stairwell.*

"He is no longer your friend." Antnoir kicked Rustant and stormed off. "He has developed a distaste for flaky old metal." She said, looking back at Rustant with disdain.

　　　　　🐜　🐜　🐜

It enraged Rustant when he discovered that Currant planned to attend a rally supporting his opponent, Antebon. His anger reached the boiling point. *I heard he's going with a FLY. FLYs are the worst!* Rustant went to the rally to convince his old friend of his mistake. On arriving, he hid behind a stack of chairs at the back of the hall to watch. He waited and fumed as he listened to Antebon's oration. *Currant and that FLY are applauding and laughing at the speech. I'll teach them.* He waited for the rally to end and for most attendees to leave. He noticed that Currant lingered behind. *Is Antnoir inviting Currant and the FLY to meet Antebon? I can't believe it.* Rage surged inside him like the rush of roaches fleeing a threat.

Rustant stepped out of the hall, grabbed a nearby rock, and waited for Currant to appear. In time, the FLY exited and flew off. Looking through the window, he saw Antebon pointing to the podium and then to a closet on the side of the hall. After seeing Currant push the pulpit toward the storage space, he ducked down as the two female black ANTs headed for the door. He stared from the bushes as Antnoir and Antebon walked out together, and his hemolymph bubbled at the thought of his best friend helping his opponent. When the Antunites were out of view, Currant exited the hall. Rustant jumped from the bushes and struck Currant's head with the rock. He hit him with the concave side of the granite weapon, and the blow rattled his brain so hard it smashed the opposite side of his skull. It was a fatal impact, but the smooth granite perfectly fit his skull's contours, and the blow spilled no hemolymph. Rustant dragged Currant's limp body over the edge of a crag and down into the ravine, placing the rock under his head to make it look like the contact occurred as he accidentally fell. Then the reddest of ANTs slipped into the crimson dusk.

CHAPTER 10

THE BREEDERS: A POTENTIAL NEW BREED MASTER

Antalonia (Rudyard's rule, the current president)

KEEGAN GREETED HIS boss as he entered the hall. "Good morning, sir."

Breed Master Vermillion lurched. "I didn't realize you were here already."

Keegan smiled like a young nanitic on the first hexay of school. "I have my passcode, and I came in early." He wiggled two claws. *I hope he doesn't think I'm sucking up.*

Keegan expected it to annoy Vermillion when he robbed him of his few hexutes of solitude before the lessons, but he hadn't let on.

"Were you just coming from the bloom room, er the nanitic wing?"

Keegan tried hard to conceal his smile. "Yes, I wanted to see where this all leads." He had difficulty hiding his desire to surge forward as fast as possible. *These halls are such a wondrous place where all cyborg life begins. The galleries may seem dingy, but it is here where breeders have the power of creation. We can shape young cyborgs in the image we choose.*

Vermillion frowned. "Well, let's not get ahead of ourselves." Without explanation, he changed the subject. "I saw Clay heading out. Did you meet him?"

Keegan revealed his smile. "Yes, he seems nice."

"Yes, and very sociable." Vermillion looked towards the door Clay had left through. "I trained him a few hexades ago. He was a talented student, but his shade was not as red as yours. The other leaders like him, but he drinks too much strong sap. He'll never be a breed master."

"As a breeder, I assume he is red and an alpha," responded Keegan. He stretched his arms wide. *I'm not so particular about shades. Yet, a pure red female always turns my head.*

"Yes, of course. It is a requirement."

Keegan shrugged. "But is not red—red, and alpha—alpha? Would it not depend on his training and aptitude?" He struggled to suppress a frown. *Are ANTs not judged by their abilities? And there's nothing wrong with enjoying some strong sap – it's natural.*

"There are many shades of red and some alphas in time become Scarlets," Vermillion explained. "Although your brain sizes may be the same, we give the purest of the reds the most advantages."

"What do you mean by advantages?" Keegan flinched.

Are there inequalities among red ANTs? I don't think he knows I started as a red beta.

They walked down the aisles, and Vermillion pointed at the liquid food sacks attached to one incubator. "As a pure red, you received the most nutrients of all ants in the incubators." Keegan noticed the different color sacks attached to the young nanitics' incubators.

"They assigned you the most intelligent of attendants and teachers. Did you notice that all your classmates were the reddest of the red?"

Keegan's eyes grew wide. "I was unsure whether this was significant other than keeping us straight." He froze, considering this information. *Did my start as a beta hinder me somehow?*

"You received the most challenging training, and your teachers primed you to excel." Vermillion patted his student on the back. "Assuming your motivation remains high, you will become a leader in our society. If you achieve scarlet status, you can become a leader. The few among many."

Although early after Rust established Antalonia, they selected a few Scarlets each hex, students were recently chosen for the scarlet program only when they determined leaders would soon need replacing. Vermillion expected to retire as breed master within a hexade, and they would need to groom a Scarlet to take his place. Keegan was the first scarlet trainee since Clay's high school hexays when they trained two Scarlets and an alternate. Vermillion considered Keegan for the breed master post but would only decide after assessing the recruit's potential in the coming hexths.

Keegan wafted a balmy bouquet. "I will try my best." He looked down. *Assuming I can overcome my start as a beta.*

Vermillion gave him a stern look. "No, you will *achieve* what we bred you for."

Keegan stood erect. "Of course, Master." He raised his chin. *I always drive myself to excel.*

Vermillion placed a claw on Keegan's shoulder. "For example, I did not teach Clay about socionics because his tasks do not require it. He only needed to learn about larval and pupal nourishment, genetic engineering, and cyborg production." He looked deep into Keegan's eyes. "You, I will teach all the steps—from egg fertilization to cyborg production to socionic training."

Keegan sagged a little, understanding that Vermillion considered training him as the next breed master. "I am honored." He rubbed his thorax, but still slouched. *But am I up to the challenge?*

Vermillion grabbed him by his shoulders and straightened him. "A breed master needs to know it all." He cracked a wide smile. "And you have it in you to learn it. Although it will take some time to complete all the training."

Keegan returned the smile. "I am young, and I have the best teacher." A pride he never knew grew within him. *I mean it, this guy is the best mentor.*

Vermillion turned and pointed at an incubator with a fertilized egg. "Now, let's start to-hexay's lesson on genetic engineering."

Keegan raised his claw. "I assumed breeders would fit the ants with bionic limbs." He tried to imagine what other purpose bionics served. *I'm keen, but I'm also naïve.*

Vermillion sighed. "Yes, one problem with your schooling is that you lead a very sheltered life. You probably don't know anything about other insectoids and how we replaced them."

Keegan frowned. "I know about the Great Insectoid War and how we defeated our enemies."

Vermillion sighed even deeper. "Yes, but were you taught about the different tasks various insectoids completed within our colony and how we took them on ourselves?"

Keegan stood his ground, trying his best to defend his education. "Our teachers told us other insectoids were useless, and we could live without them." He noticed a chart with some odd-looking ANTs on the far wall of the classroom ahead. *We didn't get the complete story.*

Vermillion laughed. "Well, that may be true now, but only because of genetic engineering. We endured hard times until we developed the methods to create replacements."

Keegan puzzled. "Replacements! What do you mean?" He stared harder at the chart while still training a few ommatidia on his teacher. *I never expected this—science to wield power.*

Vermillion continued to chuckle. "Exactly that. We had to create ANTs that could do the work of BEEs, FLYs, RoAChs, and WoBBs. Since there are now no other insectoids, we only use the term cyborg."

Keegan cleaned and straightened his antennae. "WoBBs. What are those?"

"They are Wood-Boring Buddies. Were you taught about beetles?"

"Yes, I remember something about beetles, but not WoBBs." He tried to guess which bizarre ANTs on the chart fulfilled their role. *There's no way I would have forgotten that.*

Vermillion rolled his eyes. "Beetles are the small ones, and WoBBs are the cyborgs."

Keegan shook his head and released a raw reek. "Oh, okay." He broke eye contact with Vermillion and headed toward the classroom to get a better look at the chart. *I guess I'll be learning many new things from him.*

Vermillion smiled again at his trainee. "I don't blame you. It is your schooling. The leaders are afraid to provide students with too much information and squelch the teachers' purview. You'll come to learn knowledge is everything." He put his fore-limb around Keegan's abdomen and nudged him towards the classroom at the end of the hall. "I see I have to fill in some blanks before getting to the good stuff."

The schools' curricula in Antalonia were under the strict control of the leaders. All rules and lessons were in line with the Czar's designs. The Czar communicated to the breed master and master of socionics what the students could and couldn't learn and the methods to teach them. The two masters would then instruct all teachers on which subjects they could cover, and they inspected their lesson plans daily. Not a pheromone could enter a student's scent glands without the Czar's approval, and not a pencil stroke could enter a student's note-roll that the masters did not intend. The breed master oversaw every student's upbringing from hatch to high school graduation and, with the help of the master of socionics, strove to mold their minds in keeping with the system.

Other teachers were simply the claws, eyes, and scent glands of the two masters, ensuring that the students only gained the knowledge they needed to understand how to be model citizens of Antalonia and succeed at their intended employment.

🐜 🐜 🐜

Keegan arrived early the next morning for his lessons with Breed Master Vermillion, eager to learn more about the finer points of bionics. "Breed Master, what's on tap to-hexay?"

"Hey, that's breed master, not brewmaster."

Keegan slapped his claws onto his hind limbs. "Good one. I didn't realize you had a sense of humor."

"You know we've bred red alphas to be sociable and friendly. You went to an all-red alpha school, so you know what I mean."

"Yes, I have many hilarious friends, but you imply that other groups do not." Keegan scratched his head. "And it seems you've already turned our conversation into a lesson."

Vermillion grinned, but held back a chuckle. "Yes, indeed. I am not talking so much about humor, but friendship. Black or brown ANTs cannot have friends, nor red betas and chi."

Keegan shriveled his brow. "Why is that?" He squelched the urge to shake his head. *So that's why I had no friends when I first started school.*

Vermillion answered after a pause. "Red alphas are the elites that run our society and have privileges that other groups do not."

Keegan tried to guess the real reason. "Yes, but I assume we don't want the other groups to collude and organize." His eyes brightened as if a spark had flashed in his brain. *It makes sense, but what if I'd remained a beta?*

Vermillion smiled. "For a naïve student not yet exposed to the real world, you are very perceptive."

Keegan pondered Vermillion's opening point. "Yet the more we meet, the more naïve I feel."

"Alright, then let me tell you what you'll learn to-hexay." Vermillion pointed to the end of the hall. "We'll start in the classroom and talk about genetics, then move into the hall for practical biochemical and genetic engineering demonstrations."

Keegan almost jumped out of his exoskeleton. "A practical

demonstration. I can't wait!" He couldn't control his quaking antennae. *Finally, I will learn the hands-on techniques of breeding.*

"Yes, Clay is here now, and I asked him to show you around the hall." Vermillion looked to the bloom room, where he knew Clay was working. "Although he may never be a breed master, he is an excellent chief of bionics and teacher. He can't paint the big picture, but he is a highly skilled technician who can precisely sketch many components."

Keegan grinned and oozed a bubbly bouquet. "I was hoping to get to know Clay better." His nervous excitement warmed a growing pride. *I may have some reservations about the system, but I'm ready to boost my knowledge about breeding.*

"I am sure you'll learn a lot from him, and he will be a significant influence."

CHAPTER 11

HOW ANTALONIA BEGAN: THE DEBATE

Intopia (Umberant's rule, three presidents in the past)

RUSTANT MET WITH his new campaign advisor before an all-important debate with Antebon. After violently ditching his best friend, Currant, Rustant was elated to discover another that shared his views. His new friend, Garnant, had been on a student exchange trip to Earth 14 hexs earlier and had recognized some of the same characteristics in humans and Earth ants that intrigued Rustant. Unlike Rustant, however, he did not feel in a position at the time to act on what he learned. Umberant was not so frail then, and the Antalone economy was healthier, so common ANTs were not primed for a change like they were when Rustant returned and announced his candidacy. Yet, when he heard some of Rustant's early speeches, he understood what he meant and appreciated that Rustant had the charisma and proper political environment to win the presidency.

Rustant met with Garnant shortly before a crucial debate with Antebon. "I am so thrilled to have found a red ANT who also went to Earth and had the same experiences I did." He pointed to his red shell. *If only we had gone together, instead of traveling with Antunites.*

"Yes, most exchange students are too naïve to pick up on human leaders' messages about aggression and power," Garnant replied. "I had dreams like yours when I returned from Earth, but the time was not right. I feel our time is now."

"We think so much alike, and your advice has been inspiring." Rustant shined his shell to a glittery glow. "How did you come up with the term histrionics? It's what powerful humans do on Earth." He smiled at Garnant. *With his support, I can accomplish anything.*

"They don't call it that, but they twist history and spin current events to support their ambitions," Garnant scoffed. "People don't care about facts, and neither do ANTs. They just want a great story."

"And perhaps a brief history about how aggressive Earth ants were." Rustant snapped his jaws hard. "We are a thousand times larger than those tiny critters, but we have forgotten how to fight and dominate as they do." He swiped his claws across the table and snapped his jaws again. *With your help, I can change all that.*

"We must claim our rightful place as the dominant species on Intopia." Garnant raised a clenched claw. "But in your debate with Antebon, be careful not to give away too much. We don't want to lose all the non-ANT votes."

"I learned about slave maker ants on Earth—where black ants work as serfs for their red ant masters." Rustant smirked. "Wouldn't that be great?"

Garnant jumped up from his chair. "Don't go there until you've won the election." He sneered. "Think of it as a long-term goal."

"Right. I'll only stress the need to improve the economy and give the colony an alternative to insectism," Rustant grinned. "I'll tell them the story we cooked up about the god EOW." He looked up at the sky and held his heart. *Once I get going on that, no ANT will resist our cause.*

"Absolutely. That's the best thing you've come up with." Garnant beamed at his candidate. "You are the perfect blend of charisma and creativity—everything Umberant is not."

"Thanks for that." Rustant puffed out his thorax. "While our Earth ant ancestors never had a god, we can fool the public that they did." *I've learned they are a gullible bunch.*

"Yes, tell them that this god will save them and provide a rewarding afterlife to those who believe."

"Like humans and their gods, we'll convince them EOW gives them their vigor and aggressive zeal." Rustant laughed. "That EOW, in his generosity, granted them the gift of telekinesis." He raised a glass to his mouth without using his claws. *How else can even the tiniest ants, move objects 5,000 times their weight?*

"He also gave us the power of aggression to dominate other insects." Garnant rapidly snapped his pincers. "But only spread that message among ANTs."

"Thank you, Garnant. I'm ready for the debate." He stood up and swung his arms all around. *That wimpy black ANT won't know what hit her when I'm through.*

It was traditional for opposing presidential candidates to have one crucial debate during the middle of the campaign. After the two candidates had been giving speeches for a few hexeks, the election officials scheduled a candidates' debate. Much of the colony attended the event held at the band shell in the main square. Umberant acted as the moderator for the debate, as was expected with abdications. He introduced the two candidates and asked his first question. "Antebon, tell me about your vision for Intopian society."

Antebon moved forward, thanked Umberant for his introduction, and answered. "My fellow Intopians, I am an Antunite and stand for all insectoids." She spread her forearms wide, pointing to all the insectoids in the square, projecting a shiny scent. "With me as your president, you can trust that all insectoids will be treated equally." She then looked down. "I fear my opponent does not share that view, and he will bring us back to the hexays before Poo-ponic's destruction. Rustant is no better than Antilla, who destroyed our civilization hexennia ago. The choice is simple. Do you want Antilla or Antuna?"

Umberant returned to the podium. "And how do you respond, Rustant? What is your vision?"

Rustant thanked the moderator and paused, looking up at the sky before speaking. "My friends, my vision was given to me by the magnificent god EOW. EOW came to me in a dream to tell me his plans for us. I was dying, and he saved me, and he will save you too if you follow his plan." He brought his three arms together and made an enclosure with his claws. *I'll use just enough histrionics to entice the crowd.*

Umberant interrupted, "But what is his plan, and what is yours?"

"Citizens of Intopia," Rustant began. "My plans are EOW's plans. I will follow the guidance EOW gave me in my fever dream and the path EOW set for me when he brought me back to the living." He fell to his knees and raised his arms to the sky. *I'll leave enough mystery so that the multitudes will itch for more.*

Umberant stepped forward again. "And Antebon, what is your reaction to Rustant's plan?"

Antebon fumed. "It's obvious he has no plan, just the ramblings of a lunatic. He has made up these stories to make himself seem like a prophet to win your favor. I traveled with him on Earth, and he was never deathly ill."

Looking at Rustant, Umberant asked, "How do you respond?"

Rustant stood up tall. "Messengers of the glorious EOW do not make-up stories. I was ill during the three Earth days Antebon and I were apart. To reduce our travel demands, Antebon went to Nepal while I visited Tibet. After I toured many sacred human temples and the tallest mountain on Earth, EOW came to me. My fever may have been from a virus or altitude sickness; both can be lethal," responded Rustant, concealing a spiky scent. *I'll push up the dramatics. Histrionics won't fail.*

Antebon jumped in. "These are all lies. Rustant never told me he was ill and never mentioned the so-called EOW until now."

"But is it true that the two of you traveled separately, and he may have been ill?" questioned Umberant.

"Yes, I was in Nepal while he was in Tibet," responded Antebon. "But have you ever heard of an ANT getting altitude sickness? And would not Rustant, or one of our hosts, have told me he nearly died when we were apart?"

Rustant lowered his head. "I didn't bring it up because I didn't want to worry you. And it embarrassed me. I was weak and got sick easily from climbing a mountain." He scanned at the masses with a sheepish look. *I give them just enough humility to garner some empathy.*

"So as Rustant and you separated briefly, you cannot be certain that Rustant lied about being ill?" probed Umberant.

"That is true, but sick or not, we would all be fools to believe Rustant's story about EOW saving him and inspiring him to spread his words."

"Listen, friends, Antebon just called you fools," declared Rustant. "Clearly, that's what she thinks of you. Do you want to be led by someone who calls you a fool or a leader who inspires you to follow a magnificent and wise god?" He pointed a down-turned claw towards Antebon and turned another towards the sky. *I know they'll fall for these tricks I learned from human leaders on Earth.*

"I did not call anyone a fool, " Antebon responded, emanating a blistering bouquet. "Rustant is trying to trick everyone with his words."

"Now, who's the real liar?" Rustant retorted. "You all heard what she said. And now she implies you are easily tricked." Rustant held his forelimbs up high. "Do you want to be led by an uninspired black ANT that hopes to fool you? Or do you want a red ANT president who respects you and gives you a new direction? Follow me and find the rightful path to EOW. With the poor economy, I know your lives are difficult, but EOW will give you strength, and together EOW and I will offer you prosperity and salvation." He raised his three arms to the sky. *The leaders on Earth taught me that religion is a powerful, unifying force.*

"But isn't EOW an ant god?" snapped Antebon, emitting a scalding scent. "You intend to use EOW's ways to have ANTs dominate all other insects. You say prosperity and salvation, but you mean persecution and superiority."

"By condemning EOW, you are the one that assumes superiority," countered Rustant. "And as a god, EOW is neither an ant nor any other insect. But his words can inspire cyborg insects of all species. EOW sent me as a messenger for all Intopians who need to hear his words. He is here for all insectoids on Intopia that want to strive for something better." He shuffled his three arms like he was constructing an imaginary staircase. *Some Earth leaders showed me how to turn things on their heads and use your opponent's words against them.*

"Rustant wants you to believe he is a divine messenger, but what is his message?" asked Antebon. "Is it for all insectoids to live free? Or is it for red ANTs to take control of our society and treat the rest of us as enslaved cyborgs?"

"It is Antebon that wants insectoids to be slaves," exclaimed Rustant. "Slaves to old ideas that keep our society from moving forward. Notions that keep us from pulling ourselves out of poverty and depression. Through inaction and a lack of inspiration, Antebon wants to keep you down." He cupped his six claws together, forming a small cage. *I learned that the electorate responds more to emotions than policies.*

"You must all see the game he is playing. Rustant promises you a vision while he holds a veil over your eyes," concluded Antebon. "Do not fall for his ploy."

"My only ploy is to bring you joy," responded Rustant. "To raise you and show you a better life." He elevated his forelimbs.

"You only need to choose the right path. Choose it now, with the spirit of EOW!"

Umberant thanked the two candidates for their lively debate, which made the crowd vibrate like a dragonfly hovering over a pond. Nearly all red ANTs in the colony attended the event, outnumbering the brown and black ANTs in the square. Post-debate polling showed that almost all red ANTs thought Rustant had won the debate. Although Antebon was chosen winner of the debate by 75% of black ANTs and other insectoids, the brown ANTs split the poll 50/50 when asked who won.

CHAPTER 12

THE RULERS: HISTRIONICS

Antalonia (Rudyard's rule, the current president)

BLOOD MET WITH his father, Rudyard, after spending several hexays studying in the library. "Papa, I read the entire sacred text and learned how the six insect species, spiders, and worms originally transported from Earth to Poo-ponic mega hexs ago." Blood took a deep breath and continued, "I loved the part where the insects decimated the termites and spiders, although it saddened me when Antuna and her friend Spifry died. But Malevolant and Antistry were so clever and cunning. I couldn't help but admire them, even if they wiped two species off the planet." He looked towards a pictogram of Czar Rust on the wall. *My grandfather's aggression inspires me.*

Antistry was a chemist in Antuna's time that used his supervisor's research about the chemistry of plant defensive methods to develop insect neurotoxins. Malevolant, who befriended Antistry, used propaganda to convince Poo-ponic's colony insects to use the neurotoxins as chemical warfare to propagate a familic cleansing of termites and spiders.

"Blood, I am glad you feel that way. My father always stressed that we remember Malevolant and Antistry as esteemed heroes among ants in our history, and histrionics began with them."

Blood smiled and then shrugged. "Father, I'm not sure I understand the difference between history and histrionics." A line creased across his brow. *Perhaps aggression doesn't always mean violence.*

"History actually happened, including events that leaders need to know and understand. Histrionics are the parts of history, real or imagined, that we teach our followers. Malevolant started this by distorting the truth about how many ants were being killed by spiders and termites."

Blood grinned. "So, we construct the histrionics we want our followers to think of as history." He scribbled the idea down in his note-roll. *Violence and deception are two edges of the same killer sword.*

Rudyard clapped his claws together. He explained to Blood that histrionics is both a play on words and an essential aspect of their society. He stressed how they used the word to mean history, but it is a word they took from human English. The real meaning of the word is: 'fake, over-dramatic emotions intended to manipulate others.'

Blood raised his claw, like a student trying to get his teacher's attention when he knows the answer. "So, we create a drama that stirs emotions in our followers that allows us to manipulate them. That's clever!" He flipped to the pages of the sacred text that mentioned Malevolant and Antistry. *I bet my grandfather used histrionics better than anyone.*

Rudyard raised his claws over his head and clapped them together. "I see that your studying has paid off."

Blood beamed. "I hope to make you proud." He stood and walked closer to the pictogram of Rust. *And to become the Czar of Antalonia one hexay.*

Rudyard composed himself and continued, "My father taught me a line from a play by a famous human playwright, William Shakespeare. It went: 'All the world's a stage, and all the men and women merely players.'"

Blood jumped in, releasing a slimy stench, "So, history is just a drama, so let's give the followers the most dramatic parts and make up an entertaining play they'll all believe." He grinned menacingly, imagining Rust's bright red shell. *I must store these lessons to amass the strength and power of my grandfather.*

Rudyard smiled so widely that his jaw cracked. "Absolutely! My son, you are going to make a fantastic ruler."

Blood beamed so brightly that he sparkled. "You mentioned Rustant. Was he the one who started spreading histrionics?" He imagined how histrionics could be used to fool the public. *I never knew him, but I feel like I did.*

Rudyard nodded. "Yes, it started after he returned from a student exchange trip to Earth."

"Right, you mentioned last time Grandfather went through the wormhole and learned major lessons from humans."

Rudyard motioned for Blood to take a seat. He described how Rustant learned about all the technologies that humans developed so that they could dominate their world. Rustant realized humans were not the strongest or fiercest of the species on Earth, but they created the tools to become masters of all creatures in their world. He returned from his visit to Earth convinced that ANTs should rule Intopia the way humans dominated creatures on their planet.

Blood thought for a moment. "So, they are mentally fierce?" He studied the English script on the book's pages and imaged what famous human began the practice of writing. *I need to learn more about these delightfully evil alien creatures.*

"Yes, and much more intelligent than all the other species."

Blood put the ideas together in his head. "Intelligence and mental fierceness are a deadly combination. Are all humans intelligent?" He went to the library stacks and pulled out a book entitled 'Manipulating Human Behavior: The Art of Deception'. *How do human leaders control their colonies?*

"Relative to other species, humans are more intelligent. But some humans are more intelligent than others."

Blood raised his brow. "And they become the leaders?" He tapped on his temple. *The smart ones, like me.*

Rudyard shrugged. "Yes, but there are other factors. Some human leaders are intelligent, but it is more important for leaders to be strong and charismatic."

Blood pondered what he heard. "You mean those that can best sell the histrionics and push their followers to fight for them?" He looked back at Rustant's image. *I bet that's what Grandfather did with the ANTs!*

"Humans don't call it histrionics, but otherwise, you got it right."

Blood looked out the window over the ANT nests throughout the colony. "So, to keep one's followers in line, you need to show strength and give them some drama to keep them coming back for more."

"And don't provide too much knowledge. Remember, knowledge is power."

Blood paused, thinking. "On Earth, are some followers intelligent?" He flipped through the book he had just found. *Intelligence could be a hindrance to dominance.*

Rudyard considered how to answer the question. He clarified to Blood that intelligence could be a problem when not everyone follows their leaders. Rustant realized that if too many people gain knowledge, some will refuse to obey. He also recognized that there were countries on Earth where the leaders effectively controlled the electorate by restricting access to information. He learned that propaganda might be a helpful tool. Still, it was more effective in a society where the leaders used disciplined schooling and strict societal rules to suppress individual intelligence.

Blood ventured a guess. "So, those who don't follow can rebel and try to take over?" He smiled as he discovered a chapter title that confirmed his hypothesis. *I see we must suppress our followers' intelligence.*

"Yes, in the countries where the leaders do not control the knowledge."

Blood concluded, "That explains the need for histrionics."

Rudyard nodded. "And also, for socionics to help condition the followers to be model citizens."

Blood began fidgeting in his chair. "Socionics, when can I learn more about that?" He scanned the stacks to find the books on the subject. *I see that reduced intelligence of one's followers and increased social control are crucial partners of deception.*

"When you are ready, son." Rudyard pointed towards the library. "Did you have time to read the books of EOW?"

Blood nodded. "I finished two and started a third." He pulled the third one from his book bag. *They're fascinating books.*

"So, you understand the level of organization and the fighting skills of our ancient ant ancestors."

"Yes, for tiny creatures, they organized their colonies well." Blood snapped his claws hard and fast. "They held their own against termites, spiders, and other enemies." He thought briefly about Antuna from the sacred text. *They were indeed not Antunites.*

Rudyard frowned. "They more than held their own. Many insects, even considerably larger ones, feared ants."

Blood shrunk a bit in his chair. "Yes, I understated their strength." Then he straightened himself and stared blankly across the room. *But no one will underestimate mine once I take over.*

Rudyard pointed out the window towards the moon. "It's been hexades since we lived like the insectoids on Bilaluna. Even I can't fathom what our ancestors experienced, having to share our colony and power with other insectoids."

Most ANTs on present hexay Antalonia did not know that various insectoids lived together in harmony on Bilaluna. Some didn't even realize that the early colonists came from Bilaluna or that Bilaluna was even habitable. Rustant realized the less Antalone ANTs knew about Bilaluna, the better. Once he rid the planet of other insectoids, he quickly discouraged any discussion of the insectoid civilization on Bilaluna. Mentioning Bilalunan society became a crime punishable by hard labor for life or a death sentence.

Blood gaped at his father, emitting a plump perfume. "It must have been awful having to shake claws with beetles and stroke worms' egos." He shook his claw as if shaking off a slimy substance. *It's bad enough we have to live alongside brown and black ANTs.*

Rudyard made a face like he'd bit into a lemon. "Your grandfather said he shared classrooms with six other insectoid species and was never comfortable with it. However, he couldn't complain because it was the norm, and the system required him to do so."

Blood aped his father's face. "I can't even imagine what that was like."

"Then, while he was on Earth, he read the books of EOW and realized that ANTs could do it alone and even thrive on their own."

"But didn't EOW talk a lot about altruism?" asked Blood.

Rudyard smiled, proud of his son's observation. He explained that the altruism of Earth ants meant 'ants serving other ants'. Wilson's books described how ants used altruism and self-sacrifice to strengthen the ant colony. Rustant suspected that the Intopian society had corrupted this virtue, so ANTs were generous towards other insect families, a practice encouraged mainly by the Antunites. He wanted ANTs to return to their ancient instinctual ways and use altruism to serve only other ANTs and follow their leaders. Earth ant society was highly structured and designed with a caste system where all ants in their colony accepted their roles without question. If Antalonia was to succeed, it needed to return to these ideals.

Blood put a claw to his head. "I see how that is critical."

"Yes, as leaders, we must appreciate and exploit the altruistic tendencies that our comrades exhibit towards ants." Rudyard smirked. "We can ask them to do anything for us, and they will."

"But we must squash any urge to help other species." Blood

pounded his claw on the table. "The misguided altruistic inclinations of the Antunites." He thought again of Antuna and the rebel ANT Anthiery, who challenged Antilla's rule. *I see that they were freaks of nature.*

Rudyard nodded. "Yes, your grandfather recognized this and wanted to correct it."

Blood smiled, imagining his grandfather's zeal. "So, he began the campaign to have ANTs take over the colony." He picked up a cane next to the doorway and rattled it like a saber. *And rightly so, things needed to change for the better and the redder.*

"Yes, but he had to start slow." Rudyard paused for effect. "You can't change a colony's system overnight."

"Was he supported by the other ANTs that went to Earth with him?" He imagined a friendly group of red ANTs exploring Earth together. *I assume Rustant would have convinced them all.*

Rudyard rolled his eyes. "No, only two were on the exchange, and the other was a female Antunite—an ANT with a black exoskeleton."

"A follower of Antuna's philosophy from the sacred text?" Foul bile rose in Blood's throat. "All those black ANTs have Antuna's genes and follow her altruistic ideals." His mood switched to anger as his face reddened. *She was the vile ant that inspired insectism.*

"Yes, and we revere our sacred text not because of Antuna, but the example set by Malevolant, Antistry, and the powerful Antilla." Rudyard fidgeted. "I had you read it all only because I wanted you to know how far the society regressed when our ancestors bought into the Antunites philosophy of insectism."

Although Malevolant and Antistry successfully rid ancient Poo-ponic society of their enemies, the average insects learned shortly later that Malevolant had deceived them on how much threat spiders and termites posed. Antuna's tragic death deeply moved the colony, and her descendants reminded everyone how her actions saved the early colonists from starvation. For many generations and hexennia that followed, the colony insects idolized Antuna for her remarkable life. Raised from the dead by the bite of a spider at the urging of bees and endangering herself to save a termite, she encouraged interspecies co-operation. As a gender-role-reversing scholar, war resistance fighter, and an ant who became a mother despite not being a queen, she was a hero to many. Her descendants, who kept a pheromonal history of her life, were also revered as Antunites that kept her story and encouraged everyone to follow her example.

Hexennia later, Antunites fostered the development of democratic rule, but a draconian leader, Antilla, exploited the fledgling democracy and ruled their civilization with an iron claw. His authoritarian methods led to the destruction of democracy and the planet, as he and his clones ignored a climate crisis that destroyed Poo-ponic's atmosphere. Those few that escaped to Bilaluna before Poo-ponic's demise vowed to uphold democratic principles and protect the environment on their moon. Antunites, and those who despised Antilla, advanced the values of insectism, which has been the pillar of Bilalunan society to this hexay. Early Intopia settlers maintained this view until Rustant changed everything. Although Rustant recognized Antilla's failings, he admired his ability to use histrionics to establish his authority. He idolized Antilla like Antistry and Malevolant, who had come long before him.

"So how was Grandfather able to reverse this horrible, misguided path our ancestors had taken?"

The elder sighed again, and Blood assumed he was weary of

all the questions. "All I'll say for now is that the colony at the time was very excited when exchange students returned from Earth. Everyone wanted to know what they experienced, and society paid much attention to Rustant," Rudyard explained.

"Grandfather was charismatic and knew how to speak to the masses. He used his newly gained knowledge to inspire and deceive." Blood considered his magnetism and wondered how he could use it to his advantage. *I love my father dearly, but I long to be as strong as my grandfather.*

"Yes, and he knew how to generate the drama that could support the expansion of histrionics."

Blood rubbed his claws together. "Oh, I can't wait to hear more."

Rudyard pointed towards the sacred library. "First, I want you to finish the books of EOW, since histrionics about EOW played a large role in getting all ANTs on board with your grandfather's revolution."

CHAPTER 13

THE BREEDERS: GENETICS

Antalonia (Rudyard's rule, the current president)

AFTER A QUICK break, Keegan and Vermillion returned to the classroom.

Vermillion tapped on his clipboard. "You'll meet Clay soon, but first, we'll discuss genetics."

Chemistry, biology, engineering, biomechanics, and genetics were the sciences that insectoids had mastered to a high degree. From their early hexs on Poo-ponic, scientists like Brilliant realized that the principles of chemistry underlined much of nature and insect biology. Building on their understanding of the chemistry of nature, subsequent scientists made significant discoveries that underpinned their growing knowledge in biology, bioengineering, and genetics. Around Antilla's time, inventor/scientists such as Renaissance and Innovant encouraged the opening of the University of Noble Insect Technology or the UNIT. The famous engineer Antstrong led the team that created cyborg insects many hexennia before. Antstrong's team included bioengineers that pioneered the study of genetics on Poo-ponic, parallel with the studies that the famous geneticist Mendel had performed independently on Earth. This expertise allowed UNIT scientists to genetically modify spider DNA and produce the novel insectoids called BUGs for bipedal unibodied golems. Antilla later had his scientists genetically alter these BUGs so they could once again spin webs and sting with deadly venom, but they acted as his secret police.

Keegan cracked a mischievous grin. "Okay, I'm ready for some Mendel gymnastics."

Vermillion guffawed. "Now, who's the humorous one? And you've been doing some advanced research."

Keegan smiled. "I noticed the bookshelf at the back of the classroom last time, and I saw the book with the peas on the cover. I hope you don't mind that I borrowed it." He was becoming quite at home in the breeding halls and enjoyed that. *I can guess where this is going.*

Vermillion shrugged. "Of course not. That's why the books are there. And you picked the right one. I was going to assign it to you for homework. Mendel was the human father of genetics research, and his book is the right place to start."

Keegan showed off his intellect. "Yes, it's a complex topic, yet Mendel seemed to simplify it." He stood tall, proud of what he had learned. *Ask me anything.*

"Let's see how much you learned, then." Vermillion flashed a devious smile. "If you mate a purebred tall pea plant with a small purebred one, how many tall plants would you yield in the next generation?"

Keegan answered immediately. "Well, the gene for tall is dominant. So, the next generation would have all tall plants."

Vermillion creased his brow. "And what about the F2 generation?"

Keegan thought for a moment. "I can't say exactly how many of each plant there would be, but the ratio would be about three tall ones for every small plant." He smiled. *I know I got this one right.*

Vermillion nodded. "Excellent. I see you read just as well as you listen."

"I only read about his pea experiments, but I saw from the table of contents that he also performed genetic research on other plants and honeybees. Do his principles apply to insects?" He quickly flipped to the back of the book. *I hope he sees my inquisitiveness can match my wit.*

"Yes, Mendelian genetics applies to all life-forms, from plants to insects to humans on Earth."

Keegan spread his forelimbs wide. "But they must have so many genes?" He looked hard at the drawing of Mendel on the back cover. *I know from school that humans are highly complex organisms with thousands of genes.*

"Yes, but often each gene is dominant or recessive and controls traits in the same ratio, as shown in peas. It gets a little more complicated when two or more genes influence a trait."

Keegan again sported his mischievous grin. "That explains why most humans aren't pea heads."

Vermillion doubled over in laughter. "I may be the breed master, but I can see who the pun master is." Vermillion regained his composure. "Now, back to the lesson. Did you know humans share one-third of their genes with us?"

"That's amazing! We share genes with aliens?!" Keegan threw his forelimbs in the air.

Vermillion looked down at his notes. "A question. What would you say from your mingling within our colony is the dominant ANT exoskeleton color gene?"

Keegan answered quickly. "Red is dominant, for sure."

"Would you say the ratio of reds to blacks is three to one?"

Keegan pondered the question. "No, it's about even. And of course, there are browns as well." He looked out at the incubators in the breeding halls. *He knows we aim to breed equal numbers of all ANT colors. Where is this going?*

Vermillion pointed at the book in Keegan's claw. "How is it possible that a dominant gene does not dominate a society, based on Mendelian principles?"

Keegan beamed, "Blacks must have bred with other blacks, producing black offspring to a higher degree than if we bred them with reds." He sported a crooked half-smile. *This is my best educated guess.*

Vermillion pointed out the window. "And what about the browns? Where do they come in?"

Keegan stuttered, "I, uh, I'm not sure. I haven't finished reading the book." He looked down sheepishly. *I can admit it when I don't know something.*

Vermillion projected a superior scent. "It is based on polygenic inheritance, with multiple genes controlling exoskeleton color. So, the combinations of dominant and recessive genes can create different shades."

Keegan sprayed a puffy perfume. "So, the reddest of the reds have all dominant red genes, but browns have some dominant red and some recessive black genes?" He grabbed both sides of his head and bugged his eyes to show his head might explode. *I hope I'm on the right track.*

Vermillion grabbed Keegan's book and held it up for effect. "Precisely, and all recessive genes create pure black, while a majority of dominant genes with a minority of recessive genes would yield a less pure red."

Keegan puckered his brow. "But we breed blacks, browns, and reds? Couldn't we just breed out the black and create only reds?"

Vermillion explained that they only started a selective breeding program recently. Although they were trying to create a pure red line, recessive genes sometimes popped up and contaminated the pure line. He also mentioned that mutations sometimes affected the ANT's hues, so an ANT could have two shades. Also, traits or mutations sometimes do not show until adolescence, so it is hard to prune them out in the larval stage. They also intended to produce pure black and pure brown ANTs so that it was clear to what social class each cyborg ANT belonged. Their society reflected a hierarchical system based on color and wanted to ensure everyone knew their caste. They knew ambiguity could lead to questioning, and being inquisitive was highly discouraged. Conversely, removing ambiguity would encourage a sense of belonging and a willingness to accept one's role in society and achieve the Czar's primary aim—conformity.

Keegan thought for a moment, rubbing his chin. "I see, so it's complicated. Are there other mutations?"

"Not that I know of, although…" Vermillion hesitated.

"What?" Keegan perked up.

"There is a rumor that some Bilalunan ANTs have a chameleon mutation."

Keegan did a double-take. "Chameleon, what's that?" He jumped up from his chair. *Fascinating!*

Vermillion pointed to a colorful mosaic on the wall of the classroom. He explained the term referred to some species of reptiles on Earth. Lizards that can change their color to match their backgrounds as a defense mechanism. He told Keegan there could be one climbing the mosaic, and no one would know it was there.

Vermillion added, "Some say there are mutant ANTs on moon Bilaluna that can do the same. But I don't believe it."

"Wow, that would be amazing."

Vermillion again assumed an academic demeanor. "Yes, I also read that a beetle on Earth in South America can change colors from gold to black and back again. I suppose a mutation could alter the concentrations of eumelanin, porphyrin, and carotenoid in ANT biochrome pigments, allowing them to change from black to brown or red. Though it's improbable."

Keegan swung a forelimb over his head. "Whoa, you've left my stratosphere with that one." He spun once around for dramatic impact. *I have much to learn if I want to match this guy's intellect.*

"We can talk about chameleons later, but it's not pertinent to this lesson. I got side-tracked."

Keegan tried to get serious again. "You mentioned there were three factors, and the first was a hidden recessive or dominant gene in a not yet pure breed, and the second was mutations. What is the third factor?"

Vermillion spread his forelimbs out in three directions. "Choice."

Keegan raised his shoulders. "Choice?" His ommatidia rattled a little, as if he was looking at his own thoughts. *I wasn't expecting that.*

Vermillion tapped on the blackboard. "Yes, we could choose to have a society with only pure red ANTs, but we don't."

Keegan tilted his head. "Why not?"

"We use color to differentiate our ANT castes." Vermillion pointed out to the ova cava. "So, we breed three different colors of ANTs, but we haven't yet got to 100% pure colors for each of the three castes."

Keegan pointed to the reddest part of his thorax. "So, I assume reds are in the top tier, but who's next?"

Vermillion grabbed Keegan's book again and shook it. "It's obvious when based on genetics."

"Ah yes, browns. But why are different castes desired?" He sat down, trying to understand the implications of all he had learned. *I think I'm correct, but is it right?*

Vermillion flipped to the page in the book that describes polygenic inheritance. "Like many biological systems, genes often control multiple traits, and we have determined that the dominant gene for red exoskeletons is also dominant for aggression."

Keegan opened his claws, then shut them. "And those ANTs with recessive genes are less aggressive?"

"Exactly, black ANTs are less aggressive and more altruistic."

Keegan raised his claw for effect. "So, I assume when Rustant took over the rule and started Antalonia, he wanted to squash altruism and demote black ANTs to third-class citizens." He stifled the urge to shake his head. *That's his style, as well as that of his heirs.*

"Yes, especially since his student exchange partner, Antebon, opposed him, and he resented that."

Keegan looked out to the black section of the ova cava. "Is it also because black ANTs are less intelligent?" He put a claw to his nose. *There's something else apod.*

Vermillion explained that the gene for exoskeleton color and aggression did not impact intelligence and that black and brown ants are no less intelligent when hatched. However, he mentioned they received fewer advantages during their development. The early breeders also reduced the neuronal growth factors that enhance brain size during the transformation of ants to cyborg ANTs. He told Keegan that they engineer brown ANTs' brain sizes to be smaller than red ANTs and black ANTs even smaller.

Keegan fidgeted. "Why is that?"

Vermillion pointed successively from the black to brown to red hatcheries in the ova cava. "Our caste system reflects not only a continuum from black to red exoskeletons but also intellect."

Keegan tried to hide his growing discomfort. "I assume we give black ANTs more menial tasks and less chance for advancement, with reds getting the best jobs and browns somewhere in between?"

Vermillion pressed his claws together. "Precisely, everyone is content because their jobs match their intellectual capacities and resultant skill levels."

"But what about alpha, betas, and chi within each color caste?" Keegan asked. He turned his back to his mentor and lowered his head. *That is so wrong.*

Vermillion sighed heavily, growing weary of the lesson. "As I mentioned before, alphas get more nutritional and educational advantages. And for red ANTs, since their selection to these subcastes is based on the 'redness' of their exoskeletons, alphas are more aggressive and more likely to succeed in the most challenging jobs."

Keegan squinted his eyes. "But within each color caste, are their brain sizes equal?" His stomach began to turn. *I started as a beta. Did they shrink my brain?*

"Yes, since we can't determine their final hues until adolescence, we treat ANTs equally to others in their color caste." Vermillion pointed out the window at a nearby school. "But we segregate them into alpha, beta, and chi educational classes once we know their true colors."

Keegan shrugged, sloughing a scruffy scent. "I see why you didn't want to get into this on my first hexay." He shook his head despite his urge to suppress it. *I can't believe all this, but I need to learn it to improve myself.*

"Yes, and now it's time for your practical training with Clay."

CHAPTER 14

HOW ANTALONIA BEGAN: ANTNOIR'S REVENGE

Intopia (Umberant's rule, three presidents in the past)

ANTEBON DIDN'T NEED to read the polls to understand that Rustant had won the candidates' debate. She knew she had performed well, but recognized that many in attendance had fallen for Rustant's various ploys. She knew he was never sick on Earth or had any god-like 'epiphanies'. Antebon rolled her ommatidia as she paced back and forth. She was discouraged by the debate's outcome and hoped her mother might provide some advice to help fight Rustant on his level. "Mother, how do I debate an opponent who won't play by the rules—an ANT who deceives with his every odor?" She thrust her forelimbs upward. *I think he's possessed; maybe that's why he's so red.*

"Antebon, my pupa, the voters will believe what they choose to believe, and you may lose your battle with a devil whose only goal is to seize power. Only when all learn for themselves that an ANT is false will they turn on him."

Antebon stared hard at her mother. "But that could take hexs. I need to turn this around now. Before it's too late." She pulled hard at her setae hairs. *I can't allow him to win.*

"You must convince the public that truth is more attractive than lies. But I fear our colony wants a change, and Rustant offers them the forbidden fruit they long to taste."

"I remember reading the ancient history text of Narrant," started Antebon. "Rustant talks about it like Antilla was a hero, but I see him as an autocratic tyrant. Rustant is cut from the same cloth, and he will fool the insects, then rule with an iron claw." She spoke so violently that her antennae shook like wheat shafts blowing in the wind. *He has caught insects in his spell, and I can't snap them out of it.*

Her mother stroked Antebon's dorsal thorax. "You should remind all insects of the altruistic goals of Antuna and how our Antunite ancestors, Anthiery and Gretant, stood up for insectism. Non-ANTs and many black ANTs support insectism."

Anthiery was one of the cyborgs that stood up to Antilla's authoritarian tendencies. Gretant was an environmental scientist who battled Antilla over his climate policies and later helped improve the environment on Bilaluna.

Antebon raised a claw. "Like Antuna, I would give my life for insectism, and I'll fight those like Rustant who would destroy it." She swiped the claw through the air like she was eviscerating her enemy on a battlefield. *I will defeat Rustant no matter how long it takes.*

"All you can do, my pupa, is fight for your cause and be

true to its principles. Rustant may win the vote, but if your aim is just, you will win in the long run." Antebon's mother looked down. "But before then, I am afraid we are in for hard times."

Antebon met with her old classmate Antnoir, who applied to work as her campaign manager.

"Antnoir, I am glad you applied for this position," Antebon began. "I am looking for a kindred spirit, and I know from the non-ANT friends you had in high school we believe in the same things."

"You know both my parents are black ANTs." Antnoir flashed her black thorax. "We are Antunites through and through, although my folks are not that political." She rolled her compound eyes so hard they collided. *They just like to boast about being Antunites.*

Antebon admired Antnoir's black thorax. "I get my black from my father. My mother is brown with some red genes, which makes her work harder to prove she's an Antunite. She may not be an Ebon, but you wouldn't know it from talking to her. Her altruistic views rubbed off on me."

"But I expect the red genes you got from your mother have made you more aggressive than the average black ANT. That's why you fight so hard for insectism." Antnoir bit her antennae. *Maybe I shouldn't have said that out loud.*

Antebon looked down at Antnoir's resumé. "I've had the same thoughts. Or perhaps I have an Antunite inferiority complex?" She looked up at Antnoir and smiled. "If your parents are so apathetic, why are you motivated to be political?"

Antnoir glared into space. "Rustant came to see me last hexek to tell me to stay away from Currant. He thought my

Antunite views negatively influenced his old friend. Can you believe the nerve of that hindgut?" Her blank look shifted to a burning scowl. *I told him to go "f" himself.*

Antebon's ommatidia spun. "Do you think Rustant had something to do with Currant's death?"

Antnoir turned her gaze towards Antebon. "Yes, and that's why I'll do everything I can to prevent him from becoming president." She held her claws up to imitate iron bars. *He should rot in prison, not lead the colony.*

Antebon raised her brow. "So, you'll work long hexours and fight hard?"

"I love your cause even more than I hate Rustant. No one will work harder to get you elected." She jumped up from her chair and patted Antebon on the shoulders. *How come we were never best buds in high school?*

"Antnoir, you convinced me. You're hired! Can you start right away?"

"Yes, but I also want to ask you a favor." Antnoir stared directly into Antebon's eyes. "I want you to help me prove that Rustant did it." Her gaze intensified to a laser-hot glare. *You've got a stake in this too.*

"If you truly believe he was responsible, I will help in whatever way I can." Antebon looked tenderly at her new friend. "If he is guilty, we must never let him take power."

Antnoir took Antebon's claw. "Will you come with me to the police station tomorrow? They want to speak with me about my meeting with Rustant before Currant died. It was intimidating when I went there to report him missing." She pouted and lowered her head. *I need to convince them he did it.*

Antebon put a second claw over Antnoir's. "Of course, I

feel bad that Currant died after I asked him to help put away the pulpit."

"I know. I feel so guilty I left the hall ahead of him." Antnoir pulled away her claw and put it up to her face. "If we had all left together, he might still be alive." Her stunned demeanor revealed she had not considered this before. *I allowed that devil to do his evil deed.*

"Don't blame yourself." Antebon stepped forward to hug her friend. "If it was Rustant, he could have attacked Currant at any time."

Antnoir covered her face and cried. "Yes, but we should have been more careful." She smashed one claw into another. *I know he bashed in his brain.*

"You can't blame yourself." Antebon stared hard into Antnoir's eyes. "If you're right, the only one who deserves blame is Rustant."

Antnoir forced a sad smile. "Meet me at dawn, and we will talk to the police first thing." She raised her shoulders and stood tall. *We can do this together and defeat the bastard.*

～ ～ ～

Antebon accompanied her friend to the police station the next morning, and Antnoir described her meeting with Rustant before Currant died. A few hexays later, Antnoir learned the police found no evidence of wrongdoing and assumed that the teenager was doing what young male ANTs often did, risk-taking for fun. They suggested the political rally excited Currant, and he took a slide down the cliff's edge to release steam after getting charged up. Or maybe he had drunk too much strong sap.

Antnoir rejected the final police report and tried to convince Antebon of its errors.

"Antebon, do you believe the crap the police said about Currant's death?" She repeatedly rubbed her claws as if washing them. *They're a bunch of incompetent fools.*

"They ignored your testimony?" Antebon queried.

"Yes, there was no mention in the report of my meeting with Rustant. They also ignored that Currant said he'd never talk to him again." She kicked at a stone on the ground in front of her, unable to control her anger. *It's like they are on his side.*

"The police on the case were all red ANTs." Antebon fumed more than Rustant did when he struck Currant. "I bet they support Rustant's campaign, and he probably charmed them like all the others."

"I complained when the police released the report, and they hinted I was jealous because Rustant was leaving behind his old friends as he climbed to the pinnacle of power." Antnoir smashed her claw against her hind leg. "They also said they found no hemolymph anywhere near the entrance to the meeting hall so that it couldn't be murder." She shook her head. *He covered his tracks well.*

The next hexay, Antnoir asked Antebon to help her investigate the crime scene. Antebon fully backed Antnoir's assessment and agreed to help her find potential evidence. They weren't sure whether the police were incompetent or complicit, but they were convinced of Rustant's guilt and wanted to prove it.

Antnoir shook like a butterfly in the wind while she spoke. "Let's comb the area of the hall's entrance to see if there is any hemolymph or any sign someone removed it." She held her claws in front of her eyes and furrowed her antennae. *I bet those crooked cops didn't even investigate.*

Sometime later, Antebon spoke. "Antnoir, I am sorry. We've been searching for hexours, and there's nothing here." She raised her claws in the air. "It's time to give it up."

Antnoir's eyes teared. "You're probably right, but can you help me down the crag so I can see where he died?"

Antebon nodded. "Yes, but it's steep. We'll need to take it slow."

As they stepped over the brink to begin their descent, Antnoir pointed at a small shrub. "Look, is that hemolymph on that leaf?" Her face turned grey. *I knew we'd find it, and I bet the cops never even looked here.*

As they inched their way down the grade, Antebon pointed to a bramble covered with prickles. "What's that? I think that red fabric was torn from someone's sash."

"Currant never wore a sash, but I bet Rustant does." Antnoir grinned. "And look, there are pod prints right below it." She grinned from antenna to antenna. *I think we got him! The police only need to check and see if he has a red sash.*

Soon they reached the rock on which the police presumed Currant fell.

Antebon nudged the rock with her hind claw. "Odd that the rock is not sunken into the soil." She looked at Antnoir. "It teeters when I push on it."

Antnoir trembled. "Let's gather up this evidence and show it to the police. Rustant will go to the slammer, and you'll win the election." She gestured as if swinging a gate back and forth. *It's an open and shut case.*

Crime novels and television shows about police activities and courtroom trials were not a thing on Intopia, or even Bilaluna or Poo-ponic. So, Antebon and Antnoir knew nothing about preserving evidence in its natural state. When they brought their evidence to the precinct, the police informed them that anything removed from the scene was not trustworthy. The pair got nowhere with their arguments, and the case remained closed. Antnoir left behind an acrid aroma as she stormed out of the police station.

Antnoir felt vindicated in finding the evidence, but she became enraged when the police failed to act on it. She glared out the door of the police station. *I can see an incensed Rustant striking him with the rock and Currant lying dead on the cold ground.*

※ ※ ※

The next afternoon, Antnoir decided, without telling Antebon, to seek justice on her own. *I hate Rustant and can't live without finding justice for Currant. I must confront Rustant with the evidence and force him to admit his guilt.*

Antnoir was an imposing ANT for a female and knew that Rustant would not overtake her if it came to a fight. *Rustant's secretary will let me into his office to see him. I'm Antebon's campaign manager, after all.* As his schedule was full, she pleaded with the assistant to add an extra appointment at the end of the hexay. The secretary was packing up when Antnoir arrived, so she told her to let herself out after meeting with Rustant.

Antnoir stepped through the door, scowled at Rustant, and threw the hemolymph-stained leaf on his desk. "I found this at the edge of the crag. You hit Currant with a rock and dragged him down the ravine, and your pod prints were there under the bloody leaf." She glared so hard that Rustant needed to look away. *Look me in the eye, and I'll know you're lying.*

Rustant stood up. "What are you talking about? I wasn't

even there. How dare you accuse me? It's planted evidence, and it doesn't prove anything."

Antnoir raised her arm, imitating a striking blow. "Your claw marks were on the rock, which wasn't even sunk in the ground." She kicked a door stop across the room. *We got you now, and I want to see you squirm.*

Rustant remained as cool as a wet worm's skin. "You're making this all up, and no one will believe you. The police never found such things."

"What about this?" Antnoir opened her claw and showed Rustant the patch of red cloth she found at the scene. She extended her other claws, which were freshly sharpened. *What do you say now, sucker?*

Rustant shuddered momentarily before regaining his composure. "So, what about it? That could belong to anyone—we all wear red." He sat down hard. "The case is closed, and the captain assured me they'd never re-open it."

Antnoir thought back to the look in the police captain's eyes, the disdain he showed her, and she realized Rustant was right. Her compound eyes rattled. *Rustant won't admit anything because he knows the police are on his side, and it's futile.*

Antnoir stormed toward the door and noticed a red sash hanging on a stand. She looked closely and saw a tear in the garment and a hole that matched the small patch she had in her claw. *He did it, that bastard.* Antnoir grabbed the stand and lashed out at Rustant, striking him across the head with its base. He crashed to the floor with hemolymph splattering across the room. *Now die like my poor Currant, you murderous thug.* A sizzling stench warmed the air as she dropped the rack and ran from the room as fast as possible.

The next morning, the police arrived at Antebon's nest and

found Antnoir cowering in her closet. Antnoir had not killed Rustant as she had suspected, and he described the attack to the police, omitting any discussion of further evidence. He burned the sash with the missing patch before contacting the police and had his secretary confirm Antnoir was there. The scandalous news spread around the colony like wildfires in high winds. The news that they caught Antebon's campaign chair red-clawed and charged her with attempted murder of her opponent was jaw-dropping. The additional report of Antnoir hiding in Antebon's closet was even more damning and ultimately killed her candidacy for president. Rustant won the election in a landslide, although many Antunites and non-ANT cyborgs shunned the polls. The police didn't charge Antebon, as she convinced them that Antnoir had just run into the closet on hearing the knocks on the door. The police believed Antebon did not aid her since the attempt to escape was inept. Antebon tried to make a case for her campaign chair and push her story of Rustant's guilt, but the scar on his face generated sympathy from the electorate and proved Antnoir's vengeful anger.

CHAPTER 15

THE RULERS: ADVANCED HISTRIONICS

Antalonia (Rudyard's rule, the current president)

BLOOD MET WITH his father, Rudyard, for a morning tutoring session. "Papa, I know you wanted to teach me about socionics to-hexay, but can you first tell me more about Grandfather's return from Earth and how he won the support of his followers?" He rubbed his claws together. *I want to know more about my favorite topic.*

Rudyard nodded. "Of course, my son. And the story will put the worm skins on the cake for how he used histrionics to gain favor."

Blood guffawed, "Worm skins, you're so funny. So, tell me how Grandfather got started on his plans?" Blood stroked a red sash he wore that he inherited from Rustant. *I can't wait to take over and follow my grandfather's and father's pod steps.*

Rudyard exuded a proud perfume around the room. "He wanted to take advantage of the excitement around his return from Earth and quickly announced that he'd be running for President of the colony."

Blood's eyes lit up. "Wow, that quickly, and how did Antebon take it?"

Rudyard reanimated his sour face. "She hesitated initially but then ran against Rustant since she opposed his views. I think she hoped a more established candidate that shared her opinion would step forward."

"I assume no one did." *I bet Rustant was so strong the others all feared him.*

Rudyard nodded and described how the previous leader, Umberant, had been president for one and a half hexuries, and he was getting old. The public seemed to feel that he would rule forever. Others in his party were also old and had been followers for so long that none of them aspired to take over at their advanced ages.

Blood pointed to his father. "The old president did not plan for a successor?" Then he pointed at himself. *I assume you won't make that mistake.*

Rudyard told Blood that Umberant never wanted to be president but fell into the position when his popular predecessor, Jetant, died young from cancer. Rudyard learned from his father that Umberant had been Jetant's best friend and a big supporter. The death of his friend upset the electorate, and many voted for Umberant because they saw him as the candidate that would follow Jetant's policies. As he was still young, Jetant had no offspring.

Blood shrugged. "So, Umberant won power because everyone wanted another Jetant, and they settled for the closest thing." He flexed his forelimbs. *But I can't comprehend how voters could choose such a weak leader.*

"That's right, Umberant rode in on his deceased friend's coattails, and the electorate chose him as president. But he was no Jetant." Rudyard shifted in his chair. "He was not as charismatic or creative, but he felt a duty to continue his friend's legacy. And all Jetant's closest advisors supported him."

Blood wrinkled his brow. "But if he was not charismatic or creative, how did he stay in power for so long?" He looked inquisitively at his father. *I assumed he wouldn't last even two hexs.*

"Because Intopia established a hybrid political system similar to Bilaluna's," Rudyard explained. "However, Bilaluna did not have a president, only a ceremonial queen BEE and a congress. The new settlers of Intopia elected to have a president again and no queen."

Blood squinted. "I'm not following. How did that affect Umberant's presidency?" He shook his head.

"Oh, on Bilaluna, they appointed a queen for life, and Intopians decided they would do that for their president," Rudyard explained.

"So, did Umberant die when Grandfather came back from Earth?"

"No, but he was so old he no longer wanted to hold power. He had announced he was considering abdicating." Rudyard continued, "So when he saw two young ANTs were vying to replace him, he said he would step down after an election."

"Were other insectoids eligible to run?" Blood asked. He

held his antennae at the thought of it. *Yet I can't imagine any other insectoid could attain such a powerful position.*

Rudyard rubbed his chin. "Yes, that's likely why Umberant abdicated when he did. He wanted to make sure there was a powerful candidate to ensure ANTs maintained the presidency."

No other insectoids ran because an ANT had been president since the colony of Intopia began. Everyone assumed other insectoids would not stand a chance. ANTs were the supervisors of all activities, and because they were more aggressive, they were more often the owners of businesses and those that paid most attention to politics. He described how some insectoids, like WoRMs and WoBBs, were apathetic about politics.

Blood nodded as he took in the information. "That explains how he avoided facing other opponents, but how did Grandfather defeat Antebon?" He reminded himself how poorly he thought of black ANTs. *I'm keen to know how Rustant squashed the black ANT.*

Rudyard stood and walked around the room, emanating a solid stench. "It was an uphill battle because the society cherished the principles of insectism, and many ANTs thought insectism would sustain a utopian society and uphold Intopia. And as an Antunite, Antebon was the embodiment of insectism."

Insectism stressed the principles of understanding, empathy, and caring for fellow insects, regardless of their family, a philosophy that Rustant rejected.

Blood pointed to their library. "Yes, I read in the sacred text that Antunites were the principal proponents of insectism throughout our post-Earth history." His lip curled in disgust. *I taste bile just saying the word insectism.*

"Indeed, the view at the time was the blacker your

exoskeleton, the more you supported insectism—and Antebon was among the blackest ANTs."

Blood oozed a shaky scent. "So, how was it even possible for Grandpa to sway public opinion?" He had read how long rulers had practiced insectism on Bilaluna and even on Pooponic before Antilla. *I do not doubt it, but I love the drama.*

"Rustant was extremely charismatic, but there were other issues that helped." Rudyard held up one claw.

"There were problems?" asked Blood.

Rudyard described how democratic societies always have problems, especially when the electorate has too much freedom, too many choices, and too much access to information. He said other insectoids resented how ANTs were always supervisors and business owners. Democratic societies were content when the economy was strong but grumbled when it weakened.

Blood scratched his head. "Did that happen on Intopia?"

"Umberant was aged and not very creative, so he could not solve the economic problems."

"The population got antsy and wanted something else. Something new." Blood warmed at the prospect of Rustant's success. *I see the conditions were ripe for Grandfather's ideas.*

Rudyard nodded. "Yes, especially the ANTs who were getting lots of flak from the other insectoids about the high cost of living and the poor economy."

"But what about the other insectoids?" Blood scrunched his face as he spoke. *I need to know the circumstances Rustant faced.*

"They got more apathetic, feeling that government was not helpful to their needs. They became less likely to vote."

"So Antebon couldn't drum up their support?" Blood rubbed his claws together.

Rudyard scowled and sat again. "She originally had most of the non-ANT support as the blackest of Antunites."

"I imagine Rustant had to get all the ANTs to vote for him?" He raised his arms as if cheering on a crowd. *How did he pull it off?*

"Yes indeed. Rustant needed nearly all the remaining ANT votes."

"So, how did he do it?" begged Blood.

Rudyard pointed to the library. "First, with the books of EOW."

Blood put his claws out to the side. "Using the scientific text of a human biologist who studied tiny ants?" He dug through his bag for one of the books. *I know Rustant needed to be creative, but this is not a strategy I expected.*

"Not exactly. Rustant used the ideas of EOW and the knowledge he learned about Earth ants to create a belief system that ANTs could adhere to." Rudyard put a claw over his heart. "He created a drama about the fierceness of our Earth ant ancestors and made-up stories about the glorious ant god EOW." A smarmy stink filled the air.

"EOW, I see it now. It intrigued me when you first said the word, and I finally understand." Blood clapped his claws together. *I applaud Grandfather's ingenuity.*

CHAPTER 16

THE NEW SPIES: TRANSFORMATION

Antalonia (Rudyard's rule, the current president)

AFTER A QUICK break, Keegan followed Vermillion's instructions and sought Clay in the bloom room. "The breed master said I should report to you for some practical training."

Clay extended his claw. "Yes, great to see you again, Keegan. I've been looking forward to working with you." He studied Keegan for any signs of suspicion. *I must be friendly with all new staff so no one will suspect me.*

Keegan grabbed and shook Clay's claw. "Me too, and I'm thrilled to get out of the classroom and see some live procedures."

Clay moved his claw to Keegan's shoulder and nudged him further into the hall. He instructed him to follow so that he could introduce him to a couple of nanitics that were ready for their cyborg transformations. This was a crucial moment in Beewish's grand scheme to infiltrate the Antalone leaders. Clay had been a spy for hexades and knew how to conduct himself without generating suspicion. He also knew that Rose and Jasper would be nervous and that he needed to compensate by projecting an infectious calmness the others would catch.

"This is all very exciting," replied Keegan.

"Keegan, this is Rose and Jasper. They've agreed to allow me to show you the procedures required for them to become cyborgs." He exuded a serenity to relax his comrades.

Keegan looked at the two tiny nanitics in their incubators and wanted to reassure them.

"Don't worry," replied Keegan. "The breed master says you're in great claws with Clay cause he's the best."

"I'm a little nervous, but excited to get my bionic limbs," Rose recited her practiced reply.

Jasper nodded. "M-me too."

Keegan looked closer at Rose, making her squirm. "You have a beautiful shell, and I don't think I've ever seen a redder red."

Rose turned even redder.

Jasper shook his antennae. "Yes, I call her my Triple R—ravishing red Rose."

Keegan nodded. "Ravishing Rose, indeed. Let's hope Clay's procedures don't fade your perfect hue."

Clay interjected. "The growth factors don't change one's colors; she'll only have more of it."

"Hey, I'm nervous enough already. Thanks for the compliments, but please don't examine me too much."

"I am sorry, Rose. I'm a little nervous too as a trainee,"

admitted Keegan. "Except for my own transformation, I've never seen this before."

"Well, you said Clay was the best, so I feel better." Rose flickered her ommatidia at Keegan. "You should too."

"I'm not so nervous," chimed in Jasper. "But I would like to get on with it."

"Okay," started Clay, addressing the nanitics. "Lie back." Then he looked at Keegan. "The first thing is attaching the mechanical limbs."

"Oh, I had a question about that," interrupted Keegan, consulting his copious notes. "Have the bionic frames always expanded with the growing exoskeletons? I thought they used to be full-sized."

"Long ago, we installed full-length bionics." Clay pulled out a small mechanical prosthetic. "But now we use telescoping limb frames programmed electronically to stretch continuously in three dimensions throughout the transformation." He thought back to when he had suggested the innovation. *I don't like to boast about all the successful modifications I've implemented.*

"That's ingenious!" responded Keegan. "When did they start that?"

Clay shrugged. "A little less than three hexades ago. It reduces the chances of growing pains."

Jasper bolted upright, shooting an icy incense. "Growing pains?"

Clay eased Jasper back into a prone position. "My bad. I meant to say it eliminates growing pains, and your exoskeletons grow more evenly and gradually." He considered whether he might need to change his style to put Rose and Jasper at ease. *I know there is some chance of discomfort statistically, but it's minor.*

Keegan noticed Rose trembling, and he stroked her tiny

claw. "During my transformation, everyone had the old method, and even then, growing pains were not so bad. You guys have the latest technology."

"Keegan is right," assured Clay. "You are also getting third-generation growth factors which are easier to tolerate."

Jasper bolted upright again. "Easier?"

Clay chuckled a little as he lowered Jasper again. "Yes, and by easier, I meant fully tolerated. Don't worry. We have ironed out all earlier issues, and this will be as easy as sliding into your nest after a couple of sips of strong sap." He thought for a moment how helpful Keegan was. *I could learn from him about bedside manners.*

Jasper sat again. "We've never had strong sap."

"Yes, I forgot how young you are," replied Clay. "When you do, you'll love it." *I could use a shot right now.*

"What's next?" asked Keegan.

"Now that I've attached the limbs, we'll start infusing the growth factors, antioxidants, and protein stabilizers," instructed Clay. He looked the nanitics over. "We also give them low doses of a sedative."

Rose shuddered. "What's a sedative?"

Clay bent over close to Rose and Jasper. "It's a drug that makes you sleepy, and you'll get it for a while. We're ensuring that you don't move your limbs too abruptly and disconnect your natural limbs from the new mechanical ones." He reconsidered his earlier conclusion on style. *I'll do everything to reassure them.*

Jasper continued to lie down, but stiffened. "And what were those other things?"

"You mean in the infusion?" Keegan clarified.

Jasper nodded. "Yes."

"They are drugs that cause your exoskeletons to grow over your new mechanical limbs and increase your organ sizes," explained Keegan. "They'll even increase your brain size and extend your life, and you'll live many hexades—for as long as your new bionics last."

"Yes, Keegan's right," added Clay. "Some cyborg ANTs have lived over two hexuries." He considered how this was the one breeding step that didn't discriminate between ant castes. *We make the black ANTs stupid, but at least they live long.*

To help Rose and Jasper relax while Clay worked, Keegan described some facts he learned from Vermillion. He explained that the conditions on the planet already allow ants to live six times as long as their Earth ancestors. However, they worried that the dramatically expanded size of cyborgs might cause a shortened lifespan. But with antioxidants and protein stabilizers, cyborg ANTs live twice as long or more, despite their large size.

"That's if we survive the transformation?" Jasper shivered as he got sleepy.

"Relax and get some sleep," insisted Clay. "I've never lost a nanitic yet."

Keegan gazed into Rose's eyes while she repeatedly lost focus before falling asleep.

As Rose fell asleep, her red hue began to dim slightly. While Keegan looked up to the ceiling to see if the lights had dimmed, Jasper bellowed a loud yawning noise. It was a signal the two nanitics had worked out to warn each other when their colors were off. Rose instantly stirred and reddened herself. Then she remembered to lock her color before sleeping, as they learned during their training. When Keegan looked back, Rose was as red as ever, and Clay, who witnessed the scene, mentioned how annoying it was when the lights flickered, as they often did.

Then, after Jasper also fell asleep, Clay continued his lesson with Keegan. "You did a stellar job there helping to relax our patients." He thought about how well it went working with Keegan. *I must establish a smooth working relationship with potential leaders for our mission's success.*

"Thanks. I could see that performing a practical demonstration might upset the young ones." Keegan then lowered his head. "I am sorry if I said anything inappropriate. But I found Rose so captivating. I've never seen such a dazzling red. I could almost see myself reflected in her shell."

"I expect she will grow up to be a Scarlet. She has the purest red shell of all the nanitics I have transformed." Clay winked. "You should keep your eye on Rose. She will go places." He looked at Rose and admired her evident chameleant skills. *I must encourage my Antalone colleagues to notice the new young spies and consider them potential Scarlets.*

"I guess that's why they called her Rose," Keegan gazed down upon the sleeping beauty. "It's such an exquisite name."

"Now, speaking of Scarlets," began Clay. "These nanitics are in these two columns because they are red alphas. Jasper may not be as red as Rose, but he is still a pure red." He smiled to himself, realizing that Keegan was quite taken with Rose. *I repeat the word, Scarlet, to get it to sink in.*

"I know we give lower concentrations of neuronal growth factors to browns and blacks, but how much lower?" asked Keegan, frowning.

Clay spread his forelimbs about one meter, then reduced the distance to one-half. "Browns get half the concentration of reds." He reduced his claw separation by half again. "And blacks get half that."

"That's quite a reduction." Keegan tried to hide his vexing vapor.

"Yes, it seems when he set up the bionics program, Czar Rust wanted to punish the blacks for their opposition to his leadership," replied Clay, hiding his distaste.

Keegan shrugged. "It seems harsh, but I guess it works."

Clay nodded. "Yes, the duller black ANTs no longer rebel and seem satisfied with their simple lives." He detected a reluctance in Keegan but tried to ignore it for now. *It's a conclusion I believe, but do not cherish.*

Keegan looked over at the brown and black incubators. "And do they get the same antioxidants and protein stabilizers as reds?"

"Yes, on that level, they are equals. We want everyone to live to the same age." Clay continued, "They also get the same amount of non-neuronal growth factors, so they grow just as large." He considered that some hexay he might be able to play on Keegan's sense of morality, but he must be patient. *He can learn these facts, but he must not discover my secret plan to raise the intelligence of black and brown ANTs equal to reds.*

Clay had studied for hexs how to use genetic engineering to make black and brown ANTs seem dim-witted even after increasing their brain sizes. This strategy would allow him to give all ANTs the same potential intellect, but to time it so all black and brown ANTs became smarter instantly, no matter how long since their transformation, at a chosen date when he wanted them to rebel.

"And what about nutrients?" asked Keegan.

"Brown and black ANTs get the same, and reds about 20%

more." Clay stretched his limbs as wide as the first two columns in the red section, where he placed Rose and Jasper. "And the purest of the reds, the ones we are sure will not develop any brown or black flecks; they get an additional 10%, as we expect they'll become alphas." He hoped Keegan would accept this as a given and not discuss the matter with other breeders. *This increase was one of my secret innovations for Rose and Jasper and earlier ANTs on which I experimented.*

"That makes sense, although Vermillion did not mention that."

"Well, as usual, some tricks are not in the cookbook, and we develop the best recipes on the fly. Don't worry, though. All the breeders in the bionics group do it the same way." He offered him a secret, establishing a closer bond. *And I deceive him on this since I don't want him to think Rose and Jasper are getting extra for an illicit reason.*

"Is there anything else I should know?"

"When you return for another practical training, I'll show you the prosthetics we use to create hybrids."

"Hybrids?"

"Yes, these are ANTS who perform the tasks that BEEs, FLYs, RoAChs, and WoBBs used to do." Clay snickered to himself. *I think I stunned the novice.*

"Er, Vermillion has not explained this to me yet, although we discussed ANTs replacing other insectoids." Keegan shook his head. "I see why we're not covering it to-hexay."

"Oh, and I forgot to mention vitamin S," added Clay.

"Vitamin S?" Keegan shifted his eyes from side to side.

"Yes, we give vitamin S to brown and black ANTs, although I don't know why." Clay laughed. "Given your reaction, I assume Vermillion hasn't taught you about that yet."

Since I am not a scarlet leader, I'm not permitted to know why we use vitamin S, but I hope I can wriggle it out of Keegan once he becomes a Scarlet.

Keegan shrugged. "You're right, so that's for next time, too?"

"Okay, check in with the breed master and see what he wants you to do." Clay pointed the adjacent columns. "I've got a couple more transformations to do in my section. If you don't have more classwork, you can come back and try one yourself."

Keegan smiled. "I'd love that."

"And if you're free after work, we can go for a couple of shots of strong sap. If you'd like." He considered additional ways to draw the novice closer. *I must get Keegan to take me into his confidence to provide the best for Rose and Jasper.*

Keegan wafted a bouncy bouquet. "That would be fantastic! All this learning makes me thirsty."

"Me too, my friend." Clay still longed for that shot.

CHAPTER 17

THE BREEDERS: VITAMIN S

Antalonia (Rudyard's rule, the current president)

VERMILLION AGREED TO let Keegan continue to shadow Clay for more practical training that afternoon and return to the classroom the next hexay. Keegan did well on his first cyborg transformation procedure and helped Clay replace some empty nutrient bags. Clay and Keegan later enjoyed some strong sap at the nearby tavern, but didn't stay out too late, as Keegan wanted to be fresh the following morning. Keegan tried to keep up with Clay but could only swig two shots while Clay downed four.

In the morning, Keegan arrived early and checked in on the nanitic he'd worked on, ensuring the transformation was going well. He also stopped to see Rose and Jasper, but they were both sleeping. Keegan noticed Rose's pillow had slipped off her cot, and he picked it up and placed it under her head. He saw her exoskeleton had expanded and noted how her beautiful shell was as red as ever. He wondered how she'd inherited such a pure red exoskeleton and assumed that both her parents must be high-brow Scarlets, and she would attract many mates. He decided then to do his best to ensure Rose had access to the best schools and advantages. It was the first time he realized how important it was to be a Scarlet and how much he wanted it for himself and whoever he supported. He envisioned himself in the future as an influential and distinguished Scarlet, with young protégés like Rose and Jasper following in his footsteps.

Vermillion arrived and interrupted Keegan's reverie. "Are you ready for your last bionics lesson?"

"Yes, master, I was born ready," joked Keegan. He oozed a broad bouquet.

"Aren't you cocky this morning?" noted Vermillion. "What's gotten into you?"

"Guess I'm just fired up after my practical training," offered Keegan. "It makes all the studying worthwhile." He couldn't shake the image of Rose's beautiful exoskeleton.

Vermillion smiled. "Your performance greatly impressed Clay. You have an ally in the bionics department."

Keegan stood tall, emitting a swollen scent. "I tried to be helpful without stepping beyond my bounds." His pride lessened as he worried about being too forward with the young Rose. *I can't stop thinking about her.*

Vermillion motioned for Keegan to enter the classroom. "Let's cover your last bionics lesson, and then you can spend a few hexeks each in the ova cava and the bloom room. After that, we'll move on to socionics."

"I'm keen to work hands-on with our developing ants— eggs, larvae, pupae, and nanitics, and I'm eager to learn about socionics." He considered whether he had the right stuff to take over as breed master.

As they entered the classroom, Vermillion spoke, "Let's get on with it, then. Clay told me you might have some questions."

Keegan looked down at his notes. "Yes, could you tell me about hybrids and vitamin S?"

Vermillion laughed. "That's exactly what this lesson is about." Vermillion picked up a vial with a large S on the label. "Let's start with vitamin S."

Keegan shrugged. "I've never heard of it until Clay brought it up." His curiosity peaked, but so did his concern. *I have a feeling I'm not going to like this.*

Vermillion scanned his lesson plan. "As a red ANT, you wouldn't have. We only give it to brown and black ANTs."

"What is it for?" queried Keegan, looking up from his notes. *I find it curious that even Clay doesn't know.*

Vermillion reduced the concentration of released pheromones and checked to ensure no one was nearby. "We tell brown and black ANTs it increases their intellect, but it's a drug that promotes conformity."

Keegan tried to mask his shabby scent. "Conformity? How does it do that?" His face reddened, despite his efforts to quell it. *Are we brainwashing fellow ANTs?*

Vermillion hesitated. "It's a long story, but something you need to know." He continued, "When we select tiny ants to become cyborgs, we let the eggs hatch and the pupae develop into nanitics to determine which ones are the strongest and healthiest."

"What happens to those not selected?" asked Keegan. His ommatidia turned inward as if to scan his thoughts. *I'm not sure I want to know the answer.*

"We used to release them into the wilds, so they help with soil and forest rejuvenation," started Vermillion. "But we discovered we had too many tiny ants. Of course, the wild ants mate and propagate offspring on their own. So, now we euthanize the extras."

Keegan raised a claw. "How is this related to vitamin S?" It is a practice he expected, so he was not so alarmed. *Culling tiny ants is okay, but using a conformity drug is wrong.*

Vermillion explained how they used a drug called 2-aminobutane to euthanize the unwanted ants, but one time they gave them the S-isomer of the drug by mistake, and the ants did not die. He described how rather than dying, they stayed still, waiting for instructions, instead of scattering like they usually would. While the standard form of the drug, or RS-isomer, is lethal, the other isomer, R-2-aminobutane, is a psychedelic drug like LSD, but only at high doses.

"But the S-isomer is a conformity drug?" asked Keegan.

"Yes, humans have experimented with low doses of LSD to brainwash people. And it seems like S-2-aminobutane, which we call vitamin S for short, has this effect in ants, without causing the psychedelic effects."

Keegan forced a smile. "That's amazing, and you discovered it by accident?"

Vermillion nodded. "Yes, scientific discoveries are often serendipitous."

Keegan turned and looked at the eggs and pupae in the other hall. "So, how do you administer vitamin S?" He considered that short-term use might be okay. *Maybe we only use it briefly before cyborg transformation.*

"We infuse it to all pupae so they don't scatter when they morph." Vermillion held up two bottles, clearly marked RS or

S. "The effects of the drug linger until we give the RS-isomer to kill the unwanted ants, or we sedate those we transform into cyborgs."

"So, it's important not to mix the isomers up?" assumed Keegan. He scribbled a comment in his notebook. *I must keep these drugs straight.*

Vermillion exaggerated his nod. "Yes, especially since we continue to give vitamin S to brown and black ANTs, so they follow directions."

Keegan puckered his brow and pointed to the far hall. "Do you mean when they are in the bloom room?"

Vermillion shook his head quickly. "No, I mean after they leave and throughout their lives."

"Not by repeated infusions?" queried Keegan. He took a deep breath through his spiracles. *I don't like this.*

Vermillion laughed. "No, we give them pills and tell them vitamin S will make them smarter."

Keegan thought for a moment about freedom of choice. "But what if they forget to take them or don't care?"

Vermillion smiled. "We lace them with sugar, which is addictive for ANTs who get it repeatedly."

Keegan pulled at his antennae. "So, they think they're taking vitamin S because it makes them smarter, but it only makes them conform. And they can't stop taking it because we addict them to the sugar." He wondered whether he could lead such an operation. *I might vomit.*

"Exactly! You must take your vitamin S," Vermillion joked.

Keegan forced a laugh. "Sweet!" Yet, upset about addicting the ANTs to sugar, he told Vermillion he needed to take a break. *I must process all of this.*

Vermillion pointed to the lunch and relaxation room.

"Okay, take a short pause, and when you come back, we'll talk about hybrids. By the way, we have classified information about vitamin S for leaders only. As a potential future breed leader, I can tell you. But you can tell no one else."

CHAPTER 18

THE RULERS:
THE BASE SICKS

Antalonia (Rudyard's rule, the current president)

BLOOD TWIRLED AROUND like he did when he was young and looked up at all the books and scrolls in the library. The room was circular, and there were stacks from floor to ceiling everywhere except in the study hall at the entrance and a small, restricted zone at the end. There were rails lining the main room's circumference in front of the stacks on the floor and the ceiling. They supported an elevator that looked like a dumbwaiter, with railings and a scaffold connected to the floor and ceiling tracks. Two buttons on the bar moved the elevator clockwise or counter-clockwise along the rails, while two more caused the dumbwaiter to go up or down the scaffold. Blood was as fascinated by the elevator as a youngster as he was with all the books. Yet, he always followed his father's rule that he could not ride it unless he returned with a book. As a result, he read many books and learned to love reading even more than he loved the elevator. He jumped into the lift and zoomed around on the rail to the border between the histrionics and socionics sections, spreading a sweet smell as he rode. He pushed the up button until he got to the enormous book he sought: 'Socionics as a Means to Support Histrionics.' Just as he was about to reach for the text, his father, Rudyard, entered the room and called him, "You better come down with a book, or it's off to your room."

Blood laughed so hard he had trouble grabbing the book. "I haven't heard that line for hexs." He thought warmly of his childhood. *I do love my father and respect his parenting skills. And he's an incredible teacher.*

Rudyard squelched his laugh when he saw the book his son chose. "That's a perfect book for to-hexay's lesson. And I know you are keen to get on to socionics."

"Yes, I've been eager to know more, ever since you said you wanted me to take over as master of socionics." He realized his desire to make his father proud drove his urge to learn. *Papa has given me so much care and guidance, and I love the tender way he treats me.*

"Like the title of your book, to-hexay's lesson is about the development of socionics and how your grandfather used it to build on histrionics. As you know, histrionics can only go so far, and you must use it judiciously, or the followers will catch on."

"Father, before you go any further, I have a question about the library."

"You know my feelings about this. You should learn

all there is to know in the sacred library of knowledge. Ask me anything."

Blood pointed to the group of large scrolls lining the library's top row. "Ever since I was a nanitic, those scrolls fascinated me. First, I couldn't reach them. But then they looked so old and fragile, and I was afraid to pull them out. I worried they might rip." He wanted to know everything because he understood that knowledge was power. *My father is too soft to be truly powerful and would never get mad at me.*

"You were smart to avoid them. The scrolls are delicate and sacred."

"I looked at two of them recently and couldn't read them. In what language are the scrolls written?"

"That's what we call ancient pheromonics."

"Pheromonics, I've never heard of that."

"It's the language they wrote the sacred text in before the scribe Narrant translated it into English. After that, we wrote all textbooks on Bilaluna in English because it was easier to print. That's the language we teach you to read."

Blood creased his brow. "I never realized how odd it is to speak with pheromones when we read and write English." He considered how powerful he could be as he gained more knowledge. *Father may not be the strongest leader, but I've never doubted him as a source of knowledge. So, he's taught me both the ability to be robust and what it is to be weak.*

"Well, we don't have vocal cords, so we have to speak with pheromones," explained Rudyard. "But our eyes can read anything, and English is simple."

"And although we hear some sounds with our subgenual organs, we don't have ears, so we need the syntax generator to understand spoken English."

Rudyard nodded. "Yes, the syntax generator translates English into pheromones and vice versa so humans can understand us."

"But what exactly is pheromonics?" asked Blood.

"Pheromonics are a direct transcription of the pheromones we release to communicate," Rudyard responded. "And our ancestors wrote them as chemical formulae."

"So that's why they look like chemistry books." Blood smiled. "I couldn't understand why we would have so many scrolls of chemistry experiments."

"My father taught me how to read pheromonics, but I hated it so much that I didn't want to put you through it." Rudyard laughed. "And since we've all learned to read English, there's not much point to learning the old text."

"But don't you want me to gain all the knowledge I can?" asked Blood. "I would love to read the sacred text in its original form." He realized how much he wanted to be like his grandfather since gaining his knowledge would allow him to amass strength. *If Rustant could read them all, I should, too.*

Rudyard sighed. "Perhaps some hexay. But you don't know what can of worms you're opening."

Blood laughed and rubbed his tummy. "That's OK. I love worms."

Rudyard pointed to the lounge outside the library. "So, on to socionics—but realize that Vermillion, the breed master, will teach you all the specific methods. I am just providing an introduction, letting you know the history of how it started."

Blood nodded. "I understand." He considered what he knew about socionics to control the minds of others. *I'll never turn down an opportunity to learn how to wield power.*

Rudyard shook his antennae to clear his voice. "Remember,

we spoke about how your grandfather ran against Antebon to be president of Intopia? Since he charmed all the ANTs with his talk of the great EOW, his campaign surged from the start." Rudyard beamed with pride. "Then he defeated his opponent Antebon in the final presidential debate."

"So, he won the election and became president?" asked Blood. He hoped that he would sometime need to put down a worthy adversary. *I'm glad he defeated that Ebon Antebon.*

"He won in a landslide after an enormous scandal involving Antebon's campaign manager." Rudyard spread his arms wide. "She maimed someone she accused of killing her boyfriend. And Antebon was caught hiding her." He intentionally left Rustant out of the story to not tarnish him.

"That's incredible," responded Blood. "So Antunites and other insectoids voted for him." Unbelievable!

Rudyard shook his head. "No, a large part of the population was still against him; many just withheld their vote."

Blood guessed. "Antunites?" A black cloud entered his mind. *I can taste the bile welling up in my throat.*

Rudyard nodded. "Yes, and most non-ANT insectoids."

Blood looked at the sky. "I assume the talk of an ant god did not enthuse many other insectoids?" He lusted for his own chance to manipulate the masses. *It must have been an uphill battle.*

Rudyard raised his forelimbs in the air. "No, and especially not a god that promoted ant supremacy."

"So, what did Grandpa do to get support for his policies?"

Rudyard grinned. "Remember, electors voted him in for life, so he didn't have to worry about being liked."

Blood motioned his arms forward. "So, he just pushed

through whatever policy he wanted?" A familial pride swelled within him. *Soon I'll be extending my family's reign.*

Rudyard explained that Rustant had to ensure that the public supported his policies enough that there was no rebellion. He concentrated on pleasing and convincing his base. Rudyard told Blood his father's favorite saying about gathering support—'Cover the base sicks.'

Blood clapped his claws together. "I've heard you say that, but I never understood it until now." He concluded he must always get gullible ANTs on his side.

Rudyard laughed. "Yes, appeal to the lowest of the low, those sick enough that they'll trust you no matter what."

Blood laughed too. "And give them enough histrionics to have them coming back for more." He thought of ways to inspire his loyal followers. *I see it was necessary to fool the masses.*

Rudyard spread his limbs wide. "Yes, lots of talk of how ANTs should learn from Earth ants and dominate the rest of the society." Rudyard snapped his jaws and claws

Blood emanated a shiny smell. "So, ANT supremacy was all the rage." He considered how he must follow in Rustant's pod step. *Is my father capable of such deception? Perhaps Grandfather's system was so robust he was never tested.*

"At least amongst his sick base of supporters." Rudyard grinned. "He and his advisers understood the *basics.*"

CHAPTER 19

THE OLD SPIES: NEW FRIEND

Antalonia (Rust's rule, one president in the past)

WHEN HE ENTERED high school, the leaders selected Clay as an alternate for the scarlet program. He received similar training to the intended Scarlets, including regular visits to the palace for brief sessions with the Czar. They anticipated a shortage of leaders in the coming hexs and needed Scarlets trained as replacements.

The Czar's secretary greeted Clay as he arrived early for one of his visits. "I'm just making some coffee. Go upstairs and wait for Rust, since he's in a meeting."

"Thanks, I guess I'm early." He shrugged his shoulders. *As usual, I am too eager.*

While he waited in the anteroom outside Rust's office, Clay overheard a discussion between the Czar and his minister of war and interplanetary relations. Rust was excited and projected his voice, as he often did, and his minister followed suit so Clay heard them easily. They discussed plans for a space rocket program to produce long-range missiles targeting Bilaluna if needed. Rust asked his minister whether they could place their nuclear warheads on the missiles and launch them towards Bilaluna. His minister confirmed they could do it using the knowledge they gained during their Earth exchanges but that it might take several hexs or more. The minister explained he had his best astrophysics scientist, Radley, working on the program, but accomplishing a rocket that could traverse space and reach Bilaluna was challenging. He also mentioned that they could use the rockets for space exploration or delivering warheads if they succeeded. Clay tried to hide his excitement, fanning his ion-charged incense.

Clay listened carefully to determine whether there might be other significant topics the two would discuss, but when he realized the next issue was mundane, he left the anteroom and sat and waited in the library's study hall. One could see the study hall across the circular living room from the Czar's office entrance, and most often, Rust brought him there for their sessions. He waited there to avoid the suspicion that he might have overheard anything sensitive. Rust's secretary returned and offered him some coffee, which Clay graciously refused. She knocked on Rust's office door and brought the coffee to the Czar and his minister. Their meeting went late as they lingered over their coffee. When Rust emerged, the secretary pointed to the study hall, and the Czar looked over, happy to see Clay waiting there.

Clay contacted Queen Beeutee at the first opportunity to report the highly consequential intel that he'd gotten. The news alarmed the Queen, but it was satisfying that her embedded spy could deliver such sensitive information, even while he was still a high school student. She instructed him to use his access to the sacred library to learn as much as possible about rocket science and develop a plan to sabotage Rust's efforts. Clay had already told Rust that Breed Master Vermillion wanted him to study the complicated topic of genetic engineering, and he might need extra access to the library, to which Rust agreed. Beeutee suggested he work with Darci, the spy who helped him penetrate Antalone society, to hinder the rocket program, but wait until it would create the greatest disruption. Beeutee knew it might take them a hexade or more to produce the rocket technology, and she instructed Clay to be patient. She told him the most effective attack would be so devastating that Rust would have to terminate the program, yet so covert no one would suspect that spies had anything to do with it.

When Clay finished high school, he arranged a meeting with Darci to discuss his plan. "Darci, I have been studying gene engineering and rocket science, and I think it's time to obliterate the rocket program."

Darci smiled. "It's fortunate that you've had access to the sacred library with your elevated status."

"I still need to learn more, but there's nothing more for me in the library."

"I've been thinking about something, but it's risky. You could hide a pheromonic listening device near the entrance to the rocket testing center and learn what you can about the workers there." Darci scratched her head. "Try to identify a young rocket scientist as your mark. What do you think?"

After listening to thousands of brief conversations he had recorded for hexths, Clay met again with Darci. "I think I found my mark. A clever missile designer, Rumo, is about my age." *I will befriend him.*

"Great, now you need to figure out how to meet and get to know him," Darci advised.

"I already staked out the neighborhood. There's a tavern near the test facility that many younger rocket scientists frequent." Clay was eager to take on another assignment. *I'm happy to stake out a tavern.*

Darci pointed towards the tavern. "Move your microphone into the pub and listen some more."

After several more hexths, Clay determined that Rumo patronized the tavern when he worked the evening shift and had a favorite booth close to where Clay had the listening device. Clay then regularly visited the bar, often sitting at the table beside Rumo's. He began to appreciate the sweetness of the fermented sap, which resembled a maple syrup-flavored spruce beer. Clay liked the relaxed feeling it produced and felt he'd blend in better with the crowd if he drank it. He justified his fondness for the brew, chalking it up to a necessary part of his 'spy' persona. But he also had to keep his wits about him; it could mean life or death to all he held dear on Bilaluna.

One night, after a successful test of a small rocket, the tavern was full of engineers and scientists celebrating their accomplishments. Clay had arrived in the pub before their shift ended and sat alone in the booth next to Rumo's.

As the night wore on, Clay called out to a group of junior engineers. "You guys have been standing a while. Why don't you take a load off? There's plenty of room at my table." He beckoned them with two claws. *I don't bite, at least not yet.*

One engineer agreed. "Sure, I've seen you in here before. Do you work around here?"

"No, I just got hired at the breeding halls." Clay started. "My new boss often goes to the bar nearby, and I don't want to run into him."

"New job. I understand." He pointed outside. "My buddies and I work at the rocket center over there."

"That's cool. By the way, I'm Clay. Do you know if they ever show the gladiator matches on the telescreen?" Clay deflected the conversation. "I've been coming here for a while and never seen one." He assumed that sports might provide a shared interest.

"I think the owner doesn't like RoAChants and never shows the matches," replied the engineer. "It's too bad. I love to watch them too." He turned toward his colleagues. "Hey guys, this is Clay. He works at the breeding halls and is a big gladiator fan."

Clay grinned and nodded.

The engineer introduced himself and his two buddies, and they sat with Clay in his booth.

Clay turned to one of his new acquaintances. "Why's the bar so busy tonight?" He raised his brow, playing ignorant.

A tipsy engineer gushed, "We just fired a massive rocket into the stratosphere, and the sucker didn't blow up."

"Wow. That deserves a celebration," chimed in Clay. "Let me buy you guys a round." He reached into his sash pocket for some cash. *I am glad Blood pays me well.*

His new acquaintances could not refuse the generous offer,

and his gesture started alternating round buying by his three booth mates. By the end of the fourth round, his questions became more targeted. He informed them he had studied physics and engineering before switching to genetic engineering for his career. Clay impressed them with his lay understanding of rocket science and wowed them when he mentioned he had been a scarlet program alternate. Clay said he designed small rockets to impress a youngster and expressed his love for everything about the field that he almost entered himself.

Clay so ingratiated himself with the three junior engineers that they sought his booth the next time they came to the bar. He insisted on buying a round, and the alternating pattern continued. After a few hexths of hanging out with his tavern friends, he got into a complicated discussion about multistage rockets with one engineer.

Rumo, who sat in the next booth, leaned across the barrier and said, "Don't ask that wing-ANT about rockets. His expertise is aerodynamics." He winked. "You need to talk to a real rocket ANT."

Clay noticed Rumo was a little drunk and playful, so he responded, "So, you're one of the big honchos with a missile under your shell?"

Rumo guffawed and lifted a claw to his head, "In my brain, not my shell. I design these babies."

"So, you work with the amazing Radley. I have always wanted to meet him and get his autograph." He wiggled his claws like he was writing. *He's brilliant.*

"He never signs autographs, and he only meets other rocket scientists. But I'll give you mine."

"Okay, jump over, and I'll exchange you a drink for your signature on my napkin. Maybe it'll be worth something some hexay." He tapped the booth space beside him. *I know tipsy scientists can't refuse dares.*

Rumo was drunk enough to accept a challenge, but not too drunk to refuse another drink. So, he leapt over the barrier between the booths and landed partially on one of his colleague's laps.

Clay laughed. "For that performance, you won yourself a second drink." He held up four claws to the waitress. *I must praise a completed dare.*

Rumo beamed. "Jet propulsion is my forte."

Clay released a shimmering smell. "Aha, a joker too. But are you as skilled at shots as at missiles?" He raised two of the glasses and licked his lips. *If one dare worked, I should try another.*

Rumo grinned. "Yes, especially the two-stage ones."

The two new friends tossed back their shots neatly. Rumo noted he'd overheard several of Clay's conversations over the last hexth, and he impressed him with his lay knowledge of rockets. Rumo was young and reckless and liked to boast. He also had a keen interest in the biological sciences and wanted to learn more about genetic engineering. And he loved gladiators.

CHAPTER 20

THE BREEDERS: HYBRIDS

Antalonia (Rudyard's rule, the current president)

KEEGAN AND VERMILLION returned from a short break to finish their lesson. Having completed the section on Vitamin S, Keegan was uneasy learning about hybrids.

Keegan looked up at Vermillion. "So, what exactly are hybrids?" He'd convinced himself that he must play along despite his distaste for some aspects of the program. *Vitamin S, hybrids—this is becoming devious. Still, I have to follow the plan if I will succeed in my goal of being the breed master. Maybe then I can change a few things.*

"After the Great Cyborg War, we debated killing off the remaining prisoners or keeping some as slaves." Vermillion pointed to a more prominent textbook on the shelf labeled 'Basics of Genetic Engineering'. "Then Czar Rust suggested that we just keep the genes we need from them so that ANTs could do the work of the other insectoids."

Keegan released a shocking scent. "I didn't know we could do that." He realized how little he knew about genetic engineering. *I am relieved that there are no slaves but eliminating and replacing the other insectoids—that's not right.*

Vermillion spun his forelimbs around each other to form a helix. "Yes, it's like when our ancestors first created cyborgs and developed venom-free BUGs using spider DNA, so they could use their thread to make bins."

Keegan tried to conceal his scowl. "Or when Antilla created new BUGs with spider venom to act as his secret police." He wondered whether he'd gone too far with his example. *I know science is fantastic when used for good, but malicious ones can use it for evil.*

In his enthusiasm for the topic, Vermillion missed the sarcasm. "That's correct. So, now we make ANTs that fly like BEEs and FLYs, sting like Antilla's BUGs, transport goods like RoAChs, and takedown trees like WoBBs."

Keegan held his head. "How is that possible?" Despite his distaste, he was intrigued by the scientific implications. *I must concentrate on all the fantastic techniques I'll be learning.*

Vermillion laughed and pulled the thick Genetic Engineering textbook from the shelf. "Your homework is to read this."

Keegan winced as he took the book. "All of it?" He crumpled under the weight of it as Vermillion passed it to him.

Vermillion laughed some more. "Yes, but it's simple. Since we are creating prosthetic wings and limbs from mechanical parts, we mainly need to insert the genes that control the movements of the bionics. We require a few hundreds of

motoneurons from each species and the genes needed to produce the right exoskeletons."

Keegan flipped through the textbook. "I'm sure it's
more complex than that." *Advanced genetics just got much
more challenging!*

"The goal is simple, but the methods are complicated."
Vermillion tapped on the book. "But you'll find it all in here."

"Does it describe each species and how to create different
cyborg ANTs?" asked Keegan.

Vermillion snickered. "Goodness, no, it's just the basics
of inserting the desired genes into the developing ants using
CRISPR. Once you understand that, Clay will demonstrate the
specifics for each cyborg."

"So, we are creating Franken-ANTs?" Keegan faked a laugh.

"We call them BEEants, BUGants, FLYants, RoAChants,
and WoBBants."

"How come I've never heard of this or seen any?" puzzled
Keegan. He recalled a distant childhood memory of meeting a
roach-like ANT that he thought was from a dream. *Perhaps it
was a nightmare I repressed.*

"I said before that you've led a sheltered life." Vermillion
smiled. "As a youth, you traveled from home to school in the
red alpha section of the colony. Hybrids live on the colony's
perimeter close to their work forests. We create BEEants and
RoAChants from brown ANTs, and FLYants and WoBBants
from black ANTs. They come from the chi of both castes."

"What about BUGants?" asked Keegan.

"Since they are our policemen, they come from red ANTs,"
Vermillion noted. "We need to trust them. Once again, they
are chi, but as red ANTs, they don't get vitamin S."

Keegan raised both his forelimbs. "So, besides police BUGants, what do the other hybrids do?" *I am curious now.*

Vermillion explained how BEEants collect nectar and make honey, and FLYants carry trees and transport messages. Then he described how they designed WoBBants to cut trees and make strong sap and RoAChants to transport nectar and honey or fight as gladiators. Except for the gladiators, these were all the chores previously done by other insectoids, including BEEs, FLYs, WoBBs, and RoAChs.

"Gladiators?" His thoughts crept back to his dream-like memory of a RoAChant. *He must be kidding.*

Vermillion guffawed. "It's entertaining to watch them crush each other."

Keegan winced, then thought of something. "If hybrids are all chi, what do the alphas and betas do?"

Vermillion sighed. "Most brown alphas are civil servants, while betas are soldiers. And most black alphas are farmers, while betas are sanitation workers."

Keegan cocked his head. "I read somewhere we also had insectoids called WoRMs. Are there any WoRMants?"

"No, after the Great Cyborg War, we decided we didn't need specialized ANTs to do the work of WoRMs. We realized the other hybrids could dig burrows and nests and erect buildings. I used the word 'most' before, since some hybrids from each group are also construction workers."

Keegan furrowed his brow. "I read that no one on Pooponic liked WoRMs or their small versions."

"As members of our society, we don't like WoRMs here either, but we kept the small ones around so we could eat them." Vermillion licked his lips.

"Of course, they are delicious." He considered how nutritious they were. *I have eaten worms my whole life.*

During the Great Cyborg War, nuclear blasts destroyed many of the forests on Intopia. The remaining ANTs couldn't make as much nectar or honey, even after cloning BEEants. So, Antalones ate termites and worms.

"Oh, I love termite stew. And sometimes, I grind termites and spread them over a plate of worms." At last, he thought, an innovation that was positive. *Having insects as food is fine with me, and they're a superb source of protein.*

"Yes, they reproduce quickly, and they can both feed us and still fulfill their natural role to rejuvenate the soil and keep the remaining forests healthy. So, our economic troubles are over with worms and termites to feed us and hybrids to work for us."

"It all seems so organized," noted Keegan. "And everyone likes their jobs?" he asked. He tried his best to be more accepting of their manipulations. *I see how all these controls may be necessary to keep everyone content.*

Vermillion grinned mischievously. "Given their different brain sizes and vitamin S, they don't aspire for more and follow directions without question."

Keegan raised a claw. "And what about red alphas and betas?" He considered his early childhood. *What if I had remained a beta?*

Vermillion smiled. "They can do whatever they want. Mostly they are professionals or business ANTs, and the smartest, often alphas, are Scarlets and become leaders."

Keegan raised his brow. "What do the leaders do?"

Vermillion explained that the leaders formed an exclusive club, including those running the colony. And how they have access to the most knowledge and control histrionics. The leaders also approved the socionics programs all others must follow and made all decisions about any changes in bionics.

"I assume it includes all Czar Rust's offspring?" Keegan concluded. He realized that he had no opinions about their ruler, but that he must be a mighty ANT. *I'll be meeting him soon, but I'll never have that much power.*

Vermillion nodded. "Of course."

"And the heads of all government departments, including the breed master and the master of socionics?" Keegan asked. He considered all the politics required to get ahead. *I must schmooze the other leaders, or they'll see me as weak.*

"Yes, but as we've been talking about leaders, I should mention hierarchies," Vermillion spoke quietly so no one else would hear. "For the last few hexs, I have been looking for a replacement for myself, as breed master, since I will retire soon."

Keegan shrugged. "You don't seem old enough to retire, sir." Yet he considered he would step down sometime. *But where is he going with this?*

"True, but it takes many hexs to train a new breed master." Vermillion pointed to all the books on the shelves. "The breed master heads both the departments of bionics and socionics, and there is much to learn."

"You mentioned the master of socionics and said Clay was the chief of bionics. Are these positions both subordinate to the breed master?" asked Keegan.

Vermillion took a deep breath. "Yes, since they are both trained by the breed master, an expert in both."

Keegan sighed. "I see why it would take a long time to train a new one." He thought of his current situation and his potential future. *There will be much to learn and many obstacles, but this should be my goal with my skills.*

Vermillion smiled. "Indeed, I want you to start now as my apprentice." He patted Keegan on the back. "I have trained many breeders throughout the hexs, and I know when I see an exceptional student. Clay was one of my best, and that's why he's chief of bionics."

Keegan nodded. "Thank you, Breed Master. I'm honored. And yes, Clay is incredible." Despite expecting this offer, he was stunned to hear it.

"But there's something extra special about you. You have a true eagerness, a sharp intellect, and *you* are pure red."

Keegan ejected a swelled bouquet. "I am honored to be your apprentice and hope I can live up to your expectations." The excitement of his academic success superseded his other concerns. *This is a great opportunity; I can't turn it down over a few minor objections.*

"I trust you will." Vermillion turned and looked out the window towards the schools. "But it will be a challenge for me to train both a new breed master and a master of socionics simultaneously, and that's why I am getting you started so soon."

"Oh, there will be a new master of socionics?" asked Keegan. His outlook became even more positive. *We'll be a whole new generation of leaders.*

"Yes, our current one, Ruby, announced she will retire within a hex. Czar Rudyard asked me to train his son, Blood, to take over, and he will act as master of socionics until he takes over as Czar."

Keegan lined his brow. "So, I assume that Czar Rudyard is your boss?"

Vermillion explained that one of his cabinet ministers, the minister of social order, was his direct boss. Yet, since the Czar made all the decisions about bionics and socionics, he was the real boss. He further explained that most cabinet ministers had minimal power since Rudyard controlled everything.

Keegan shrugged. "So why does he need cabinet ministers?" He recalled how he detested micromanagement. *It seems to me he's all-powerful.*

"For appearances, and they act as advisors," responded Vermillion. "Of course, they are all his best friends."

Keegan rolled his eyes. "What other ministries are there?" *I must understand the politics of my position to succeed.*

"The ministers change all the time, depending on which friends the Czar favors. I believe there is a ministry of war and inter-planetary relations, one of social control, a ministry of business and economics, and one for the environment."

CHAPTER 21

THE NEW SPIES: TRANSFORMED

Antalonia (Rudyard's rule, the current president)

AFTER CLAY HAD been chief of bionics for some time, Darci returned to working as the night cleaner at the breeding halls, a job she had when she first received the nanitic Clay. She followed Clay around one evening, as she often did when he worked alone on the night shift. She wanted to meet the two young nanitics whose futures they depended on so much.

Clay showed Darci the incubators with Rose and Jasper. "They've been in these larger hatcheries for about four hexths now."

Darci peered at the two emerging ANTs. "Have they been sleeping all this time?"

Clay placed a stethoscope on Rose's thorax. "Yes, we don't want them moving while their limbs are setting." He pulled out a large needle from his bag.

Darci cringed at the sight of the needle. "What are you giving her?"

"It's some non-neuronal growth factors to stimulate the expansion of their exoskeletons over their new mechanical cyborg frames." He inserted the needle and started pushing the plunger slowly. "Oh, and a full dose of neuronal growth factors allows her brain to grow to the maximal size." He smiled at Darci. *We want Rose and Jasper to be as brilliant as they can be.*

Darci noticed Jasper was twitching a little. "Are you giving them something to make them sleep some more?"

Clay checked Rose's chart. "No, I want them to wake up so I can start their physio."

Clay then connected a new nutrient bag to a feeding tube inserted down Rose's gullet.

Darci winced. "Is that how you feed them?"

"Yes, and these two get the highest concentration of nutrients." He examined the inserted end of the feeding tube to ensure he correctly positioned it in Rose's gullet. "I'm giving these guys 10% more than other red alphas to enhance their development further."

Darci looked Rose all over. "Is that everything? No more needles or tubes?"

Clay snickered. "No, she won't get more needles, and that's the only tube." He turned the value on the feeding tube and tapped on the nutrient bags for Rose and Jasper. "But these also contain the antioxidants and protein stabilizers they need for long, healthy lifespans. Like you and I, they will continue to take them in pill form for the rest of their lives."

"I hate taking those pills." Darci gagged. "I always wondered if they work."

Clay's eyes widened. "They double your lifespan. Make sure you take them." He considered how vital Darci was to the spy program in Antalonia. *Don't mess around. We need you.*

"Don't worry. I will. But now I'd better get back to work, or my boss will shorten my life."

As Clay and Keegan projected, Rose and Jasper experienced no growing pains, and their exoskeletons grew perfectly over their cyborg frames, which gradually telescoped to full length without a hitch. In just over four hexths, the small nanitics had increased from about two millimeters to two meters. The breeders also rearranged their six limbs from the standard three sets of two legs to a single set of three legs and another set of three arms. Thus, they converted them from tiny ants into giant, human-sized ANTs or Allied Noble Tripods, with tripods referring to their three hind limbs or legs.

Ants on Antalonia already lived about six times longer than their ancient relatives back on Earth, but after these treatments, they lived over two hexuries. Cyborg ANTs spend two hexades in low school and another in high school. They became full adults or 'of age' once they graduated high school and were ready to take a position in society. As cyborg ANTs lived much longer than their Earth ancestors and had significantly larger brains, it took them longer to mature. Unlike their ancient Earth forebears, who could breed and mature rapidly, typically, it took over three hexades or half a hexury from one generation of cyborg ANTs to the next.

～ ～ ～

After Darci left, Clay gave all the same treatments to Jasper and then moved on to another emerging ANT in the next row. As he did, Jasper stirred and pulled out his feeding tube.

Jasper rubbed his eyes, stretched his new bionic limbs, and called Rose. "Hey, sleeping beauty, how are you feeling?" Jasper was groggy but animated. *I'm excited about starting our next phase of life.*

Rose rolled over gingerly and turned towards the column from where Jasper was calling, but her eyes were hazy and unfocused. She pulled out her feeding tube and spoke, "I'm dizzy and very thirsty, and I have milkweed mouth."

Jasper sat upright. "Me too, but have you checked out your new limbs?" His eyes widened at the sight. *They are so great!*

Rose sighed. "I've barely tuned my eyes." She shook her ommatidia and looked down the length of the long incubator bed. "Oh my, I'm a gi-ANT!"

Jasper lifted a leg off the bed. "I don't think it's finished. We're still going to grow some more." He thought back to their first meeting with Clay. *I was a little nervous, but I remember everything Clay told us.*

Rose shook, trying to clear her head. "Yeah, I think Clay said we'll wake up after our limbs have set enough that our movements can't harm them, but we will still grow another 20%."

Jasper began moving an arm back and forth. "And we're supposed to move them so they don't lock up." He feared that inaction might cause problems. *We got to exercise right away!*

When Clay arrived a little later, he noticed his new cyborgs had awakened and sidled up to them. "Now that you're awake, you need to start physio." He thought back to all the times he had done this before. *This task won't be easy.*

Rose protested. "Physio, already?"

Clay nodded hard. "Yep, start by doing leg lifts, arm swings, knee and elbow bends." He grabbed one of Rose's three hind limbs and bent it at the knee. *You may be my little spies, but you're like all the other nanitics turned into cyborgs.*

Rose complained, "Hey, your claws are cold."

Clay smiled. "Perfect, you have normal temperature sensitivity." He then pulled out a pointy object from the pocket of his lab coat. "Do you feel this?"

Rose's hind claw jerked sideways. "Ouch, that hurt!" She sprayed a searing scent.

"Fantastic," Clay exclaimed. "Appropriate reflexes and acute pain reporting." The finding met his expectations. *Perhaps she's a little overdramatic.*

"You're right about the pain." Rose pushed Clay away from the bed. "But there was nothing cute about it."

"Sorry, Rose, I have to check all your limbs to see if you respond normally to hot, cold, and pricking pain," explained Clay. He got down to business. *Be a big girl now!*

Rose slid over to the far side of her incubator. "I thought you said physio, not torture."

Clay laughed. "It'll be over in no time. Don't be a cry-larva." He continued to prod other limbs. *I see pain cripples even the brightest of young cyborgs.*

"Okay, but I hope the first physio includes leg extensions so I can kick your hindgut."

"Hilarious, girl. I can see you woke up on the wrong side of the incubator." He snickered to himself and thought about how sassy Rose was becoming. *I think it's time I move to Jasper.*

Clay gathered up his probes and crossed over to Jasper's

incubator. Jasper lay back down and smiled at Clay. "Don't worry about me. I have a high pain threshold."

Clay first pricked him with his sharp needle. Jasper winced but made no noise while his hind limb swung forward and kicked Clay in the foregut.

"Sorry, Clay, are you okay?"

"No worries, Jasper. It happens all the time." Clay took a deep breath. "You may not find it that painful, but you have hyper-normal reflexes." He made a note on his patient chart. *Quite the kick for a young tyke, I'd say.*

Rose sat up and started laughing. "I was only kidding, but I'm glad Jasper got you back."

Clay smirked. "Okay, it's time for leg lifts." He pulled out a stopwatch. "When I say go, lift all three hind limbs, and hold it for 30 hexonds until I say drop 'em."

Rose stared back at Clay. "I just woke up, and you want me to lift those massive legs?"

Clay laughed. "We need to start your physio immediately if you want to walk again." He waited for a reaction. *That should snap them into shape.*

Jasper bolted up. "What! We have to learn to walk again?"

Clay explained how they needed to re-establish connections between their brains and limbs. He told them how he had rearranged their limbs, and they needed to teach their brains which limb was which and how to coordinate their movements. He described how much their brains had grown and how important physio was. The physio included both biofeedback and telekinesis.

Jasper shrugged. "What's biofeedback?"

"Let me demonstrate," Clay responded. "See, I am holding up Rose's legs. I will let go, and Rose, I want you to keep them in the air." He put on his most authoritative voice, concerned they would not improve if they didn't heed his instructions. *They must listen to me if the physio is going to work.*

Clay let go of Rose's legs, and two remained elevated, but the third dropped and crashed on the bed.

"What the hell?" Rose exclaimed. "I can't move the third one."

"Don't worry," reassured Clay. "It happens to everyone." He laughed inside at Rose's reaction. *And I thought you were the calm one.*

Jasper tried to raise his legs and could only lift two, although the third one quivered.

"That's wonderful, Jasper," Clay exclaimed. "That quaking means your brain recognizes you have a third leg." His worries about their progress subsided. *Maybe they'll catch on quickly after all.*

"Mine moved a little," cried Rose.

"Excellent, Rose," Clay replied.

Clay then explained that biofeedback is when one tries hard to recognize what they've done to make their limb move. He told them one of their arms would probably act the same, and they'd need to teach it to move. Clay then explained how they needed to use telekinesis to help carry the extra weight. The physio would require much practice since they needed to coordinate motoneuron nerve signaling with telekinetic messaging.

"I can see why we need physio," admitted Jasper. "But how long will it take?"

"It depends on how hard you work." Clay looked closely at the two new cyborgs. "Some new cyborgs can effectively walk and use their arms in a few hexays, and others take a few hexeks."

Rose's eyes grew wide. "What's the slowest you've seen?"

"Well, some black ANTs can take up to a hexth." Clay scratched his head. "But I've never seen a red alpha take longer than two hexeks, except the paralyzed ones." He dropped Jasper's chart. *Oops, I shouldn't have said that!*

Jasper bolted up. "Paralyzed ones!" He oozed a rumpled reek.

"Don't worry." Clay laughed. "It rarely happens, and I've already checked your reflexes. Neither of you is paralyzed." He picked up Jasper's chart and made some notes. *Guess I asked for that.*

Just then, Keegan walked up. "Hey, guys. Nice to see you're awake and doing physio." He smiled at Rose. "I am working in the ova cava to-hexay, but I'll come to see you later. You are looking so red that you shine, girl."

Clay looked up at Keegan. "I'll check in on you later, don't forget to turn over all the eggs in the brown sector." He smiled, satisfied that all their plans were working. *I'm pleased he's still into Rose, and that'll work to our benefit.*

CHAPTER 22

THE RULERS: THE TAKEOVER

Antalonia (Rudyard's rule, the current president)

AFTER BREAKING FOR a quick worm salad, Rudyard and Blood continued their lesson. Blood looked out the window towards the schools. "So, when did Grandfather start socionics? Ever since you mentioned I'd be the new master of socionics, I want to know everything from the beginning."

Rudyard smiled knowingly. "Rustant realized histrionics could deceive and animate his base, but he needed additional methods to keep them loyal. He reduced taxes on businesses and their wealthy owners." He pointed out the window at the nearby schools. "Then he pushed for segregated schools."

"I expect that Antunites, and other insectoids, resisted that." Blood swallowed hard.

"True, but the ANT supremacists in his base loved it." Rudyard raised his claws. "There were protests, but there was nothing the public could do about it."

"What about the Congress?" asked Blood. "Did they support him?"

Rudyard explained to Blood that Congress had to follow Rust's lead when a president was elected for life and had many in his base supporting him. If they didn't, he'd pick another candidate the base liked in the next elections for Congress and oust the non-supporters. Some Antunites and other insectoids in Congress had enough support to get re-elected, but most members were ANTs who got there because of the ANT supremacists. None of them dared any actions that would counter Rustant.

Blood looked out the window. "So, he got his wish for segregated schools." He compared his father to Rustant. *My father would never have done this since he was not ruthless enough, but Grandfather had it in him.*

Rudyard described how Rustant restructured the schools, so ANTs got the best teachers. He also changed the school curriculum so that they taught young ANTs all of EOW's laws. These were not EOWs laws, but edicts designed by Rustant to achieve his aim. He taught the students that ANTs were the masters of all other insectoids.

Blood thought briefly about the enemy. "What about the non-ANT schools?"

"Rustant forbade other insectoids from speaking anything but the common insectoid language and taught them to respect red ANTs as their lords and masters." Rudyard waved his claws up and down. "Their teachers drummed into them that they were inferior to ANTs and that without the mercy of their ANT masters, they would be nothing more than savages."

Blood rolled his eyes. "Why didn't they rebel?" he asked. He reflected on his feelings about Antunites, misguided but zealous. *I think I know the answer.*

Rudyard grabbed a cane by the doorway and described how young insectoids in school were beaten by their ANT teachers if they did not follow the rules. He also explained how Rustant forced their parents into re-education classes to learn about the new social norms, and if they resisted, he threw them in jail, where the lessons included torture. Rudyard slammed the cane down on the table and said if they still fought, the police tortured them some more and then released them, but somehow, they never made it home.

Blood jumped and emitted a shimmering stink. "Rustant terrorized them into following his directives?" He imagined what he would do in the same circumstance. *Grandfather was formidable, and I could do that.*

Rudyard tossed the cane back into its stand. "He had them all in his snare, except for some that followed Antebon and other rebels that fought back."

"So, how did Rustant stop them?" The thought of Antunites boiled his hemolymph. *I hope he crushed the black ANTs and other insectoids too.*

Rudyard smiled. "He kept calling the protestors thugs, EOW haters, and enemies of ANTs. He convinced everyone that the protestors were treasonous and needed to be defeated."

"So, what happened?" Blood asked. He cherished the thought of arresting and jailing opponents. *I know Grandfather stood triumphantly over his enemies.*

Rudyard explained that as more young ANTs and other insectoids graduated through the school system, the socionics program created many devoted ANT supremacists. The schools also turned out more non-ANTs who were demoralized and felt inferior to ANTs. Some young insectoids believed they couldn't survive without the mercy of benevolent ANTs that ran the new society.

Blood raised a claw to his temple. "So, ANTs hated non-ANTs, and non-ANTs believed they deserved to be hated?" He guessed at Rustant's intent. *I must remember these lessons.*

"Exactly, but the non-ANTs were conflicted because some insectoids, including Antunite ANTs, tried to convince them to fight for their rights."

Blood rattled one limb like a saber. "So, Antunites and non-ANT dissenters started a rebellion and tried to take over the colony." His eyes turned red. *I know Rustant crushed them.*

"Well, not so fast. Protests and struggles went on for hexs." Rudyard pushed two claws together. "With ANT supremacists and Rustant's police fighting the protestors, almost every hexek."

"So, what changed to start a war?" asked Blood. He assumed that the rebels pushed Rustant too far. *I can imagine my grandfather dressed in dazzling armor.*

Rudyard held up two claws and described the steps Rustant took. First, he changed the Earth student exchange program, so only ANTs visited Earth and went every three hexths. He charged several of them to work with Earth's military leaders, weapons manufacturers, astrophysicists, and atomic energy scientists. Those who worked in countries with authoritarian leaders understood Rustant's plight and allowed them to acquire the plans to develop simple nuclear weapons.

Intopia had many large iridium deposits and would trade the mineral with humans for manufactured goods and technological plans. Earthlings craved iridium which they used to produce radioisotope thermoelectric generators as batteries that store energy much longer than outdated fuel cells.

Blood's eyes lit up. "And what was the second thing?"

Rudyard slammed his claws down on the table next to them. "The Antunite leaders on Bilaluna secretly sent troops through the shorter wormhole to reinforce the rebels."

"How did Rustant find out about it?" queried Blood. He expected that would have made his grandfather furious. *It's unimaginable that foreigners would try to hinder Rustant's plans.*

Rudyard told Blood that many rebels left the colony to join their military force. And when Rustant found out, he forced all remaining non-ANT insectoids out of the settlement and executed some diplomats heading back to Bilaluna. Then the non-ANT insectoids and Antunites from Intopia joined forces with the Antunites from Bilaluna. Under Antebon's leadership, they repeatedly raided the colony, trying to destroy government buildings and the ANT schools.

"How did our ANT loyalists respond?" He deemed Rustant wouldn't stand for this. *I know I wouldn't.*

"As well as sending more ANTs to Earth for training, Rustant had also built up a massive ANT military." Rudyard marched back into the library and pulled out a book on military strategy. "His military was rife with the most ardent ANT supremacists that would do whatever he asked." Rudyard grinned from antenna to antenna as he handed Blood the book. "They mercilessly killed many insurgent Antunites, taking no prisoners. But Rustant waited until they perfected their nuclear weapons before he mounted a large counter-offensive."

Blood opened the book to the table of contents. "Sometimes patience is the best strategy." He looked for a chapter on tactics.

Rudyard nodded. "Yes, and when they knew their weapons were effective, they began Rustant's plan."

Blood oozed an itchy incense. "What was the plan?" He imagined Rustant was a brilliant strategist. *I envision titanic explosions with non-ANT cyborgs blown to pieces.*

Rudyard explained that the main thing was to keep their new weapons secret as they started their counter-offensive. They used their massive, well-trained, super-aggressive ANT armies to drive the Antunite forces back several miles. He described how one night after they pushed their enemy back, Rustant's armies retreated but left dirty bombs as hidden land mines as they backed away. When the Antunites and non-ANT soldiers advanced after the retreating colony ANTs, they were blown sky-high by explosives or subjected to poisoning by the clouds of radioactive isotopes. Those that retreated and gathered in a clear area behind the radioactive clouds were then rained on by missiles with small nuclear warheads developed by Rustant's Earth-trained ANT weapons experts.

Blood slapped his claws together. "So, the war was quick?" He opened the book to a chapter on nuclear weapons. *I get a warm feeling picturing a battlefield full of dying foes. All will dread me when I'm ruler just like they feared Rustant.*

"Very few survived the attack and were taken as prisoners." Rudyard pointed to the bionics halls. "We kept them as slaves until we used genetic engineering programs to produce hybrid ANTs, and the other insectoids were no longer needed."

Rustant originally intended to have ANTs subjugate other insectoids, to become the master race or insect family. Yet, he altered his original goal by replacing other cyborgs with genetically engineered hybrids. Rustant changed his plans after being angered that so many non-ANTs fought against him in the ensuing war. Also enraged at the Antunite ANTs that fought alongside the non-ANT insectoids, Rustant shifted the targets of his intended bionic and socionic programs to Antunites and brown and black ANTs, which he saw as less evolved.

Blood broached one last topic. "Whatever happened to Antebon?" asked Blood, squeezing his claws together. *I hope her charred body melted into the ground.*

Rudyard shrugged. "No one ever saw Antebon again, and Rustant presumed a nuclear blast incinerated her and all her officers."

Rustant never realized, and therefore did not inform Rudyard, that some Antunite forces, including Antebon's platoon, escaped through the wormhole to Bilaluna.

Blood whined. "Antebon and the Antunites almost ruined everything."

Rudyard nodded. "That's why Rustant had to develop the caste system within our ANT society. Antebon taught him that genetics are a powerful force, and it is impossible to use histrionics alone to control all one's followers."

Blood smiled. "So, everything worked according to plan. Then he dropped the ant from his name and became Rust."

Rudyard's smile waned. "Yes, the only hitch was that one of the nuclear blasts landed too close to the wormhole to Earth and destroyed the portal. Given we don't have the technology to produce spacecraft, we can never travel to Earth again."

CHAPTER 23

THE OLD SPIES: CLAY AND ROCKET ANT

Antalonia (Rust's rule, one president in the past)

AFTER CLAY GOT to know Rumo well, he invited him to tour the breeding halls. He hoped that Rumo would reciprocate and show him the rocket testing facility.

Clay started, "Not just any breeder can give tours of the breeding halls. You're lucky you befriended the chief of bionics." He tried his best to let Rumo know he owed him. *And I want something from you.*

"I hope this didn't create any problems for you," replied Rumo. "I've always wondered where they make gladiators."

"Not at all. The breed master trusts me. But we'll have to

claw print you and take a sample of your DNA to ensure you are not a security risk."

Rumo's eyes broadened. "You guys are strict."

Clay laughed. "I'm just kidding, but don't go around boasting about your visit. We can't give these tours to every red and brown ANT that loves gladiators." He wanted Rumo to feel special. *I need your trust.*

Rumo guffawed. "Right! Of course, I'll be discrete."

Clay showed Rumo around the ova cava and the bloom room but saved the chi section of brown ANTs to the end. He showed him the room where they transform nanitics into RoAChants and separated RoAChants into transports or gladiators.

Clay stroked the hind limbs of one hybrid. "Remember, I told you in the ova cava how we used CRISPR to insert RoACh motoneuron genes into black ANTs to make hybrid RoAChants?"

"Yes, it was very complex," began Rumo. "But I understood most of the process."

"Well, this is where we attach the frames and arrange them in the right position to produce working RoACh limbs." Clay smiled. "We not only insert DNA for motoneurons but also the genes needed to generate a hard roach shell. Otherwise, we'd have ANTs that crawl on all six legs instead of the tripod kind."

"Yeah, we wouldn't want ANHs." Rumo laughed at his own joke. "Allied noble hexapods!"

"Exactly. RoAChants need to have armored shells," Clay explained. "Especially the gladiators. Look, you can see the shells forming on the ones in the next row." Clay didn't really like gladiators, but played along. *I hope you get your fill of gladiators.*

"Wow, this is amazing." Rumo shook his head from side to side. "True RoAChs are obsolete since we can create them from brown ANTs."

"Brown ANTs and RoACh DNA, of course." Clay rubbed his claws together. "And a little know-how in genetic manipulation." He pointed towards the door to show the tour was over. *I hope I've ingratiated myself.*

"Genetic magic!" Rumo laughed as they headed out. "You are the genies of gene modification. Just rub your bottles, and we get our wishes for BEEants, FLYants, and gladiators."

Clay chuckled his appreciation, leading Rumo to the nearby tavern. "But you guys are genies too. Rocket en-ge-nie-eers, that is! Rust asks for rockets, spacecraft, and missiles, and you grant him his wish."

Rumo walked along with Clay but abruptly stopped laughing. "Hey, I've said nothing about spacecraft and missiles."

Clay grinned coyly. "You didn't have to. Why else would you be building rockets?" He tried his best to cover his mistake.

Rumo paused and nodded. "We're just rocket ANTs, and we leave it to the AstroANTs and military hawks to figure out how to use them."

"But you've got to ensure they launch safely and can blast off into space." He used his mistake to initiate his ploy. *Not if I can help it.*

Rumo chuckled. "You just explained my job, and those of a few hundred of my co-workers, in fifteen words."

Clay snickered. "Easier said than done." He chose flattery before fraudulence. *And I hope to undo it.*

Rumo made a loud sound like the boom of thunder. "We are careful not to have any mishaps."

Clay smiled as they sat at a booth and ordered two shots

of strong sap. "I recently read about the human space race and came across a description of the Nedelin catastrophe." He got right to the point. *As a slow-plotting spy, I've waited so long. Yet now I prepare my luring brew.*

Clay brought up the Nedelin disaster to prepare the way for his scheme, which was for Rumo to implement a manual trigger for igniting the second-stage rocket. Clay could override a switch with manual ignition and cause the second-stage rocket to fire prematurely. He just needed Rumo to take the bait, and his hexs of study and planning would pay off.

Rumo laughed, "I know you are a dedicated lay rocket nerd, but I can't believe you could dig that up." He shook his head. "I haven't read about that since studying for my Pupa degree."

Clay continued after ordering two more shots, "There was an article about it in the *Popular Journal of Human Science History.*" He assumed Rumo was too serious a scientist to read a popular science magazine. *It's a plausible story to add some ingredients to my broth.*

"That's cool." Rumo nodded. "They rarely cover Astroscience, let alone rocket science."

"Well, as far as human scientific history goes, it was a big deal," suggested Clay. He tried to emphasize his case. *He's sure to agree as I add some salt.*

"I guess." Rumo replied. "Especially for us rocket geeks."

"I wondered whether humans could have avoided the disaster if they weren't so preoccupied with automation," Clay pondered as he zeroed in on his crux. *I thicken the broth.*

"What do you mean? Automation is the way to go with rockets." Rumo threw his arms out. "Even with manned human space travel, their rockets could fly themselves."

"Aren't you producing two-stage rockets soon?" Clay quizzed, hoping he was right. *I stir in some spices.*

"How would you know that?" Rumo bolted up from his chair.

"Come on." Clay frowned. "All amateur rocket geeks know you need a two-stage rocket to reach deep space." He guessed to further his case. *And I turn up the heat.*

Rumo frowned, "But what were you getting at with your point about the Nedelin disaster?"

"Well, I read a short circuit accidentally triggered the second stage rocket to fire while the rocket was still on the launch pad," Clay began, masking his smoldering stink. *I'll just waft the aroma of my broth his way.*

"I think so," said Rumo.

"So, automation caused it." Clay tapped a claw on his other arm. "I'm guessing the short circuit wouldn't have happened if they manually triggered the second stage rocket."

"I don't remember exactly what caused the explosion." Rumo pondered Clay's theory.

"It just makes sense to have someone on the ground trigger the second stage rocket after it's clear the rocket is off the ground," Clay argued as he quaffed a third shot. *I fill him up with a bowl.*

"I suppose it's a trade-off between potential electronic and manual errors." Rumo thought some more. "The main thing about designing these suckers is to consider all potential problems before they happen and ensure they can't and don't."

Clay nodded. "That's my point." He wished he'd agree. *Will he drink from my bowl?*

"Well, at least your breeding halls don't blow up if you get

your gene sequences wrong when you make the gladiators."
Rumo laughed.

"Thankfully, although we could accidentally create a
Franken-ANT that tries to kill its master." Clay guffawed. He
stepped back. *Humor always works with Rumo. Take a sip of
my broth.*

"There's more risk of blowing yourself up with your amateur rockets," teased Rumo.

"I try my best to be careful," responded Clay. He grinned
inside, hoping the seed he planted would germinate. *I believe
my recipe worked.*

"Didn't you say you were building models to impress a
youngster?" Rumo tapped his skull. "He must be high school-
aged by now. Is he still into rockets? We can always use more
rocket scientists. You should bring him around next time. He'd
probably love to meet a real rocket ANT." He laughed.

Clay paled. "We haven't shot any off in a while, and I'm not
sure he's still into it." He panicked a little. *He put down the bowl
and spit the soup in my face.*

"Come on," Rumo exclaimed. "Have you ever known a
young ANT who loves rockets to stop loving rockets?"

Clay paused before answering. "I'll inquire."

Rumo looked at him curiously. "Clay, I've never seen you
so tongue-tied. Is there some reason you don't want me to meet
this kid?"

"No!" Clay squirmed. "I just have to see if he's still interested." His desperation peaked. *What can I say?*

"Well, I've built this cool home rocket, and I'd love to show
it to both of you. Promise me you'll ask him," Rumo insisted.

Clay fidgeted. "I can't promise anything." He bailed. *I must
think about this and how to get him back on my brew.*

Clay fretted about the imaginary youngster but convinced himself that Rumo would eventually forget it. When Rumo brought up the subject several hexeks later, Clay realized he would not let it go. He thought long and hard about it and realized there might be a way to use it to his advantage. Clay stopped showing up at the bar and turned down Rumo's invitations to get together. After a couple of hexths, he agreed to meet Rumo at his insistence. He had devised another plan to solve the non-existent youth problem and speed up his potential rocket facility visit.

Rumo frowned when he met Clay. "What's going on? Did I offend you?"

"No, it's not you." Clay looked at Rumo earnestly. "I've just been so depressed lately." He began a new ruse. *I must start more slowly, and I cannot lose this one—I've been fishing for too long.*

"I can't believe it." Rumo furrowed his brow. "You're always so chipper. What happened? It must be serious."

"Well, you keep asking me to introduce you to my rocket-loving youngster." He turned panic into a ploy. *I'll pause for effect.* "And I can't."

"It's not that big a deal. Bring the kid or not." Rumo raised his arms. "It's not worth losing our friendship over."

"But it *is* a big deal." Clay scowled at Rumo. "And it's why I'm so depressed." He stared down at the ground. *My wile should lure him in.*

Rumo shook his head. "I don't understand."

Clay looked down. "The kid is dead." He looked up into Rumo's eyes. "He made his own rocket, and it blew up in his face," He exclaimed while scowling. *Now I cast out my line.*

"Oh, no!" Rumo froze. "I understand now."

"It's my fault for getting him interested," Clay cried as he trembled. *My lure is spinning.*

"It wasn't your rocket. Was it?" Rumo asked.

Clay shook his head. "No, he made it himself." He hid his smoldering stench.

"Then you shouldn't blame yourself," Rumo insisted.

"I don't, but I do." Clay sank into his chair. "Now, I want nothing to do with rockets, so I don't come around to the tavern." He pried for some sympathy. *I jig it a little.*

"I understand, but you must see it for what it was—a freakish mishap," Rumo urged. "You can't give up something you love over an accident."

"But it's hard to be reminded of him." Clay looked down again. *I'll project some guilt.*

"I am so sorry I pushed you." Rumo tilted Clay's head up to look into his eyes. "I didn't know."

Clay nodded. "I'm still feeling down about it." He rubbed it in a little. *And hope he bites.*

Rumo stood up quickly. "I know something that will cheer you up."

Clay tilted his head. "What?" *Have I hooked him at last? Will my spy skills work their magic?*

Rumo smiled a little. "I'll give you a tour of our control room and the launch pad."

"Is that even allowed?" asked Clay.

"I'll tell my boss you were a scarlet alternate and almost a leader. Not to mention you are chief of bionics, and my boss is a gladiator fan also," replied Rumo.

"I don't know." Clay shrugged. "I fear it might depress me more." He stepped back so as not to look too eager.

"I'm betting it's your lifelong dream." Rumo grinned. "We'll call it implosion therapy."

Clay grinned. "Now, who's practicing outside his profession?" He again used humor. *It gets him every time.*

Rumo fluttered his eyes, "Just call me Doctor Rumo. And I'll take that grin as a yes." Rumo's eyes lit up. "Oh, I have a special surprise for you."

"Aside from making my lifelong dream come true!" Clay chuckled. "I just hope it comes before I die." *I can reel him in now.*

Rumo chortled. "You're not that depressed, I hope."

Clay shook his head and laughed. "No, I just know how slow you guys work."

CHAPTER 24

THE BREEDERS: SOCIONICS

Antalonia (Rudyard's rule, the current president)

AFTER SPENDING A few hexeks in the ova cava and bloom room, Keegan entered the breeding halls, expecting that he'd meet Vermillion on his own and begin his studies of socionics. It surprised him to find Vermillion in the classroom meeting with another student. Since Blood would train to take over as master of socionics, when Keegan started his sessions on the subject, Vermillion instructed them together. A secondary purpose was to get the two to know each other and foster a constructive relationship. The breed master and master of socionics were vital players of the Antalone system, and they needed to work side by side as a well-oiled machine.

"Here's Keegan now," Vermillion addressed the novice. "Blood, this is my apprentice, Keegan, training to be the next breed master." He looked towards his apprentice. "Keegan, this is Blood. He's Czar Rudyard's son."

The pair shook claws, and Vermillion continued. "I decided that I would train you both together."

Keegan smiled. "So, we can be sociable studying socionics together?"

Blood laughed. "As long as there's nothing sociopathic about it."

Vermillion guffawed. "I knew you two would hit it off. And I'm glad you're both getting into sociologese." He suppressed his laugh. "I also thought it would make sense to train you together, as you'll both need to work as a unit over the hexs."

"So, how do we start?" asked Blood.

Vermillion pointed to the doorway. "First, I want you to walk out into the breeding halls."

A little annoyed that they might be back-tracking, Keegan complained, "I just spent the last three hexeks there." He tried to hide the fact that he didn't want to share his mentor. *I hope for something new but without all the Blood.*

Vermillion smiled. "But you were probably looking down at eggs, larvae, and pupae the whole time." He pointed up. "Did you ever look up at the ceiling and high on the walls?"

Keegan shrugged. "No, what's up there? And what's it got to do with socionics?" Still bothered, he wasn't his usual cheerful self. *I must get out of this funk.*

Blood, as a newbie, was already looking all around. "All the signs. I guess."

"Yes," Vermillion exclaimed. "Socionics is all about messaging and getting our youth to read the signs."

"Funny, I've been here so long now I forgot all about them," noted Keegan. His demeanor slowly shifted. *Guess it surprised me to have a classmate.*

"But did you forget their messages?" Vermillion put a claw to his head. "We want our youth, especially brown and black ANTs, to forget the signs but remember the messages."

"I expect that's easier to say than accomplish," noted Blood.

"But is that enough? Just having signs around the room?" questioned Keegan. He reacted negatively to its simplicity. *I was so keen to begin complex socionic training.*

"Both of you, cover your eyes," Vermillion barked. "Now, Blood, finish my sentence 'Altruism is ….'"

Blood replied without hesitation, "Ailing!"

"Excellent," responded Vermillion. "Now Keegan, 'Friendship is…'"

Keegan paused. "Uh, forbidden." He reeled in disbelief. *How did I know that?*

"Excellent," commented Vermillion. "You both got it right, and were you ever taught these sayings before?"

Blood and Keegan both shook their heads.

Vermillion smirked. "So, Keegan, you forgot the signs were there, but you remembered the message?"

"It seems so," replied Keegan, nodding, still dumbfounded. *That's incredible.*

"In a nutshell." Vermillion paused for effect. "That's socionics."

"Do you mean subliminal messages?" asked Blood.

"Sometimes, yes. But socionics don't have to be subconscious." Vermillion pointed up to the placards. "You both saw the signs." Vermillion laughed. "You both saw the writing on the wall."

"So conscious messaging can work as well as subconscious?"

asked Keegan. He cleared his head to consider the possibilities. *I see this has considerable implications.*

Vermillion explained it didn't matter whether the methods were covert or overt; the crucial thing was repetition and consistency. He pointed to the sign halfway down the hall that read: 'Learning is loathsome.' He noted that diverse ideas and new horizons inspire exploration and free will. He pointed to a sign closer to the back of the hall that read: 'Sameness is soothing.' He stressed repetition, consistency, and uniformity encourage compliance and conformity, key elements of social control.

Keegan crumpled his brow. "But there must be more than these signs." He still craved some complexity. *I can imagine many ways to train young minds, some from my schooling.*

"Yes, of course." Vermillion nodded. "We reinforce the messages by repetitions every hexay, quoting verses, singing songs, playing games."

Blood looked around the hall. "But why do you use signs like 'Empathy is evil', and Friendship is forbidden?" He could imagine the answer but wanted to drink from Vermillion's cup of knowledge.

Vermillion pointed to the sign, 'Histrionics is Heavenly.' "I'm sure you have probably heard your father use the human expression 'divide and conquer.'"

"Yes, it's a strategy for battle. A way to get troops disoriented and mistrusting each other," replied Blood.

Vermillion grinned. "Well, it works well in socionics, too."

"How is that?" asked Keegan. He was stunned by a flood of ideas. *The possibilities are endless, but I need to know what is best.*

"If everyone mistrusts everyone else, has no empathy for others, and has no friends to share ideas with, they fall back on the authorities. If you can't believe in your fellow students, you're more likely to trust the teacher."

"I'm not sure I follow," declared Blood.

"If a teacher told you that you needed to shock your best friend so that he would follow your directions better, would you do it?" asked Vermillion.

"Probably not. I'm sure I could reason with my friend instead," responded Blood.

"What if it was your enemy?"

"Then I might," responded Blood, leaking a burly bouquet. "Because I can't reason with my enemy, and I don't care if I hurt him." He imagined himself shocking most of his classmates, who largely ignored him.

"Exactly. That's why the teachers discourage empathy in brown and black ANTs, and friendship is forbidden." Vermillion beamed. "Because when the teacher says you need to beat your classmate for not following the rules, you'll do it. Especially when you know they will do the same."

"That makes sense," responded Blood. Although he could never imagine himself as a brown or black ANT, he could see himself beating a classmate if instructed, or perhaps even the teacher, if he detected some insubordination to his family's rule.

"But why do you say for brown and black ANTs?" queried Keegan. He again expressed his empathy for the lower castes. *Why do we pick on them?*

Vermillion explained that black and brown ANTs were the ones they needed to control most, as they were the ones that would object to the conditions of their lives and perhaps collude to fight the authorities if socionics did not condition them. One approach was to decrease their intellectual potential by reducing their brain sizes. By reinforcing this with socionics, they better learned how to behave in a manner consistent with their social position. They could not imagine any other way to comport themselves. And they learned to respect and even admire authority so they would not question the motives of their leaders.

"So, we don't use socionics on red ANTs," assumed Blood, expecting that reds would only need encouragement and not conditioning.

"No, we still expose them to socionics," Vermillion explained. "But we don't discourage empathy and friendship for red ANTs."

"Yes, my father has explained why red ANTs receive more privileges," replied Blood.

Keegan tapped his temples. "And I've been learning from you that black and brown ANTs are more likely to express altruism. So, we need to discourage them." He tried to align himself again with the program.

After he provided them many other examples over a few hexours of lectures, Vermillion smiled while glancing at the clock on the wall. "You both are catching on quickly, as I expected you would." He turned back towards his office and sighed. "Okay, students, let's call it a hexay. We'll cover a little more theory before visiting the schools for a practicum next time."

"I'm looking forward to it," responded Blood, as he thought about taking a ruler to a disobedient young black ANT.

"Me too." Keegan nodded. The sheer scientific nature of it excited him, if not the immoral purpose. *I can see myself teaching a classroom a song about proper etiquette and following the rules.*

Vermillion pointed to the exit. "You two go on ahead. I've

got some paperwork to complete." He turned and headed to his office.

As the two trainees passed through the ova cava and headed to the exit by the bloom room, Blood noticed Rose and Jasper.

Blood nudged Keegan. "Do you see those two young cyborgs in the first columns? They are definitely in the right sector. Alphas, for sure!" He poked Keegan in the abdomen. "And that female, what a beauty! I'm sure she'll be a Scarlet." He oozed a silken scent.

"Yes, that's Rose. I've been following her progress." Keegan blushed. "She's smart as a whip, too."

CHAPTER 25

THE OLD SPIES: EXPLODING ROCKETS

Antalonia (Rust's rule, one president in the past)

SOON AFTER RUMO promised a tour, he called Clay and told him his superior approved it, as long as he came between shifts and the visit was brief. Rumo suggested they do it that evening before Radley could change his mind. Rumo also wanted to do it soon because he had a surprise for Clay and couldn't wait to spring it on him.

That evening, Rumo met Clay at the front doors of the control center. "Clay, I am glad I could do this to cheer you up."

Clay smiled. "Yes, I'm as excited as I was on the first hexay of classes." Yet his enthusiasm also reflected a spy getting close to achieving his goal. *On this point, I couldn't be more honest.*

"As I was once a keen young student like you, I know the feeling." Rumo smiled. "I'll show you the launch pad before dark and then the control room." Rumo beamed like a fire-fighting ANT, sliding down the bamboo in front of cheering nanitics.

Clay looked up and shot an electrified essence. "Wow, that's some rocket!" He leaned left and then right. "Is that a two-stage rocket?" All his reading of rocket science piqued his desire to see them up close. *I feel like a bee in a wildflower garden.*

Rumo paused briefly. "I'm not sure if I'm allowed to tell you." He waved his claws towards the ground, deciding to speak anyway. "No, we won't have the two-stage ones ready for several hexths. I'll let you know before we launch the first, so you can watch it blast off into space," he said.

Clay gasped. "That will be amazing. I can't wait." He beamed at Rumo. "I'll take time off to see the launch." He couldn't wait for the hexay this long ploy ended. *I wouldn't miss it for anything.*

Rumo wiped off his smile. "You know you can't watch it from here, though."

Clay nodded hard. "Yes, I know. I'll watch from home. There's a patio on my roof." He considered how close to the blast he could safely stand. *Where can I get the best view to see the culmination of my mission?*

"Let's go inside now, and I'll show you the control room."

Clay nodded, emitting a vivacious vapor. "Super, this is all so exciting." *These rockets pump me up so much that I am not deceiving him.* Yet he knew the control room would be his primary access point.

They walked into a room littered with desks, video screens, and claw pads, and Rumo pointed to an extended counter at the front. The long desk sat next to a floor-to-ceiling window that covered most of the wall and framed the rocket launch pad.

Rumo cracked a big smile. "That's the main control panel. And if you look closely in the middle section, you'll see the surprise I told you about."

Clay shrugged and squinted, looking hard at the extended desktop. "What, is there something on the counter?" He wondered whether all his hard work had paid off. *What is he getting at?*

Rumo laughed. "Yes, the green button is halfway through the panel with the 'Stage 2' sign underneath it."

"I don't get it." Clay twitched. But get it, he did! *Could my wish come true after all this time?*

Rumo walked over and pretended to push the button. "Stage two," he stated, looking hard at Clay.

Clay did a double-take. "You took my suggestion?" He knew that he would. *It's true. I'm almost there!*

"Yes." Rumo smiled widely with bright eyes. "I convinced my colleagues that a manual system was better than an automated electronic switch." He beamed even more. "And I get to push it when systems are a go for the second stage rocket."

"I can't believe it!" Clay teared up. "That's the best surprise I've ever gotten." He had a hard time not jumping for joy. *It's not a surprise but a fait accompli. It's what I have been working toward since before I even met you. I can't wait to tell Darci.*

Rumo patted Clay on the back. "Well, you can't pass on a stellar idea, no matter where it comes from."

"But how does it work?" asked Clay. His spy instincts pressed him on. *Will he put the worms on the cake for me?*

"Well, since the two-stage rocket won't be ready for hexths, it's not functional yet." Rumo pulled the button and its socket off the panel. "The button is a switch, and these two wires will connect to a transmitter picked up by a receiver that triggers an ignition of the second rocket."

Clay laughed. "Guess you better ensure not to mix up the wires when you connect it up." He dug for more intel. *Could I have a termite on top?*

Rumo guffawed. "I can see why you're a genetic and not an electrical engineer. It's all color-coded to make it simple, red to red, black to black."

"Yeah, I'll never do wiring. I'd electrocute myself for sure." Clay howled as he stepped back his inquiry. *I must go back to humor to keep him from getting suspicious.*

Rumo slid the button and socket back into place and continued, "I think our time is up. I hope you enjoyed the tour."

Clay smiled. "Yes, I especially enjoyed the short lines to get in."

Rumo shoved Clay in the spiracles. "Go on, get out of here!" he laughed.

Clay looked back at the control panel as they were leaving. "Don't forget to tell me when the first two-stager is going up. I want to envision the blast you'll have pushing that button." *I can only imagine my goal going up in smoke—in the right way!* He sighed on a mission well done.

Rumo nodded. "I won't forget, and you won't be disappointed."

🐜 🐜 🐜

Later, Clay met with Darci, who began working as a night janitor at the rocket testing facility nearly a hex earlier.

"Darci, it has taken some time, but my plan worked. Rumo took my suggestion and made the firing of the second stage rocket manual. He even showed me the button on the control panel that triggers the ignition." Clay rubbed his claws together. "Now, installing the receiver for my remote switch is your job." He was sure she wouldn't fail. *Then all our systems will be a go.*

"I'm a cleaner, not an electrician," Darci replied. "How am I supposed to do that?"

Clay looked into Darci's eyes. He told her not to worry and explained that the receiver had the latest wireless technology. One only needed to snap the red and black wires from the green button into the color-coded matching grooves on the box. Clay described the exact location of the controller and panel, how the cables extend down through the table-top board below the button, and how to snap them to the receiver.

Clay smiled. "Just locate the wires, snap this on, and use the two-way power tape to stick the box to the underside of the table." He thought back to all Darci's accomplishments. *It'll be a piece of cake for her.*

"That easy, huh? I could do it in hexonds while hand washing the wall and floor below the panel."

"Exactly, it's simple," Clay continued. "I wired the receiver, so you only need to put it in place. It won't interrupt the normal function of their switch, which they will test regularly." He raised a single claw. "But when I push my button on this remote transmitter, it will override their button and trigger the ignition of the second-stage rocket."

Darci grinned. "And then kaboom!"

Clay laughed. "No, KABOOM!"

"You'd better stand back a little." Darci snickered.

Clay pointed towards the hills at the back side of the rocket testing site. "My remote has a radio-controlled signal with a five-mile range, so I'll be a safe distance away."

Launch hexay was beautiful, and there were no delays. Clay watched from the far-off hills through his spyglass as the countdown began. He planned to start the engines for the second rocket immediately after the first rocket fired to make the accident seem realistic. They would assume that the explosion occurred after some error associated with the first engine's start, which triggered the second engine's misfire. He looked at his watch, and remote-control button, then lifted the spyglass to his eye.

I need to wait for the flash of the first rocket and then press, he reminded himself. *I can't blow the second rocket until I'm sure the launch is on.*

When the first rocket fired, Clay pressed the remote, closed his eyes and listened for the bang. Clay was far enough from the explosion that he wasn't injured, yet he sensed a sudden rush of warm air even before he heard the blast. Only then did he consider what the explosion did to his friend Rumo and his associates.

In the next hexay's newspaper, he read how a catastrophe at the rocket testing site had killed Radley, his assistant Rumo, and hundreds of engineers and scientists that worked at the site. The article noted how the blast destroyed the plans needed to make nuclear warheads since they were only in the secure area there. It also stated that all atomic warheads previously constructed were used in Rust's war against the Antunites. Clay marveled at how the journalist mentioned the similarity of the accident to the Nedelin disaster that plagued humans' early attempts at multistage rocket development. After the explosion, Rust canceled the rocket program and concentrated on developing a powerful antimatter gun.

That evening Clay visited the tavern near the rocket testing facility and raised a glass to Rumo and all his rocket scientist drinking buddies. He downed the shot and pointed at his empty glass, which the shot-tender refilled. A single tear rolled down his face. *A shot for each of them, and then it's home to bed—If I can make it.*

CHAPTER 26

THE REFUGEES: THE ESCAPE

Bilaluna (Beeutee's reign, two rulers in the past)

ANTEBON CAME TO as she felt cold water dousing her face. She shook herself, startled by the sight of the raging river next to Bilaluna's wormhole entrance. "Lieutenant, where are we? What happened?" She coughed and tried to get her bearings. *Tell me our troops are okay.*

Her lieutenant lifted her to her pods. "The nuclear blast blew us over the edge of the crater. Radioactive clouds were approaching, and I ordered everyone through the wormhole." The lieutenant pointed in the colony's direction. "We're on Bilaluna now, and I'm taking you to see Queen Beeutee."

"Lieutenant Obsidian, you saved us all. The clouds would

have poisoned us for sure. Did everyone make it?" She emanated a fluffy fragrance of pride and concern. *I am forever in your debt.*

"We are all here, although the fall injured many, and there are three that perished." The lieutenant pointed to their bodies. "We brought them here for burial."

"That was not only thoughtful but strategic." Antebon patted her lieutenant on the back. "By bringing everyone, Rustant will not know of our escape, and he'll assume the blast incinerated us all." She smiled warmly at the soldier. *Your actions have saved us and fooled Rustant.*

"I had to act fast, and my motives were based on empathy, not a strategy," replied the lieutenant.

"Well, regardless of your reasons, your quick actions saved many and concealed our getaway. I'm sure the families of the fallen will be grateful as well." Antebon smiled. "I will recommend you to the Queen for the highest commendation." And I'll never forget your bravery. *I believe you truly deserve it.*

"Thank you, Captain." The lieutenant bowed to his superior. "I just did what anyone else would under the circumstance."

"No, not all soldiers react with valor and wisdom under duress." Antebon returned the bow. "And thank you for saving my life and the surrounding dozens." His actions moved her, and a sudden attraction overcame her. *I believe this ANT is a hero!*

Obsidiant smiled and motioned for Antebon to follow the river towards the colony and the Queen's palace. They marched downstream for about a hexour, and the Queen's patrol met them. The lieutenant spoke to the guard and introduced Antebon. The guard captain escorted them to the palace and arranged for Antebon to have an immediate audience with the Queen.

Queen Beeutee looked down at Antebon, who was resting in a chair when she entered the hall. "Antebon, you must be exhausted, injured, and soiled by your fall." She waved to her attendant. "I will call for our medic to see you. And then have my attendant draw you a warm bath."

"Please, no fuss. I only bumped my head. I am okay now." Antebon bowed before the Queen. "But please have your medic check over our troops. Some are injured worse than me." She smiled. "I will take you up on the warm bath, though. That's just what I need." Antebon looked the monarch up and down. She gaped in a state of awe. *I never expected the Queen to be so young!*

"Yes, that's the least I can do." Beeutee clapped her claws together, and her attendant ran off to alert the medic and prepare the bath. "Once you are cleaned up and rested, we will meet again to discuss the battle and how to proceed."

Antebon looked hard at Beeutee. "I apologize, Queen, for staring. But I did not expect you to be so young and beautiful." The pageantry of the surroundings overcame her. *I have never met royalty before.*

"Beautiful perhaps, and so young I hope my subjects look at me and think it is so." Beeutee fluffed her fuzzy, yellow mane. "I only recently succeeded my deceased grandmother Beewary."

Antebon gasped. "I am sorry. I didn't know." She extended her claw towards the Queen. "I hope she passed peacefully." She suddenly sensed the young queen's vulnerability.

Beeutee took Antebon's claw and smiled warily. "Yes, but my mother, Queen Beehold, was not so fortunate."

Antebon's eyes widened. "Oh, what happened?" She feared

the worst. *I know this war is hell, but I thought Bilaluna was spared from the worst of it.*

Beeutee continued to hold Antebon's claw as she spoke. "My mother, who had been Queen since I was a pupa, paid a diplomatic visit to Intopia to visit Rustant after he drastically changed Intopian society, and the Antunites and non-ANT insectoids rebelled. While there, she protested Rustant's latest actions and was leaving to come back through the wormhole to Bilaluna."

Antebon put a second claw over Beeutee's. "Did she not make it?" Her heart sunk a little.

Beeutee slid her claw out of Antebon's grasp and put her claws to her cheeks. "There was a mix-up, and the Congress thought my mom had already come back." She turned and looked towards the wormhole site. "But Rustant detained her and delayed her transit."

Antebon released a freezing fragrance. "Oh, no!" She turned pale at the news. *I don't have to guess what Rustant did.*

"In the meantime, the Congress sent our troops through the wormhole to help your valiant rebels." Beeutee dropped her head low. "We heard later that Rustant executed my mother in cold hemolymph."

Antebon grasped Beeutee's claws once again. "I am so sorry." She wanted so much to hold and comfort the young queen, but her thought turned to her hated foe. *Rustant makes my hemolymph boil, but Beeutee, despite her youth, is a leader I could follow.*

"Don't blame yourself. Our Congress sent our troops even without your request. But my grandma was so distraught after my mother's death, and it aged her so." Beeutee looked out the window to her gravesite. "She briefly took the throne, but only so she could convince the Congress and public that I was mature enough to reign."

Antebon extended a deep, warm look. "That must have been so devastating for both of you."

"Yes, but Grandma asked me if I would take over as queen." Beeutee returned the warm look. "I agreed, and when the Congress and populace concurred, she told me she found peace and would die contented."

"Still, it must have shattered you to lose your grandmother and mother so fast," added Antebon. She again felt strong compassion for the young queen. *I can't even imagine how much that would hurt.*

"Yes, but I take strength from my promise to grant my grandmother's last wish."

Antebon looked hard into Beeutee's eyes. "Pardon me if I ask. What was that?"

Beeutee stared hard back at Antebon. "To tear down the evil Rustant and defeat him, no matter how long it takes."

Antebon matched Beeutee's gaze. "In that quest, you see your most devoted ally before you." She spewed a scorching stench. She imagined it was Rustant standing before her. *I'll kill him with my bare claws!*

Beeutee looked softly at her newfound supporter. "I believe I do. But for now, you need to bathe and rest. So, we'll talk more later."

～ ～ ～

After Antebon cleaned up and rested, she met again with Queen Beeutee. She requested the Queen commend her lieutenant for his life-saving actions at the wormhole canyon. The Queen was happy to oblige, and the following hexay, they stood together at the dais in the main square as Lieutenant Obsidiant marched up the aisle with his Sergeant and Corporal. Obsidiant refused to accept any commendation unless they lauded the two under his command. The two non-commissioned officers and the lieutenant carried the dead and most injured to the wormhole, repeatedly risking their lives returning to the canyon floor as the radioactive clouds descended. The three soldiers survived the ordeal and were humble recipients of their just rewards. Antebon stood and watched them approach, marching up the aisle between the multitudes, including most of the Bilalunan capital. She could not help but notice how dashing the three soldiers looked, all washed up and with their shells shined to a dazzling sparkle. In the dirt and grime of warfare, she never noticed Obsidiant's shiny black thorax. For a moment, she gaped at the sight of him, her valiant savior, and smiled, knowing that ANTs had no ethical issues with commanders dating lower-ranked officers.

Queen Beeutee read the text of the commendation, proclaiming the heroic deeds of the soldiers, and presented them with their medals. She then invited Antebon, the three awardees, and their guests to a reception in the palace ballroom. First, the three officers left the dais and mingled amongst the crowd, where their troop mates, families, and friends congratulated them. Antebon and Queen Beeutee shook claws with the public, who were in awe of the Queen. The insectoids also adored the courageous Captain Antebon, who stood up to Rustant politically and in battle. In the commotion of the post-award ceremony greetings, Antebon lost sight of Obsidiant and eagerly awaited his return so she could congratulate him herself. The gathering waned in time after the ceremony, save for several of the Queen's distinguished guests, including all members of Congress, who had unanimously approved the commendations. Queen Beeutee had her attendant call the guests into the palace, and Antebon watched as the sergeant and corporal approached with their dates. She scanned the crowd for Obsidiant but could not find him. Her heart skipped when she saw him leave the restroom and walk alone towards the palace steps.

When he reached the top of the stairs, Antebon approached him. "Lieutenant, I wanted to offer you my congratulations." Antebon couldn't ignore her rapidly growing crush on her lieutenant. She tried to hide her flush. *Be still my pounding heart.*

Obsidiant bowed his head. "Thank you, but I assumed it was you that arranged for all this."

Antebon extended her claw. "Yes, you and your junior officers deserved it." She thought back to their heroic actions.

Obsidiant softly held his captain's claw. "My charges did what was required. Me, I would do anything for my captain."

Antebon flickered her ommatidia repeatedly. "Well, soldier, would you be my escort for this reception? I see you are on your own." She held her breath, anticipating his response. *This ANT is such a drone. I may be his superior, but he weakens my three knees.*

"As a mate-less bachelor, it would be my privilege to join you and honor any further requests."

Antebon could tell Obsidiant returned her friskiness, and she suspected he had equally strong feelings for her.

Antebon smiled and emitted an alluring aroma. "Well, take my limb, Lieutenant, and count on additional demands." She sported a playful grin. *I feel a solid connection to a male ANT for the first time in my life. I'm giddy with surviving the war; he inspires my naughty side.*

Obsidiant chortled. "What! Saving your life was not enough?"

Antebon gazed into her lieutenant's eyes. "Don't you know? Once you save a life, you are forever responsible for it." She imagined them in a passionate embrace. *I want him so much.*

Obsidiant matched his captain's gaze. "That's an obligation I've felt since I first met you."

Antebon knew he, too, could not ignore their overwhelming mutual attraction.

Antebon smiled brazenly. "Well, now that duty may come with some perks." She brazenly twirled in front of him. *I think my heart will explode.*

CHAPTER 27

THE RULERS:
THE BIG PICTURE

Antalonia (Rudyard's rule, the current president)

BLOOD MET WITH Rudyard after returning home from his lesson with Vermillion. He was excited about socionics since he understood that it was a key component of their society that kept their subjects under control. As a future ruler, he wanted to know everything about their system, and he was learning it from the inside. He realized that Rudyard suggested he take the position for that reason, and he was grateful for his father's insight.

Rudyard walked up to Blood as he headed towards the library. "How did it go with Vermillion this morning?"

"It was fascinating, and I met his new apprentice, Keegan." Blood showed him the outline of the course Vermillion provided him. "We will do some sessions together, since Keegan also needs to learn about socionics."

Rudyard abruptly looked up from the outline. "He's not going to get in the way or take away from your training?"

"No, quite the contrary. Keegan is knowledgeable and asks questions that aid my learning," Blood answered. "He's a superb student, and I expect he'll make an excellent breed master."

Rudyard nodded. "Yes, I believe I understand Vermillion's plan. When he retires, you two will work closely together." Rudyard smiled. "It's clever of him to pair you up for training to encourage you to get along now and in the future."

"I agree, and I couldn't be more impressed with Vermillion." Blood tapped his temple with a claw. "He really knows his stuff." He thought back to earlier lessons with his father. *He's an excellent educator, like you.*

"I'm glad you're immersing well in the program and with your peers." Rudyard looked down again at the outline. "I notice you will soon meet our outgoing master of socionics. Ruby is tough, but you'll learn much from her." Rudyard spread his forelimbs wide. "You and Keegan have large pods to fill."

Blood took the outline back from his father at his offering. "I understand, Father. I won't let you down." Blood stuffed the prospectus into his bag. "But father, I still want to understand how our system came to be. When we last spoke, you described the Great Cyborg War, but what happened after Grandfather's forces won?"

Rudyard rubbed his claws together, eager to continue the story. "After the defeat of Antebon and the Antunite armies, Rust pushed his politics hard."

"So, the socionics program continued?" asked Blood.

"Yes, but Rust decided it was necessary to create a bionics

program to complement the socionics." Rudyard pulled out another book from the restricted section of the library written by Rust entitled: 'The Onics of Complete Societal Control: The Trinity of EOW's Plan' and handed it to Blood.

Blood studied the book's cover. "What's 'The Trinity'?" he asked. He shivered at the use of the word. *Rust was so creative.*

Rudyard raised his brow. "Histrionics, bionics, and socionics, of course."

Blood shrugged. "But didn't we already have a bionics program to create cyborgs from small insects?"

Rudyard nodded. "Absolutely, but we needed to expand the program to include genetic engineering to produce hybrid ANTs with genes from other insects so that they could do the work of the now decimated insectoids."

"Yes, of course," responded Blood. "But wouldn't it have been easier to enslave the captured insectoids?" He imagined a scene with Rust marching detainees into dungeons. *With a whip in my claw, I see myself ordering those non-ANT slaves around.*

"There were very few non-ANT insectoids taken as prisoners. And Rust hated them all, and he insisted ANTs wipe them off the face of the planet after he collected their DNA for genetic engineering."

Blood nodded and grinned. "That makes sense if there were so few survivors." He concluded that Rust knew what was best. *And I can see why he hated them so much.*

"He also called himself 'Czar Rust-the-Robust' and banned the use of species identification within names."

Blood spewed a beaming bouquet on hearing the title, Czar Rust. "I guess it wasn't necessary anymore if the society now only included ANTs."

"But there was more," Rudyard smirked. "Rust wanted the

remaining black and brown ANTs to pay for the disloyalty of their Antunite brothers and sisters who'd led the rebellion."

"Even if they did not rebel themselves?" Blood asked. He imagined the powerful Czar wielding his might. *I love that title, Czar Rust-the-Robust, and I like Czar Blood-the-Stud too.*

"Yes, there was a feeling that even those black and brown ANTs that did not rebel were sympathetic to the Antunite cause." Rudyard made a fist with his claws. "We can't trust ANTs with Antunite genes, and we need to control them."

"So, he used bionics to place controls on brown and black ANTs?" Blood thought hard about Rust's motivations.

"Yes, he required that we breed all insectoids in hatcheries to control their numbers and early upbringing," Rudyard smirked. "He realized it was only because of Antuna that our ancestors had their own families, and he wanted to reverse that."

Blood's pupils grew wide. "Did anyone object to it?"

Rudyard shook his head. He explained that Rust convinced his subjects that this was EOW's way, which is why the book had 'EOW's plan' in the title. He noted that Earth ant ancestors did not have parents. There was only one queen who laid all the eggs. Rust told everyone the breed master was like the colony's queen and would ensure the security of all ANTs. Then he described how the breeding hall was like a sizeable cozy nest, where all developing ANTs would be safe. Rust enthralled the public with his stories about Earth ants, and they bought into Rust's suggestion that they live as their ancestors had. Also, many ANTs, particularly red ANTs, were not really into family life, so they saw it as a burden that Rust removed from their shoulders. This point allowed Rust to build the breeding halls, where he started various biological manipulations that suppressed black and brown ANT intelligence and facilitated the mass production of hybrids.

"But you are my father, and we were a family with mother," Blood noted.

"Although we preach the opposite, we understand the importance of early childhood education in an intimate family environment. It is a perk we reserve for top leaders," replied Rudyard. "And the entire society understands they need a ruling class, and they know the leaders need to teach their offspring the knowledge required to lead."

"So, red ANTs have families, but brown and black ANTs do not?" enquired Blood.

"No, to appease the public, red betas and chi ANTs also do not have families. Even many red alpha ANTs do not have families, though most males know which female's eggs they fertilized."

"Why is this necessary?" puzzled Blood. "I thought Grandfather Rust only wanted to punish ANTs with black genes." He briefly questioned Rust's methods. *Shouldn't superior red ANTs be free?*

"As I mentioned, it appeased the public and ensured societal uniformity." Rudyard sneered. "I'm sure Vermillion has taught you uniformity breeds conformity."

Blood nodded, "I can see that it would be easier to expose them to socionics from an early age." He reconsidered his conclusion. *It must be right if Rust implemented the policy.*

"Exactly. We don't want other red ANTs to feel they have a right to take over our positions whenever they get disgruntled."

Blood lined his brow. "So, only the leaders have genuine families? And the rest have no family roots."

Rudyard smiled. "That's right. The system is their family,

and the leaders are their parents. And as parents, we are strict enough so they don't rebel. Yet, we provide them with all their needs, so they are content."

"I understand. What else should I know about bionics?" asked Blood.

Rudyard smiled. "Just the bit about smaller brain sizes and vitamin S."

Blood did a double-take. "What?" He couldn't believe his antennae. *I'm surprised he'd go that far.*

"Fearing that the genes of Antunites were innately rebellious, Rust wanted to make sure that ANTs with Antunite genes were less intelligent and would conform," Rudyard explained. "So, the bionics program limits neuronal growth factors for brown and black ANTs that carry the Antunite gene. The breeders also use vitamin S, a drug that promotes compliance."

Blood released a brassy bouquet. "I assume this was also a means to punish the Antunite breeds for the disloyalty of their genetic siblings." He considered what would be required. *I see that Rust's tactics were not only needed, but justified.*

Rudyard clapped his claws together repeatedly. "Absolutely. Now I believe you see the big picture."

CHAPTER 28

THE REFUGEES: SETTLE DOWN

Bilaluna (Beeutee's reign, two rulers in the past)

A FEW HEXAYS after the commendation ceremony and reception for Obsidiant and his junior officers, Antebon asked for another audience with the Queen. Something about the Queen drew her, and she wanted to get to know her better. Antebon was the farthest thing from royalty, but she had become a leader in fighting Rustant politically and in war. She now craved power, not for its own sake, but with the explicit purpose of opposing her enemy—not the Antalones per se, but Rustant himself.

They let Antebon into the Queen's chamber, and she approached her on her throne. "Your majesty, I am thrilled you agreed to see me." She hoped to get close to the Queen because she liked the Queen and shared her objectives. *She seems like a kindred spirit, but I wonder whether befriending her violates some royal protocol.*

"Let's get things straight from the outset, Captain." Queen Beeutee signaled her attendant to leave the room and close the door.

Antebon cringed and braced herself to be put in her place by the Queen.

"A female ANT that stands up to that monster Rustant, and leads a squadron against his armies, does not need to make appointments to see me or call me Your Majesty."

Antebon wafted a waffling whiff. "Wait, what...." She stood frozen and perplexed. *What am I to think?*

Beeutee interrupted, "Queens don't wait. You may be a captain, but I know you're close to my age. I may be a queen, but you can call me girlfriend." She took off her crown and put her scepter down.

I think she wants me to be a friend. "How about just Queen?" Her heart swelled at the prospect of having a close girlfriend again.

"No, call me Tee."

I'll bite my tongue and play along. "If you insist, Tee," replied Antebon.

"I do, and I'll call you Ebon. That is a beautiful black shell."

Antebon smiled. *Perhaps she and I can become close.* "I clean up well when I'm not on the battlefield." She tried her best to reduce the formality in her demeanor.

"So did your escort, Obsidian." Beeutee snickered. "I expect you noticed."

Antebon had not had a close girlfriend since Antnoir, but she let down her guard and spoke to the Queen in such a manner. "Yes, and I assume we made a dazzling pair at the reception."

"Indeed, and he is a handsome devil," teased Beeutee. "How is he?"

"I haven't seen him since the reception." Her thoughts returned to her military conquest. *There's a war on, and I must prepare.* "I was planning a counter-attack to get a pod-hold back on Intopia."

"Have you not heard the word?" asked Beeutee.

"What word?" responded Antebon. Again, her body stiffened with confusion. *She must realize I'm new here and do not have many connections.*

Beeutee described how another small group of Bilalunan troops escaped through the wormhole the night of the reception. They were hiding in the jungle on the far side of the crater and dashed through the wormhole after Rustant's troops cleared the area. She learned that they were the last of the rebel troops. Rustant killed all the others with nuclear warheads, except a small group of insectoids he took as prisoners.

She looked Antebon in the eyes. "The war is lost, and it would be futile to return to battle." A poignant perfume filled the room.

"But Queen... I mean, Tee, we must do something," Antebon urged. She could not accept defeat. *I cannot fathom losing a war to that piece of Rust, and I'm desperate to get back into action.*

"We will, Ebon. Just not a military-style assault—rather, we will soon begin covert operations."

"You are right. Things are too hot right now." Antebon held her claws to her face, disappointed at the setback but buoyed by Beeutee's plan. *I'll never admit defeat, but there's nothing we can do right now.*

"You know Rustant's calling the colony Antalonia now, and the ANTs, Antalones."

"That is confusing. The planet is Intopia, but its only colony is Antalonia." Antebon spun her ommatidia. "I guess Rustant thinks ANTs can do it alone." Her heart grew cold. *I long for the hexay I can pay him back for his atrocities.*

"The rest of the planet is a toxic wasteland with radiation everywhere, so they don't call the planet anything and focus on the colony. And Rustant is calling himself Czar Rust-the-Robust." Beeutee chortled.

"I'd like to discuss what we can do to take him down." She saw no humor when it came to the tyrant. *I can't bear the thought of Rust as a Czar.*

"Ebon, you will be the first one I call." Beeutee held up a single claw. "But first, I want you to relax and take it easy for a time. You have been fighting Rustant for hexs, and it's time for you to settle down and think about starting a family." She rattled her claw. "We need you to produce some shiny black offspring to join us in our fight."

"Funny that you bring up offspring." Antebon blushed. "I've been thinking a lot about that recently." Her thoughts turned to Obsidiant, a male that she held as exemplary. *I need something to take my mind off Rust; he's been living in my head for too long.*

"Well, sister, we're not getting any younger, and it's time to attract the mates while we're still hot." Beeutee laughed and spewed a radiant bouquet.

Antebon searched her mind for a positive male image. "I have been meaning to call on Obsidiant again."

"I had his sergeant and corporal in my chamber last night." Beeutee snickered.

"But they're ANTs, and you're a ...." Her heart warmed, despite the lightning shock that first stabbed her foregut. *I must learn from my Queen how to be young and carefree again.*

"Oh, I'm not looking for a mate yet, just a fun time. I'm all for diversity, and a Queen deserves some privileges."

"Tee, I can see you are a very progressive and inclusive ruler." She laughed at her image of the soldiers doting upon the queen. *I must drop the soldier title and embrace the role of Queen's close friend and confidante.*

"You got that right, and I have an order for you." Beeutee chortled. "Get out of here!" She pointed at the door. "You have a mate to find."

"I'll take that as a royal decree." Antebon laughed and gave her young friend a big hug. She turned and looked towards the colony. *I wonder what Obsidiant is doing right now.*

﹏ ﹏ ﹏

Soon after Antebon came to Bilaluna, she and Obsidiant fertilized her eggs to have offspring. When the larvae metamorphosed into pupae, Antebon noticed something odd, which she brought up with Obsidiant. As a new mother, Antebon was excited but also worried about the well-being of her young. She had no child-rearing experience and no younger siblings to base her judgment on, but she could tell something was off with her new hatches.

Antebon pointed down at one of her pupae. "Sid, do you think that's normal?" Her concern heightened as she looked back towards Obsidiant. *It seems odd to me.*

Obsidiant stooped down to look at the tiny being. "What do you mean—how small it is?"

Antebon slapped Obsidiant lightly on his shoulder. "No, watch closely. It changes color from dark black to brown to bright red." She raised her arms in the air. "Shouldn't they just stay black?"

Obsidiant squinted and shook his head. "Wow, that *is* weird. Let's ask the medic about it."

Antebon asked if Queen Beeutee could send her medic, which she did. The doctor called for a wise old ANT grandmother, who had hatched many eggs and had many grand ants. The two of them each noted that they had seen nothing similar. They called in a FLY that the ANT grandmother knew had been on a student exchange to Earth before the wormhole, which had a branch to Bilaluna, collapsed.

When the medic returned, Antebon spoke to the FLY. "Are you also a medic?" She craved all the expertise they could get. *What is this freakish behavior?*

The FLY was already inspecting the pupae and flung his head up. "No, I'm not a physician—I'm an entomologist and study insects of all kinds. I observed some interesting ones on Earth while on my student exchange."

Antebon pointed to a pupa that was changing color at that moment. "Have you ever seen anything like this?"

"Yes, I observed flower crab spiders and tortoise beetles on Earth, which can change their exoskeleton colors." He picked up the pupa and examined it. "Those spiders and beetles were like some Earth reptiles called chameleons that changed their colors to match their background environment. It's a defense mechanism."

Antebon frowned. "But did they change colors as pupae?"

She desperately hoped his research applied to her offspring. *Can this explain what my pupae are doing?*

The FLY nodded. "I once saw a flower crab larva changing colors like this pupa in its egg sac." He placed the pupa back with the others that were also shifting hues. "I expect when these pupae metamorphose into nanitics, they might have chameleon-like abilities, like the spiders and beetles I saw."

Antebon and Obsidiant were worried that it was a hatching defect, which might be fatal, but the pupae grew and otherwise developed normally. Then, sure enough, the healthy nanitics could change colors from black, brown, and red when they emerged from their cocoons. Shortly later, Obsidiant's sergeant settled down and mated with a female ANT who had been under Antebon's command while fighting in Intopia. They discovered that their pupae and nanitics had the same ability to change colors. Yet, the offspring of Obsidiant's corporal, who mated with a female that had never gone to Intopia, did not develop the color-changing ability.

The medic and FLY returned to visit Antebon after her nanitics emerged from their cocoons.

The medic stated, "From what you tell me about the sergeant and the corporal's offspring, I'd say you have a novel mutation here."

Antebon pulled at her antennae. "What? My kids are mutants?" She fixated on the word mutation. *Will everyone see them as freaks? Can we live this down?*

"Yes, but I wouldn't say it negatively," reassured the FLY. "Mutations happen all the time, making individual ants or flies look slightly different from others."

Antebon shook her head. "But this isn't a small difference."

She stared at one nanitic changing hue. *No ants have ever done this before.*

The FLY let one of the tiny ants crawl up onto his wing. "No, your radiation exposure when you escaped Intopia likely caused it."

"But they are all very healthy," added the medic. "Don't worry so much. You should be proud that they have this extraordinary ability. Superpower, you might say."

The FLY entomologist added, "You have bred a new mutation into Bilaluna ants that may be useful at some point. You have produced a strain of chameleants."

Antebon beamed on hearing this and realized there might be an upside. *We should see this as a wondrous thing!* "Perhaps by having the ability to choose the hue they show, my children will bring color to our world and bring all ANTs from Bilaluna and Intopia together." An effervescent essence permeated the area.

CHAPTER 29

THE BREEDERS: MORAL EDUCATION

Antalonia (Rudyard's rule, the current president)

WHEN NOT TAKING socionic classes with Blood, Vermillion asked Keegan to shadow Clay for practical training in the breeding halls. Keegan was eager to get out of the classroom and enjoyed working with Clay. The two had developed an excellent working relationship and continued to visit the local tavern after their shift, engendering a close friendship. Yet, at work, Keegan appreciated Clay's amiable but down-to-business attitude. Keegan saw Vermillion more like a father figure from whom he needed to learn key life lessons, but he saw Clay as a big brother whom he could befriend and emulate.

Clay met Keegan after their lunch break. "You'll be happy

to know that Rose and Jasper have finished their physio and are now full-grown cyborgs ready to leave."

"That's fantastic." Keegan rubbed his claws together. "My first graduates from the breeding halls."

"Yes, I thought you'd like to join me to send them off."

"I appreciate that." Keegan smiled. "As the first cyborgs I saw in my practicum, I am interested in following their progress." He thought back to his earlier fantasy about supporting the young red alphas. *They will become fantastic apprentices.*

Clay winked. "Now that you're studying socionics, you can follow these two young cyborgs into the school and see their development."

Clay wanted to encourage Keegan's interest in the two young cyborgs. He would have been charmed to know Keegan dreamed about taking them under his wing.

"Yes, it'll be like the future teacher learning alongside his first students." He wondered whether Rose might some hexay see him as a close friend. *And I can groom Rose from a young age.*

Clay patted Keegan on the back. "I envy you. As a breeder, I never see the breeding hall graduates finishing their growth, and it will be rewarding for you to see them grow mentally and socially."

Keegan looked into Clay's eyes. "Are you disappointed you were not selected as the breed master's apprentice?" His thoughts returned to his training and his future dealings with his colleagues. *I hope my advancement doesn't cause resentment that could harm our relationship.*

Clay turned and stroked the growing limbs of a developing cyborg in a red alpha column near Rose and Jasper. "No, I wanted to remain a bionics specialist. I love seeing the eggs develop into pupae and choosing which nanitics become cyborgs. And genetic engineering was my favorite subject." Clay stretched his forelimbs to encompass all the incubators in the hall. "I am delighted to foster the physical growth of all these cyborgs."

Keegan rumpled his brow. "So, you are not jealous about my selection?" He sighed.

Clay shook his head. "No, I am very thrilled for you, and you are much more keenly interested in socionics than I ever was." He pointed directly at Keegan. "You will make a wonderful breed master, and I look forward to when I can call you friend and boss."

Keegan extended his claw to Clay, emitting an affable aroma. "My friend, you have made my hexay." He looked Clay directly in the eyes. "You and I will achieve wondrous things together." He looked forward to a time when he would be the head honcho at the breeding hall. *I am so relieved, and I believe Clay will be as solid a supporter as he is a friend.*

Clay shook Keegan's claw. "I'm sure we will. Now let's go release Rose and Jasper."

~ ~ ~

Vermillion later met with Keegan and Blood in the classroom next to the ova cava for their third socionics lesson. "Okay, trainees, I just wanted to give you a quick review before heading to the schools for your practicum."

"You mean now?" asked Keegan. He was so thrilled that he nearly lost his lunch. *I can't wait to get out of the breeding halls.*

"Yes, Master Ruby has graciously agreed to bring you into her classroom for moral education lessons."

When Rust first established the breeding halls, Ruby became the master of socionics, and it was around the same time that Vermillion became breed master. When Rust took power, Ruby was a young teacher who quickly recognized and supported what Rust was trying to do. Rust appreciated how Ruby championed his goals and selected her to be a moral education teacher. When he saw how she excelled at enforcing socionics in the classroom, he promoted her to master of socionics. Some thought Ruby was having an affair with Rust, which explained her rapid ascension through the ranks. But these were just false rumors since Rust preferred older females to the spry young Ruby.

On a professional level, Vermillion and Ruby were ideally suited, and together they rapidly constructed the complete socionics program. They even took a few suggestions from Rust's son Rudyard, who worked with them briefly at Rust's urging. A young Rudyard encouraged the implementation of various video games intended to promote loyalty to the Czar and the leaders. Vermillion and Ruby designed them to be manipulative, yet enjoyable for youth. They also made them addictive, so the students would keep returning for more. The students thought they were only playing, not realizing the socionic messages they were absorbing.

"Moral education?" asked Blood, thinking the term might be more oppressive.

Rudyard nodded. "Yes, that's what we call the class. The young students won't understand the term socionics. They only see it as a class that teaches them how to behave with others."

Keegan pointed to the signs over the columns of incubators in the ova cava. "Which classroom will we visit? Brown or red? Alphas or betas?" He stared at the black beta sign, hoping it would be them.

Vermillion pointed to the breeding hall columns inside

the farthest right ones. "Ruby and I thought it would be most instructive for you to visit a black beta class."

"Why would you say most instructive?" asked Blood, although he thought he knew.

Vermillion took a deep breath. "If you remember, brown and black chi ANTs are hybrids. Hybrids spend most of their time learning to perform the tasks previously done by other insectoids." He pointed to a chart on the wall with pictures of BEEants, FLYants, RoAChants, and WoBBants. "They learn to fly, chop down trees, or transport goods. The most aggressive RoAChants become gladiators. Once they gain their skills, they work long hexours at their jobs. The point is, they don't need much socionics since their lives are too busy for them to think about social interactions."

"Whereas betas have more time to think?" queried Keegan. He thought back to his earlier bionics lessons with Vermillion. *And need to be controlled, I assume.*

Vermillion looked at the clock on the wall. "Yes, but let's not dwell on this too much. Ruby is waiting."

As the three walked through the breeding halls toward the schools, Keegan noticed Clay placing two new nanitics into the incubators Rose and Jasper had previously occupied. He nudged Blood and pointed at the incubators. "Those two red alphas left the bloom room and are off to school."

Blood shined his thorax to show off his redness. "Oh, you mean that red beauty and her buddy?"

"Yes, Rose and Jasper," replied Keegan.

Blood sported a cocky grin. "We'll have to watch that one. All the young alpha males will be after her."

Vermillion squirted an alert pheromone to get his trainees' attention. "Okay, on your best behavior. Remember, Ruby is an excellent master of socionics because she's tough. You'll want to make a good impression."

※ ※ ※

When Master Ruby heard the knock at the classroom door, she slammed her pointer down on the young black beta ANT's desk in front of her. All the ANTs in the classroom snapped to attention. Ruby organized her classroom as strictly as possible. The best or most cooperative students were at the back of the room, and the unruliest ones were at the front. These were the students she wanted to keep her compound eyes on and those she wanted to be within her pointer's reach. A few cracks on the claws with her stick, and it wasn't long before they switched positions with those in the second row, as they quickly conformed to her will. There were no restrictions on teachers for corporal punishment, as it was strongly encouraged by the Czar. It was better to learn it early rather than experiencing the wrath of his BUGants later in life.

"Now remember, class, when I raise my claw, you should all give Master Vermillion a warm greeting," barked Master Ruby. She opened the door and invited the breed master and the two trainees into the classroom. She eyed Blood up and down. *He's the Czar's son, no less—I hope his skills match his famous ego.*

As she turned and raised a claw, the entire class broke into a robotic chant: "Welcome, Breed Master Vermillion. May your hexay be drab and fertile."

Vermillion addressed the class, "Yes, a perfect hexay, nothing out of the ordinary, yet productive. I wish you all the same."

Master Ruby stepped forward. "Now, class, Master Vermillion has brought in two of his students, and they want to learn from me how I teach this class." She pointed to the trainees. "This is Blood, and beside him is Keegan. Blood is Czar Rudyard's son." She noted the similarity of Blood's features to his grandfathers. *Is he supposed to fill my pods?*

Before Ruby spoke again, there was an audible gasp throughout the room. "Quiet, class. Both Blood and Keegan deserve your utmost deference. I will meet any acts of disrespect with severe punishment." She turned and raised her pointer. "Now, as the breed master leaves the room, I want everyone to show Blood and Keegan how well you know your alphabet." Her thoughts waffled between Blood and her young charges. *I hope Blood learns quickly. These kids need constant supervision. No, make that governance. No, domination!*

As Vermillion left the room and Ruby pointed at the single letter A on the wall, all the students chanted, "A - Altruism is ailing."

Blood grinned while looking at the stern expression on Ruby's face.

Ruby noticed him eyeing her and correctly read his thoughts. *I think he likes my creative, fierce, and demanding style.* An ominous odor clouded the classroom.

CHAPTER 30

THE REFUGEES: THE FIRST CHAMELEANT

Bilaluna (Beeutee's reign, two rulers in the past)

ANTEBON RECEIVED A message that Queen Beeutee urgently wanted to see her, and she immediately proceeded to the palace.

Antebon bowed before her queen. "Your majesty, I am so glad you called for me. It's been too long since our last meeting, and I brought one of my nanitics, as you requested."

Beeutee's smile changed briefly to a scowl. "Drop the 'Your majesty' stuff, my friend. Just because you're a mother now doesn't mean we aren't best buds, Ebon." Still an isolated young BEE, the Queen craved friendship.

"Sorry, Tee, all the royal stuff around here must make me think I have to be formal."

Beeutee laughed. "By the way, I might soon join you in motherhood. I found myself a proper mate." As she was still young, she wondered whether he was the one.

"I'm so happy for you." Antebon snickered. "I assume he's a BEE!"

"Ha-ha. Yes, his name is Beeast." Beeutee poked Antebon in the thorax.

"Beeutee and the Beeast. That sounds strangely familiar." Antebon pondered her point. "I'm sure you make a wonderful couple."

"Yes, and he lives up to his name." Beeutee chortled. "He's quite the animal, if you get my meaning." Her youth and position explained her tendency to be crass, particularly with her close friend.

"So, you'll be bringing up some little beeutees?" Antebon laughed.

"Perhaps. And I'm glad you brought one of yours." Beeutee grinned at the nanitic, hiding behind his mother. "I hear they have some special qualities." Her crassness quickly switched to craftiness.

Antebon exuded a sunny scent. "Yes, I was worried at first, but now I see it as a gift." She pulled her little one up front and put her claws on his shoulders. "They're special." *And I'm so proud.* She thought back to the FLY's positive comments about novel mutations.

"Indeed. What's this one's name?" asked the Queen, smiling at the tot.

Antebon looked down lovingly at her son. "His name is Clayant. When he turns red, he looks like a polished piece of baked clay. He has a twin sister we call Antonyx. She is also a chameleant but is better at turning dark black, much blacker than Obsidiant or me."

Beeutee tilted her head. "But Clay has your shiny black coloring now."

"Black is his natural color, like Antonyx, but he can switch to brown or red." Antebon beamed. *I've seen few ants redder.*

"Could you have him go through his colors?" the Queen requested as she considered a bold plan. "I'd love to see it."

Unbeknownst to Antebon, Beeutee had already started covert operations in Antalonia. Once she learned about the lunar winds clearing the radioactive clouds and dust, Beeutee immediately sent over the spies she had been training. However, her lack of understanding of how far Rust had gone to alter Antalone's society after the war caused her plan to fail abysmally. All but one of the spies she had sent to Antalonia had been discovered, captured, and killed by Rust. She realized she needed another approach, and hearing about Antebon's young nanitics sparked a radical idea. She needed to convince Antebon that it was the only way.

"Sure, he loves to show off." Antebon turned from Beeutee to Clayant. "Baby, could you show Queen Beeutee your hues?" Her pride in her son's unique skills overtook her. *Wait till she sees this.*

The young ant smiled and nodded his head. "I'll show off my rainbow shades to the Queen." He then changed his color from black to brown, and then, after a hexute, he morphed from brown to a brilliant red.

The Queen stepped back. "Wow. That is amazing!" She looked at her reflection in his shell. "I've never seen a nanitic so red." The term 'red alpha' popped into her head.

Antebon rubbed a small piece of brown dirt off her son's abdomen. "I dare say he can make himself even redder than Rustant."

"Funny that you bring up Czar Rust-the-Robust as he now goes by." Beeutee cracked a cynical grin. "He is why I asked you here." After seeing the nanitic go through his colors, she concluded her plan would work.

"What has he done now?" Antebon clasped her claws together hard, trying to suppress her intense hatred. *I can't wait to get that tyrant.*

"Nothing recently," Beeutee assured. "But over the last several hexths, he has captured all but one of our spies. Five of six." She revealed her secret to Antebon.

"Spies?" Antebon shrugged.

"Yes," the Queen replied. "Remember, I mentioned we would start covert operations. I have been sending spies over to infiltrate the Antalone colony."

Antebon huffed. "Didn't you say you'd call me when you started?" She recalled Beeutee's promise to call on her first. *That's my job!*

"Well, I didn't want to bother you when you and Obsidiant first got together or later when your eggs hatched." Beeutee lowered her head. "That's when we started. But I contacted you now."

Antebon raised a claw to her chin. "But how were they all captured?" She quickly dropped her disappointment and focused on the moment. *Wasn't it supposed to be covert?*

Beeutee shrugged. "It seems most spies gave themselves away, since they were too smart for black ANTs."

Antebon could feel Beeutee's hemolymph pressure rising as she discussed it.

"How do you know that?" Antebon asked.

Beeutee described how she communicated with the remaining spy. She told Antebon how the female spy evaded capture by playing stupid. She had discovered they bred the black and brown ANTs on Antalonia to have much lower intelligence than red ANTs. And Rust forced the few black ANTs that survived the war to have surgery to reduce their brain size so that they were all dull, like the newer ones.

"All black ANTs in Antalonia are dim-wits." Beeutee lowered her head, then looked up at Antebon with a twinkle in her eyes. This failure is what compelled her creative plan.

"Oh, my!" Antebon raised two claws to her cheeks and shot a shrill stink. "He's punishing ANTs with Antunite genes. What a tyrant!" *Please let me go to Intopia and quash him.* She thought about various ways she could eliminate the rusty autocrat.

"My thoughts too," responded Beeutee. "And all remaining ANTs on Bilaluna are black or brown." The Queen pointed up to the planet in near space. "It seems when we first sent colonists to Intopia, all our red ANTs volunteered to go since red ANTs are more aggressive and adventuresome." She gave her friend the background that required alternative thinking.

"There are no red ANTs on Bilaluna?" puzzled Antebon. She thought hard about all the ANTs she'd met on Bilaluna. *I never noticed!*

"Hard to believe, but true." Beeutee scratched her head. "But we just had 1,000 insectoids in total on Bilaluna at the time of the Great Migration, and of that, only about 140 were ANTs. My grandma told me we sent over about 70 of each insectoid family to Intopia, and I checked the numbers, and half of the ANTs that went were red ANTs."

"So, we sent 35 red ANTs; the remainders were browns and blacks?" Antebon queried.

"Yes, we didn't formally track how many ANTs of different colors we transformed, as an ANT's color was not so much of an issue on Bilaluna," Beeutee explained. "I guess we had fewer red ANTs, and all of them left." She looked towards the ground.

"As I think of it, I realize Bilaluna now has mostly black ANTs. Why are there so few browns?"

Beeutee shrugged. "I assume it's because brown ANTs are usually hatched when black ANTs mate with red ANTs. So, if there are no red ANTs to mate with, few brown ANTs are hatched." Young Beeutee had excellent schooling, and her brains matched her beauty.

"So that's why you sent black ANTs over as spies?" Antebon surmised.

Beeutee nodded. "Yes, but it would be much better if we could send red ANTs." She hinted at her plan.

"Can't we just ask all our spies to act dull, so they avoid capture?" suggested Antebon.

"That would work, except that lower intellect brown and black ANTs all work in menial jobs and have no power within the colony," explained Beeutee, justifying her scheme.

"So, we'd only be supplying them with more laborers, and we need someone in a position of power where they would have influence," surmised Antebon. "But can't we selectively breed our brownest ANTs together and get redder offspring?"

"Yes, that's possible." Beeutee slumped. "But it would take many hexades, maybe even hexuries, to achieve a bright enough red to crack the red alphas. And it would take even longer to create a Scarlet, from which they take their leaders."

Antebon could tell that Beeutee had considered all possibilities.

"But what else can we do?" Antebon shrugged as her little one tugged on her hind limb. *There must be something.* She thought back to the evil Rust, suppressing the intelligence of black and brown ANTs.

The Queen looked down. "The answer is pulling your leg." Her heart pounded hard.

Antebon threw her claws in the air. "What, you've been kidding me?"

Beeutee pointed at the nanitic. "No, I mean Clayant. But we'll have to call him Clay." She bit her claw and held her breath.

"What, send over my baby!" Antebon's antennae straightened. "I hope you're joking. You must mean when he comes of age." *He's too young to be a spy.* She couldn't imagine sending one of her babies.

"No, they watch red alphas too closely. We can't just send over a full-grown ANT—everyone would know they are new and therefore a spy." The Queen picked up the tiny nanitic. "He needs to grow up there." She sighed, awaiting her friend's response.

Antebon perked up from her funk. "I know. There must be some wild, tiny red ants we could send."

"No, our constitution forbids us from transforming wild insects." Beeutee shook her head. "Wild ants have evolved away from us so much for the hexennia, and we are not even sure they would survive the process."

"But some must be recently released ones that haven't evolved," Antebon surmised.

"None are that recent as we have no red breeders, and even if there were, how could we tell which are more recent?"

Beeutee gave Antebon a stern look. "We can't take a chance and send one that doesn't transform correctly."

"I see. But I'm not sure I can give Clayant up. We would have to separate him from his sister Antonyx and me." Antebon snatched the tiny nanitic from the Queen, oozing a sticky smell. "I'll have to think about it." She cuddled her youngster. "I need to discuss it with Obsidiant." Her thoughts rapidly vacillated between her love of her offspring and her hatred of Rust. *But how else can we defeat that evil tyrant?*

"Sure, take some time." Beeutee smiled at the young ant and his mother. "But remember, this may be our only chance to get back at Rust." She crossed her wings behind her back.

CHAPTER 31

THE RULERS: MOLDING MINDS

Antalonia (Rudyard's rule, the current president)

RUBY INSTRUCTED BLOOD to stay in the classroom after the class finished. Keegan had trained with Ruby for only two hexays, but as a future moral education teacher and master of socionics, Blood needed more intensive instruction. Ruby could see that Blood had the right temperament for the job. She saw a lot of Rust in him but wanted to ensure her guidance would stick with him and not peel off. Meeting Blood reminded her of an earlier time when Vermillion, Rust, and her had started everything off. Ruby saw it fitting that Rust's second coming would take over as she retired. Yet she wanted to ensure he learned all he could from her.

She wiped the chalk off the blackboard and turned towards Blood. "How did you enjoy your first hexek on the front lines?"

Blood grabbed the pointer off the desk and slammed it into his claws. "Oh, I saw some behaviors that got me riled up." He recalled instances dealing with some insolent brats. *If I had been in charge, they might have tasted this wood.*

Ruby grinned. "You need to be stern, but fair." Ruby took the pointer away from Blood. "Remember, the purpose is to mold minds, not create angry young rebels."

"I like how you get all the pupils to mistrust each other," Blood smirked. "I love the games where we encourage cheating and back-stabbing as the best way to win in the end." He recollected a scene with the youngsters all glaring at each other. *That should keep them all from colluding against authorities.*

Ruby packed up the game boards and shoved them into a closet. "Yes, that's the goal of socionics, to get all the students thinking they can't trust each other."

Blood flashed a wide grin. "But the games inspire fear and loyalty to the leaders and the system." He pondered about his future in the position. *I'm sure I can develop my style by playing such games with the young ANTs and teaching them not to defy me.*

"When they learn to mistrust each other, we encourage them to seek support from authorities." Ruby chuckled. "Then the system becomes their best friend."

"My favorite game was where all the students secretly named two other students they wanted out of the class." Blood laughed. "Then you tallied up the scores, and the winner was the one most other students threw out."

Ruby clapped. "Yes, and if someone was not picked, they had to stand in the corner for the rest of the hexay."

Blood snickered, spewing a thorny stink. "And the other

students got to shoot spitballs at them." He thought back to his school hexays. *I would have loved to spit at all the popular kids in my class, but they don't condition red alphas the same way.*

"Yes, we designed it to encourage the students to be disliked," Ruby noted. "With unpopular students winning and popular students getting derided for being liked."

"These are amazing techniques." Blood bowed before the master. "My father tells me how your efforts helped shape the minds of so many students. I can learn much from you." Again, he pictured himself dominating a class of young students. *You have nothing to worry about.*

"Well, now I have a novel challenge—to pass on what I know to a new master of socionics." Ruby smirked at Blood. "If I fail, it will counter all I've accomplished."

"Remember, the new master, as a future czar, has the most to lose if you fail." Blood winked at Ruby. "So, you couldn't have a more motivated trainee." He conjured up a vision of Rust, Vermillion, and Ruby starting the socionics program. *I'm more like Rust than you could imagine.*

Ruby opened the door and motioned Blood to leave the room. "I don't doubt your motivation, but it is your mind and your manner I must mold."

Blood stepped through the threshold. "It seems molding minds and manners is your forte."

"Yes, shaping behavior is like working clay; you are my final *master*-piece."

~ ~ ~

Blood returned home after his socionics lesson, excited about everything he had learned from Ruby. He enjoyed the hexek immensely and sensed a connection with Ruby, inspiring him to excel. He knew that Rudyard thought the world of Ruby, but he didn't realize that she and Vermillion had started the socionics program and that Rust claw-picked her for the position. In Blood's eyes, anyone with Rust's seal of approval had to be incredible, and he saw in her the same characteristics that appealed to his grandfather hexades ago. He was sorry that she was retiring, but excited to learn from her and take her place when ready.

When Blood got home, his father met him at the front door of the Czar's palace. "How did the socionics lessons go this hexek?"

Blood rolled his eyes. "I am learning how harsh Master Ruby can be."

Rudyard grabbed a cane from its stand and slapped it into his claw. "She's a tough one." Rudyard handed the cane to Blood. "You'll need to be strict, too."

Blood waved the cane like a conductor commanding his orchestra. "Yes, but Ruby taught me subtle ways to coerce the students to follow my directions."

"Yes, I remember creating some games with Ruby when designing the new course curriculum." Rudyard scratched his chin, thinking back. "Many of them involved behavioral manipulation during social interactions."

"And there are video games where they have to fight attacking rebels and defend our leaders and institutions." Blood raised the cane and pretended it was a laser gun, and he was shooting at imaginary targets. "At the highest level, they must reverse an attempted Antunite coup and execute all the traitors to win the game."

Rudyard slapped his claws on his hind legs. "They still use that one? I suggested the plotline for that game."

"Cool!" Blood twirled the cane like a baton and squeezed it into the tight gap between his thorax and abdomen. "I didn't know you were so creative." He imagined his father as a dashing young ANT. *Well, you have Rust's hemolymph, after all.*

"Hey, I wasn't chosen to be Czar for my looks."

"But you *were* Rust's only child." Although he respected his father, he never considered him creative or powerful and saw him as only maintaining all his grandfather had gained.

"Yes, apparently, my mother had fertility issues," replied Rudyard. "Although I heard she had laid eggs several times before my batch."

"So, why didn't they create any other cyborgs?" Blood cragged his brow. "You could have had siblings."

"With earlier eggs, Rust disposed of them because they were not red enough." Rudyard threw his arms in the air. "At some point, my mother said she would only lay one more clutch."

"Why didn't they create more cyborgs from your batch of eggs?" asked Blood. He assumed there would be at least one more aggressive offspring. *You wouldn't have stood a chance.*

"I heard someone released all the nanitics into the wild by mistake," started Rudyard. "My father heard about it and found me at the release site; I hadn't fled like all the others."

"That's why they say you were 'The One that Chose Royalty.'" Blood raised a single claw. "It was a stroke of luck." *I am gratified you continued the family line.* He thought about those that got away. *But your actions were weak. You couldn't even flee when you had a chance.*

"Yes, that's why I insisted on three cyborg heirs. But succession isn't required to be familial." Rudyard chuckled. "Better remember that next time you want to throw me a left-clawed compliment."

"Well, my two brothers are dead, and you wouldn't dare choose someone else." Blood challenged. *I always enjoy this playful banter with my father.* He considered how much his father loved him.

Blood noted that Rudyard paused for a moment and thought he might be grieving his lost offspring.

"Yes, it was many hexs ago, but that's why having three heirs was a smart plan."

"I don't remember my brothers that well. What were they like?" asked Blood. He recollected the broken memories he had of playing with his older brothers. *Sometimes I regret my sudden only child status.*

"Well, we assumed the oldest would succeed me, and I trained him to be a forceful leader from birth." Rudyard paused, lost in thought. "And the younger tried his best to follow the elder's lead, so both were capable, mature young ANTs."

"What caused the fire that killed them?" asked Blood. Though he had blocked the memory from his consciousness, faint impressions from that hexay still haunted his dreams. *Yet their loss was my gain.*

"The investigators said it was an electrical fire, but I sometimes think someone started it intentionally." Rudyard fumed. "But we could not prove it."

"But weren't all the black and brown ANTs under control by then?" Blood asked. He considered how it was his father's role to protect them. *How could you let it happen?*

"Yes, but we detected and executed a few Bilalunan spies several hexs earlier."

"It is possible you missed some?" Blood shrugged. "And they lit the fire?"

"If there were other spies, we never found them, and they

did nothing else," Rudyard concluded. "But fortunately, you left the toxic wing. You were young and untrained as a leader, but you survived."

"So, I guess I was just an afterthought," surmised Blood. He tried, but could not conjure up any feelings about either of his brothers' true sense of character. *But you ended up with the best leader, anyway.*

"Yes, we thought of you as insurance but never expected you'd have to lead."

"So, I had more time to play and lead a normal life," deduced Blood. "At least when I was very young."

"Yes, but when you were the only one left, we gave you a crash course in leadership," explained Rudyard. "Fortunately, you caught on quickly."

"You were stuck with me, the only survivor." Blood looked down. "And the circumstances took Mom away from us." He recalled how much he blamed Rudyard for his mother's death. *I can't believe you couldn't help her.*

"Despite all the tragedy, you were stronger than I expected." Rudyard beamed. "You have a lot of your grandfather in you—a born leader."

"So, I survived and thrived. And now you should go with the survivor, not some outsider." He pushed aside the emotions from his past. *I'll try to re-trigger the repartee.*

"We'll see how competent you are as the master of socionics." Rudyard laughed. "Do a poor job, and my advisors might pressure me to look elsewhere. But do a stellar job, and I'll have no choice."

"You still think you have to push me to become a leader?" Blood scoffed.

Rudyard cracked a wide smile. "There are born leaders,

those that follow the leader, and those born to follow after the leader."

"You're using socionics on me now?" Blood twirled the cane again and holstered it. "You always have."

Rudyard roared, releasing a syrupy stink. "Yes, and I've been a superb role model."

CHAPTER 32

THE NEW SPIES: ANTI-SOCIONICS

Antalonia (Rudyard's rule, the current president)

ALTHOUGH MOST STUDENTS had school every hexay, as red alphas, Rose and Jasper got one hexay off each hexek. They could leave the school grounds and explore the rest of the colony with their friends, which they could possess. Rose and Jasper mostly stuck together and did not have other close friends. As bloom room neighbors, it surprised no one when Rose and Jasper became best buddies and spent considerable time together. After their second hexek of classes, Rose and Jasper visited Clay as they shared the same hexay off. They told no one about Clay and ensured no one followed them when they traveled to his place.

Clay offered them some honey and poured himself some

strong sap. "Even though you are alphas, I know you never get this in school." He held the bowl close to each of them. "Take some. Use your claws—don't be shy."

Jasper dipped his claw in the bowl, then licked it. "This stuff is amazing! How come I never heard of it before?"

"They don't make it on Bilaluna." Clay shrugged. "It's banned within the constitution."

Rose tried some, too. "This is tasty! Why would they ban it?" She struggled to remember her brief time on Bilaluna. *It doesn't make sense.*

Clay thought for a moment. "I believe the original settlers feared that greed for honey was an evil that destroyed Poo-ponic and forced them all to escape to Bilaluna."

Jasper took another dollop. "I love this. I know why it could cause problems. Insectoids would fight over it."

Clay nodded. "Yes, but mostly ANTs couldn't get enough." He raised his glass. "I prefer this."

Rose furrowed her brow. "How come honey is available here?" She faintly recalled her great-grandmother's hatred of her foe. *I bet Rust had something to do with it.*

Clay downed his glass. "Czar Rust brought it back because he loved everything Antilla loved."

Jasper raised his claws. "Who's Antilla?"

Clay explained Antilla was the emperor when Poo-ponic declined. He told Rose and Jasper how Antilla's society treasured honey, and it was not only a tasty treat, but was also their currency. He explained the greed ANTs had for honey and how they could never get enough. They destroyed the environment as they continued to over-produce it, despite the climate crisis threatening their world.

Rose vented a scalding scent. "And Czar Rust brought it

back so that he could destroy the planet again?" Her diluted memories flooded back. *My great-grandmother hated Rust, and so do I.*

Clay shook his head. "Because it's no longer currency, and we eat other foods like termites and worms, it hasn't created the same problems."

Jasper took a large scoop from the bowl. "That's good because we really shouldn't ban it. It's the best."

Clay laughed and put the bowl back in the cupboard. "Now, let's discuss anti-socionics."

Jasper cocked his head. "Auntie, who?"

Clay roared, "You've had too much honey, Jasper. I mean countermeasures to socionics."

Jasper blushed. "Oh, right."

Rose raised a claw. "I don't think our teachers use much socionics." She scanned her brain for any evidence of attempted coercion. *Or maybe I'm just naïve.*

Clay moved his chair closer to them. "As red alphas, you two have few restrictions, and they won't pit you against your classmates. But there's always socionics—it's just subtle."

Jasper interjected, "I'm with Rose. I didn't notice anything."

Clay jumped in. "Are there sayings posted around the classroom? Do you play video games where you must kill rebels?"

Jasper's ommatidia rattled. "Yeah, they're fun."

Clay continued, "Do the bad guys have black shells?"

Rose jumped up. "Yeah, sometimes it is hard to tell, but they flash their black thoraxes when they come in for the kill." Her eyes lit up. *So that's how they brainwash us.*

"And what are the sayings on the walls?" asked Clay.

Rose tapped her temples. "One of them says: 'healthy

aggression trumps everything,' I think." She pictured the poster in her mind's eye.

Jasper added, "I remember one that says: 'Trickery reins unruly empathy' or something like that."

"And is the first letter of each word uppercase or a different color?" asked Clay.

Rose replied, "Yes, all the other letters are black, but the first letter is bigger, uppercase, and red." Her fuzzy vision of the sign became focused. *I'm surprised Clay can describe it so well.*

"So, what does it spell if you put together only the first letters?" Clay inquired.

Rose thought briefly, "HATE." Her hemolymph grew warm.

Jasper spat out, "TRUE."

"So, it's a mixed message to convince you that to hate is virtuous and that the truth is trickery." Clay twisted himself like a pretzel. "That's socionics."

"Wow, I didn't even realize," concluded Jasper.

"That's the point," said Clay.

Rose rubbed her chin. "If we don't know it's going on, how can we counter it?" She imagined herself as a broken, brainwashed child. *As a spy, I need to know.*

Clay perked up. "Take AIM against it. 'Assume' it's going on and do your best to 'Ignore' it. And most of all, remember the 'Morals' of your roots."

Rose thought hard. "So, if we're aware it's going on, we'll recognize it, and we can ignore the signs around the classroom. But I don't know what you mean by morals of our roots." She considered their little time on Bilaluna, which she could scarcely remember. *It isn't comforting, but I trust Clay.*

Clay started slowly. "You both began your lives on Bilaluna.

And as soon as you hatched, your mother spoke to you. And when we determined you were chameleants, you had others come to speak to you around the clock, even while you slept."

Jasper jumped up from his chair. "Yes, I remember someone outside my cocoon always reading poetry or singing songs. It was nice."

Clay continued, "These were your parents, family members, and Bilaluna moralists teaching you right from wrong. You received extra doses of it since we knew you'd be coming here."

Rose wafted a breezy bouquet. "It surprised me how much I knew about the world before I emerged from my cocoon."

Clay explained that because of their early instruction on Bilaluna, Rose and Jasper knew the correct meaning of hate and true or love and false. He pointed out that the other Antalone students missed this pupal training and were more vulnerable to social manipulation. Clay described how Antalone students didn't recognize the deception of falsehoods, the glorification of hate, or the perversion of truth and love. He told them they had an excellent moral base and could resist the twisted messages and corruption that socionics breed. Rose and Jasper's souls would not be tainted if they recognized what was happening and remembered their roots.

Rose smirked. "I'm sure you'll help us stay on track."

Clay patted both Rose and Jasper on the back. "As long as I'm still here to coach you."

"You're not going anywhere, are you?" asked Rose. *You've got me worried.*

"No, but a spy's life is always at risk," Clay warned. "If anything happens to me, seek out Darci."

"Who's Darci?" queried Jasper.

"She's the spy that got me into the breeding hall and taught me how to combat socionics." Clay paused and thought back. "She is getting older, but is still an incredible resource. She even helped my mother, Antebon, get back at Czar Rust."

"What did Great-Grandma do to Rust?" asked Jasper.

"It's a long story." Clay laughed. "I'll tell you another time."

CHAPTER 33

THE REFUGEES AND OLD SPIES: HATCH A PLAN

Bilaluna (Beeutee's reign, two rulers in the past)

ANTEBON LEFT HER meeting with Queen Beeutee distraught over the idea of sending one of her nanitics to Antalonia. However, she also committed herself to the cause of overthrowing Rust's rule. She convinced herself that she would need to release most of her developing nanitics into the wilds. But Clay would become a cyborg, though, in another world. She gave Clay a crash course on everything she knew about the evil Rust and all that was good about Bilaluna. Antebon strived to impart on Clay her zeal to take down the Antalone society and return Intopia to its former glory. Queen Beeutee assured Antebon that she was communicating with the remaining spy on the planet. The spy would meet Clay and arrange for him to enter the breeding halls and go through his transformation to a red alpha cyborg.

Antalonia (Rust's rule, one president in the past)

Fortunately, the Antalone colony paid little attention to the lives of black beta ANTs, and Darci could blend into the society if she continued to play dim-witted. Although she needed to pretend she was stupid, Darci was far from it. She was a well-trained fighter and was loyal to the cause. Darci suggested and implemented a plan the Queen approved. The first step was to determine which black ANTs were part of the sanitation team at the breeding halls and befriend the group's dullest one. The second step was eliminating and replacing a janitor at the breeding hall. The third step was to substitute Clay for a nanitic selected for transformation.

Darci scouted the breeding halls and tailed each sanitation staff member as they walked home. Janitors at the breeding halls were easy to identify, as they were all black betas, and they wore a badge with a picture of a broom on it and a depiction of a cluster of ant eggs, which was a symbol for the breeding halls. Because of their tiny brain sizes, black beta ANTs were often dull and sometimes needed help to find their way around. The badges allowed red ANTs to assist the black betas, directing them to the breeding halls when required.

During her surveillance, Darci noticed that one of the sanitation staff at the breeding halls often had difficulty finding her way to the breeding hall as she reported for her overnight shift. One night, when the worker was far off track, she asked the flustered black beta if she was lost. Darci discovered the ANT was a new employee at the breeding halls and had not yet memorized the best route to work. Darci befriended her and helped her find the breeding halls, telling the sanitation worker that she worked at the school next door. When asked about her badge, Darci told her new friend Pepper it was her hexay off. She offered to meet her each evening and walk with her to work until Pepper knew her way.

🐜 🐜 🐜

Worried that the lack of a badge might blow her cover, Darci broke into the high school next to the breeding halls late at night. She wandered through the building looking for the janitors' locker room, which she assumed was in the basement. Darci found the locker room and desperately searched for a badge that might have been left behind by one of the sanitation workers. Before giving up, she noticed one unlocked locker. Her hope was dashed when Darci opened the locker and discovered it was empty. She slammed the locker door shut. As she lamented the loud bang from the metal cabinet, Darci heard pod steps. She turned around and saw a young male black beta ANT with a mop in claw.

The school's overnight janitor spoke, holding the mop menacingly, "What you doin' here?"

Darci thought quickly. "I'm new here and came for orienting this morning." She pointed to the locker. "I got this cubby."

The night janitor lowered his mop and laughed. "The one with the loud clanging door. That's always what's left for newbies." He shrugged. "But why you here now?"

Darci used the time while he spoke to devise an excuse. "Silly me, I forgot my badge." She reflected hard on her spy training to remain calm and think on her pods. *I must still my racing heart.* "My trainer said she'd leave it here. So, I come for it."

The janitor's eyes grew wide. "How you get in?"

"Don't know if you're here, but I try anyway." Darci smiled nervously. "I knocked at front, but no answer. Then I find back unlocked." *This excuse better work, or I'll lose everything.* She considered her options for escape if he didn't buy her story.

"Oh, dang! I did it again." The janitor banged a claw on his head. "Promise you no tell. I'll get fired for sure if the boss finds out."

"Yeah, no problem," replied Darci. She breathed deeply. *He's buying my story.*

"You get it?"

"What? Oh, my badge." Darci raised two claws in the air. "No, I guess she forgot to leave it."

"Ain't we all mindless black betas?" The night janitor guffawed. "I think I got one in my locker."

Darci sighed, emanating a bright bouquet. "Oh, thanks. You a kind un."

The janitor laughed harder. "That's what they say about us. Forgetful, but kind. Dull, like when moon don't shine."

The janitor opened his locker and found three badges hanging on a hook. "They give me lots. Cause I'm ever losin' mine."

Darci patted the janitor on the shoulder. "I better bring it ta-morrow." She laughed and walked out of the locker room.

Darci escorted her new friend Pepper to the breeding hall the next evening and told her she would meet her to walk back to the black beta district together in the morning. She gave her pointers about how to remember markers she could use to help her find her way. She taught her a mnemonic, 'Robin likes stringy red licorice and sugar rockets,' so she would remember whether to turn left, right or go straight at the intersections along her walk to work.

Grateful for her help, Pepper invited Darci inside her nest for some honey after her shift. Darci was excited to join her as she had never tasted honey before, although she did not let on.

Darci responded to the invitation. "That's very nice. I'd love to."

"Well, in you get." Pepper motioned her through the doorway. "It's the least I can do to thank ya back. I get you honey." She brought some honey and two bowls from her cupboard and poured some into each bowl.

Darci watched as Pepper dipped her claws into the bowl and then licked them off, and she then did the same. "This is darn yummy honey, sis." She considered her next steps and what she needed to do to Pepper. *I like Pepper. So, I regret what I must do.*

"It's fresh. I get it last morn," replied Pepper.

"Pepper," Darci started. "When I waited for you at the breeding hall, your boss said you not working out." She shrugged. "He wants to fire you." She felt sorry for Pepper. *I'm sorry, but I must start my sting.*

Tears welled up in Pepper's eyes. "Can't be! I just begin."

"He said you forget which aisles you do, and breeding hall need be extra clean," Darci misled Pepper. "I tell him I'm unhappy at my job."

"Really? You not like it?" asked Pepper.

"He handed me a mop and told me what to do." Darci swayed her forelimbs back and forth. "He said he liked my moves, and we could swap." *I hope that Pepper buys my story.* She briefly considered the alternative. *Else, I'll have to switch to Plan B, which is much messier.*

"Swap?"

Darci nodded. "Yeah, you work school, and I work breeding halls." Her heart pounded as she knew her response was vital. *It's the moment of truth, although nothing about it is true.*

Pepper wiped the tears off her face. "You kiddin'?"

Darci shook her head. "No, for real. The school job's much easier." She sighed hard. *Super—my ruse is working.*

"I don't believe it." Pepper jumped up. "You do that for me?"

"Yeah, it's worth it. I get delicious honey." Darci dipped in three claws and licked them off with a sticky smile. "Here, you have my badge. And I get yours." She winked at Pepper. "I introduce you to the night sweeper. He's nice and funny, and you'll like him." She sighed.

᙭ ᙭ ᙭

The next evening, Darci brought Pepper to the school and entered the unlocked back door. Then she called out to the night sanitation worker.

The janitor laughed when he saw her. "You get in by the back again?"

"Hey, me no tell!" Darci chortled. "This is Pepper. We swap jobs." Again, her heart throbbed. *This better work.*

"No kidding? But it happens lots." The janitor smiled at Pepper, to whom he took an instant liking.

Darci smiled and swayed her forelimbs back and forth. "Boss said to bring her round tonight and you can show her the ropes." Her hemolymph pressure fell. *He's bought my story.*

"Well, the ropes on me mop are wet and ready to dance." He wiggled his hips a little and laughed.

"You're funny." Pepper beamed back at the janitor. "I like you."

"Okay, I'll get you a mop, and she can dance with my guy." The janitor flashed his crooked pincers.

Pepper sparkled her ommatidia. "Yeah, we dance."

"I must get to breeding halls." Darci interjected, "You two have a nice dance."

Pepper's eyes never left the janitor as she spoke. "Great swap, thanks."

🐜 🐜 🐜

Darci had arranged with Queen Beeutee that Antebon send her nanitic through the wormhole at the peak hexour of lunar winds a few evenings later. On the appointed evening, Darci left the breeding halls and rushed to the crater, arriving just before Clay exited the wormhole. They were fortunate that the winds picked up for a few hexours after her shift, so the radiation was cleared at the rendezvous time. Clay was a little late since Antebon wanted to tell him as much as she could about his new planet and kept remembering things at the last moment. Perhaps she was stalling, so she'd have more time with him. However, it worked out, since Darci had underestimated the time needed to get there and was equally tardy.

Darci spoke to Clay briefly, before slipping him into her bag. "You are a red one, aren't you? I see why they call you Clay. You'll fit right in with the red alphas." She held up an open claw. "I'll get you into an incubator tonight, and they'll start your transformation in the morning. From now on, you are an Antalone, and you'll soon be a cyborg." She watched Clay nod, and she placed him in her unzipped bag. "Once you start school, I'll meet you and give you further instructions. Come to the recreation center on your first hexay off." Darci winked before zipping up the bag, discharging a firm fragrance. "I'll be the cleaner there."

CHAPTER 34

THE BREEDERS: A NEW BREED MASTER

Antalonia (Rudyard's rule, the current president)

SIX HEXS PASSED since Keegan began training as the breed master's apprentice, and Vermillion decided he was ready to take over the reins. By this time, Ruby had long since retired, and Blood had been the master of socionics for five hexs. Blood rotated between classes of red, brown, and black alpha and beta ANTs, teaching the moral education classes to all these groups, interspersed with other courses taught by their regular teachers. He also supervised an assistant who spent time in the red, brown, and black chi classrooms, ensuring that the BUGants and other hybrids got their dose of socionics. But now, it was Keegan's time to step up and take over as breed master, as Vermillion was retiring.

Keegan arranged a small party with Vermillion, Blood, Clay, Blood's assistant, a few breeders working the afternoon shift, and one of the teachers on break. "Welcome, everyone," Keegan began. "I think you all know why we are here. It's hard to believe, but this is Breed Master Vermillion's last hexay in the breeding halls." He realized his long-term goals were about to be realized. *I'm excited to take over the reins.*

"Yes, you will finally see the last of me." Vermillion laughed.

Blood interjected. "So, how long have you worked here?"

Vermillion thought for a moment. "It's been over a hexury." He spun around slowly with his forelimbs stretched wide. "I was here when this all started 50 hexs ago."

"Well, it's about time you scram and let others take over." Keegan laughed and patted Vermillion on the back. He recalled all the good times he had while training with the master. *I'm going to miss this guy a lot.*

Vermillion guffawed. "Yes, and I fully expect I am leaving the place in capable claws." He wrapped two of his forelimbs around his former trainees. "Keegan will be a superb breed master, and Blood has already distinguished himself as a great and terrible master of socionics."

"Terrible?" Blood puzzled.

"No, not terrible, terrifying—at least that's what some students say. And that's a great thing." Vermillion smirked. "A master of socionics should be feared."

"Yes, Blood is doing a super job." Keegan patted him on the shoulder. "Master Vermillion was smart to get you started first." Keegan smiled. "It's going to make my job so much easier."

Clay stepped forward. "At least until I retire, at the end of the hexury."

Keegan laughed. "Clay, you'll never retire. You love your

job too much." He pictured Clay and himself working through any problems in the breeding halls. *I foresee a delightful working environment with my two supportive colleagues.*

Clay snickered. "We'll see. I must determine how the new breed master works out."

Vermillion straightened his antennae to draw attention to himself. "All kidding aside, a lot of serious work gets done here." He looked over at Clay. "I should have included our amazing chief of bionics in my earlier praising. The smooth operation of our whole colony depends on what we do here. And I leave knowing that the work will be supervised by three of the best. Our breeders' and teachers' skills and diligence are a tribute to their management."

Keegan stepped forward. "Thank you, Vermillion, for your praise and hexades of service. Everyone in this room and all those working in the halls and schools have benefited from your leadership. And we wish you all the best in your retirement." Keegan pointed to a table with several glasses and a bottle of strong sap of the finest vintage, expelling a festal fragrance. "Now enough with the formalities—let's party."

As the senior supervisor, Clay stepped forward while Masters Vermillion and Blood handed full glasses to everyone. "One last formality, a toast to the new Breed Master, Keegan."

All in the room raised their glasses and spoke in unison, "To Master Keegan."

※ ※ ※

Shortly after Vermillion's retirement, Keegan asked Clay into his office for his advice. He debated whether to change the program to reverse some of the more egregious controls on the black and brown ANTs. He trusted Clay's judgment and wanted his perspective. The two of them were close enough that Keegan didn't worry that Clay might be shaken by his ideas. He also sensed that Clay shared his concerns about the color inequalities, though he did not find it that odd. He detected no serious insubordination that would require reprimand or reporting to the Czar.

"Clay, I wanted to ask your opinion on some possible new directions I have been considering with the breeding program," Keegan started with a frown.

"Sure, boss. You're in charge now," Clay replied. "What are you thinking about?"

"I am not comfortable reducing black ANTs' brain sizes so much." Keegan made a face like he bit into a lemon. "Do you think it would mess things up too much if we increased the volume to the level of the browns?" He held his breath.

Clay squirmed a little, worried that Keegan might just be testing his loyalty to the program. "Well, the system works well the way it is, and we wouldn't want black ANTs craving more challenging positions."

"You might be right, but they could aspire for a little more." Keegan scratched his head. "Or at least they wouldn't get lost all the time coming to work." His pulse sped up. *Am I going too far?*

"It's your call, Keegan." Clay rubbed his claws together. "I can do whatever you ask me to."

"Okay, let's increase the brain sizes of both black and brown ANTs by 50%," Keegan suggested. He slowly realized that he was now in charge and could call the shots. *I don't need Clay's permission, do I?* "That way, they'll each do better, but still know their place."

"Sure, and the browns will still be less intelligent than red ANTs," Clay surmised. "But don't we need Rudyard's approval?"

"Don't worry about Rudyard." Keegan looked towards the palace. "I'll let him know after we get it going and we see everything is still running smoothly." He sported confidence he didn't expect as a new boss. *I'm grateful for Clay's support.*

"It's your call." Clay smiled. "Just let me know when to start."

"Start immediately, but don't tell the other breeders and prepare the growth factors yourself," Keegan insisted. "I want to keep this quiet until we see how it goes."

"Yes, of course." Clay winked. "You can trust me." Though Clay omitted to tell Keegan that he had already increased the brain sizes of black and brown ANTs to that of reds. Yet no one had discovered it because of some additional genetic modifications he had implemented.

"Perfect." Keegan turned and looked at the books on his shelf. "And what do you think about vitamin S?" He continued to lean on Clay to forge a good boss/subordinate relationship and to forward his agenda. *Perhaps I can push it further.*

"Well, if you want them to be smarter, we could increase the dose," Clay replied.

Keegan did a double-take. He suddenly remembered what Vermillion told him about leaders-only information. *I forgot Clay doesn't know what vitamin S does.* "Maybe increasing their brain sizes will be enough for now." He sighed.

Clay only said, "If you say so."

"Okay, you know what to do." *I must change track to defuse the vitamin S issue.* "Now, can you tell me what you know about the progress of those two red alphas, Rose and Jasper?"

"Rose and Jasper, yes, I remember them." Clay tapped his

temples. "They set the record for completing physio in the shortest time. After that, I sent them off to low school, and they've been there for a few hexs now."

"Has Blood mentioned them at all?" He remembered how he intended to support them. *Have they excelled as I expected?*

"Nothing about Jasper." Clay rolled his eyes. "But he's always going on about Rose."

Keegan stood erect. "That's a little odd." His red shell turned a little green. *He can be such a creep sometimes.*

"He is her moral education teacher, so he's the one to ask about her progress." Clay turned away. "She's still young, but it seems she's Blood's master's pet. I'm not surprised, though, since she's a bright one and has the reddest shell."

"Yes, I know Blood adores redness, and Rose's shell impressed him from hexay one." Keegan looked Clay straight in the eyes. "Tell me if you see or learn about anything inappropriate. He may be royalty, but I don't want him doing anything improper with a young female." Keegan vented a fiery fragrance.

"I only know what he tells me." Clay matched Keegan's gaze. "But you'll be the first to know if he tells me something improper or if I hear anything."

"Thank you. I appreciate it." Keegan smiled. "Rose and Jasper were the first two nanitics I helped transform, so I feel very responsible for their wellbeing."

CHAPTER 35

THE RULERS:
LEADERS IN TRAINING

Antalonia (Rudyard's rule, the current president)

BLOOD HAD BEEN the master of socionics for almost two hexades, and Keegan was the breed master for a hexade when Rose and Jasper were about to enter high school. When they did, the breeders needed to make important decisions about their futures. As the master of socionics, Blood had taught the two students in their moral education classes for hexs and had followed their progress closely. He continued to be intensely interested in Rose, but never misbehaved. Blood now lived in his own palatial nest but visited his father Rudyard often. Blood discussed Rose and Jasper with the Czar during one of these visits.

Rudyard greeted Blood on this visit. "Blood, my son, visit

more often." He hugged him. "Now that you've proven your-self as the master of socionics, I need to train you further to succeed me when it's time. I can tell my hexths are numbered."

"Oh, so you're not going to bump me off and find another Czar to be." Blood laughed.

"There was never any question about that," Rudyard snorted.

Blood stood tall. "Well, I'm glad to hear that." He pictured himself taking over to rule the realm. *Czar Blood! It's getting so close I can taste it. But maybe not Blood-the-Stud.*

Rudyard shook himself. "I already have some royal busi-ness for which I need your advice."

Blood beamed. "Whatever I can do to help. I will." *Royal business, you say?* He cherished the idea of getting a taste of such duties.

"As the master of socionics, I am sure you get to know all our students well."

"Yes, of course," replied Blood.

"You also know that every few hexs, we pick a couple of high school-age red alphas for the scarlet program." Rudyard shined his shell. "This program is essential to maintain the ranks of our leaders. So, I see it as one of my most important tasks."

"As it should be," responded Blood. His thoughts turned to Rose and Jasper. *I think I know where this is going, but I won't let on.*

"Could you provide me with a recommendation for two students entering high school you think would succeed in the scarlet program?"

"I have recognized some students that have risen above the others." Blood smirked.

"Do you need time to whittle them down to the top two?" asked Rudyard.

"Actually, no. There are a few talented students, but two are outstanding, and I wouldn't hesitate to endorse them." He got a warm feeling thinking of a beautiful red flower. *Especially Rose—I want her promoted.*

"What are their names?" Rudyard picked up a pen and note-roll.

"There's a young female named Rose who's as sharp as a bee's stinger and a real red beauty." Blood smirked. "She is so radiant red you can see yourself reflected in her shell. She'll excel at whatever role we give her."

"And the other?"

"A young male called Jasper. He's almost as red as Rose. His science teacher says he's as bright as a firefly, and she's never had a student with such an excellent memory and creative mind." Blood thought for a moment. "I remember they went through their cyborg transformation together, and Clay did it while Keegan was training with him." He smiled, thinking back to the first hexays of his socionics training.

"That explains it. Clay showed off to Keegan and did his best with the two." Rudyard snorted. "Vermillion told me the red alphas Clay breeds and transforms always turn out the best, and he guessed he gave them extra nutrients."

"I don't know about that, but it makes sense. These two were far ahead of the other students from the start." Blood thought back. "In their first few moral education classes, it was like they already knew what socionics was all about." His heart pulsated, awaiting his response. *I hope he agrees.*

"You've convinced me, son. We need to bring students like

this on board as Scarlets. We want them to work with us. You never want the smartest ones out of your sight."

"I've been watching Rose. It's hard to keep your eyes off her," Blood admitted.

Rudyard flashed a cheeky grin. "Give her a few more hexs, and she could be a breeder for a leader."

Blood emitted a spindly scent. "I've already thought about that." His hemolymph warmed. *More often than I'll admit.*

~ ~ ~

Rose and Jasper had the hexay off following their convocation and were taking a short-cut through a meadow towards Clay's nest. They couldn't contain their excitement about graduating. They had worked hard during their low school hexs, and their efforts paid off. Most of their teachers, including Blood, were impressed with their intellect and captivated by their bright red shells. Both Rose and Jasper recognized that Antalones highly valued their redness.

Rose shined her thorax. "One thing I learned at school is everyone is obsessed with how red they look."

"It's funny." Jasper scratched his head. "You're the reddest in the class, yet are not so concerned."

"Maybe we should be." Rose looked at herself reflected in a pond they were skirting. "If we want to be Scarlets, we need to be as red as we can be."

"You're right." Jasper nudged Rose aside so he could look at himself. "Have you noticed the reddest ANTs always get the highest grades?"

"It's because the teachers give us the most attention," Rose started. "They want us to succeed."

"Then we should figure out ways to give them more of what they want," replied Jasper.

Rose frowned. "What more can we do?"

"I know." Jasper scratched his head. "Remember how we used biofeedback during our physio? Maybe we could use it to enhance our chameleon skills."

"That's brilliant." Rose thought for a moment, while surveying their surroundings. "Wait, when I did my project on the Earth bird called the cardinal, I learned they get so red because they eat lots of cherries and red berries." She grabbed some fruit from a cherry tree next to the pond. "We might get redder if we eat more of these."

"Great idea. I expect eating cherries increases the levels of porphyrin and carotenoid in their feathers." Jasper gave Rose a high-six. "It should work for our exoskeletons, too."

"You once said we make a great team." Rose popped a cherry in her mouth and jokingly shoved Jasper, so he almost fell in the pond. "You were right, and we'll be Scarlets before you know it."

Jasper snatched a cherry from Rose and pelted it into her thorax; then he pointed at her image in the pond. "Hey, look, you're redder already."

When they got to his place, Clay greeted the two at the door, a little tipsy from celebrating early but sober enough. "Welcome, graduates. You must be excited to be entering high school." He remembered back to the slough where he found the two nanitics. *I'm so proud.*

"Absolutely," exclaimed Jasper. "I got the top math and science prize, and Rose was the best student overall?"

"You guys are amazing. Rose, your valedictory speech was the best I've ever heard." Clay beamed.

"I was very nervous but proud of myself." She pulled the royal envelope out of her pouch and handed it to Clay. "And we got this letter from the palace."

"I know. Blood told me but made me promise I wouldn't tell anyone." His limbs twitched. "Keegan was excited to endorse you, having followed you throughout your schooling." Clay remembered how sassy Rose was during their first physio session. *You've charmed these guys even more than I expected.*

Jasper jumped up and down. "We did it. Not only alphas but Scarlets."

"Yes, you achieved our goal. You're the first chameleants to become Scarlets." Clay extended his claw to the youngsters. *My hexade-long plan is finally coming to fruition.* He remembered how disappointed he was when the leaders didn't appoint him a Scarlet. Yet he was thrilled now. *Sometimes things happen for a reason.*

Rose shunned his claw and gave Clay a big hug. "I couldn't be happier. And thanks for all your help."

"Just remember, you're only into the scarlet *program*," Clay cautioned. "You must work hard, keep up your grades, and graduate to become Scarlets." He threw his forelimbs into the air. "But you're almost there." His heart swelled.

Beewish was ecstatic when she learned the news. Their selection as red alphas didn't surprise her, but she never expected them to become Scarlets. As Scarlets, these two young spies could set the wheels in motion for the revolution her mother Beeutee and Rose and Jasper's great-grandmother Antebon had envisioned so long ago. Antalonia could be free again, and their evil masters would no longer enslave Antunites. Beewish urged Clay to start his long-term scheme's ultimate steps and ensure Rose and Jasper succeeded in their scarlet programs. But she cautioned Clay the revolutionary movement would have to wait until the two Scarlets became established in their leaders' positions.

Rose released Clay from the hug and looked into his eyes. "Did they consider you for the scarlet program? You became chief of bionics, after all."

"It was hexades ago when I was starting high school." He thought back to his youth. *It seems like hexuries to me.* "Vermillion told me I was an alternate and would be a substitute Scarlet if one of the chosen two turned it down or flunked out." He rolled his eyes. "It didn't happen, but I got all the training."

Jasper interjected, "That's fantastic and probably why you got your current position."

"Yes, as an alternate, I followed along with the scarlet curriculum in case anything happened to the selected ones," responded Clay, smiling. *I remember meeting all the challenges thrown at me.* He recalled being a better student, but their parents supported the other two.

"I guess nothing did, and the two Scarlets graduated," surmised Rose.

"They did. And one of my fellow students was being geared for bionics chief, even though I scored much higher in our genetic engineering class." He exhaled.

"So, what happened?" asked Jasper.

"After graduation, I heard he got the black measles or something." Clay cracked a wide smile. "Anyway, the black spots never went away." He snickered. "And you can't have a Scarlet marred with black spots." *This recollection is making me giddy.* He felt vindicated as the student robbed of his rightful selection.

"So, you got to be chief of bionics?" Rose inquired.

"Yes, but since it was after graduation, they couldn't go back and make me a Scarlet." Clay sighed and poured himself some more strong sap.

Jasper looked mournfully at Clay. "That must have been disappointing."

"It was," Clay started. "But I now realize it was the best thing for our goal." His hemolymph warmed.

Rose creased her brow. "Why is that?"

Clay smiled, discharging a sprightly scent. "Because I still became chief of bionics." His smile shifted to a wry grin. "But I could do the job under the radar, and the leaders largely ignored me and let me do my business." He was gratified that this allowed him to cultivate Rose and Jasper. *The spy in me allows me to focus on my lifelong task, not petty status symbols.*

Jasper said, "We're glad you can spend so much time with us."

Clay smiled. "I often see you during leaders' meetings, as they don't invite me." He considered it as his way to retaliate for being left out. *It reinforces my loyalty to Bilaluna.*

Rose beamed, letting her black shell shine through for a moment. Clay spread his forelimbs wide, inviting his two young comrades in for a group hug. "Be careful you don't flash anyone else, Rose."

THE REFUGEES AND OLD SPIES: ANTEBON TURNS RED

Bilaluna (Beeutee's reign, two rulers in the past)

ANTEBON MET WITH Clay's twin sister Antonyx several hexays after the daughter laid her first eggs. Antebon was excited about becoming a grandmother and visited as the larvae metamorphosed into pupae. Antebon and Antonyx were close ever since Clay needed to leave for his Antalone mission when the twins were still nanitics. Although ANTs are not too family-oriented, black ANTs appreciated familial attachment more than red ANTs. Bilalunans valued family life to a greater extent, as they knew these bonds would fortify the support of insectism.

They knew a strong love of family encouraged altruistic ideals that could spread to others of all insect species.

Antebon vibrated. "Antonyx, this is so exciting! Do you think they'll be chameleants like you and Clay?"

Antonyx shrugged. "I don't know. I guess we'll see soon enough."

Antebon pointed down at the cocoons. "Here's one coming now; look, it's black at the moment." She shivered as she waited. *I'm not sure what I'm hoping for.*

Antonyx pointed at another. "This one's black too. Wait, it changed to brown, and now red. It's definitely a chameleant."

Antebon pointed back at the first one. "That one's still black. I guess it's not a chameleant—unless it's just slow to change." Her heart pounded, wanting but waffling. *Beeutee wants more chameleants, but do I?*

Antonyx raised her claws. "I think you can only tell when you watch them for a while."

Antebon pointed at another one. "It's funny how they randomly switch colors. It's not like they need to hide or anything." She considered the difficult life as a spy far from home. *I can't decide what's better.*

"Must be a way of developing their range," surmised Antonyx. "I know if I don't change myself regularly, it gets harder to change colors."

Antebon shrugged. "I don't think I ever asked you or Clay how you do it."

"Do what?" asked Antonyx.

"Change colors," replied Antebon. She entertained an alternate strategy. *I wish I could turn my shell red, and then I could go instead of my descendants.*

"I don't know what Clay does, but I imagine I'm sitting on

a giant apple, tree bark, or some cooled black lava." Antonyx thought for a moment. "The nuclear blast's clouds irradiated you. Maybe you can change your colors, too."

"No, that's just something that happens to my offspring." Antebon pointed to the eggs. "Another one hatched." She decided it was a bad idea after all. *I need to get her off this topic—I'll just be disappointed.*

"How do you know if you don't try?" Antonyx pressed.

"To change color? No." She shuddered briefly.

Antonyx nudged her mother. "Try it. Maybe it'll work."

"I am not very good at imagining stuff." Antebon tapped her temples. "And I don't think it'll work, anyway." Her thoughts turned to Rust and how to kill him. *Yet, I've dreamed of it from time to time.*

Antonyx grabbed her mother's claw. "There's a strawberry field just over there. As we stand within it, imagine yourself blending in."

Antebon pointed back to the nest. "But what about your pupae?" She tried to detract. *I don't want to fail.*

"There's thousands." Antonyx raised her shoulders. "You think I am watching every single one? They're not going anywhere till they come out of their new cocoons. It may take one to two hexeks."

"Okay, but it won't work," Antebon surmised. Curiosity took her over. *I'll try just this once.*

When they got to the strawberry field, Antonyx instructed her mother. "Cover your eyes and just imagine yourself blending into the background."

"This is silly." Antebon sighed. "I'm not a chameleant; I would know by now." Her fear of failure intensified. *But wow, if it works.*

Antonyx placed her claws on her mother's shoulders. "Take deep breaths, relax, and let the redness take you."

Antebon relaxed and inhaled and exhaled slowly. After two hexutes, she lamented. "It's no use." *I don't have it in me.*

Antonyx chortled. "Uncover your eyes."

Antebon exuded a shrill smell. "Oh, my! I'm redder than hot lava."

Antonyx guffawed. "See, I told you, ma."

Antebon began hyperventilating and fled from the strawberry field. "I have to see our Queen."

"Whatever for?"

"I want to go to Antalonia to see Clay and get Rust." Antebon's hemolymph boiled.

"You must practice first and see how long you can hold it," urged Antonyx.

"I will." Antebon stroked her daughter's forelimb. "But I know what to imagine to turn myself red." She smiled coyly. An image came to her in the strawberry field and etched itself in her brain.

"What?"

"That dirty rotten red ANT Czar Rust dead on the floor." Antebon's eyes went blank. "I imagined standing on his burning red corpse while we stood in the strawberry field." Her shell reddened brighter than Clay's, more brilliant than Rust's, and she shone like a beacon while she spoke. *Beeutee better let me go.* "When I'm done with him, Rust-the-Robust will return to dust."

Antalonia (Rust's rule, one president in the past)

Beeutee arranged for Darci to meet Antebon after she transited through the wormhole to Antalonia. Darci had been tracking Rust's movements since she finished her assignment setting up

Clay as a cyborg. In the meantime, Clay had graduated from high school and worked as chief of bionics for several hexs. He insisted Darci bring his mother straight from the wormhole crater to his place but not tell Antebon her destination. The wormhole transit and rendezvous at the crater were uneventful as Antebon arrived during the evening of the high lunar winds. Darci pretended to be Antebon's servant, carrying her bag so no one would suspect a red and black ANT walking together. Since Antebon's hatching predated the Great Cyborg war, she was one of the older disregarded red ANTs that weren't tracked by the system, and she could move around freely.

When they arrived at his burrow, Clay opened the door and greeted the two older female ANTs. Once the door was closed, he spoke, "Hello, mother, long time no see."

Antebon gaped. "Is that you, Clay? It is! I'd recognize that shine anywhere." She opened her forelimbs for a hug as her heart swelled.

Clay jumped into his mother's claws. "And look at you. You're redder than red. I think you're brighter and shinier than me."

Antebon laughed. "I can get even brighter with the right motivation." She squeezed Clay even tighter. "I've missed you. What a nice surprise." She looked her son up and down wistfully. *We've lost so many hexs.*

Clay updated his mother on his transformation, training, and efforts to counter the socionics imposed by the Antalones. He explained how Darci had helped him along the way. Then he mentioned his alternate status in the scarlet program and how he became chief of bionics. "I studied molecular biology and genetic engineering hard so that even if I didn't get the position, I would be an assistant in the breeding halls."

Antebon beamed. "I could tell right away when you hatched that you'd be a smart one, and it was difficult to let you go." She sighed, proud yet remorseful. *But here you are, leading the cause.*

"Well, I'm good at what I do, and I have some brilliant ideas on how to use my genetic engineering studies to advance the rebellion." Clay showed Antebon and Darci into his parlor. "But there's something important you should know before I get into that." He turned toward Darci. "Mother, Darci has been studying Czar Rust and has some interesting information that will help you with your mission."

"Yes, I do." Darci smiled. "But first, let me tell you what a marvelous young ANT and spy Clay has become. If we succeed with our goal of a revolution, we will have Clay to thank for it."

Antebon beamed. "I am extremely proud of him."

"I hear Beeutee wants him to receive and transform some new chameleants down the road," continued Darci.

"I am honored to help, and my family can provide chameleants as soon as Clay is ready." Antebon smiled. "Beeutee suggests we wait for another generation, maybe in three hexades, after Clay establishes himself." Although eager to get Rust, she knew their greater goal would be more difficult. *It'll take some time to destroy Rust's regime and bring Intopia back as it was.*

"Okay, mother, but first, listen to what Darci has to say about Rust so that you can complete your current mission," suggested Clay.

"Darci, tell me what I need to know to get that scoundrel," replied Antebon, taking a little sip of strong sap Clay handed her. She thought back to the petulant young Antunite hater who had been her travel mate.

"Listen to this," Darci began. "After I helped Clay get

started, Beeutee asked me to trail Rust to see if he had any vulnerabilities we could exploit." Darci sighed. "I followed him for many hexths whenever he left the palace he had built for himself."

Antebon smirked. "That sounds like Rust—he's got to have a palace." She thought about his lack of empathy, which allowed him to kill thousands of insectoids. *That selfish bastard.*

Darci chortled. "I discovered he likes to frequent a tavern that red ANTs call the Widows' Nest."

Clay shrugged. "The Widows' Nest? Funny, I've never heard of that one."

Darci nodded. "It's not your style, Clay. After the war, many female ANTs who lost their mates would gather there to console each other." She snickered. "And maybe so they could meet new mates."

Antebon interjected, "Let me guess, widows still go there? And Czar Rust goes there to find mistresses?" Her heart pounded. She considered that lust would be Rust's downfall. *That will play right into my claws.*

Darci nodded vigorously. "Exactly! After I saw him go there repeatedly, I applied to work there as a cleaner." She straightened her antennae for clarity but lowered her voice. "And I discovered some interesting things about Rust."

Antebon leaned in closer. "Do tell all." Her antennae stiffened.

"Well, Rust likes mistresses sure enough, but he likes them older." Darci beamed. "Or rather, he likes them to be close to his age. And he likes them as red as they get."

Clay raised his brow. "Do you know why?"

Darci took a deep breath. "One time, while I was cleaning up, I saw him with an older widow."

"Did they leave together?" Antebon asked, her interest piqued.

"No, they argued in a private room off the main bar." Darci looked all around. "I heard him yelling and her crying, and then he left."

Clay cleaned his antennae to hear better. "Do you know what happened?"

Darci sighed. "I grabbed a bottle and two glasses and went into the room to console the widow, and I held her till she stopped sobbing and offered her some strong sap."

Antebon rubbed her claws together. "Darci, you are terrific." Curiosity overtook her. *I'm glad you're on our side.*

Darci chuckled. "Then, as I primed her with more and more strong sap, she poured out her heart."

Clay sipped his sap and pulled his chair closer. "What did she say?"

Darci told Antebon and Clay that the widow had been Rust's mistress for hexs, and he'd just dumped her. Darci said his jilted mistress told her why Rust liked widows. Rust grumbled that the Queen he mated was too young for him, and he desired relationships with older females who remembered the election and the war so they could reminisce. And the widow said that a hex after Rust took her for his Queen, his young bride developed some black spots on her abdomen.

Antebon gasped as she and Clay looked at each other with wide eyes. "Nooo."

"Yes, they were small and, in a place only a mate would see." Darci creased her face. "But they repulsed him. So, he never mated with her again."

"I'm sure he didn't want any black genes in his family line," Antebon surmised. She thought of how Rust suppressed the intelligence of all black ANTs. *I taste bile when I think of Rust procreating.*

"Yes, so when he wanted to sire an heir, he pretended his mistresses' eggs were those of the Queen." Darci sighed hard. "So, his son Rudyard is a bastard son. Although Rust said to his mistress: 'At least he's a red bastard.'"

Clay gasped. "Oh, my!"

Darci continued, noticing she had dumbfounded Antebon, "Then she said he dumped her because his advisors thought they were too close and common ANTs might find out about her."

"So, he never saw her again?" Antebon asked.

"I don't think so. The widow never came back to the tavern." Her eyes widened. "Maybe he 'offed' her."

"I wouldn't put it past him." Antebon sighed. "But he still comes to the Widows' Nest?"

Darci smiled. "Yes, and he still goes for females his age. And the redder, the better."

"Perfect. That's me!" Antebon oozed a shifty stink. "He'll see me as a red mistress, but I'll be his black widow."

BREEDERS AND RULERS: OLD RULES, NEW RULER

Antalonia (Rudyard/Blood's rule, the current president)

BLOOD AND KEEGAN met one afternoon when Blood was not teaching socionics. They needed to discuss the additional parts of Rose and Jasper's courses that would make up their scarlet training. Scarlet training was a serious endeavor and required the utmost planning and care.

Blood pointed to the Czar's palace. "I spoke with my father about the scarlet program, and he suggested Rose and Jasper spend one hexour per hexth with him to receive training on being a leader in Antalonia."

Keegan nodded. "Yes, he has done that with all previous Scarlets."

Blood scratched his chin. "We must also decide what leadership roles the two will play once they become Scarlets." An image of Rose's red shell colored his thoughts. *I know what role Rose should play.*

"Of course, that's the main purpose of the scarlet program." Keegan thought for a moment. "It should reflect our needs and their respective talents."

"My father isn't getting any younger, and he hopes I succeed him as Czar when he abdicates or passes on." Blood smiled wryly. "When I do, we will need a new master of socionics." He imagined closely supervising Rose and winning her heart. *Will he guess what I want?*

"What about your assistant that teaches the chi hybrids?"

"She does a reasonable job with that group since they don't need a lot of moral education." Blood shrugged. "But she could never handle the challenges of brown and black alphas and betas."

Keegan lined his brow. "So, you think we should prepare Rose or Jasper for that?"

Blood nodded. "I think that since Jasper scored so well in math and science, he should probably take a position that requires an analytical mind." He rubbed his claws together. "But Rose's all-around scholastic skills would make her the best candidate for master of socionics." His hemolymph pressure soared. *He must support me in this.*

Keegan nodded. "I agree." He thought for a moment. "I believe the chief chemist and pharmacist will retire in the next hexade, and perhaps that would be a suitable position for the science-talented Jasper."

Blood clapped his claws together. "Wonderful idea! Father will be so pleased. I think we nailed it." *Keegan can be very supportive, and I shouldn't have worried.* He exhaled and considered how to introduce part two of his plan. *Will he accept my next request?*

"I'm sure Rose and Jasper will have no trouble achieving these goals." Keegan smiled.

Blood turned slightly away from Keegan, leaking a syrupy stench. "I know that normally the breed master and the master of socionics split the training of the two Scarlets." He looked out the window towards the school. "But since Rose will take over my position and Jasper's training will be closer to your area of expertise, I suggest I take Rose under my wing and you tutor Jasper." *My ultimate desire.* He looked closely at Keegan's reaction.

Keegan shook his head. "I don't think we should change a system that's worked well for hexades."

Blood now stared harder at Keegan. "But Rose needs to learn socionics, and that's my expertise." He twitched, understanding it would not be easy to sway Keegan. *You can't disagree with me on that.*

Keegan frowned. "You teach moral education, but the principles of socionics have always been the purview of the breed master."

"But it makes the most sense," Blood pleaded. "And what can I teach Jasper if he's learning to be a chemist?" His thoughts turned back to Rose. *You've got to agree.*

"They both need a rounded scarlet education. Our plans for their careers are only proposals." Keegan raised his claws. "They may show aptitudes we don't expect at this point."

Blood stood tall and rubbed his shiny red exoskeleton. "Maybe we should discuss it with Czar Rudyard and let him decide." He became increasingly desperate. *I'll play my trump card.*

Keegan shot a scalding stench. "As breed master, I make the call." He stared hard back at Blood. "Remember, you are my subordinate, and I don't care who your father is. Jumping over your superior in the chain of command can be grounds for dismissal."

Blood shriveled. "You're right, Keegan. It was only a suggestion; we can do it the usual way." He took some solace as he realized Rose still needed much tutelage from him learning the practice of socionics. *Keegan wins now, but I'll have my way in the end.*

Keegan cooled down. "Yes, and she'll learn the theory behind and basics of socionics from me."

🐜 🐜 🐜

As the hexs passed, Rose and Jasper excelled in high school, including their scarlet training. Rudyard, who was getting older and frailer, enjoyed his time with the two young trainees. As he aged, he fed off their youthful exuberance, yet he slowly became feeble. He explained the importance of the social controls placed on society and encouraged them to learn as much as possible from the books of EOW and Rust's books on histrionics. After six hexs, when Rose and Jasper were about to graduate, Rose noticed that Rudyard had aged considerably, and his health had deteriorated. She mentioned to Blood that she was worried about Rudyard. Blood at first was not overly concerned, but after he heard that Vermillion, a few hexs younger than Rudyard, had died, he visited his father more regularly. One morning, Blood received a message to rush to the Czar's palace as his father was gravely ill.

Blood walked up to Rudyard's bedside. "Father, I am pleased I reached you in time." He thought back to all the fun times he had with his Papa. *Seeing him like this, my concern for my father outweighs my desire to take over the reins.*

Rudyard extended his claw towards Blood. "Come sit, son. My time is now short."

Blood noticed how dehydrated Rudyard appeared and looked down at the floor as he held his claw. "Have you been looked after well since my last visit?"

"Yes, my medic has been constantly at my side." Rudyard looked into Blood's eyes. "But I know I won't last through the night, and I've just held on so I could see you one last time."

"Perhaps if you rest, you'll live longer." A desperate longing for more time flooded his mind. *Can't we return to the old hexays when exchanging our friendly barbs?*

"No, I've been resting for hexeks." Rudyard squeezed Blood's claw. "I want to know all is in order for the succession."

"You trained me well. And as master of socionics, I have learned the fundamentals of our system and how to be strict when I need to be." Blood beamed.

"Will anyone run against you?" asked Rudyard.

Blood shook his head. "The leaders will acclaim me, as no one will stand against me." His heart swelled as he remembered his father's lessons that prepared him well. *I love you and am proud of your steady stewardship of Rust's regime.*

"Who will take over as master of socionics?"

"I will fill both roles for a few hexths." Blood put a second claw over Rudyard's. "Until Rose is fully ready." He beamed. He pictured them standing together on the palace balcony. *And soon, she'll be by my side as I rule.*

"Rose. Is she the pretty scarlet student? I like her." Rudyard twinkled his eyes. "She'll do a wonderful job."

"Yes, we have been grooming her for the position, and she graduates next hexth." Blood smiled. "She will become a Scarlet, and I'll ease her into the role as the moral education teacher. She will assume the master of socionics role by next quarter." His heart raced, thinking that she would be his, at last. *I will soon realize my long-desired plans.*

"All is set, then? I only have one regret." Rudyard sunk deep into his bed. "That I'll never meet your queen or my grand ANTs."

Blood's eyes lit up. "You may have met my queen already." He pictured Rose walking uphill to the palace. *She visited you every hexth.*

Rudyard used his remaining strength to sit up. "You fancy Rose? She would make a delightful Queen. She reminds me of your mother—rest her soul."

Blood beamed. "Yes. I see that." He leaned over to give his father one last hug. "She's of age now, so I can finally push to win her affection." He recalled the short time he had had with his mother. *And you will soon be with your mate.*

Rudyard sank into Blood's forelimbs. "Thank you for this news. Now I can die carefree knowing that my descendant's genes will be the purest red." He wilted in Blood's arms. "Goodbye, my son." Rudyard collapsed and slowly expired within Blood's embrace.

Blood's eyes welled up with tears as he watched the life leave his father. "Goodbye, Papa." He briefly thought of his grandfather and how he would fill his father's shoes and reconstitute Rust's majesty, but he quickly thought back to all the wonderful times he had with his loving father. Then an azure aroma flooded the room.

THE NEW SPIES: GRADUATED AND READY

Antalonia (Blood's rule, the current president)

AFTER ROSE AND Jasper completed their high school graduation ceremony, they met with Clay again. The two of them were jubilant to have achieved the first critical step of their life goals. Although Beewish desired that they become Scarlets, it seemed to everyone it was just a pipe dream. But the closer they got to it, the more reality set in. They could almost taste it—scarlet graduation, becoming Antalone leaders and leading a Bilalunan-inspired revolution. Their destiny was within reach.

Clay extended a claw to each of the graduates. "Congratulations, you finished high school and the scarlet program with flying colors."

Rose beamed. "Yes, and we're ready to take on our assignments."

Clay smiled. "The next step is to accept the positions Blood and Keegan present to you and do well enough that they confirm your scarlet status."

Jasper rumpled his brow. "Do you know what positions they will offer us?"

"Yes, and you may suspect it yourselves," Clay responded. "They've prepared you for your positions throughout your training."

Rose raised a claw. "I think they want me to replace Blood to teach moral education." She quivered at the thought.

Clay nodded. "Yes, and if you do well, you will become the master of socionics." He patted Rose on the shoulder. "This is better than we ever expected."

Jasper rubbed his chin. "I can tell they want me for a science position, but I am unsure which one. I had a lot of chemistry classes."

Clay sported a wry smile. "I planted a seed with Blood and Keegan hexs ago that you should replace the chief chemist and pharmacist when he retires." Clay rubbed his claws together. "He is getting to that age. And I informed him repeatedly that there was a top-notch chemistry student in the scarlet program."

"But will he retire soon?" Jasper enquired.

"He is keen to meet you and pass on his knowledge," Clay smirked. "He's ready."

Clay turned towards the female scarlet candidate. "And Rose, I overheard Blood and Keegan arguing hexs ago." His sardonic smile returned. "They were fighting over who would take part in your training."

Rose tilted her head. "Really?" She reddened herself and smiled.

"Yes, it seems Blood wanted to be your sole supervisor, but Keegan, as boss, insisted that he also contribute." Clay laughed. "They both like you and want to spend time with you. I'm sure it's still true. We could well use that."

Rose blushed. "I can see that. They pay me attention and always comment about my beautiful shiny red shell."

Clay snickered. "Now that you're of age, they will probably pay you even more attention. Don't discourage it. There is nothing better than a female spy that can get close with their mark."

"I'm okay with Keegan. He's mostly just been nice to me. He's like a big brother encouraging me to succeed, and it's sweet." Rose first smiled, then squirmed. "But Blood gives me the creeps. Since low school, he's been my moral education teacher, and it's weird when a teacher gets too close. And lately, his advances have increased."

Clay stiffened. "Rose, you must steel yourself from your feelings. Remember your duty to Bilaluna. You are foremost a spy and must do what you can to progress our cause." He grabbed Rose's claws. "I know it's difficult, but you must encourage both. They may offer you more and more privileges if they feel they are competing for your affection."

Rose stood tall. "I will do anything for Bilaluna, my Queen, and Antunites." Her heart warmed, knowing she could please Clay. "And it might be fun."

Jasper smiled and raised his forelimbs. "Rose, you are a credit to all Antunites."

Clay raised his forelimbs and moved close to the graduates. Rose raised her forelimbs and initiated a high six.

After graduation, Rose was asked to report to the breeding halls for her first work hexay. She would start as a socionics teacher, and if she excelled in that position, she would eventually become master of socionics. This plan was an outcome so outstanding that not even Beewish could have imagined it. As the master of socionics, Rose would have ample opportunity to manipulate the minds of young Antalone students, but not how Blood imagined. Instead, she could replace much of the socionic conditioning with proper moral education and engender an optimism in her students that could inspire a rebellion.

Keegan invited Rose and Blood into his office to discuss how her practical training would proceed. "Welcome to you both, especially Rose, on your first hexay as a socionics teacher."

Rose stood tall and beamed her reddest red. "I am very excited to begin. You both have provided me with a lot of basic knowledge in the field, and I am ready to put it into practice." She remembered Clay telling her how the two had fought over training her. *They both want me so much. Let the bidding begin.*

Keegan jumped in. "You will continue to get specific theory instruction from me, and Blood will start your practicum."

Blood interjected. "Yes, that's when the real fun begins. There's nothing like getting your claws on the young students. Rather, I mean getting into the heads of your charges."

Keegan released some alert pheromones to draw attention back to him. "I have taken tremendous pride in supervising you through the hexs, Rose," he started. "I knew from the moment I met you that you were something special. And I foresaw the hexay when you and Jasper would stand beside me and help continue our colony's vital objectives."

Rose smiled nervously. "I hope I can live up to that vision and do what I can to strengthen our colony—to make Antalonia even better." She gave Keegan a wide smile. She thought warmly about all the support he had given her. *He's had my back from hexay one.*

Blood stamped a pod. "Rose, you and I have worked closely together for many hexs. First, you were one of my top moral education students. Then I was an intimate mentor for your scarlet training." He ogled her. "Now, as you have come of age and will soon be a full-fledged Scarlet, I want us to work even closer." He shined his abdomen, oozing a portly perfume. "I soon will spend all my time working at the palace as Czar, but I want to do everything I can to help you become the best master of socionics ever." He leered at her. "I want the contents of your mind to match the beauty of your shell."

Rose swallowed hard, but hid her repulsion and smiled. "I look forward to working as closely as possible with you to achieve the most we can together. Maybe I can come to the palace to see you for additional tutoring if I have the urge." She squelched the desire to turn away. *I will if I must, but keep your claws off me.*

Keegan sported a wry smile. "Remember, too, that when Blood returns to his palace, I will be close by to provide you with whatever you need as you continue in what I know will be a long, successful career."

Rose cracked a genuine smile. "I am heartened to have such a powerful leader so close by to help fulfill my needs, and I am sure I will rely on you often." Her mood elevated as her thoughts turned to Keegan. *My distaste for Blood is intensifying my connection with Keegan.*

"You are such a fit young female," Blood flattered. "I am sure you'll have no trouble marching up to the palace." Blood smiled. "I assure you I will clear my schedule whenever you call."

"It seems," Keegan started, "you will have plenty of support during your practical training, and later we will promote you to master of socionics. As your senior and continuing supervisor, I will offer that to you soon." Keegan grinned sardonically at Blood. "But now I will ask Blood to leave, as I will launch you off towards that goal with a few more valuable theoretical tips. I will escort you to the school when we have finished, and Blood will introduce you to the students of your first class."

Blood offered his claw to Rose and winked. "I await your arrival and count the moments until we can practicum together." As Rose placed her claw in Blood's, he kissed her claw, turned, and left the office.

As Blood exited, Rose looked toward Keegan, rolled her eyes, and smiled demurely. Keegan grinned knowingly and beamed back at Rose while motioning her towards the small classroom next to his office. Like Blood, Keegan adored Rose, but he was too much of a gentle-ANT to push her affections. He planned to support her fully to the best of his ability, and if she developed a crush on him, he would not resist, but if she didn't, it was not meant to be.

CHAPTER 39

THE REFUGEES AND OLD SPIES: HOT LAVA

Antalonia (Rust's rule, two presidents in the past)

DARCI DIRECTED ANTEBON to the Widows' Nest tavern on the night Rust routinely came. It was highly predictable since he took advantage that his queen retired earlier that night each hexth, since she had a choir practice first thing in the morning. Rust told her that he didn't like to be awakened that early in the morning, so he slept in the extra bedroom on those nights. Rust insisted she not bother him, and he would wake himself after she left. The Czar was always sure to lock the spare bedroom door, so she would not disturb him.

Antebon turned her reddest red when she imagined herself doing her planned deed. She shined herself with the finest beeswax so Rust could not miss her. Antebon was also sure not to cover her face or neck so that he could tell she was not a young ANT, but a mature one about his age. She knew her pure red shell would captivate Rust so much he would never recognize her, but she was extra careful to dab herself with strong sap to disguise her scent. Antebon entered the tavern moments after he arrived. Rust had already invited a widow he knew to his private room in the bar. But he turned when he heard the tavern door swing open and thud against a table.

Antebon had flung it open wide to ensure no one missed her entrance. All eyes turned towards her as she sidled into the bar. Rust did a double-take and gravitated nearer the newcomer. She was everything he desired—a mature ANT and the reddest he had ever laid eyes on. He lamented that they had not met earlier when they were both younger, and he could have harvested her genes to sire the purest red offspring. Yet he still wanted her with every urge in his loins.

Rust forgot about the other widow and offered his claw to the new arrival. "I haven't seen you here before. Are you new?" Rust knew that his wealth was apparent, and he didn't even attempt to open with an original line.

Antebon laughed. "I expected to hear a line like that, but perhaps not so soon." She readied herself for the task she so long desired. *My heart is pounding like a trapper finding fresh tracks in the mud.*

Rust smiled and didn't hesitate to boast. "Coming from a palace, I am not accustomed to making small talk. Everything about me is large."

"A palace, you say." Antebon flashed her eyes. "I'd love to see that sometime."

Rust kissed her claw. "Well, let me buy you a drink, and perhaps I can grant your wish later."

"I wish big." Antebon teased. "Can you grant me that?" She toyed with her prey. *Now I set my trap.*

Rust chortled. "As big as you can handle." Emboldened, he wrapped an arm around her abdomen. "Come to my private room, and I'll order the best strong sap."

Antebon smiled deviously. "Oh, just a little. I like to have my wits about me when I'm handling precious goods." She nearly drooled at the quest. *I spread the jaws of the snare wide.*

Rust's ommatidia popped out so far that he had to refocus his gaze. "So, what is your name, my mysterious red beauty?" He pulled out a chair for her. "And what brings you here?"

"It's Lava, and my mate died some hexths ago." Antebon gazed into Rust's eyes. "I've been mourning so long my loins began to ache." She continued her game. *I lock the jaws in place.*

Rust nodded and smiled. "A widow, at the Widow's Nest. Who would have guessed?"

Antebon gave him a knowing look. "I assume you have met widows here before."

Rust laughed. "A gentle-ANT never tells."

Antebon smiled coyly and oozed a sizzling scent. "Gentle, you say, but I bet you know rough." She knew he couldn't resist her. *I set the bait in its place.*

Rust's loins began to throb. "For a widow, you are very astute."

"My mate knew how to treat me right." Antebon grinned. "And now I need another. Will you fulfill my needs?" She stroked his engorged ego. *I ready the trigger.*

Rust bragged, "Widows are my forte—your satisfaction is guaranteed."

"I'm counting on it." Antebon downed her glass and licked her lips wet. "Can I see that palace now?" *Will my prey be drawn into my trap?*

"Yes, we'll go out the back way." Rust chugged his mug.

When they arrived at the palace, Rust showed Antebon around but asked her to be quiet.

Antebon whispered, "I understand. We wouldn't want to be seen by a queen."

When they reached the spare bedroom, Antebon handed Rust a small package containing the poison jinsome weed. "I have something for you." She brightened her redness to inspire more naughtiness. *I waft the bait's aroma toward him.*

Rust took the gift. "What is it?"

"Hexades ago, they selected my mate to go on a student exchange trip to Earth."

"Oh really? So did I." Rust cragged his brow. "What was his name?"

Antebon stroked Rust's hind limb. "Let's talk no more of him, or I might lose my mood." She pointed at the package. "He brought black licorice from Earth," she lied. "It's an aphrodisiac." She sparkled her ommatidia. "We're not getting any younger, and this stuff works wonders." She pushed his claw up to his nose while rubbing his thigh. *I know I can fool him because jinsome weed smells just like licorice.*

"I tried some of that back on Earth." Rust smirked. "It had a pleasing taste, but I didn't know it had that effect."

"One piece, and my mate could go all night." She winked and pinched his hindgut.

Rust smiled. "Luckily, my night is wide open."

Antebon smirked. "You can see I'm wide open, too." She quivered as he neared her trap. *Come prey and examine my bait.*

Rust opened the package and took a tentative sniff. "I remember that aroma, but something else smells familiar."

Antebon puzzled. "It smells like anise."

"No, I detect another black smell." He looked long and hard at Antebon's face.

Antebon shuddered. "I could bring you red licorice, but it doesn't have the same effect."

"I do like red best." Rust smiled.

Antebon wiggled her pure red abdomen. "I'll give you my reddest parts, but that black stuff will make it last longer." She pouted and posed her sexiest leer. *Come closer. You know you want my bait.*

Rust stared hard at the package. "I don't know."

"My mate took it till the night he died." She rocked seductively. "And he died a happy ANT." She wiggled her hips some more. *Prey are often most suspicious right before they bite.*

Rust paused further. "Perhaps I don't need it."

"I'm used to high performance." Antebon laughed. "You wouldn't want to disappoint me." She dared him to jump. *Come, touch my trigger.*

"No, you're right. That's the last thing I want." Rust leered at her as she swayed her abdomen from side to side. "Here's to a long night." Rust took several large bites.

Antebon smiled and danced seductively in front of the Czar. "Lie back on the bed and let Antebon take care of you. You'll be stiff as a board in no time." She'd never grinned so widely. *And now the jaws snap.*

Rust brazenly smiled as he watched her rhythmic dance. "You are hypnotizing me with your moves. Wait! Did you say Antebon? Now I know what I smelled."

"So, now you meet your black widow." She glared at him hard. *Squirm, you bastard.*

Rust's tongue popped out to match his bulging eyes. "Antebon, what did you give me? You witch. I can't brea…."

As Antebon saw Rust's eyes glazing, she transformed her shell to her darkest black. "This is why they call me Lava. Some widows are too hot to handle." She pulled Rust off the bed onto the floor. "And when they cool, you see how black they can get." She ached with anticipation. *I have such skill at the kill.*

Saliva drooled from Rust's mouth. "Help me. I'm dy…"

Antebon pressed a hind pod hard on Rust's chest. "Help you die? That's my goal." She withheld the cackle on her tongue. *I tighten the snare.*

Rust fought back his convulsions for one last word. "Dye?" A seasoned stink permeated the room.

After she was sure Rust was dead, Antebon grabbed the package, turned herself red again, slipped out of the palace, and crept back to Clay's nest. Clay broke open a bottle of his finest strong sap to celebrate their successful mission. Later, when the lunar winds returned, Antebon discretely headed back through the wormhole to Bilaluna.

CHAPTER 40

CZAR BLOOD: THE CRYPT AND THE LIBRARY

Antalonia (Blood's rule, the current president)

AFTER BLOOD SPENT the afternoon overseeing Rose's practical socionics training, he returned to his new home at the Czar's palace. He still hadn't gotten used to calling himself Czar Blood, but he always thought it had a nice ring. It took several hexays before he moved from his bachelor's nest to the palace, and he was just settling in. Of course, he grew up in the court, but that was when at least one of his parents was alive. Hexades after his mother died, Blood moved out but regularly visited his father.

Blood had two older twin brothers who died together during a mysterious fire at the palace. Blood survived as he was frightened and had left the boys' room, seeking his parents just before the fire. Heartbroken at the loss of the twins, his mother took her own life a few hexths later. His father assumed that having three male heirs would ensure a viable successor. So, he sired only three cyborgs, and all the other small nanitics were released into the wilds. With the deaths of his parents and brothers, Blood was the sole cyborg descendant in Czar Rust's line. This situation had two significant effects on Blood when his father died. First, he became very lonely and despondent at the passing of his father, with no siblings or mother to share his grief. Second, although he enjoyed the bachelor lifestyle, he felt pressure to find a mate and generate some heirs. These two effects did not take away from his knowledge that he was now in charge, and all should yield to him.

Feeling lonely in his large palace, Blood visited the tombs of his father and grandfather, Czars Rudyard and Rust. He had already visited the crypt multiple times since his father died, as it gave him some solace. The mausoleum contained statues of his father and grandfather, and they were larger-than-life granite carvings of the two dressed for battle. At one and a half-scale, the stones towered over Blood, standing almost ten feet tall. Blood draped them in armor, with their three arms brandishing a spear, sword, and shield. ANT soldiers typically didn't carry these weapons as they fought with their pincers, sprayers, claws, and jaws. Chain mail and weaponry were reserved for the leaders to reduce their chance of injury.

He would speak aloud to his deceased ancestors and imagine the answers they would provide in the crypt below the palace. These actions didn't seem odd to him since he had many conversations with his imaginary friend Flash over the hexs. Blood first faced the statue in front of his father's tomb. "Rose is working under my supervision, and we are getting very close." He thought of Rose's warm smile. *I think she's falling for me.*

Blood conjured his father's reply. "That is fantastic, son. I can see the two of you get along very well. Do what you can to win her heart. She is an amazing female ANT and would make a perfect mate."

Blood next looked over at the sculpture of the grandfather he had never met. Czar Rust was less than a hexury old when he died under mysterious circumstances before Blood was born. Some believe he died accidentally, but others thought one of his advisors became jealous and poisoned him. Yet, there was not enough evidence to charge anyone.

Blood spoke to his grandfather's statue. "Grandpa Rust, you never met Rose, but I am sure you would approve. She has the reddest and shiniest shell I have ever seen." He swelled with pride, having made such a find. *If you were alive, I could show you my prize.*

Blood sensed his grandfather's booming response. "Blood, nor have I met you, but you are the last in my line. It is on you to keep our hemolymph flowing. Do not disappoint me." Blood almost believed he saw the lips on the figure move. "You must win Rose's affection and mate her at all costs. Our line needs to be the reddest of the red, and there should be no genes redder."

Blood turned back to his father's effigy. "Father, you have taught me the meaning of love, and I am forever grateful for that. I will use your lessons as best I can to win her heart." He thought of ways he could impress Rose. *I learned from you how to love, and I only need the patience to foster a close relationship.*

He looked again at his grandfather's image and seeped a seasoned stench. "Grandpa Rust, I will make you proud, and your hemolymph will live on and rule forever. Rose will be my

mate, even if I must kill Keegan to remove my competition."
He took a claw and sharpened his pincers. "And our children
will be the reddest ANTs Antalonia has ever seen. And we will
have many cyborgs." His heart swelled as he thought about a
large family in the palace once again.

Blood had to convince himself that he did not see the statue
of Rust nod as the word "terrific" crossed his mind. Blood then
returned to the other part of the palace he liked to visit when he
felt lonely—the sacred library.

🐜 🐜 🐜

Clay also had the sacred library in mind when he invited Rose
and Jasper to discuss their new assignments. Indeed, both his
comrades were progressing well in their practicums, and it was
clear they would achieve their goals of becoming Scarlets. They
met with Clay at his place for further instructions. The sacred
library was a key topic of discussion. The library that Blood loved
provided the strength of knowledge for Antalone society. Still,
it also afforded a weakness, as it was a tool that his enemies, the
Bilalunan spies, could exploit, as Clay had before.

Clay once again congratulated his friends. "Keegan and
Blood are ecstatic about your development, and they will promote you to Scarlets. Our Queen will be delighted, and I am so
proud of you two." He hugged Rose and then Jasper.

Jasper looked up at Clay, who was taller. "I am enjoying
life as a working chemist and pharmacist. We have many chemistry books from Bilaluna and Earth that are more advanced
than the ones in high school. I am learning a lot and discov-
ering I not only have a pheromonographic memory, but also
what humans call a photographic memory." Jasper rubbed his
claws together. "I can read a page from an Earth textbook and

instantly remember it. Although, I may eventually lose some information as I take in more and more."

Although Jasper's position as Antalone chief chemist and pharmacist wasn't the apparent coup Rose's station represented, Clay knew it was essential. He purposefully manipulated all leaders involved in the decision to adopt his plan in this regard. Clay designed it because he needed Jasper in that role to perform the final step of his genetic engineering to boost the intelligence of the black and brown ANTs. The fact that Jasper trained his mind to be a sponge for scientific information would aid them as they raided the sacred library for valuable information.

"That is amazing, Jasper, and useful to our cause." Clay patted Jasper on the back. "This talent will come in handy in meeting our first specific objective." Clay looked over at Rose. "I have instructions from the Queen about your assignments; a key one is for us to gain as much information as possible from the Czar's sacred library."

Rose's eyes lit up. "You want me to steal books from the library when I visit Blood at the palace?"

Clay shrugged. "I wouldn't risk stealing them. But borrowing them for a time could help enormously, especially if Jasper can read them and remember the contents."

Jasper interjected. "I'll do my best. I'm a fast reader, so you won't need to borrow them long."

Clay clapped his claws together. "Breed Master Vermillion often quoted a saying he heard from Rudyard: 'Knowledge is power, and power is everything.'" He looked out the window at the moon. "Our Queen understands this too, which explains your first assignment." He tapped his claws on his temples.

"We must absorb the knowledge of our enemy if we are to gain the power to over-take them."

Rose stared into Clay's eyes. "Once I become master of socionics and Blood no longer comes to the school, I am sure he will invite me to the palace." She put her claws together. "I will ask him to show me the library so I can learn more about the birth of socionics."

Clay jumped up from his seat. "That's perfect! He'll assume that if you learn more socionic theory from the library, you won't need to visit Keegan as much." He put his arm around his female protégé. "Rose, I am certain that Blood wants you to be his mate. I know he obsesses about you and wants his queen to be the reddest of the red. All in Antalonia will be in awe of his line if there are none redder than his offspring."

Rose stood up abruptly. "But I can never mate with him, nor would I want to." She wrinkled her face. "My offspring may be black or brown or even chameleants."

Clay nodded, venting a baked bouquet. "You are right, but you must lead him along as far as possible. We need to gain as much knowledge as we can." He pointed to Jasper. "You must feed Jasper as many books as you can. Remember, knowledge is power."

Jasper laughed. "You know I am always hungry."

"And Jasper, find out as much as you can about vitamin S. Either from your chemistry texts or books Rose brings to you. It is odd that although I am chief of bionics, both Vermillion and Keegan would never tell me the real reason brown and black ANTs are given it." He shrugged. "All they would say is: 'S for survival, S for strength', the line they give to those taking it. We'd give it to red ANTs if it were for survival and strength." Clay creased his brow.

Jasper stood tall. "I'll be sure to keep my eyes open for that."

Clay noted it was time to go before curfew; he raised a claw, and Rose and Jasper each raised a claw in solidarity.

CHAPTER 41

ROSE: COURTING KEEGAN AND BLOOD

Antalonia (Blood's rule, the current president)

A FEW HEXEKS after Rose started her practicum, she met Keegan in his office. She wanted to test him to see how much he was interested in her. Rose planned to flirt with him, get him to trust her, and fall for her, to get information from him. Although spying was her primary objective, she liked Keegan and wanted to know him better. It thrilled some part of her that Keegan might be attracted to her, and Rose wanted to test her sex appeal. She had been so married to her role as a stellar student and a spy that she never had time for the opposite sex. Rose had no connections with anyone besides her brother Jasper and her mentor

Clay, but she had always felt a tiny spark with Keegan from their first meeting.

Rose stepped up to his doorway at the prescribed time. "Breed Master, I am glad you had time to meet with me." Her pulse rate quickened. *I'm punctual, as usual.*

Keegan straightened his antennae. "Please call me Keegan. We're colleagues now." He motioned for her to enter. "And I'll always make time for you."

"Yes, Keegan." Rose moved up close to the breed master. "I've always loved that name. It's so red, but also exotic sounding." She breathed in deeply.

"And Rose." Keegan stared into his junior associate's eyes. "It's that beautiful flower on Earth."

"Yes, I never met my mother, but I was told she called me that because she thought I'd blossom among the ranks of the red alphas and shower all Antalonia with the pollen of my wisdom." She made up a story to impress Keegan. *I'm sure he'll respect this line.*

"And so you have. There's no doubt that you will soon be a Scarlet and a leader."

Rose beamed at Keegan. "I couldn't have done it without your guidance." Then she rolled her eyes. "And without Blood's too, I guess."

"Oh, about him. He has trouble controlling his urges, a problem he got from his grandfather, Rust." Keegan looked down, embarrassed as a male ANT. "I will speak to him if you'd like."

Rose smiled knowingly. "No, I can take care of myself." She wiped her brow. "He adores me, but he bores me. I'll let him know." She shuddered to shake Blood off her mind. *You must know I prefer you.*

"I suppose a stuffy older breed master bores you too," surmised Keegan.

"You are the farthest thing from stuffy. Since I first met you, I have been in awe of you, and I know you had just graduated high school when I arrived." Rose stroked Keegan's shoulder as if to say: 'you're not much older than me.' "I'll be so happy when we are no longer teacher and student but colleagues working side by side."

"Well, your wish will soon come true." Keegan caressed Rose's forelimbs in return. "And Blood will soon be off your antennae."

Rose flashed her ommatidia to show she was comfortable being touched by him. "Speaking of Blood, I came to you to ask if you knew whether there are books on the development of socionics I should borrow from the palace library. I saw the library when I visited Rudyard during my scarlet program training, and I've never seen such an amazing treasure trove of knowledge."

"Once you are the master of socionics and a leader, Blood will grant you access to the palace library." Keegan nodded. "We encourage leaders to gain as much knowledge as possible. As Vermillion said: 'Knowledge is power.' And I could direct you to some excellent resources there on socionics."

Rose pouted. "I guess I have to wait until my promotion, then?" She had difficulty hiding her disappointment. *I can't wait!*

"And you'll also have to deal with Blood." Keegan creased his face. "Again, I could go to the palace for you if you like."

Rose laughed. "No, no. I'm a big girl now and can handle the Czar." She stood tall and puffed out her chest. *You must see me as a capable adult female.*

"I'm sure you can." Keegan grinned coyly. "You seem to bewitch everyone you meet."

"Are you calling me a witch?" Rose pretended to be offended.

"No, not a witch." Keegan pondered. "But you certainly have both Blood and me under your spell."

"How about I serve you a love potion and make Blood disappear, then?" Rose's eyes sparkled, and she turned on her charm. *I can't restrain a playfulness Keegan brings out in me.*

"And you read minds, too!" Keegan laughed. "But remember, technically, you are still my student, so any potions will have to wait."

"Look now, who's trying to exert control over another's affection?" She lingered on the last word. *The only magic I need is my red shell and my smile.*

"Affection. I like your choice of words." Keegan reached for Rose's claw. "But bide your time, else it will be my affliction."

"I understand. Dating students is taboo." Rose placed her claw on Keegan's. "For now, just get me that book list." She squeezed Keegan's claw firmly, radiating a silky scent. "And once I become master of socionics, we can master getting to know each other more intimately." She boldly annunciated the final word. *I like this game and can't wait to see where it leads. Keegan is so witty—it's sexy.*

"If I didn't know any better, I'd say you were flirting with me." Keegan beamed.

Rose pulled her claws away from Keegan, flashed her shiniest red thorax, and headed towards the door. "No, I'm just continuing to weave my spell so I can catch you with my web in time." Her demeanor danced as she left. *I know he's a sucker for my bright red abdomen.*

Keegan opened the door and headed to the fountain to get some water while watching Rose leave. He wiped his brow.

* * *

A few hexeks later, Rose and Jasper completed their practicums, and Blood promoted them to scarlet status. As expected, Rose became the master of socionics, and Jasper took over as chief chemist and pharmacist. Blood elevated them both to the rank of a leader. As leaders, they could borrow books from the regular stacks at the sacred library at the palace, although they needed to be returned within three hexays, no exceptions. Rose or Jasper could enter the restricted section, but these reference books could not leave the library.

It disappointed Jasper when Clay suggested only Rose visit the library, and he complained to her. "I can't believe Clay said I shouldn't go to the library." He stamped one hind pod. *It's not fair.*

Rose shrugged her shoulders, "He doesn't want Blood to get suspicious with both of us suddenly making several trips to the library."

Jasper turned quickly towards Rose. "But he knows I'm the one that loves to read and learn all I can." Then he turned towards the library. *I bet Clay can go whenever he wants.*

Rose patted Jasper on the shoulder. "It's because the pharmacy has its own library, and Clay expects Blood will assume you have enough to read there."

"There's only a handful of books, and they're all chemistry or pharmacology books. I want to learn all there is to know in many fields of science." Jasper gasped. "The sacred library has so many books about the scientific discoveries of Earthlings, and I want to know it all."

"Don't worry." Rose smiled. "I can take out books for you."

"I don't want you to have to take out my books." Jasper pounded the desk. "And I don't want you going to Blood's palace, anyway. That guy is a letch, and he's always had a creepy thing for you." He made a sour face. *I think you should stay as far from him as you can.*

"Don't worry about me. I can take care of myself." Rose hugged Jasper. "But thanks for caring."

"I guess our mission is more important than my desire to go to the library." Jasper released Rose from their hug. "But promise me you'll be careful and bring me lots of books."

🐜 🐜 🐜

Despite Jasper's objections, and at Clay's suggestion, Rose made an appointment with Czar Blood the next hexay to visit the palace library. She was strongly attracted to the library, which she often visited during her scarlet sessions with Rudyard. She missed Rudyard, who treated her well. A gentle-ANT despite his stewardship of an evil empire. Although she could see in Blood some characteristics that Beewish used to describe the malicious Rust, who had killed her great-grandmother, Rudyard didn't seem that aggressive. Something about him exuded a tenderness, despite his position and his policies. She feared Blood's aggressiveness on the other claw and shunned his interest in her. Yet, the spy in her knew she had to play along. Like Keegan, she knew she must toy with Blood's affections to exploit his knowledge and power.

Blood met Rose at the palace doors and escorted her through the grand entrance hall. "Rose, I am so proud that you graduated, and all the leaders approved your promotion." Blood grinned from antenna to antenna. "You will make a fabulous socionics master, and I am dying to introduce you to the other leaders."

Rose blushed. "Everything is happening so fast, and I still feel like a high school student." She wilted to make herself seem shorter. *I may slow down his advances by stressing how young I am.*

"Well, you have earned everything you achieved. You are not only a radiant red beauty, but also a brilliant mind."

Rose tapped Blood on the claw. "You flatter me too much." *I'll play with Blood like Keegan, but with more caution.*

Blood shook his head. "That would be impossible. You are amazing." He extended his claw to Rose. "And now that you are no longer my student, I hope we can get to know each other better—on a new and more personal level."

Rose placed her claw in Blood's. "I would like that too." Then she pulled back her claw. "But we need to take it slow. We wouldn't want anyone to think we were too close as teacher and student." She turned away but kept a few ommatidia tracked on him to gauge his reaction. *I hope he gets my caution signal.*

"Of course," Blood replied as he straightened himself. "The last thing I need is a palace scandal. But I am not getting any younger, and my court pressures me to find my Queen." Blood looked into Rose's eyes when she turned back. "If I don't sire an heir in a reasonable time, other leaders will take it as an invitation to oust a childless Czar."

Rose wrinkled her brow. "They would never dream of such a thing." She swallowed her repulsion. *Damn, this guy is driven.*

Blood leered at Rose. "They have dreams, just as I have dreams."

"Well, for now, keep me in your dreams." Rose sparkled her eyes, emitting a sultry scent. "And in time, you may awake with me beside you." She crossed her claws behind her back while walking towards the library. *I'll throw him this bone.* "But for now, I have some studying to do. I need to understand how socionics came to be, so I can truly be the best master."

Blood spoke softly, so Rose could not hear him. "Yes, and I will dream of the hexay when this pretty master becomes my mistress and queen." He then spoke louder. "I will leave you to your studies for now. I assume Rudyard explained to you the sacred library rules."

Rose turned back to the library doorway. "Yes, you can trust me with your heart and precious books." Her attempt at a warm smile quivered. *I must keep my smile until he can't see my face. Hold that scowl, girl!*

CHAPTER 42

THE OLD SPIES: TARGET THE NEW CZAR

Antalonia (Rudyard's rule, one president in the past)

BEEUTEE ABDICATED NOT long after Antebon assassinated Rust, and her daughter Beehope became Queen of Bilaluna. Beehope watched Rust's heir, Rudyard, for several hexs to determine whether he would continue his father's draconian ways. When she realized he would not depart from Rust's policies, she sent a message to Darci stating that she needed to target Czar Rudyard and his family. Rust might have been dead, but the evil empire he created was alive and well, and they needed to take it down.

Darci met with Clay to explain Beehope's objectives to him so they could devise a plan.

"Beehope suggests we kill Rudyard and his sons to end Rust's line."

Clay thought, then replied, "You should scout out the palace and determine if there are weaknesses in its construction that we could exploit."

Rudyard was an adult when Rust died and took over as Czar immediately. He was already a father, and his mate and first two cyborg sons moved in with him at the palace. About a hexade later, his third son, Blood, was transformed into a cyborg, and the three boys lived in the palace with their parents. Darci was pleased to join Antebon's plot to kill Rust and thrilled when the plan worked. After all, Rust had five of her comrades killed, all her close friends. She regretted not being more actively involved, so she was elated when Beehope gave her the green light to target Rust's descendants more than a hexade later.

⁂

A few hexths later, Darci met with Clay again. "I've frequently broken into the palace grounds and studied the structure's layout." She sported the smile of one who had done their job well. *I know this place inside and out.*

Clay rubbed his claws together. "So, what have you learned?"

Darci took a deep breath. "The building is two stories high with three wings emanating from a circular structure with a 120-degree angle between each extension."

Clay nodded and queried, "What about the rooms?"

"The lower floors contain a circular reception hall, meeting halls, offices, a dining hall, and a kitchen." Darci sighed. "From what I can tell, peering through the windows, the circular space on the second floor is the Czar's family room."

Clay salivated. "Do you know where the bedrooms are?"

Darci nodded. "The Czar and his mate's bedroom, his private office, and a second bedroom are on the upper floor of the northeast wing. The upper floor of the northwest wing contains the bedroom and a playroom of his three sons." She bit her tongue, trying not to blurt out her whole scheme. *We should target the bedrooms.*

Clay smiled. "Please tell me more."

Darci continued to explain the whole layout of the building. She described that the sacred library was in the upper south wing and included a rectangular study hall off the family room, circular floor-to-ceiling book stacks in the middle of the wing, and a small, square restricted section at the end. But it was the northeast and northwest wings on which Darci wanted to focus. She assumed it was best to target them while they slept, so she concentrated on the bedrooms.

Clay shook his head. "How did you figure this out with such detail?"

Darci pointed to a tree outside the window of Clay's nest. "I've become adept at climbing fences and trees and blending in. While camouflaged, I peered into all the upper floor windows and avoided detection by the palace guard or others."

"That's brilliant, but I'm glad you were climbing trees—I'd fall and break my neck for sure." Clay scratched his chin. "Knowing the palace's layout, have you considered a plan?"

Darci grinned. "I hope to set a small fire to burn toxic materials that will seep through the palace ventilation system and poison all those in the bedrooms within the palace's northeast and northwest wings." She thought of her dead friends and how to even the score with a family of five. *We can get them while they sleep, and they won't wake up.*

Clay smiled in return. "That's perfect. Hopefully, the fumes will kill the Czar and his heirs, but not cause much damage to the building. And it should seem like an accidental electrical fire."

"Yes, that's what I intended." Darci darkened her shell at the thought of executing her plan. "I hope to avoid damage to the south wing so we don't destroy the valuable books in the sacred library."

"Exactly. The books contain information we'll need to implement a coup successfully."

Darci stretched her antennae. "I need to know now which ventilation shafts lead to the bedrooms." Darci then pulled her antennae through the setae hairs and brushes on her forelimbs. "But I believe I know a way to find out." She recalled a small detail she noted the previous hexek. *We need an inside track.*

Clay stood up. "Don't keep me in suspense. What is it?"

Darci smirked. "While staking out the palace one hexay, I noticed the palace guard inspecting and approving the entrance of a ventilation cleaning company. I can apply to join the company and see if they have the plans for the palace vents." She envisioned poisonous gases seeping through the ducts. *We can then see which vents supply the bedrooms.*

"That's a fantastic plan, but let me help you." Clay scratched himself. "I'll stake out the company and figure out a way to get you in."

"Okay, I've had it with stake-outs for now." Darci wiped her brow. "But what else can I do to help?" She itched to move forward. *I'm not sitting on the sidelines on this one.*

Clay thought for a moment. "You can talk to the inspectors at the breeding halls and find out what insulation is the most toxic during an electrical fire." He spun around, looking at the vents in his nest. "Tell them you had a small fire at your home, and the smoke almost got you. Say you want to find out what caused such toxic fumes."

Darci beamed. "And when we find out, we'll be sure to burn some of it in the palace vents." She imagined five burial plots filled in the palace crypt. *We'll exterminate Rust's line where it lives.*

After their meeting, Clay found the address of the palace ventilation cleaning company and surveyed all its employees. During his stake-outs, he noticed two cleaners frequented a nearby tavern, particularly on the last evening before the hex-ek-end, when they would stay until closing. One night, while the two were getting drunk on strong sap, Clay sat alone in the bar drinking shots while remembering the good times he had with Rumo. Yet, he could not drink enough to overcome the overwhelming guilt he felt for what he did to him. Before the bar closed, Clay dismantled the side door light source and removed the cover over the drainage pit in the middle of the path. He stood by the hole to warn other customers of the danger, but when he saw his targets, he hid behind the bushes and waited to witness the accident. Sure enough, as the two ventilation cleaners exited the bar and staggered down the path, one of them fell into the pit.

The following hexek, Darci waited until the uninjured worker arrived at his company. She showed up moments later with her resumé, complete with a list of multiple cleaning positions, including cleaning ventilation shafts. The supervisor hired her on the spot and couldn't believe her timing, since he had just learned he needed a new employee. A seasoned smell lingered in the office.

Shortly after starting, she offered to work late one night to sanitize the brushes. After everyone else left, Darci examined the files and searched for the plans for the palace ventilation system. She noticed one file drawer had a lock and assumed the palace ventilation plans would be there. Darci felt around the back of the cabinet, hoping to find a key, but had no luck. Then she felt under the bottom of each unlocked drawer and found the key two levels down. Darci unlocked the secure one and found the plans under 'P' for palace. She copied the drawing and slipped the duplicate into her bag.

Clay met Darci the next morning after she called to say she had the plans. "That didn't take long—you only had to clean three sets of ventilation shafts." Clay laughed. "I guess they'll need to find another cleaner."

"Yes, that job is the worst." Darci coughed. "I'm glad to be out of there."

Clay raised his brow. "You got the plans?"

Darci reached into her bag. "Yep, right here. The shafts are on the outside walls like I thought." She pointed to a spot on the schematic. "The intake vent is the grill I noticed on the exterior wall of the central circular block between the two north wings. I didn't know what the grill was for or whether ducts ran from it to the bedrooms." An image of Rudyard and his boys cooking on the grill popped into her head. *But we hit the bull's eye.*

Clay's smile grew wide. "I see from the plans they do."

Darci grinned and rubbed her claws. "Yes, we're in business." She envisioned the ductwork making a noose around Rudyard's neck. *And if we're lucky soon, Rudyard won't be.*

After talking to the safety officer, she prepared a scheme that did not require a full-scale fire devastating the palace structure. Instead, it involved a strategic burn of highly toxic materials she would place within the ventilation systems for the upstairs bedrooms. The fumes would infiltrate the ducts and poison the air they breathed while they slept. As the rebels only intended to target the inhabitants, they planned a small fire that would cause minor damage to the palace.

"Clay, I know what materials to burn, but how can I make it look like an accident?" Darci looked at him pleadingly. *I know this is your expertise.*

Clay flipped through a book on terrorist tactics and small explosives he had stolen from the sacred library when he was a student. "We must prepare a small amount of C-4-like explosive putty and use the ventilation fans wiring to cause a spark to detonate it and start a small fire."

"Okay, but just enough to burn all the putty and the toxic materials placed in the ventilation shaft." Darci jumped up and down. "Look here on the plans. The fan motor is next to the intake vent, with an access hatch on the other side. It's perfect, and I know what to do." Her look quickly shifted from pleading to assertive. *I know how the system works now that I've cleaned such vents.*

One moonless night, after the residents were asleep, she scaled the fence and crept through the palace grounds on the north side. She located and removed the grill that covered the intake vent, and she reached through to the back of the shaft and popped off a circular cleaning access cover. Darci then used a fishing wire to locate the nearby electrical cables connected to the ventilation fan, scraped them to remove the insulation, and placed the explosive putty on the bare wires. She quickly filled the vent with polyisocyanurate foam and closed the outside grill before slipping away into the night.

When she returned to see Clay that night, she explained all the steps she had taken. "The next time the fan turns on, which it often does, the electrical current passing through the bare wires will detonate the explosive putty and start a fire that will burn the toxic foam and a small part of the wall next to the cleaning access." She looked like the spider that just caught the fly. *If I did it right, there'd be a small boom like thunder, and then poof, the vents will be full of smoke and toxic fumes.*

Clay nodded his head, then frowned. "But what materials did you use?"

Darci chortled. "It's an old foam insulation that generates carbon monoxide and hydrogen cyanide when burned, and it should poison the air in all the bedrooms." She pictured dancing with her spy friends over the Czar's grave. *I imagine Rudyard will soon take his last breath.*

Clay looked out the window towards the palace. "Are you sure they won't suspect arson?"

Darci grinned. "The fire should only burn the insulation lining the wall next to the shaft around the access opening. The only evidence of tampering will be the removed cover for the cleaning access, but I know this is a frequent error." She wiped her claws clean. *They'll suspect nothing.*

Clay looked back at Darci. "I hope you're right."

Darci nodded. "Yes, cleaners often forget to close the cover. Or a slight misalignment during replacement, coupled with the vibrations from the nearby fan motor, could also dislodge it." She spoke with authority. *I learned a lot in my hexek at the ventilation cleaning company.*

Clay furrowed his brow. "What about the wires?"

Darci flexed a single claw. "I only stripped the wires slightly, making it look like an accidental nick or the wearing of a weak patch of insulation." She swiped her claw from right to left. *And I didn't want to get shocked.*

"So now we wait and see." Clay looked out the window again.

The plan was perfect, except Darci did not account for a small ANT waking up in the middle of the night to take a pee. Blood was a young cyborg, only four hexs old, and often wet his bed. That night, Blood awoke and walked to the flush hole near the family room. He was lucky as a shaft from the intake vent on the south side of the building provided the ventilation for the family room, so the fresh air in this vent probably saved Blood's life. He also heard the minor explosion at the northern intake vent, which startled him enough to run toward his parents' room. Frightened, he yelled out, "Thunder, thunder!" Startled, his mother jumped up and dashed to comfort him. As she leaped out of bed, she awoke Rudyard, who rolled over and tried to go back to sleep. Rudyard bolted when he smelled something odd, but the fumes overcame him. Rudyard collapsed when he hurried to the family room. His mate heard his fall and raced towards him. After pulling him into the family room, she opened all the windows.

It wasn't until she opened the last window that she noticed Blood was missing. She ran to the northwest wing and saw that Blood had opened a window and had pulled both his brothers there, so their heads hung out the window. He was squeezing their spiracles, but neither boy was breathing.

Blood was panting and crying when his mother picked him up and carried him to the family room. Although in her heart, she knew the other boys were dead, she ran back and dragged them both to the family room. Rudyard revived and saw his two eldest sons dead on the floor, fell to his knees, held both boys, and wailed. His mate told Rudyard of Blood's efforts to save his brothers. Rudyard stopped crying and hugged his youngest son tightly, and they both trembled as an indigo incense fogged the room. It devastated the Czar's family when they lost Rudyard's first two heirs. Yet it disappointed Darci that Rudyard and Blood lived, although she was satisfied to have exacted some sweet revenge on the evil Rust's descendants. It also pleased her when the investigator did not suspect arson and attributed the deaths to an accidental electrical fire. Indeed, they concluded that faulty wiring caused the fire when sparks from the fan motor jumped through the uncovered cleaning access and set the nearby insulation ablaze.

CHAPTER 43

THE NEW SPIES: CLAY ENLIGHTENS THE NEW SCARLETS

Antalonia (Blood's rule, the current president)

ROSE VISITED THE library at the end of the hexek so that she and Jasper could read the borrowed books over the hexek-end. To maintain Blood's trust, she did not even approach the restricted book zone and only took out a couple of books on the development of socionics and one on bionics. Rose knew Jasper would be excited to receive some books, so she immediately brought him the bionics text. She planned to meet Jasper and Clay at Jasper's burrow the following afternoon. She and Jasper would have some time to read through the books so they could report the contents to Clay.

The next afternoon, Jasper answered the door when Rose knocked. "Come in. I am so glad you arranged this." Jasper beamed. "I want to celebrate our promotions with you, and Clay is already here." He pointed to the back of the nest. "And he brought us some vintage strong sap. I'll get some glasses." Jasper bounced across the room.

Jasper brought out his best shot glasses, and Clay filled them to the brim and shook his antennae.

"I'd like to make a toast." Clay raised his glass. "To the best of Bilaluna, now leaders in Antalonia."

Rose raised her glass. "Yes, to the three of us!"

Clay and Jasper replied together. "To the three of us."

Clay pointed to Rose's bag after they toasted each other and downed their glasses. "Did you borrow some books from the palace library?"

Rose grabbed her bag, nodding while handing the sack to Clay. "Yes, two on socionics and one on bionics I gave to Jasper last night."

Clay poured himself another glass of strong sap and pulled the books out. "They're from the regular stacks?"

Rose smiled. "Yes, I didn't want to be too brazen on my first trip."

"Next time, try to get either the Trinity book or the Encyclopedia of Human Discoveries," Clay suggested. "Vermillion mentioned both to me. The first one, you'll know when you see it. It's the thick how-to book on histrionics, bionics, and socionics."

Jasper pulled out the bionics book in which he had placed multiple bookmarks. "The bionics book Rose gave me is amazing." He looked over at Clay. "You'll be happy to know there's a chapter on vitamin S." He waved the book in front of Clay and teased him by turning away. *I'm so excited.*

Clay peeked over Jasper's shoulder. "What does it say?"

Jasper flipped to the bookmark for the chapter. "It's a type of mind control drug." He smiled at Clay. "The books in my library include a recipe for making vitamin S but provide no information about why we use it." He gave a claws-up sign to Rose. *Isn't this intel amazing?*

Clay raised his brow. "I can't believe this book was not in the restricted section. Someone must have made a mistake."

"You're right. Look at the code on the binding." Jasper shrugged. "That's the code for restricted books in my library. Someone messed up," he continued. "But at least I have it now and can learn from it." He showed Clay all his bookmarks.

Rose puckered her brow. "Wait. Your library has restricted books?"

Jasper nodded. "Yes, but there's only one other than this book, and it has the recipe for making vitamin S, growth factors, antioxidants, and protein stabilizers given to nanitics being transformed. The restricted zone is just a small, locked cabinet."

Clay encouraged Jasper to flip through the book. "But what exactly does vitamin S do?"

Jasper turned the page. "See here. It says it's the S-isomer of a drug like LSD." He smiled brazenly at Rose. *I know Clay will understand me.*

Rose shrugged. "S-isomer, LSD. Can you speak ANT?"

Clay interjected, "S-isomer is just a unique form of an active drug."

Jasper followed up. "And LSD was a psychedelic drug sometimes used by humans for brainwashing." He stuck up a claw. "But vitamin S isn't a psychedelic agent, and we use it to make ANTs conform to instructions—it's a mind-control drug." He laughed nervously. *For once, I get to explain something to Rose.*

Clay threw his claws in the air, spilling the remaining strong sap from his glass. "A conformity drug is given to black and brown ANTs, so they don't rebel."

Rose pointed at the book. "We should take them off it, so they'll join our cause."

Jasper beamed. "Yes, I could change the recipe to give them a placebo. Then we can start a revolution." He bounced up and down. *I found the key.*

Clay motioned his claws towards the ground. "Yes, but not so fast. We need to change a few other things first."

Rose shrugged. "Like what?"

Clay beamed and revealed the secret he'd kept for hexs. He explained that they could reverse everything the leaders had done to keep black and brown ANTs down, with the three leaders now in position. Clay took the book from Jasper and flipped to the chapter on growth factors. Then he told them that as chief of bionics for hexades, he had secretly increased the neuronal growth factors given to brown and black ants that were transforming, so their brains grew as large as reds. He mentioned how Keegan wanted them a little bigger but that he had already increased them to full size.

Jasper jumped up. "But how is that possible? Wouldn't everyone notice they were getting smarter?" He struggled to control his impulsiveness. *I can't believe Clay is springing this on us.*

"Normally they would, but I used advanced genetic engineering to suppress brown and black ANTs' intelligence until we start the revolution." Clay rubbed his claws together. "I did it this way so we could generate many smarter rebels all at once, and Blood would suspect nothing." He looked around at all the doubting faces. "Trust me, genetic engineering is my life, and I had hexs to work this out."

Jasper's eyes widened. "But how is that even possible?" He froze in awe of the marvels of science. *I know if anyone could do it, it's Clay.*

Clay grinned from antenna to antenna. "When you make vitamin S, is there anything else you put in the capsule?"

Jasper shrugged. "Uh yes, we also put doxycycline in the capsule." His ommatidia rattled. *What is he getting at?*

"And why do you do that?" Clay snickered, hinting he knew the answer.

"It's an antibiotic. The chief before me said many black and brown ANTs were dying of a bacterial infection, many hexs back—it was an epidemic. And a few are dying every hex since, and they need prophylactic antibiotics to prevent another epidemic."

Clay sported a wry grin. "I caused that epidemic and sporadic infections ever since."

Rose raised her claws. "Why would you do that?"

"So, the chief chemist and pharmacist would give brown and black ANTs doxycycline every hexay," Clay spoke as if he was about to spill some beans.

Jasper smiled. "I'm no genetics expert, but I think I see where you are going with this." He looked at Clay in amazement. *Clay is so brilliant, but he is drinking too much strong sap.*

Rose creased her brow. "I don't. What are you talking about?"

Clay downed his strong sap and thought about how he could say it simply. He explained that to keep the big-brained black and brown ANTs dull-witted, he performed cre-lox gene manipulations, reversibly knocking down the FMR1 gene. He told them the gene stayed knocked down if they gave the ANTs doxycycline, and the antibiotic activated a Cre-recombinase that inactivated the FMR1 gene in black and brown ANTs.

Jasper nodded knowingly, despite a slight confusion. "And what does the FMR1 gene do?"

Clay grinned. "It's essential for normal neuronal synaptic function; without it, ANTs become mentally deficient. But gene production returns to normal if we stop administering doxycycline, and that's why I say it's reversible."

Rose twirled around. "You're getting me dizzy with all this geeky talk."

"Forget the fancy science mumbo jumbo about cre-lox and recombinase. Clay means he can reactivate a brainy gene that doxycycline turns off, so he can make them smarter." Jasper beamed. *I can't believe I followed all the details of Clay's scheme.*

Rose jumped up, confused about the means, but gaining clarity on the end. "So, they all get smart if Jasper takes docky, docksee… the antibiotic out of the vitamin S capsule."

Clay exuded a buffed bouquet. "You got it. So, we do that first, before we remove vitamin S."

Rose shrugged. "But what about socionics? Can we reverse all the conditioning they've had?"

Jasper tapped his temples. "I read another chapter in the book about an amazing memory drug called PKM-zeta." He beamed again. *I can be at least half as creative as Clay.*

Rose pulled on her antennae. "PKM-zeta?"

Jasper laughed. "Yes, it stands for protein kinase M-zeta." Jasper opened the book to the chapter. "It explains that humans discovered the kinase dramatically increased the memories of lab rats and mice, but didn't work so well in humans. Yet, it worked even better in invertebrates—that includes us." He raised his three forelimbs to his head and spread them like his head was expanding. *It's an insect memory booster.*

Rose jumped up and down. "So, we give it to black and brown ANTs, who can quickly unlearn all their socionic conditioning." She picked up the socionics book. "I scanned this book last night, and there's a chapter on socionics deconditioning. So, we can reverse it."

Clay grabbed Rose's claw and twirled her around. "Especially if we've already stopped their doxycycline treatment, and they are smarter."

Rose turned and twirled Clay the opposite way. "Maybe I can recommend older ANTs that have finished school come for socionic retraining. But we'll do the opposite and teach them to unlearn socionics." She smirked, now confident of her plans. "But I'll tell them it is top secret, and they should not change their behavior just yet."

Clay smiled. "And when all black and brown ANTs get smarter and are unconditioned of their socionics, we stop vitamin S and encourage them to rebel."

Rose stilled herself. "But what about Keegan? He might figure out what we're doing."

Clay squeezed Rose's forelimbs. "Someone needs to keep him occupied and put his mind on something else."

Rose chuckled. "Someone! I can see why Queen Beewish wanted to send a female spy here."

Jasper poked Rose in the abdomen. "Starting to! I think you've known all along, and you're good at it." He smiled warmly at Rose and raised a glass towards Clay. *The three of us can easily outsmart our enemy.*

Rose guffawed. "I do like all the attention. But mostly, I enjoy messing with their minds."

Clay patted Rose on the back. "Well, mess with Keegan's mind enough that he can't see what we're up to."

"But what about Blood and the other leaders? Will they notice all the black and brown ANTs getting smarter after we stop giving them doxycycline?" asked Jasper. A look of worry crossed his face. *I don't think Clay considered this pitfall.*

"That's easily solved," added Clay with a firm fragrance. "If they still take vitamin S, we tell them to act stupid, and they'll conform. They'll learn what we teach them but act like they haven't. They won't appear smarter until we say so, and then we remove vitamin S."

"I'll drink to that." Rose wiggled her hips and then raised her forelimbs to high-six Jasper while Clay raised his glass and drank.

CHAPTER 44

ROSE: STEALS AWAY AND ROMANCES KEEGAN

Antalonia (Blood's rule, the current president)

ONE HEXEK, AFTER Jasper replaced doxycycline with PKM-zeta in the vitamin S capsules, Rose began a course of socionic deconditioning with her students. She also started mandatory adult classes where she pretended to reinforce socionics but used deconditioning methods to reverse the effects of socionics. She also taught all ANTs about Bilalunan society and how various insectoid families, and ANTs of all colors, lived together harmoniously, without castes, both on Bilaluna now and on their planet several generations ago. This action primed the black and brown ANTs for rebellion.

A few hexeks later, she prepared her last lesson on her hexay off. It would inform black and brown ANTs of all the detrimental histrionics, bionics, and socionics that the leaders had imposed on them throughout the last several hexades. She realized she needed the text Clay called the Trinity book, which was in the restricted zone of the sacred library. She planned to meet Blood at the Czar's palace. Blood mentioned he would have to leave within a couple of hexours to meet with business leaders at the burrow of commerce, so she should come immediately. Rose was eager to visit, as she remembered that Jasper also wanted to read the restricted book *The Encyclopedia of Human Discoveries*. Before substituting PKM-zeta into the vitamin S capsules, Jasper had tried the memory drug on himself and discovered its powerful effects. The drug enhanced his photographic memory, allowing him to memorize an entire textbook. He could even tell you how many commas there were on each page.

When Rose got to the palace, Blood was in an antsy mood. She could tell he wanted to woo her further, but Blood was stressed about how little time he had before his meeting. He made his typical flattering comments and showed her to the library. When Rose mentioned she wanted to enter the restricted section, he agreed, reminding her not to remove any books. Blood then said he needed to prepare for his meeting and suggested Rose visit his office when she finished in the library. Rose agreed, and Blood left her in the restricted zone, jamming the door open. She found and flipped through the Trinity book, reading some significant chapters there. Then Rose located the human discoveries book and scanned through it. When she realized that only about 15 hexutes remained before Blood needed to go, Rose took the two restricted books, moved them out of the restricted zone, and hid them among the books in the regular stacks. She then closed the door to the restricted area, which automatically locked when shut. She passed through the study hall and family room and entered the wing leading to Blood's office and bedroom.

When Rose reached the office, Blood was not there, but he heard her arrive and called out from his bedroom. "Rose, I am just getting ready to leave. Come in here, and I can give you a proper send-off."

Rose crept into Blood's boudoir. "I have to hurry out too, but I chose some books in the regular stacks that I'll pick up on the way out."

Blood smiled, eager to push forward their relationship and feeling pressed for time. "Oh, you and your books. You can't learn everything about life from books." He leered at her. "Some things you need to experience first claw."

Rose smiled back. "Yes, I have much to learn. But I must prepare my lessons, and you have a meeting." Her smile slowly turned to a frown. *And I don't like your mood.*

Blood lost his cool. "Rose, sometimes you forget I am Czar, and I decide things around here."

Rose looked at Blood sternly. "I think you're forgetting how to be a gentle-ANT." She looked at Blood like he did when scolding unruly kids in their moral education classes. *I'll try the 'shame you' tack.*

Blood fumed. "I choose when to be gentle and when to be rough." He grabbed Rose and forced a kiss on her. He slapped her face with his claw and shoved her onto the bed as she struggled to escape. A bitter bouquet filled the room.

As he moved forward and prepared to jump on top of her, she kicked him so hard that he fell back onto the floor. "If you ever want me as your queen," Rose said, "you will stop right now and leave immediately for your meeting." She scowled like she never had before. *I hope this works.*

Blood picked himself up from the floor, dusted himself off, and fled from the bedroom. When Rose heard the front door slam, she wiped a tear from her face and headed down to the library. Self-composed, she grabbed the two restricted books, feeling no guilt for her betrayal. She stomped out of the palace and left for a pre-arranged meeting with Clay and Jasper.

❦ ❦ ❦

When Rose reached Clay's place, she was breathless and disheveled. Clay looked at her closely. "What happened to you? Your cheek is swollen."

Tears flooded Rose's eyes. "Blood hit me and tried…"

Clay stepped forward and embraced her. "You're safe now. Try to calm yourself."

Jasper stepped forward and handed Rose a handkerchief. "I knew we couldn't trust him. And I also knew you were strong enough to fight him off."

Rose chuckled. "Yes, I kicked him so hard he fell on his hindgut." She stood tall and feigned a kick. *I can still see his shocked face.*

Clay released Rose from his hug. "That's my girl! I knew you had it in you."

Rose wiped off her tears with Jasper's handkerchief. "And he stormed out of the palace. And then I took these." She held up her bookbag and smiled. *I both kicked him and tricked him.*

Jasper grabbed the bag and pulled the books out. "Oh, Rose, you are amazing. You raided the restricted zone."

Rose blew her nose. "Yeah, it was the least I could do after what he tried." She grinned at Clay. *I don't linger on devastating events.*

Clay smiled back. "Well, thanks to you, we are well on our way to getting our revenge."

Rose looked solemnly at both Clay and Jasper. "Thanks to all of us."

Jasper raised a claw, and Clay wrapped an arm around Rose, who was still trembling—but now out of an urge to pay Blood back. Then Rose and Clay raised a single claw, signifying their conviction for the cause.

🐜 🐜 🐜

After she left Clay and Jasper, Rose arranged an evening meeting with Keegan to inform him about how the adult education classes were going. Rose wanted to deceive him that the program was worthwhile and that she could reinforce socionics in the older brown and black ANTs. Keegan was eager to meet Rose again now that she was no longer a trainee. Rose wondered whether Keegan would get friskier without the teacher-student dynamic that restrained him before. She craved his witty banter and the opportunity to flirt with him again. As a spy, Rose had ulterior motives; to distract him from what Clay and Jasper were doing. As a female, she wanted him to think of nothing else but her. Secretly, Rose wanted Keegan to discover what Blood had done to her. She wanted her knight in shining armor to ride into the scene.

Keegan met Rose at the front door. "Rose, what happened to your cheek?" He touched her face softly. "It's all swollen."

Rose turned away. "Oh, nothing. I tripped and hit the table—I can be clumsy." She forced out a tear. *I hope he figures out it was Blood.*

Keegan gently grabbed Rose and turned her toward him. "You didn't trip." He looked into her eyes. "That looks more like a bruise from a claw strike."

"I don't want to talk about it." Rose looked down, and the tear dropped to the floor. *And yet I do.*

Keegan seeped a blazing bouquet. "It was that brute Blood, wasn't it?"

"He wanted more than I would give." Rose looked up with true tears welling in her eyes. *I can no longer deceive Keegan.*

Keegan clenched his claws. "Did he . . ? I'll strangle the bastard."

Rose grabbed Keegan's claws. "No, I kicked him, and he backed off." She stared hard at him. "I told you I can take care of myself." Her momentary hatred for Blood fueled a passion for Keegan. *He is so sweet.*

Keegan relaxed. "You should stay away from him." He stroked Rose's forelimbs. "You're not safe around him."

Rose trembled. "I think I put him in his place." She tried to put Blood out of her mind. *Don't worry about me.*

Keegan pulled Rose closer, hugged her, and caressed her with his claws. "His place is as far from you as possible. And your place is here within my embrace."

Rose swooned. "I've never felt safer." She gazed deeply into his eyes and kissed him, letting go of her undercover games.

Keegan kissed her back gently, careful not to press her cheek. "I will always love and protect you."

Rose looked upon him tenderly, wafting a steamy scent.

"You have from the beginning." She thought back to the first time they met. *You have done nothing but help and encourage me.*

"But my little shining rosebud has blossomed into a flower beyond compare." He wiped her tears and softly stroked her face. "A beautiful red rose has pollinated my heart, and her nectar now satiates my lips."

Rose melted further into Keegan's arms. "You have been the steady scaffold for my growth and now the over-arching trellis that will forever hold my heart." She forgot all about her mission and got caught up in the romance.

Keegan looked out the window. "But to support you, I must protect you from that scoundrel." He looked back at Rose. "I know he wants you for his queen. And he will do anything to get what he wants."

Rose shrugged. "He has been persistent." She smiled at Keegan. "A thorn in my side, a burr in my brain." She craved more banter. *I feel dizzy, yet I can still show my wit.*

Keegan sighed. "He gets it from his father and mostly his grandfather. That one was a letch, a creeping Charlie among ANTs." He paused and looked woefully at Rose. "Sometimes, I think we have landscaped our entire society to fulfill that family's desires."

Rose chuckled. "With fruit trees that only the rich land-owners can pick from." She stared into Keegan's eyes. "We are the gardeners who maintain the Czar's royal orchards." She tested his loyalty to the program. *He may have me under his spell, but I am still on a mission.*

Keegan sighed. "You feel like that too?" He thought for a moment. "Without the breed master, the master of socionics, and chief chemist and pharmacist, the regal groves would wither."

Rose smiled. "What is a garden without gardeners, an orchard without arborists?" Her heart warmed. *Do I see a kink in Keegan's Antalone armor?*

Keegan looked at the sky. "Perhaps a healthy wildflower garden and *Agrius Rubi*."

Rose prodded him on. "What are you saying?" Her heart pounded hard. *Perhaps I can turn him.*

"Wildflowers and wild blackberries." Keegan scratched his head. "I've wondered whether our colony has taken a wrong turn." He looked solemnly at Rose. "What if our black ANTs were wild blackberries?"

Rose sported a crooked smile. "But you are the breed master, the master tree planter. How do you carry on if you think like this?" She stepped back. *I can't seem too keen on his revelation.*

"I did it for the challenge, to achieve the ultimate, and become a leader. I treasure you, Clay and Jasper." Keegan held Rose close and watched for her reaction. "But as for Blood, his cabinet, and the business leaders, I am not comfortable with the company I keep. We are like lilies among thistles."

Rose grinned. "I couldn't agree with you more." She cracked a smile. "But we made our flower bed and must toil in it." She prodded him for more. *I know he is being true, so I'll egg him on.*

"You're right." Keegan sighed. "But I want to punish Blood for what he did to you."

"Bide your time." Rose smiled coyly, oozing a syrupy smell. "You never know when opportunity will bloom."

CHAPTER 45

CZAR BLOOD AND ROSE: BROODING AND PLOTTING

Antalonia (Blood's rule, the current president)

THAT SAME EVENING, Blood became angry, both because Rose had kicked and rebuffed him and because he discovered later that she had taken books from the restricted zone of the sacred library. He tried to reach Keegan to complain about the library issue, but Keegan did not answer his calls. Blood then did what he usually did in times of crisis—he visited his father's and grandfather's crypts.

Blood spoke to the statue in front of his father's crypt. "Papa, what am I to do? Rose, my future queen, has refused me and defied me." He tried to conceal his anger, as he rarely saw his father get mad. *My father should share my anger, but I fear he won't.*

Typical of such visits, he meditated, closed his eyes, and waited for an answer from his father. In time, Rudyard spoke to him. "She is young, and the young don't always understand the importance of rules." Blood opened his eyes. "And did you not force yourself on her?"

Blood defended himself. "I am the Czar—everyone should submit to me." He did not accept Rudyard's subtle ways. *Your answer angers me.*

His father popped another response into his head. "You cannot force a mate to love you. You must be persistent and win her heart through kindness and generosity. To share your life fully with your queen, she must be a willing partner."

Blood closed his eyes and tried hard to suppress his dark mood. *I will consider your advice despite my distaste for it.*

Blood looked over at his grandfather's sculpture. "What say you? You created this colony." *This should be good.*

Blood perceived a tremor in the crypt and imagined his grandfather shaking with anger. "You are the Czar, and you have a right to seize the queen you choose, and you can take her when you want her." Blood detected a coolness in the air as Rust spoke to him. "She is young and foolish and needs to be taught a lesson."

Blood looked again at the figure at Rudyard's tomb, who spoke to him. "You are the Czar, but a Czar must show mercy—especially if he craves love."

Blood cringed at his father's words. *But I am the all-powerful Czar, and I can demand love.*

Rust's voice boomed in his head even though he did not gaze upon his effigy. "Love is not important. It is her genes you want and the pleasure she gives you when you fertilize her eggs and sire your heirs." Rust's words incredibly moved Blood. "She is the reddest among the red. She must be your queen—even if you need to keep her in a dungeon. It's our line, not her love, that matters."

A vile vapor clouded the crypt as Blood announced his conclusion to his ancestors. "Father, you taught me much about love and tenderness. And I cherished our time together, but Rust is right. He created this colony, and I must follow his counsel. I know Rose will never truly love me." He raised his voice. "But she will obey me!" He headed out of the crypt. "If she loves classified books so much, she will be restricted to the library until she submits to my will. And if I can't have her shining love, I will at least take her bright eggs."

Before he left, he turned and looked at Rust's tomb. "And you'll be proud of me, Grandfather. As I'll do something about my competition." He sported a sinister grin. "Keegan will no longer be around to tempt Rose's affections."

🐜 🐜 🐜

Rose was still with Keegan when Blood sent his BUGants to Keegan's nest to do the deed. As Rose left Keegan's burrow, she noticed two of Blood's goons approaching it from the other side of the path. Rose slipped around a corner so no one could see her and watched the police enter Keegan's door. She crept closer, hearing Keegan and the BUGants yelling through the partially open door.

As she approached the threshold, she heard one of the BUGants say: "You will not steal the Czar's intended queen."

She then heard Keegan's reply. "Rose can choose her mate."

The other BUGant responded with a spiny scent, "Her

choice will be easy after we finish with you. And don't worry, Clay can replace you as breed master."

Rose heard a BUGant spit at Keegan and then Keegan's painful cry. She cocked her sprayer with two shots of formic acid and jumped through the doorway. She sprayed the first assailant in the back before anyone knew she had entered the room and drenched the second with formic acid as he turned to see who was there. Rose had generated a highly concentrated dose of formic acid while overhearing the conversation, a trick that Clay had taught her and Jasper. She needed to use the higher concentration quickly; otherwise, it might burn through her venom sack and fatally injure her. But she made no mistake with the task, and the highly lethal spray hit her targets straight on. The formic acid both paralyzed and burned the intended victims. The paralysis prevented the BUGants from spitting or fleeing. Yet it did not suppress their convulsive writhes as the acid burned through their exoskeletons.

While the thugs lay prone and twitched, Rose quickly unwrapped Keegan, who was stunned. The venom in the BUGant's spitting thread was not strong enough to kill, but temporarily paralyzed and burned if left too long. Fortunately, the assaulter had not yet pierced Keegan with his fangs, which would have produced a fatal sting. After unwrapping him, Rose licked Keegan's exoskeleton to remove the small amount of venom that seeped from the toxic thread, spitting out the poison as she progressed. Then, as she waited for Keegan to recover from his paralytic state, she turned and instinctively twice snapped her pincers, decapitating the two BUGants in case their stunning might ease.

Rose held Keegan tightly as he slowly recovered. Although his body drooped like a dead slug, and he couldn't hug back, she could see tenderness and admiration so intense in his eyes that it touched her soul. She held him closer and warmed as the life returned to Keegan's body. As he slowly recovered, she detected his intensifying embrace. Her heart swelled as his clumsy squeeze transformed into a gentle caress. She smiled like a young nanitic tickled by her mother, encounters that her early departure from Bilaluna had truncated. And she pressed her body against him to convey how she never wanted to lose him and was thrilled that he survived. All the while, his compassionate look never wavered. Rose saw in his gaze more than gratitude for a saved life, more than caring for a close friend, more than a longing for physical gratification, but the look of a lifelong promise of selfless love. It was a look she could not ignore and a look she returned with more feeling than she had ever experienced in her young life.

Once Rose knew Keegan was okay, she left his nest and told him not to answer the door for anyone. As she left, she dragged the two dead BUGants out back in the dark of the night. Rose opened a jar Clay had placed in her spy pack and sprinkled a silver powder over the bodies. She then sprayed the bodies with formic acid from a distance and walked away as the powdered sodium and formic acid reacted and instantly incinerated the two would-be assassins. It was so late by then that all ANTs were asleep; if not, they would have mistaken the resultant burst as a flash of lightning.

❧ ❧ ❧

Unwitting of Blood's sinister intentions for her and angered by the attack on Keegan, Rose awoke the next morning, strongly motivated to advance her plan. She completed her final socionics undoing lessons and inspired all her young and old students to take up arms against Blood's regime. The brown and black ANTs still took vitamin S, so they felt compelled to follow her commands. Also, the reversal of the FMR1 gene knockdown by removing doxycycline meant their larger brains were no longer mentally deficient. And the enhancement of their memory by PKM-zeta allowed them to understand better and remember the lessons Rose was teaching them. Though they comprehended what they had to do, she told them to wait for her command.

Rose met with Clay and Jasper to tell them she had completed the brown and black ANTS deconditioning and about the attack on Keegan. "Guys, the black and brown ANTs all understand the injustices they have endured, and they have heeded my call to revolt, and they only await my signal." She stood tall, shining her red abdomen. *I believe they are ready!*

Jasper grinned. "And what will be your signal to them?"

Rose smiled coyly. "When my shell turns as black as a stormy night sky." She turned her abdomen black. *Reading the Trinity book inspired my plan.*

"You are a genuine leader, my girl." Clay laughed. "All will be in awe when you turn before their eyes."

Rose oozed a sneaky scent. "I told them it would be contagious, and my lieutenants will change their coats too. One brown and one black." She raised two arms. "It will be the time for all Antunites to unite when a trinity of Scarlets change their hue." She smirked at the irony of it. *It is the target I have aimed for my whole life.*

Jasper laughed. "You read the chapter on histrionics."

Rose smiled. "Whatever works. Don't you agree?" She imagined herself with Blood under her pods. "The end justifies the means." *I savor using Rust and Blood's own tactics against their regime.*

Clay interjected. "But we must remove the conformity drug vitamin S from their capsules first." He raised a single claw. "They must have a choice, and the revolution must reflect free will, not bionics or socionics." He raised a second claw. "Otherwise, we're no better than Blood and the other leaders."

"Yes, and after Blood's attack, I think I can turn Keegan, so he'll join the revolution," concluded Rose. She wondered how Keegan was doing. *I am convinced his reservations about the system and our budding love will prevail.*

"Will Blood be suspicious that you helped Keegan fend off the attack?" asked Jasper.

"He didn't know we were together, and I disposed of the bodies," Rose smirked. "I had a messenger send a note, dated yester-hexay, stating Keegan would work from his country burrow for a few hexays." She recalled all the steps to ensure she hadn't missed anything. *I get a warm feeling knowing that Clay has taught me well. And I'm at the top of my game.*

Clay smiled. "It seemed you took care of everything." He patted her on the back. "Now, Jasper and I will work on removing vitamin S from their capsules, and then we can start."

Rose and Jasper nodded. Jasper raised his two claws, and the three flashed their true colors together.

CHAPTER 46

ROSE: REVEALED

Antalonia (Blood's rule, the current president)

AFTER THEIR LAST discussion and the attempted assassination, Rose was certain that Keegan would support the Antunite cause. Despite herself, she had also fallen for him and desperately wanted to see Keegan again before the revolution began. Rose was concerned about him, so she planned to meet Keegan again the following night. She ached to hold him again and see if he still had that look in his eyes that took her away. She craved the gaze that told her she was his and he was hers, and nothing else mattered.

Keegan greeted Rose at the door, "You look beautiful. Your cheek has healed."

Rose smiled. "Yes, it wasn't that bad." She inspected

Keegan. "What about you? Did the BUG venom burn you anywhere?" She looked him up and down. *I've been worried.*

"No, I'm fine, thanks to you. I'm very cautious now that I know what Blood is capable of."

"I was worried about you," Rose continued. "And I missed you." She realized she never wanted to part with him again. *He must know how I feel about him.*

Keegan took her claw. "Come in. I have been longing to see you, too."

Rose squeezed his claw. "I have thought of nothing else."

Keegan stared into Rose's eyes. "I didn't mean our last meeting to end as it did before the attack."

Rose furrowed her brow. "What do you mean?"

Keegan looked down. "With a silly discussion about politics."

Rose laughed. "Politics are never silly." She thought back to her mission and how she must turn Keegan. *Oops, but I am a spy.*

Keegan gazed upon Rose's face. "It is when there are much more important things to discuss."

Rose sparked her eyes repeatedly, releasing an enticing essence. "Like what?" She hoped his feelings matched hers. *Oh, still my heart.*

Keegan smiled. "Like how radiant you are and how much I want to hold you forever."

Rose laughed and moved in close to Keegan with her arms spread. "Yes, compared to that, politics seem silly. And I too wished our embrace lasted for an eternity." Her mind erased all thoughts of her mission. *Spy rules be damned.*

Keegan pressed his shell against hers and wrapped his arms

tightly around her. "I want you for my queen. Blood does not deserve such a pure heart."

Rose tightened their embrace. "Blood, who's Blood?" She lived for the moment. *Can it be true?*

Keegan eased his grip, held one of Rose's claws, and twirled her once around. "Will you dance with me tonight?"

Rose stabled herself and gazed into Keegan's eyes. "It's a dance I've waited for my entire life." She imagined her future with Keegan at her side. *I'm so dizzy. What's going on?*

Keegan cradled one limb under Rose's abdomen and another below her thorax and supported her as she leaned back slowly. He caressed her face with his third arm and raised Rose from the floor, twirling her to the bedroom. "My sweet rose, are you ready for this?"

Rose swooned and tilted her head back, letting herself go with dizziness. "For you, I'll always be ready." Her basic instincts overtook her. *Take me now.*

With a gentleness contrasting Blood's brutality, he deflowered his sweet rose as she smiled and glowed with a carefree vitality she had not known since leaving Bilaluna.

A radiant Rose gazed at the strong ANT beside her and breathed, "I never expected …."

Keegan sat up quickly. "Rose, what's happening? You're all black!"

Rose pulled a sheet over her darkened shell, spewing a fuzzy fragrance. "I am overwhelmed, you have …." *What's happening? I can't focus.*

"Don't hide." Keegan pulled on the sheet. "You already blew your cover."

Rose tugged the sheet back. "My body reveals my true colors." *He'll know I'm a spy.*

Keegan bolted upright. "Yes, a spy I should turn on, just as you have turned color."

"So, my passion for you will be my downfall. All you can see is black." *Will this be our undoing?*

Keegan ripped back the sheet. "Yes, and it's the most breathtaking sight I have ever seen. My rose has transformed into a shining black beauty, like the majestic black Raven on Earth."

"Raven, I haven't heard that name for many hexs." Her mind raced to her larval infancy on Bilaluna. *I forgot—it's what Mama first called me.*

Keegan held Rose's claws. "You are not from here."

"No." She turned her head, afraid to see if he was angry. *How can I lie to him now?*

Keegan squeezed her claws. "So, it's true?"

Rose frowned. "What's true?" She looked back at him, confused. *Once a spy, now I'm an open book.*

"Chameleon ANTs from Bilaluna."

"You knew about us?" Rose sighed and wondered how long he might have suspected. *I thought he turned for me. But wait!*

"I only knew of a rumor." Keegan shook his head. "And I did not believe it."

"Well, it's true, and you have one in your clutches." Rose looked away again, fearing the worst. *I'm doomed!*

Keegan squeezed her claws even tighter. "And I never intend to let you go."

Rose tried to pull away, but couldn't break Keegan's grasp. "Will you take me to Blood, then?" She sensed his grasp tighten. *He loves me, and I've turned him. Or have I?*

Keegan first nodded, then shook his head. "Then I'd

lose you forever." He pulled Rose close and released a radiant reek. "No, you are mine, and I am yours! We will resist Blood together."

~ ~ ~

Buoyed by her encounter with Keegan, Rose garnered the courage the next morning to return to the sacred library with the borrowed books and face Blood. She first went to Jasper's nest, picked up the book he had read, and contacted Blood. When he answered, Blood did not let on that he knew about her book theft and agreed to meet her. Rose did not think she had been found out and assumed that Blood would be ashamed of his earlier abusive behavior and be on his best behavior.

Rose thanked Blood as she stepped through the doorway. "I appreciate you receiving me so early in the morning."

Blood smiled. "I said you could come here whenever you wanted." He looked at her sheepishly. "I hope you will forgive me for my brazenness the last time we met."

Rose grinned as she entered the library. "At least we established the ground rules for the game."

Blood's eyes went blank for a hexond. "Yes, rules are fundamental, especially to rulers." He tried hard to suppress his anger. *I must conceal my intentions.*

Rose walked towards the small room at the back with her bag on her shoulder. "I'll need access to the restricted zone. There's a reference book I hope helps with my program to re-educate older ANTs." She smiled as Blood unlocked the door to the small room. "I want to reinforce socionic training with those out of school."

"That's a worthy effort," Blood smirked. "And I'll give you plenty of time in there." He looked at the bag on her shoulder and blocked the exit with his body. "And be sure to return the books in your bag to their rightful place." He spoke with an emotionless cadence. *I caught you in the act, you insolent girl.*

Rose squirmed in the chair where she sat. "I'll be sure to." She feared the worst.

Blood spoke as he swung the door shut. "You stay here and think about the rules you've violated. And I'll let you out when you are ready to play the game by my rules."

Rose jumped out of her chair and tried to block the door, but she was too late. The door slammed, and she couldn't open it as it locked from both sides.

Rose desperately called out. "I only took them out briefly and returned them. Please let me out."

Blood fumed on the other side of the locked door. "It's not only the restricted books, but also your attitude. You need to recognize who is in charge." He kicked the door. "You have knocked me down for the last time. Now, you can be my queen, my prisoner, or both. It's your choice." He emitted a solid stench as his anger seethed out. *I'll follow my grandpa's advice.*

Rose heard Blood's pod steps as he left the library and stomped down the stairs.

CHAPTER 47

ROSE: RESTRAINED

Antalonia (Blood's rule, the current president)

CLAY WAS HELPING Jasper prepare the last step for the revolution—packing vitamin S capsules with placebo instead of S-2-aminobutane, the active mind control ingredient in the vitamin S tablet. They ensured the new capsules still contained PKM-zeta but also lacked doxycycline. This combination would cure brown and black ANTs of mental deficiencies and improve their memories. But they will no longer feel compelled to follow orders. They'll have free will and be smart enough to make their own choices. They had just filled enough capsules to supply all the brown and black ANTs in the colony, including the hybrids, for at least one hexek. They had informed all brown and black ANTs to discard their remaining vitamin S capsules because of a recall and only take new ones delivered overnight.

Keegan arrived as they finished packing the capsules into RoAChant hybrids for delivery. "Have either of you seen Rose? She was supposed to meet me for tea a hexour ago." He pointed at his watch. "She is usually very punctual."

"Rose came by to get a textbook from me early this morning," Jasper replied. "I think she was going to the palace library. Since Rose said she was in a hurry, we didn't talk."

Clay's ommatidia shook. "I told Rose I would return them, and I didn't want her going anywhere near the palace." Clay took a swig from a small strong sap bottle he began carrying around.

"She never should have gone there." Keegan got all flustered. "I know what Blood is capable of. He wants Rose as his queen, and he'll stop at nothing."

Jasper pulled at his antennae, discharging a scrawny scent. "I am sorry. I was preparing these capsules, and I didn't think." He remembered their brief morning encounter and how careless he had been. *What have I done?*

"Why are you filling capsules?" asked Keegan. "I thought we had enough for hexths."

Jasper froze like a cockroach, with nowhere to scurry. "Ah, we could always use more."

Clay interjected. "Yeah, the flood contaminated many lots."

"There's been no flood," Keegan smirked. "It hasn't rained for hexths. You guys are up to something."

Jasper stuttered. "N-n-no, we were preparing for a flood." His mood deflated further. *Gadfly! It just keeps getting worse for us.*

"I know." Keegan smiled. "You two are working with Rose."

Clay shrugged and took another swig from his bottle. "On what?"

"It's okay." Keegan patted Clay on the back. "Rose came clean to me, and I know she's a chameleant from Bilaluna." He motioned for Clay and Jasper to sit down. "Rose saved my life, and I promised to help her. But she didn't tell me her plans yet."

"Rose said she was what?" Clay replied.

"Rose and I are lovers." Keegan insisted. "Her true colors shone through in a moment of passion. I told her I no longer support Blood and will join her resistance effort." He raised his claws in the air. "Would I be confessing if I was not on your side? I am risking my life telling you this if you are not also rebels."

Clay extended his claw to his colleague. "Keegan, I have known you since you began at the breeding halls, and I trust you." He shook his claw hard. "Rose told us how Blood tried to kill you. Welcome to the resistance. We can explain our plans to you soon, but right now, we need to save Rose."

Keegan extended another claw to Jasper. "Rose is in grave danger with that brute, Blood. What can we do?"

Jasper thought for a moment. "Where would he be keeping her?" He perked up for a moment. *I need to redeem myself.*

Keegan tapped his temples. "He would want to keep her close, and he wants her to submit to his will."

Clay thought hard about the palace. "There are no jail cells at the palace, no place to lock her up."

"Maybe he's got her down in the crypts," suggested Jasper. "They say it's like a dungeon down there." His desperation rang loud. *I bet he has Rose chained to an icy wall.*

"We could try there, but it may be difficult to get in," noted Clay. "We'd have to go through the palace."

"Wait, the sacred library, the seat of our colony's knowledge. It's protected like a fortress." Keegan raised a single claw.

"And the restricted zone doors lock from both sides. I accidentally got locked in there once when I shut the door by mistake."

"Of course, she borrowed restricted books," Jasper interjected. "I bet he found out and locked her in there." *I can right my wrong.* Bold confidence overtook him. "We should go there first."

Clay banged his claws together. "But how will we get her out?"

"There's a window." Keegan raised his claws like he was grabbing two rails. "I tried to get out that way, but bars blocked the opening." Keegan shrugged. "Can you believe Rust made them of gold? Royal gold bars to block access to the palace library."

Jasper banged a claw on his head. "Aha, royal water." His infectious smile returned. *My inspiration warms me.*

Keegan stretched his antennae. "No, I said royal gold bars, like prison bars."

Jasper laughed. "No, 'royal water' is a solution that dissolves gold." He pointed over to his lab bench. "It's a hydrochloric and nitric acid mixture, and I have them both in stock." He snickered some more. "If they were steel or iron, I couldn't help you, but gold, I can dissolve." He imagined Rose slipping through the bars. *I knew my extensive reading would help.*

Keegan shook his head in amazement. "How do you know about royal water?"

Jasper smiled. "I read it in *The Encyclopedia of Human Discoveries*, the book I just gave back to Rose." He shined his shell, emitting a bulged bouquet. "I memorized the entire volume this past hexek-end." He buoyed at the prospect of saving Rose. *My pride now overcomes my guilt.*

Clay stood up. "Let's hurry. You get the chemicals, and I'll get a ladder from the breeding halls."

Keegan put out a claw. "No, we can't bring a ladder up to

the palace. It will create too much suspicion." He tapped on his shoulders. "Clay, you stand on my shoulders, and Jasper can climb up on yours. The second floor is not that high. Jasper should be able to reach the bars."

Jasper dissolved nitric acid to 65% in one large vial and hydrochloric acid to 35% in another. He explained that he'd mix them when they got to the palace. Royal water is explosive when mixed and jostled and loses its corrosive effect quickly. He grabbed two sponges and a pair of rubber gloves. He explained that he'd soak the sponges in the solution and wrap them around the bars to dissolve them.

Clay noted, "Rose is slim. You probably only need to dissolve one bar." He patted Keegan on the back. "Let's go rescue your girl."

～ ～ ～

As most of Antalonia's population had sub-par intelligence and those that would oppose Blood's regime had been taking a conformity drug, there wasn't much need for security at the palace. Blood stationed a single guard at the gate outside the palace grounds. Keegan approached the guard and told him he requested that Clay and Jasper meet him in the library to do some urgent research. He explained that the antibiotic they were using to ward off the lethal bacteria that caused the earlier epidemic was losing effectiveness. They had to find another that would work. He said this was a scientific matter that Blood would not understand, so he should just let him in and not disturb the Czar since it was dinnertime. The guard bought the story and began escorting him to the front doors when Clay and Jasper showed up. He then accompanied the three to the front doors, which he unlocked. The guard was about to walk them through the palace when Keegan told him he knew the way around the palace and the guard should get back to his post. After the guard left, the three ducked around the corner towards the library window.

Keegan stood directly under the window. "Okay, Clay, climb up my back." When Clay was in place, he grunted, "Now, Jasper, pass the vials up to Clay so you can climb. Work fast; he's heavy." Keegan took charge, eager to save his love.

Clay reached down and grabbed the two vials. "Okay, Jasper, climb aboard."

Jasper climbed up Keegan's back and then Clay's. "Okay, Clay, pass me the vials, and I'll mix them on the ledge." He first tapped on the window. "Rose, are you in there?" he whispered.

Rose peaked out the window and opened the glass panes when she recognized Jasper. "How did you get here?" She looked down and saw the tower of Keegan, Clay, and Jasper. "My three saviors. Hurry, Blood might come up here looking for dessert after dinner."

Keegan called up, "Are you okay?"

Rose sighed. "Yes, he just locked me up in here."

Jasper poured the hydrochloric acid into the nitric acid and swirled the solutions around. "This will dissolve the bar," he explained to Rose. "Then you can squeeze through and climb down over us."

Rose smiled. "Brilliant, you read about it in the book I gave you?" she surmised.

Jasper nodded and put on the gloves. "Yes, I'll pour some solution on these sponges and press them against the bars. Stand back. There may be fumes."

As the solution hit the first sponge, it melted into nothing. "Oh no, a sponge won't work." Jasper peered through the window. "Is there anything in there I could use?" He was desperate to salvage his plan.

Rose looked around and found a loose metal bookend on the stacks. "How about this?"

Jasper grabbed the metal divider. "Perfect."

He used the narrow end of the bookend to chip away at the stone wall at the base of one of the gold bars, creating a slight depression around the bar. He then dribbled his royal water solution into the stone well and waited for it to react.

"That should do it." Jasper smiled, proud of his idea. "The solution shouldn't affect the stone, but will eat through the bar." He looked up at Rose. "Cross your claws."

Light yellow fumes emanated from the pool as the solution turned orange. Jasper and Rose watched as the gold bar slowly dissolved. Jasper added more royal water to the well as the gold bar thinned. After a few hexutes, Jasper shook the bar, which remained solid. Jasper quickly yanked on it, but it didn't move. Then he pulled as hard as he could, and the bar bent outward, severed at its base. The momentum of his tugging caused him to lurch away from the ledge, and the gold bar broke free, and Clay had to use his free limb to brace Jasper's back. Rose squeezed through the remaining bars and climbed down Jasper, Clay, then Keegan, whom she hugged hard before jumping to the ground.

While Rose and her comrades hid in some bushes on the palace grounds, Keegan approached the palace gatekeeper and told him he had forgotten one of his bags in the palace library. It was a rouse to get him to leave his post, and when he did, Clay, Jasper, and Rose slipped off the palace grounds. Yet, before they slithered away, Blood finished his dinner and headed up to the library to confront Rose. He smirked when he observed the door to the restricted zone, unperturbed and locked shut. A draft blew the door open as he unlocked it. He scanned the empty room. The window was open, and a small pool of gold sat where the missing gold bar once was. He looked out the window, first down to the ground and then across the property. When Blood noticed the guard was not there, he scanned the area around the gate more closely. As his focus peaked, he saw Clay, Jasper, and Rose exiting the grounds.

Blood ran down the stairs as fast as his three hind legs could. He reached the front doors just as the guard opened the door for Keegan. The three stood in stunned silence before Keegan bolted toward the gate. Blood ordered his guard to chase him, but Keegan had a head start. Blood crossed the hallway and pushed the button that remotely closed the gate. The mechanism clanged into gear, and the gate slowly began to shut. As the barrier rolled along its track, Keegan sprinted towards the opening. With each of Keegan's strides, the gate edged nearer to closing. Keegan was still several steps from the exit when the gap matched his own width—he sighed and slowed as he realized he would never make it. Then Rose's claw swung out from behind the palace fence, and the automatic sensor triggered the mechanism to halt the closing gate. Rose stepped out into the breach and encouraged Keegan to keep running. As Keegan slipped through the opening, Rose glared at Blood, who watched, defeated, at the palace doorway. The gatekeeper, much heftier than Keegan, could not pass through the aperture and could only watch as Keegan and Rose disappeared into the night.

CHAPTER 48

CZAR BLOOD AND JASPER: CLUE IN

Antalonia (Blood's rule, the current president)

AFTER ROSE'S ESCAPE, Blood called for an early morning meeting with his ministers and the chief of police. He wanted to capture and interrogate the rogue leaders. He needed to determine whether this was just a plot to break Rose out or was there some grander scheme apod.

Blaze, the chief of police, arrived first and asked, "What is the matter that you called us here so early?"

Blood explained to Blaze how three of his top leaders had crossed him and helped break Rose out of the palace. "I know Rose and Keegan are now mating, and I expect Keegan forced Clay and Jasper to help him." He stared hard at Blaze. "You need to find them. We must punish them all, but Keegan has to go." He wondered what happened to the BUGants he commissioned to kill Keegan. *I will eliminate Keegan for his insubordination, and because he has stolen my queen.*

"And what about the female, Rose." Blaze polished his red thorax. "What should I do with her?"

"Bring her here. She may never love me, but she will be my queen." Blood pointed towards the windows and doors. "Have your security experts reinforce the palace to restrict her movements." He considered how long it would take to break her. *She'll be my queen and my prisoner.*

Terracotta and Alhambra, the ministers of social control and war and inter-planetary relations, arrived shortly after that.

Blood complained to his ministers, "My servant was nowhere to be found this morning, and I had to make my own breakfast." His thoughts turned to the three that broke out Rose. *I think something is going on.*

Minister Alhambra responded, "The same thing happened to me."

Minister Terracotta added, "As I walked here, I noticed the streets were dirty, and brown and black ANTs refused my directions."

Alhambra chimed in again. "Did you notice that many browns and blacks now communicate better than usual?"

Terracotta replied, "Now that you mention it, I did. And many are congregating in the main square."

Blood fumed. "I am worried that Rose and our other leaders are colluding with the brown and black ANTs." He looked to Blaze. "Call in all the BUGants. We may soon have an unruly crowd." He then turned to Alhambra, wafting a brawny bouquet. "Prepare our ultimate weapons for use and aim them at Bilaluna and the main square." He pounded his claws on the table. "If my suspicions are right, we may need to use them." He thought of Rust's war with the Antunites. *I can be just as ruthless as my grandfather.*

🐜 🐜 🐜

After leaving the palace grounds, Rose, Keegan, Clay, and Jasper hid at the now elderly Darci's burrow. Clay filled Keegan in on all the plans for the impending revolution.

Keegan looked at his watch. "When are the brown and black ANTs assembling in the square?"

Jasper responded, "They all received the vitamin S placebo this morning, and S-2-aminobutane has a short half-life. They will already be defiant—no longer complying with colony rules and the leaders' instructions."

Rose interjected. "But they've been smarter for hexays and understood my suggestions for why they should revolt."

Clay jumped in. "We knew we'd have to act fast once the vitamin S wore off. The leaders will notice their insubordination." He looked at his watch. "We arranged the assembly for noon to-hexay." He thought of the mayhem that might ensue. *We'd better get moving.*

Clay was fervent about climbing the ultimate step after masterminding his staircase of a scheme. Yet as they approached the pinnacle, he feared everything could still fall apart. He fretted most of the night and needed to imbibe a bottle of strong sap to help himself sleep. Not yet sober when he awoke, he drank more to calm himself. Clay thought of all the friends he double-crossed along the way, and how they had almost lost Rose. He long suffered from the guilt of killing Rumo and his other young rocket scientist friends. Clay also felt remorse for using genetic engineering to keep so many ANTs dim-witted for hexs and killing innocent ANTs with bacterial infections. He also worried that they would fail despite all his preparations.

"That's within the hexour. We should leave to greet the multitude soon." Keegan looked around the room. "We should figure out some disguises."

Rose snapped her claws, knowing her comrades would catch her drift. "Only you need to worry about that."

Keegan watched in amazement as his three colleagues all turned brown. "I guess that's true."

Keegan fashioned a disguise rubbing his abdomen with old ashes from the fireplace, and they prepared to leave.

🐜 🐜 🐜

Just before they left, Clay received a panicked message from Beewish: 'Blood has figured out our plans and is threatening to destroy moon Bilaluna with an antimatter blast. They have stored tons of antimatter which will destroy our moon when the package is released and reacts with matter.'

Rose shrugged, "What is antimatter, and can it destroy the moon, or is Blood just bluffing?"

Jasper replied. "I read about this in *The Encyclopedia of Human Discoveries*. When antimatter combines with matter, it's the most powerful explosive known. It can be multiple times more devastating than the biggest nuclear bomb if there's enough of it." He recalled a picture from the book which showed a demolished test site. *I can't believe they'll use it.*

Clay interjected, "But isn't it hard to produce and even harder to store?" It was not his expertise, but Clay was widely read.

"There were three entries about antimatter in the

encyclopedia." Jasper pressed his temples. "The first described what it is, the second discussed how to store it, and the third explained how to use it to make a weapon." The pages of the volume sailed across his mind. *I know all the details. Just don't panic, think!*

Rose frowned, "So, Blood's military could have an antimatter weapon?"

"I'm afraid so. The section on weapon production was very detailed," Jasper explained. "But there's something that's a little off." He knew that something was amiss. *I think we can drop the Defcon from two to three.*

Keegan shrugged. "What do you mean?"

"Wait." Jasper held up a claw. "Let me think. Darci, do you have a marker?" He yearned to see it written. *I must get my cortical wheels spinning.*

Darci reached in her desk drawer, pulled out a marker, and passed it to Jasper.

Jasper grabbed the marker. "Do you mind if I write on your walls?" He could reproduce the words, but could he grasp their meaning? *Focus, focus. I can do it.*

"Not if it'll save Bilaluna," Darci replied.

Jasper wrote two pages of scientific text about antimatter storage, underlining the words positrons, antiprotons, and octupole trap. He then scribbled six pages of scientific text about antimatter weapons production, highlighting the same three words. Words were splattered all over Darci's living room walls. Jasper looked at what he had written, concentrating on the underlined words.

"It seems like it's the same, but I keep thinking something is different." He wondered whether he could solve the puzzle. *Something is amiss, but what is it?*

Jasper backed up to see the two sets of text from a distance. He stared at the text on the wall, pulled on his antennae, then closed his eyes and pictured the book's pages in his mind. Something about the text had Jasper in a tizzy; there was a clue there, but he couldn't find it. After several hexutes of pacing, reading, and pacing, he halted.

Jasper spewed a popping perfume, "That's it!" He tossed the uncapped marker towards the wall like a dart spinning end over end and the point splatted against the wall on a phrase to the left 'expose to cold electrons.' "Do you see it?" He chilled as a nectar-filled bee that returned to the hive before the rain. *I got it! There's nothing to worry about.*

Keegan and the three Antunites stood with their eyes glazed, and their mouths gaped, trying to understand the scientific gibberish, until Rose spat out, "What?"

"The weapons instruction omits the step needed to cool the antimatter when it is being stored." Jasper threw his arms in the air. "Without exposure to cooled electrons, small amounts of antimatter generated during each production cycle would react with matter before being stored in the octupole trap." He stared hard at Darci's wall and all the equations and text.

Rose shrugged. "Can you skip to the point?"

"The authors left a key step out of the weapon building instructions, probably to prevent ignorant scientists from using the methods to produce a weapon of mass destruction." Jasper jumped up and tapped the word 'cool' on the wall. "This step is missing, so if Blood's military scientists used these instructions," he pointed to the text on the right, "they never actually stored any antimatter." He sighed like he never had before.

Clay interjected, "What happens to the antimatter if you don't cool it?"

"If it's not cool, the antimatter would react with matter when generated." Jasper pointed to some equations on the left. "But you must produce antimatter slowly, and the small amounts generated during each cycle could barely light a light-bulb." *I'm right. I know I'm right.* He thought of Blood's military scientists. *Those guys are imbeciles.*

"But what does this mean for our cause?" Keegan asked.

"Blood thought he was generating and storing tons of anti-matter over hexades." Jasper laughed. "But the antimatter was burning up. His weapon is full of blanks." Jasper flopped himself back into a chair. He imagined Blood's face when the blast did not blow. *Blood is surrounded by idiots.*

"Are you sure about this? It's kind of important," noted Rose.

"I have met the scientists at the war and interplanetary relations ministry." Jasper rolled his eyes. "I can say with near certainty they would have followed the recipe on the right and not even considered there was anything wrong." He rubbed his claws together and retraced his thoughts. *I couldn't be surer.*

"Near certainty?" Keegan queried.

"There's a lot of uncertainty in science, but less with the military." Jasper smiled. "I'm betting we're okay." He stood and pointed again to the word cool. *Don't worry. Bilaluna is safe.*

Keegan grinned. "I don't know astrophysics, but I know Blood's military, and it's never recovered from the loss of scientists since the explosion at the rocket test site." He patted Jasper on the back. "And I trust your judgment."

"Clay, message Beewish and tell her it's a bluff." Rose pointed towards the door. "And let's get to the square."

Clay grimaced at the mention of the killed scientists but nodded and punched out the message on his transmitter.

CHAPTER 49

ROSE:
A DARK REVOLUTION

Antalonia (Blood's rule, the current president)

AFTER CLAY SENT his 'All Clear' message to Beewish, the four rebel leaders dashed to the colony's main square, where thousands of angry brown and black ANTs had amassed. As they left, Clay took another long swig from his mickey, and Keegan rubbed more soot over himself. The others remained brown until they approached the bandstand in the center of the square.

As they neared the square, they spotted a line of police BUGants inspecting everyone who arrived. Rose leaned towards the others. "Look down and project your brownest brown. We need to blend in."

Keegan was slow to react, and a police BUGant grabbed

him as he approached. "I know you—you're that head breeder guy we're looking for."

As Keegan stumbled for words, Rose grabbed his claw and said, "Keep up, Soot, we don't want to lose you."

The BUGant looked over at the mocha-colored Rose, then back at Keegan, observing his black soot-colored chest. "Sorry, I didn't realize you were one of those halfwits. Move along."

Blood's BUGant police were in force, but they could not impose their will over the mob, as it outnumbered them by over six hundred to one. The BUGants simply watched the hordes, which until then were assembling peacefully.

After they passed the police line and were almost at the band shell, the four paused and ensured they were undercover, surrounded by the masses. As all eyes in the gathering were looking up at the stage, waiting for Rose's arrival, the three spies discretely turned their shells back to red. Clay and Jasper then picked up Rose on their shoulders and climbed up the stairs to the stage. There was at first a murmur in the crowd as the three appeared on stage. Then, as the three leaders reached the podium, the mob cheered louder than an orchestra of crickets at dusk.

Keegan, who wrapped himself in a red robe to hide the black soot, jumped on the stage and grabbed the pheromonic microphone at the conductor's podium.

"Attention, attention! As promised, our esteemed master of socionics, Rose, has come to you. But she is not who you think she is. Like a majestic bird that soars on Earth, she has flown to you from Bilaluna. Your master has come here to free you all from tyranny, but you must fight for her. You must fight for your freedom. Although you know her as Rose, a beautiful red Scarlet, she is an Antunite like all of you." Keegan pointed at the crowd. "All of you brown and black ANTs have the Antunite gene, and they punished you for it. You must stand up to those who oppress you and join Rose as I have." He pounded his thorax. "But know now that her name is not Rose, and she is not a Scarlet. You will see right before your eyes within hex-onds why her true name is Raven. She's the purest black beauty you have ever seen." He stood tall and orated loudly. "She is an Antunite through and through, and she will show her true colors here to-hexay."

When Keegan mentioned the name Raven, Rose's shell slowly changed colors. Her shiny pure red color first dulled, then transformed gradually from red ochre to shiny copper and then the light brown of polished amber. Rose paused at each stage until she turned from cocoa butter to the dark brown of a coffee bean until she was as black as the darkest night. Clay and Jasper also changed color as the crowd oohed and aahed. Clay turned black and Jasper brown.

And Keegan spoke again. "Her color is infectious, and her cause is contagious." He handed the microphone to Raven with pride he'd never known.

As Clay and Jasper turned her, Raven pointed at the crowd in all directions. "You all know my message. I have spread it throughout the colony in my classes of late." She pointed to her heart. "Join me now with your words. Join me with your actions. Join with your hearts. Join me now with your pincers, claws, and sprayers." She again pointed towards the crowd. "Antunites unite! Antunites prevail!" She repeated, "Antunites unite!" The crowd responded *en masse*, "Antunites prevail!" She imagined herself standing up to Rust like her great-grand-mother. *I am like Antebon leading her troops into battle.* She dis-charged a robust reek.

Keegan reached up to grasp Raven's claw, and as his claw reached hers, she called out, "I am Raven, great-granddaughter of Antebon!" And her blackness cast such darkness that her shadow enveloped Keegan, who dropped his red robe and appeared to turn black along with Raven with his soot.

And then Keegan called out, "Antunites unite," and an even louder crowd chanting like the drumming of thousands of deathwatch beetles replied, "Antunites prevail!"

Just then, several BUGants stormed the stage and charged toward Raven. Still elevated, Raven saw them coming and sprayed the lead BUGant with a concentrated formic acid she had been generating. The spray scorched his exoskeleton and his guts spewed from his abdomen as he fell to the floor. The violence spurred a multitude of ANTs to leap on stage and overwhelm the BUGants that had rushed Raven and her crew. Then Chief of police Blaze jumped onto the scene with a claw-held pheromone amplifier, blasted a siren, and yelled, "Stop, halt! I have a message from the Czar. You must squelch this revolt immediately. If you do not yield and surrender these rebel leaders to the authorities, Blood will use our ultimate weapon to destroy Bilaluna. He will bombard it with antimatter that will blow it to pieces." He pointed to the ministry's roof. "And we have another antimatter gun aimed at this square."

Keegan took the microphone from Raven. "It's a bluff, and the ultimate weapon is a dud. They will not harm Bilaluna or us."

Half of the ministry of war headquarters roof opened as the crowd heeded Keegan's words and pummeled the police BUGants surrounding them. Then the barrel of a giant cannon extended and cast a long shadow over the square. The crowd gasped as the chief of police spoke again. "This is your last warning. You must attack those here on the stage and not the police."

Raven once again seized the microphone. "Blood only has power over those he deceives? He is bluffing. Fight for your rights. Antunites unite." She again recalled the stories of her great-grandmother's plight. *I can imagine Rust launching the warheads that killed all Antebon's troops.*

As the crowd attacked the surrounding police, the chief fired a flare into the sky toward the palace. The cannon swiveled and stopped when aimed directly at Bilaluna. Soldiers pointed a second shorter mortar sitting on the closed part of the roof towards the square. Blood fired another flare from the palace towards the war ministry to approve the attack. The crowd recoiled, unsettled by the red streak. Within hexonds, millions of particles blasted from the enormous gun towards Bilaluna. All eyes turned towards Bilaluna as a jet of particles left the cannon's barrel and zoomed towards the moon. Every ANT held their breath until the glowing particles, reflecting the light from the solar star, rained down on Bilaluna, and … nothing happened.

Raven shone like a polished black mirror, releasing a brilliant bouquet. "As I told you, listen only to those who tell you the truth. Blood's weapon was a dud. But my weapon. All of you! Will take him down." She thought of Antebon's delight seeing Rust under her pods. *We can win this. We can prevail.*

The crowd turned on the BUGants as they seized on Raven's words. The smell of formic acid overtook the square. "Take him down! Take him down!" the crowd chanted.

The BUGants fought back, spitting at and biting as many rebels as possible. The crowd of mostly black and brown ANTs overwhelmed the BUGants with their burning acid and their sheer numbers, but Blood used the emergency warning system to call all red ANTs in the colony to come to fight. Alhambra also ordered thousands of soldiers from the headquarters to march toward the square. The BUGants were retreating until the red ANTs arrived as reinforcements, then they forged forward into the crowd. The more distant soldiers quick-marched from their position behind the band shell.

Together, the BUGants and red ANTs corralled the black and brown ANTs. Raven and Keegan urged the Antunites to fight, while Clay and Jasper jumped the chief of police, who was still on the stage. Jasper held the police chief while Clay used his pincers to slice his throat. Yet the drunken Clay stumbled when he pulled away from the falling victim, and the BUGant's right fang pierced the exoskeleton of his upper abdomen. Nearly pickled with strong sap, Clay did not flinch at the stab and raised himself as if nothing had happened. Only sustaining a half dose of venom, which squirted as Blaze fell, Clay was not immediately disabled.

The scene urged the black and brown ANTs on, but in time, the red ANTs and BUGants got the upper claw and closed in on the black and brown ANTs. The four rebel leaders jumped off the band shell and started surging the crowd towards the palace, in the opposite direction of the war ministry. The surge could not break through as more and more red ANTs arrived. A daunting red ANT grabbed Raven from behind, but Keegan sheered his hind legs with his pincers as Raven fell to the ground. Additional red ANT reinforcements arrived, and the revolution seemed doomed. They assumed things would only crash and burn once the army arrived.

Raven and Keegan were considering surrendering when they saw a line of gladiators flooding the square. Two by two, the RoAChant gladiators flanked groups of red ANTs, crushing their victims as they squeezed together. A small group of the gladiators, including Dolomite, the current gladiator champion, stormed over towards the platoon of brown soldier ANTs marching up to the band shell. Brown ANTs soldiers were among the most avid fans of gladiator matches since they knew gladiators were RoAChants derived from brown chi ANTs, their color mates. The gladiator needed no words. The brown ANT soldiers knew what Dolomite wanted, and they all stopped marching. A small group of soldiers broke ranks and aligned themselves with the gladiators. The general leading the soldiers was a red ANT that couldn't care less about gladiators and treated his brown ANT troops with disdain. When another soldier attempted to join the gladiators, the general grabbed him and sliced his throat with his claw, ordering the soldiers to march again.

As he turned to urge his troops on, the general did not notice that Dolomite and his tag-team mate had flanked him while he barked. Then, in less than a hexond, the tag team collapsed and squeezed the general so ferociously that his insides popped out of his exoskeleton, with his guts shooting several feet in the air. The shock and awe dissipated quickly as the transfixed troops roared like spectators at the Colosseum and stepped in line behind their heroes.

Throngs of brown ANT soldiers, no longer brainwashed by vitamin S, jumped the clawful of other red ANT commanders, and the troops broke ranks and swarmed the square. Most soldiers joined the rebels and began fighting the BUGants and red ANTs surrounding them. One surviving commander tried to rally those soldiers who had not joined the insurgents. Then an army of newly arrived hybrids closed in on the red ANTs and BUGants from all sides, thwarting his efforts. More gladiators rushed in first and tossed red ANTs around like crumpled paper thrown in the trash.

The remaining RoAChants arrived fully loaded with cargo and crushed the red ANTs that still stood. FLYants dropped trees, and the BEEants stung them while they were down, while WoBBants bored into the skulls of all the foe they could find. In just a few hexours, the rebels slaughtered most BUGants and many red ANTs while others scattered. But a large group of red ANTs begged the rebels for mercy and joined their fight to free all of Antalonia from their oppressors.

Raven and Keegan led the mob to capture Czar Blood in his palace. They crashed down the gates and burst through the doors. They scoured the residence but could not find Blood till Keegan suggested the crypts, and they descended the stairs. It was now dusk, and the stairway was dark, but the crowd lit torches. Without arteries and veins, hemolymph courses through ANT's bodies quite slowly, so it took some time before the BUGant's venom reached Clay's heart, but once there, it quickly pumped to his brain. He marched with Raven and Keegan, but he lagged, and his life spirit wavered as he staggered into the crypt.

Blood hid in the crypt where he had buried his idols as the crowd combed the palace. He locked the double-steel doors and trembled, alone in the dark. He spoke to his grandfather and Rudyard one last time. "Papa, how could you let the missile program die? A nuclear attack on Bilaluna would have stopped them, I'm sure. And Rust, you were so powerful, but your antimatter gun shot blanks." He pounded on the chest of Rust's effigy and kicked the carving of Rudyard's knee. "I am surrounded by rebels and deserters and inept relatives of stone.

I assumed your defenses would protect me, and what do I get?"
He shook the rock figures violently. "Two silent statues mock
me and don't answer my call." A raging reek fogged the crypt.

The capture and slaying of Blood are best told through the
verse below that his demise inspired:

A Raven, Two Stones, and the Crush of Blood

The mob used tree limbs to batter down the steel doors
and found Blood in the crypt as he crawled on the floor.
Raven led the crowd through the now wide-open portal
to settle the score with the evil mere mortal.
She thought of Beeutee and Antebon as her shell shone dark black.
She thought of Currant and Antnoir as she led the final attack.
Blood hid behind Rust's image as the crypt crowd did swell.
And the hordes pushed Raven up on the busts o'er Blood's shell.
She pressed so hard against the imposing stone papa
that it leaned midst the force on the daunting rock grampa.
Blood angrily shot his spray at his foes
And the mace hit Clay amidst his death throes.
The venom and acid took down the brave Clay,
but the mass of his corpse further pushed on the display.
Then domino Rust squashed the cowering young Czar,
whose hull snapped like a twig in his final hexour.
Guts oozed out Blood's shell as Raven topped the stone sires.
Before Keegan and Jasper smashed the statues of Czars.
Then they buried the dried Blood atop the earth's crust,
neath Rudyard rubble and pieces of Rust.

Raven, Keegan, and Jasper were so pumped up by the stress
of battle that they didn't discover Clay's lifeless exoskeleton until
after they buried Blood. Raven found Clay leaning against the

pedestal where Rust's statue once stood. She could tell from his dehydrated shell that there was no chance to revive him. Raven tapped Jasper on the shoulder and pointed at Clay's body.

She trembled uncontrollably as her hormones converted her state from stress to shock. Jasper clung onto her to both still her quivering and steady himself. They both thought back to all the times that Clay had supported them, their lessons, their lively discussions, and all their plans. Their plot succeeded, but neither expected that the rock that provided the foundation for their scaffold would collapse as the Antunites rose. The revolution was always Clay, and Clay was forever the revolution. Raven may have led the final charge, but Clay set it in motion. And it was Clay that Raven and Jasper looked to for inspiration, courage, love, and support.

Keegan approached slowly as he took in the dreadful scene, and Raven fell to her knees before him. Jasper and Keegan raised Raven, and the three held each other for what seemed like hexours as the surrounding crowd cheered, acclaiming their freedom. Only the three truly knew Clay's vital contribution to the cause. Although they, too, would celebrate their success and the Antunites liberation, this moment was for Clay, their mentor and friend, and for Raven and Jasper, the ground ever beneath their pods.

CHAPTER 50

THE NEW LEADERS: HOMECOMINGS

Antalonia (Queen Beelight's reign, the current ruler)

IT WAS A time of massive upheavals on Bilaluna and Intopia, but joyous ones except for Clay's death. Perhaps the most triumphant news was that Antnoir was at long last released from prison. Waiting for Raven's return from Bilaluna, Keegan invited Antnoir over to surprise her. Antnoir was elderly now, but her time in prison had not dulled her wit, and she still followed politics with a passion she had when young. She still hated Rust and the empire he had created and was ecstatic that the Antunites had dismantled it.

Keegan helped secure Antnoir's emancipation, and she expressed her appreciation, "Thank you, Keegan. I thought I was going to rot in that jail." Antnoir started. "There's no way an heir of Rust would ever let me out. And you even got me a job at the community center."

"Well, thankfully, we ended his family line and evil regime." Keegan laughed. "And I needed some help at the center."

"I hear that our government will be more like Bilaluna's." Antnoir raised her claw. "That's the direction Antebon would have taken us if we could have beaten that tyrant Rust."

Keegan nodded. "Yes, there is no longer a czar or even a president. A Congress of thirty-two senators and thirty-two members of the Hive of Representatives will rule our society."

He explained to Antnoir how the voters would elect two males and two females from the seven cyborg families and two male and female hybrids to each branch of the new Congress. The election would take place once the insectoids migrating from Bilaluna had settled.

"I hear too that the authorities imprisoned Alhambra, the former minister of war and planetary relations, and other surviving ministers of Blood's cabinet," noted Antnoir.

"Yes, and a clawful of BUGants and some loyalist red ANTs who survived the revolutionary war have joined them," Keegan added. "But we offered many an amnesty if they agreed to move to Bilaluna and live there in peace or work on farms within Intopia with the former black alphas."

"Is it true that fifty members of each cyborg family on Bilaluna are coming to Intopia?" asked Antnoir.

Keegan nodded. "Yes, they'll be coming to the immigration center in the old breeding halls. You'll be a greeter there when they all arrive."

"And what about your belle, that beautiful Raven that

led the revolution?" Antnoir tapped her temple. "Isn't she the great-granddaughter of my best friend, Antebon?"

"She is," replied Keegan. "And she just returned from a diplomatic visit to Bilaluna. The masses elected Raven as the interim Senate leader."

"Doesn't she have a twin brother that aided her?"

"Indeed, her brother Jasper. He's now the acting speaker of the Hive." Keegan paused as he poured Antnoir a cup of tea. "Raven and Jasper just escorted our new Queen Beelight through the wormhole."

"It's so exciting." Antnoir took the cup from Keegan. "Queen Beewish is stepping down, and her two daughters will be queens. Beelight here, and her twin sister, Beejoice, will be the queen of Bilaluna."

Keegan poured a cup for himself and sat down. "Antnoir, you don't miss a beat."

"I may be old enough to be your grandmother, but I used to be very political." Antnoir put her claws to her cheeks. "Even if they cut short my time in the game."

"Jasper is ensuring Queen Beelight gets settled in at the palace." Keegan looked at his watch. "And Raven should be home soon."

"Why didn't you join Raven and Jasper on their trip to Bilaluna?" asked Antnoir.

"I've been too busy converting the old breeding halls to the new community center." He put his teacup down. "And the Congress convicted me for crimes against Intopia as a long-time former leader. Since I helped lead the rebellion, I received a suspended sentence for my crimes, but I can't leave Intopia."

"So, you must do community service," concluded Antnoir.

"Yes, you probably noticed I'm shutting down most activities at the breeding hall."

He described to Antnoir how it was now a community/immigration center, but they will use a small part of it as a cyborg transformation center. He mentioned how all cyborgs would have families again, but they still needed somewhere for incubation and physiotherapy for the young cyborgs.

Antnoir put her teacup down and stood up, interrupting Keegan. "I think there's someone at the door."

Keegan jumped up. "Fantastic, Raven is back!"

Antnoir began walking towards the backroom. "I'll just nap and let you two lovebirds get reacquainted." She smiled and left the room.

≈≈ ≈≈ ≈≈

Keegan met Raven at the threshold of their new nest and hugged and kissed her several times. "Darling, I missed you so much. How was your trip?"

Raven stared into the eyes that stole her heart many hexeks earlier and replied, "It was splendid, but I was so distraught without you." She fell deeper into his brawny arms. *Now I'm home.*

Keegan smiled, having waited too long for her return. "How are Queen Beewish and all your relatives?"

Raven held up a claw. "Jasper is coming over soon, and we'll tell you together about our trip." She grabbed Keegan's claws. "First, tell me what's happening here and what you've been doing." She was so excited to be home with her dashing mate. *I'm bubbling like a pot about to overboil.*

Keegan sighed and told Raven all that had transpired while she was away. He told her he had been busy and had accomplished a lot. Keegan stood and faced the breeding halls feeling a warm breeze blowing in through the window. He described how he removed all the incubators in the ova cava, and the area was now a community center and an immigration hall for newcomers from Bilaluna. Keegan was proud that hundreds could sleep there until they found nests in the colony. He mentioned Congress released Antnoir from prison and told Raven that she'd be soon working as a greeter at the center.

Keegan looked towards the back room. "She is old but loves meeting new cyborgs after being locked up for so long."

Raven's eyes lit up. "That's fantastic. She's finally out. I didn't know whether Antnoir died in prison or what." She recalled the stories about Antebon's campaign and how it miserably failed with Antnoir's arrest. *Justice, at last. Rust was the guilty one.* "I'd love to meet her."

"I have a surprise for you—she's here." Keegan pointed to the family room. "She's resting now, but she's dying to meet you too."

Raven led Keegan to the loveseat. "That's wonderful. But tell me more about your work at the breeding halls."

"Some incubators remain in the bloom room for cyborg transformation, but the rest of the space is now a retirement center for hybrids," Keegan continued.

Raven nodded. "So, some hybrids opted for the full pensions we offered?"

"Yes." Keegan clapped his claws. "The rest look forward to working with the BEEs, FLYs, and other cyborgs coming from Bilaluna."

"Wow!" Raven cracked a wide smile. "That's what you call multiculturalism." She turned and looked at the door. "That's Jasper now." She danced toward the window and waved at her twin.

Keegan jumped up and opened the door. "Jasper, my young friend. Come in and join us." Keegan gave Jasper a big hug. "Raven was just about to tell me about your trip, and I'll get us some strong sap to celebrate your return."

Raven tapped Keegan on the shoulder. "Sit down. I already got it." Raven filled all their glasses.

Keegan stood again. "A toast to our new Queen Beelight and the returning envoys."

Jasper straightened his antennae. "To the Queen."

"And to finally getting back home." Raven laughed. *Intopia, it seems like my planet at long last. We are no longer spies.*

Keegan threw back the rest of his sap. "Now tell me about your trip."

Raven sighed. "We did so much. There was the reunion, the funeral, and then the visit to the palace." She stared down and then buoyed. "Darci is now senior attendant to Queen Beewish and supervising the palace cleaning staff. She loves it." She thought about all Darci's contributions to their cause. *I'm so happy Darci's choices are now all her own.*

"It was sad to say goodbye to Clay, but the honorary funeral was a fitting tribute," Jasper interjected.

"Queen Beewish even came to the funeral and the reunion after that." Raven grinned from antennae to antennae. "And she gave Darci, Jasper, and me special medals for our service to Bilaluna." She beamed, thinking of how much Jasper had grown. *I'm so proud of everyone.*

"That all took place on the farm. Right?" asked Keegan.

"Yes, it was a beautiful setting for the funeral and the obvious choice for the reunion," Jasper replied.

"Why, of course, it's Beeutee and Antebon's farm." Keegan surmised. "So, they didn't need to travel."

"Yes, they are elderly now, and their mates have passed." Raven looked tenderly at Keegan. "And I am so happy Clay was buried at the farm so he could be with his mom in the end." She thought fondly of Clay and all he had sacrificed. *I miss him so much.*

"Isn't Antebon your great-grandma?" asked Keegan.

"Yes," Jasper interjected. "And it overjoyed her and Beeutee when we got our awards."

"And they got their own citations for starting the chameleant spy program." Raven emanated a sparkling scent as pride overtook her. *Those two were my inspiration, my valiant great-grandma and the majestic, old queen.* "But I know the revolution and the end of Rust's line were the only rewards they ever craved—seeing that Antunites united and Antunites prevailed!"

The End

APPENDICES

APPENDIX 1

Insect time units using heximal counting system as compared to human time

Insects count using a heximal system (i.e., base 6), and insect time reflects this counting. One hex is approximately equivalent to an Earth year and reflects one orbit of Poo-ponic around its solar star. Other time units use hex as a base and endings similar to a decade, century, and millennium. Except the rise is based on the power of 6 rather than 10. Thus, six times a hex is a hexade, 6X6 or 36 times a hex is a hexury, and 6X6X6 or 216 times a hex is a hexennium. Similar terms are used for months, weeks and days; except that a hexth is one-sixth of a hex (about two months), a hexek is one-sixth of a hexth (or about ten days), and a hexay is one-sixth of a hexek (or 10/6 days = 40 hours, which matched a full rotation of the slowly spinning planet). The terms hex-hexay (1/6 hexay), hexour, hex-hexour (1/6 hexour), hexute, hexond, and hex-hexond (1/6 hexond) are roughly equivalent to 6.67 hours, 1.1 hours, 11 minutes, 1.8 minutes, 18 seconds, and 3 seconds in human time.

APPENDIX 2

Pheromonic-English dictionary of insect emotions/non-verbal speech

abashing aroma: humiliation
abrasive aroma: annoyance
achy aroma: regret
acidic aroma: sarcasm
acrid aroma: hatred
affable aroma: contentedness
airy aroma: carefree
alluring aroma: attractive, sexy
anorexic aroma: saying nothing
antsy aroma: disturbed
appalling aroma: cruel
azure aroma: sad
babbling bouquet: gossipy
baked bouquet: conviction
ballooning bouquet: egotism
balmy bouquet: positivity
beaming bouquet: admiration
beefy bouquet: resistance
biting bouquet: sarcasm
bitter bouquet: ill-will, badness
blaring bouquet: angry crowd noise
blazing bouquet: hatred
blinding bouquet: overwhelmed
blistering bouquet: very upset
bloated bouquet: intense pride
blubbery bouquet: big lie, bold lie

blustery bouquet: argumentative
bold bouquet: defiance
booming bouquet: yelling
bouncy bouquet: excitement, happy
brassy bouquet: arrogance
brawny bouquet: strength
breezy bouquet: cheerfulness
bright bouquet: happiness
brilliant bouquet: optimism
brisk bouquet: petulance, crabbiness
bristly bouquet: grumpy, cranky
broad bouquet: confidence
broken bouquet: verklempt
bubbly bouquet: excitement, happy
buffed bouquet: strength, leadership
bulged bouquet: gratified, proud
bulky bouquet: hardy, resilient
buoyant bouquet: optimism
burly bouquet: overzealous
buxom bouquet: greedy
delicate fragrance: soft voice
dim perfume: uncertainty
earthy essence: grounded
eased essence: targeted speech
echoing essence: stuttering
effervescent essence: optimism
electrifying essence: excited crowd
engorged essence: yelling by a crowd
enticing essence: alluring
explosive essence: deafening noise
fat fragrance: obvious message

feathery fragrance: whisper
festal fragrance: merriment
festive fragrance: cheer, optimism
fiery fragrance: anger
firm fragrance: confidence
fishy fragrance: mysterious, devious
fizzing fragrance: uncertainty
flabby fragrance: stretch the truth
flaky fragrance: desperation
flapping fragrance: uncertainty
flashy fragrance: optimism, flare
flat fragrance: no emotion, monotone
flickering fragrance: idea
flimsy fragrance: fragile, weak
flowing fragrance: verbose, talkative
fluffy fragrance: gratefulness
fluttering fragrance: nervousness
foggy fragrance: confusion
foul fragrance: rotten, obscene
fragile fragrance: soft speech
freezing fragrance: fear
fresh fragrance: naïve, truthful
frigid fragrance: cold message
frosty fragrance: cold, unfeeling
fluid fragrance: articulate
fuming fragrance: angry
funky fragrance: strange
fuzzy fragrance: uncertainty
icy incense: cold fear
indigo incense: depression
inflamed incense: anger

inflated incense: egotism
intense incense: tension
intense perfume: insistence
ion-charged incense: excitement
itchy incense: eager, anxiety
odious odor: revolting
ominous odor: menacing
onerous odor: burdensome
padded perfume: guarded speech
pale perfume: soft speech
pealing perfume: screaming
piercing perfume: sudden loud noise
plaintive perfume: pleading speech
pleasant aroma: thrilled, happy
pleasant scent: sociable
plump perfume: arrogance, haughty
poignant perfume: dejected
pointed perfume: coherent message
polished perfume: eloquent speech
popping perfume: inspiration
portly perfume: pompous
prickly perfume: bristling speech
pudgy perfume: pushy
puffy perfume: pride
pulsating perfume: fearful
pungent perfume: irritation
puttering perfume: mumbling
radiant bouquet: enthusiastic
radiant reek: overjoyed, proud
ragged reek: cranky, disheveled
raging reek: anger

rambling reek: gossip
rasping reek: needling speech
ratty reek: annoyed
raw reek: naivety
rickety reek: anxiety, nervousness
ringing reek: scream
ripe reek: wisdom
roaring reek: loud, boisterous
robust reek: captivating
rocky reek: hard message
ruffled reek: panic
rumpled reek: alarm, terror
rutted reek: cringing, uncertainty
sapphire scent: sad
sapphire smell: gloomy
sapphire stench: suicidal
sapphire stink: depression
scalding scent: anger
scalding stench: evil, intense anger
scalding stink: angry response
scorching scent: hatred
scorching smell: anger, hatred
scorching stench: burning anger
scratchy stink: annoyed
scrawny scent: meek, guilty
screaming scent: obvious message
screaming smell: urgency
screaming stench: obvious deceit
screeching smell: urgent talk
screeching stink: urgency
scruffy scent: disheveled

searing scent: anger
seasoned scent: wisdom
seasoned smell: a well-developed idea
seasoned stench: evil plan
seasoned stink: devious plan
secretive scent: whisper
seething stench: anger
seething stink: rage
shabby scent: upset
shabby smell: distressed
shabby stench: panicked
shabby stink: desperate
shadowy stench: deceit
shaky scent: uncertain
sharp scent: come back, rebuff
sharp smell: panic
sharp stink: sarcasm
shifty smell: deviousness
shifty stink: scheming
shimmering scent: happiness
shimmering smell: overjoyed
shimmering stink: ecstatic
shining scent: joy, contentment
shiny scent: happiness, joy
shiny smell: pride for others
shocking scent: surprise
shrill smell: alarming talk
shrill stink: alarmed
silken scent: smarmy
silky scent: romantic speech
sinewy scent: tough talk

sizzling scent: sexy
sizzling stench: anger, hatred
skinny, slim scent: shy
skinny, slim smell: cautious
skinny, slim stench: wary
skinny, slim stink: vigilant
slender scent: submissive
slender smell: gentle
slender stench: acquiescence
slender stink: compliance
slight scent: whisper
slimy scent: an obvious lie
slimy stench: deceitful plan
sludgy scent: unsure
smarmy scent: pleading
smarmy smell: beseeching
smarmy stink: evil plan
smooth scent: reassurance
smothering scent: frustrated, trapped
smoldering scent: passion
smoldering stench: lasting deceit
smoldering stink: growing deceit
sneaky stink: devious plan
snug scent: friendly
soft scent: caring speech
soggy scent: disinterested
soggy smell: unsure
solid scent: a simple message
solid smell: rule
solid stench: evil rule
solid stink: unfair rule

soothing scent: reassurance
sour scent: resentful, bitter
sour stench: hostile
sour stink: sullen
sparkling scent: pride, joyfulness
sparkly scent: excitement
spiky scent: scheming
spiky smell: deceitful scheme
spiky stench: evil scheme
spiky stink: devious scheme
spindly scent: embarrassed, humbled
spiny scent: bullying
spiny smell: offensive
spiny stench: evil
spiny stink: cruel
sprightly scent: happiness
sprightly stench: ecstatic
squeaking stink: bothersome
squealing scent: screaming
stabbing stink: harsh insult
stale scent: dull, boring
stale smell: tedious
stalwart scent: brave
stanch scent: confidence
stanch smell: authoritative
steadfast scent: conviction
steamy scent: passion, sexy
steely stench: hard advice
steely stink: insistence
sticky scent: worry
sticky smell: anxiety, worried

sticky stench: devious
sticky stench: trickery
sticky stink: deception
stifling scent: oppression
stifling stench: overbearing
stinging scent: insult
stinging stench: sarcasm
stinging stink: insult
stirring scent: energized
stocky scent: unconvinced
stout scent: honest
stout smell: frank
stout stench: moral superiority
strangling stink: deep oppression
strapping scent: defiance
strapping stench: rebellious
stringy scent: tough talk
strong fragrance: pride
stroppy smell: awkward obstinate
stroppy stink: belligerent
stuffy scent: arrogance
stuffy smell: conceit
suffocating scent: worries, anxiety
suffocating stink: cringeworthy
sulking smell: brooding
sultry scent: sexy
sunny scent: cheerful
sunny smell: overjoyed
sunny stench: ecstatic
sweet scent: nice
sweet smell: enjoyment

sweet stench: greedy
sweet stink: overindulgent
sweltering stink/stench: domineering
swollen scent: pride
swollen stench: megalomaniacal
syrupy scent: sentimental
syrupy smell: tricky
syrupy stench: devious
syrupy stink: cunning
thorny stink: devious scheme
vague vapor: uncertainty, hesitation
vacillating vapor: unsure, frightened
vexing vapor: confusion, upset
vibrant bouquet: proud
vibrant scent: ecstatic
vibrating vapor: trembling
vigorous reek: with authority
vigorous vapor: energized
vile vapor: evil
vinegary aroma: acidy smell
vinegary vapor: sarcasm
viscid vapor: sticky feeling
vivacious vapor: lively, excited
volatile vapor: aggression
waffling whiff: uncertainty
wafting whiff: uncertainty
wailing whiff: soft cry
warm whiff: tenderness, hope
wee whiff: whisper, quiet talk
wet whiff: rebuff
whining whiff: complaining

whispering whiff: subtle
wispy whiff: whisper
whistling whiff: brief shrill speech
wily whiff: cunning, tricky
withered whiff: muttering

ACKNOWLEDGMENTS

The author wishes to acknowledge a few individuals who played a vital role in completing this novel. First, I want to thank my wife, Ann Birdgenaw, for I would not have written this book without her inspiration. She was also essential as a reading partner, copy editor, and proofreader. I also want to thank my book coach and developmental editor Nina Munteanu, a fellow author and scientist, and a creative writing instructor. Nina inspired me to expand my work from a novella to a trilogy, and her suggestions taught me the essentials of fiction writing. Thanks to my kids, Kelly, Sophie, and Justin, for their encouragement and comments.

ABOUT THE AUTHOR

The author, Terry Birdgenaw, is a Metis of Oji-Cree, English, Scottish, Dutch and French-Canadian heritage, whose mother's first cousin is a long-time lead elder of the Metis Nation of Canada. However, Terry would argue that his family assimilated into European Canadian culture by moving away from the Oji-Cree territory a few generations ago. Yet, Terry has long been fascinated by the story of his ancestor, Mistigoose, the indigenous Canadian woman who was the first to welcome a European into his mother's family line.

Mistigoose was both a tragic figure and an inspiration for this series. Her tragedy was that she drowned herself while distraught over the loss of her first son William, whom her British husband Robert had taken permanently to England. Against her will, the author's fifth great grandfather wanted to ensure their son would be eligible to receive a handsome inheritance promised to his heir. Ironically, as British law prohibited Metis from owning property, William never received his rightful inheritance, so his translocation and mother's death were both in vain.

The translation of Mistigoose, an Oji-Cree word, inspired parts of the story told in *The Antunites Chronicles*. In English, Mistigoose means little branch or twig. The title character of *Antuna's Story*, whose own mother drowned, used a twig in a selfless effort to save her newfound friend Dinomite. The resolution of the second book in the series, *The Rise and Fall of *, also depended on the insectoids' realization that they needed tiny insects to break down little branches to generate the new soil required to rehabilitate their spent lands.

Visit Terry at:
TerryBirdgenaw.WordPress.com
https://twitter.com/TerryBirdgenaw
https://www.instagram.com/authorterrybirdgenaw/
https://www.facebook.com/TerryBirdgenawWriter

ABOUT THE SERIES

Antuna's Story is the first book in *The Antunite Chronicles*. It follows the lives of Earth insects transported through a wormhole to a far-off planet they call Poo-ponic. Young Antuna encouraged the settlers to work together, but hexs later, conflicts resumed. Despite her convictions, Antuna could not save herself or her diverse friends from the devastation of war. Still, surviving stories told how Antuna fought discrimination, saved the colony from starvation, reversed gender roles, became a scholar, and led the resistance effort. And though just a tiny ant, Antuna's actions changed society forever.

*The Rise and Fall of * is the second book in *The Antunite Chronicles*. This *Animal Farm*-like story tracks the insects' evolution to cyborg insects, the growth and decline of a fledgling democracy, and the destruction of life on the planet caused by a long-ignored climate crisis. It also follows the utopian society created by a group of cyborg insects that escape to Poo-ponic's moon Bilaluna before Poo-ponic's atmosphere collapses.

The Antunite Chronicles' third book, *Antunites Unite*, begins several generations after insectoids from Bilaluna recolonize their old planet with its revived atmosphere, which they rename Intopia. Despite their optimism, an authoritarian leader takes control of the colony, designs genetic modifications of ANTs to replace unwanted insect cyborgs, and uses biological alterations and sociological rules to dominate its inhabitants. It is an allegory reminiscent of *1984* and *Brave New World,* where rebel spies must overcome a dystopian regime that uses histrionics, bionics, and socionics to subjugate its citizens. It's a brave new world that's out of this world!